MW00890116

Nickie Krewson

Book One in the Forest of Fontainebleau Series

To Midge,

We are, each of us, more
than meets the eye.

Nickie Krewson

iUniverse, Inc.
Bloomington

The Poet

Book One in the Forest of Fontainebleau Series

Copyright © 2013 Nickie Krewson

This is a work of fiction. All of the characters, names, incidents, organizations, and dialogue in this novel are either the products of the author's imagination or are used fictitiously.

iUniverse books may be ordered through booksellers or by contacting:

iUniverse
1663 Liberty Drive
Bloomington, IN 47403
www.iuniverse.com
1-800-Authors (1-800-288-4677)

ISBN: 978-1-4759-6055-6 (sc)
ISBN: 978-1-4759-6056-3 (hc)
ISBN: 978-1-4759-6057-0 (e)

Library of Congress Control Number: 2012920997

Printed in the United States of America

iUniverse rev. date: 1/7/2013

Cover photo courtesy of John Varljen

In memory of my father, Robert R. Krewson,
who spent his life serving his country,

and

in memory of Chad Edmundson, a small-town boy
who willingly gave his life for his country.

With grateful thanks to my mother, Jean Krewson. Behind every
great man, there may be a great woman, but behind every great
woman, there is often another great woman—her mother.

CONTENTS

PART TWO   TEMPTATION

PART THREE   REDEMPTION

Author's Note

Write what you know. What writer hasn't heard this? Still, as counterintuitive as it might seem, I go out on a limb and write what I can only imagine.

This tale begins as a Shakespearean-inspired fantasy but evolves into a contemporary romance set in Achères-la-Forêt, a real place a stone's throw from Paris, which may or may not resemble my fictional town. I chose this village as the site of my story, as it is intimate and small, the kind of place where you can imagine that people all know one another and are willing to take some measure of responsibility for their neighbors' well-being. It is hugged by the massive forest of Fontainebleau, a perfect haven for faeries and other naturally occurring creatures, and has its roots sunk deeply in the agricultural tradition of Isle de France. The restaurant, Denis à Achères, and the stone church of St. Fare are there, but don't look for de Gaul and Son, the Achères Herb and Natural Foods Store, or the café and pub frequented by my locals.

The story, you will note, though set in France, has a decidedly American flavor to it. The expressions and language are meant to convey to an American reader the casual kind of conversation people use every day. It is the feel of the conversation I have attempted to express, contrasting the formal, Shakespearean style with the more contemporary speech. Metric measurements are used in the dialogue, but the American/British system appears in the text, so as to give a better idea of the information for readers more familiar with the latter units.

Names are important in this novel and often have meanings related to the characters. Embedded in many of the chapters, the title of each is referred to, either overtly or more subtly, twice in the text. Just a little fun with words, for those who take pleasure in such things.

The search for understanding of the spiritual world is a major theme of this story. The value of work, the unglamorous reality it presents, and how we define ourselves through our occupations is a primary theme of the entire series. The young residents of Achères face the challenge of growing up and shouldering the responsibilities of adulthood in these pages and in the ones yet to come. The magic of the Fae is subtle and invisible to the unsuspecting humans.

The second novel carries the group of friends forward into their adult roles, but the interference of the Fae continues to cause mayhem, as the faeries manipulate the oblivious humans to achieve their own ends. The final story plunges the reader into the invisible realm of the Fae, as a human becomes trapped in a world he never knew existed, while the woman he loves is enmeshed in the gritty reality of inescapable responsibility that binds us all.

Suspend disbelief, enjoy the read, and maybe find a little bit of yourself in one of my fictional Achérois.

PRONUNCIATION GUIDE

As recommended by one of my early, nonfrancophone readers, I provide the following simplified guide to pronouncing French names. In the French language, the accent is always on the last syllable, and it often sounds like the end of the word just disappears without being actually pronounced. There are two exceptions to this rule. Paolo is an Italian name, so the accent is on the second to the last or penultimate syllable. The name Latif is Pakistani, so it, too, would not follow normal French pronunciation.

Achères-la-Forêt	Ah *share* la For *ay*
Achérois	Ah share *wah*
Arcenciel	Ar kahn see *ay*
Claude Bessette	*Clod* Bes *ayt*
Denis à Achères	Den*ee* ah Ah *share*
Gilbert de Gaul	Jill *Bear* day *Gauh*
Guiscard	Gwees *card*
Guillaume Paysanne	Gee *ohm* Pay *sah*
Jacques de Gaul	*Zhoc* day *Gauh*
Latif Nasiri	La *teef* Nah *seeh* ree
Luc Flambert	*Luke* Flam *behr*
Michelle Bertrand	Mish *aya* Bear *trahn*
Marie Durrand	Mar *ie* Dur *ahn*
Natalie Bertrand	Nat a *lie* Bear *trahn*
Paolo	*Pow* low
Rene le Roux	Reh *nay* leh *Roo*
Vincent Durrand	Vin *sahn* Dur *ahn*
Yasmine du Bois	Yahs *meen* du *Bwah*

PROLOGUE

Fey arrived at the dead oak tree and stood over Paolo as he lay shivering on the forest floor. The dark-haired young man opened his eyes and looked up hopefully at her as she stood in all her former glory, a fiery-haired daughter of the Fae with eyes of deep, glittering violet and skin the delicate hue of lavender.

"Why can't I move?" he asked her weakly.

"Don't try," she answered.

She stayed with him, her hand pressed gently against his face, patiently keeping watch, hoping to impart some amount of strength through the touch of her skin on his. He gazed upon her with his large, dark eyes, which she saw as if for the first time. She could see clearly that he adored her completely, and her heart skipped faster under his intense regard, which reminded her of the way he had looked at her when they first met. He had frightened her then, with his unflinching gaze. He hadn't meant to intimidate her, she later realized. The sight of her, completely unexpected, was just so captivating that he couldn't look away.

Now, though, he closed his eyes again and muttered hoarsely, "I'm so cold."

She squeezed back her tears, not wanting him to see her cry.

"I'm sorry," she said simply.

There was nothing she could do. René's vicious attack in the alley had left him with a very serious head wound. She could see by his pallor that he had lost a significant amount of blood. His skin had begun to show a bluish tint, and his breathing was very shallow. He seemed to hover at the edge of the sleep that lies beyond dreams. She had arrived with little time to spare. She only hoped her presence would be enough to keep him alive.

"I don't think I can stay awake much longer," he added, his voice growing very quiet, his eyes closing.

"Please try," she pleaded, struggling to keep the desperation she felt from creeping into her voice, "for me. After all, we don't get to spend much time together, and I came all this way, just to see you."

The corners of Paolo's mouth turned up in an attempt at a smile as he struggled to meet her concerned gaze.

"Promise me you'll stay?" he begged, his features growing anxious.

"As long as you need me," she answered softly, settling down beside him to keep vigil. She knew that it was his worst fear—that he would die alone, a friendless wanderer.

Reassured, he closed his eyes again, and they waited together in the cold, dark November night.

PART ONE
The Fall

And the Lord God said, behold, the man is become as one of us, to know good and evil and now, lest he put forth his hand, and take also of the tree of life, and eat, and live for ever:

Therefore the Lord God sent him forth from the garden of Eden, to till the ground from whence he was taken.

—Genesis 3:22–23

1

Heart's Desire

The summer's last sunset cast a bright-orange glow over the forest, which stretched as far as the eye could see from east to west and for miles from north to south. It was the vast Forest of Fontainebleau, preserved as a national treasure in France, as valuable as any painting in the Louvre. Crisscrossed by several highways that carried travelers from one side to another like arteries, the vast wilderness, for the most part, was a peaceful haven for wildlife, as well as a refuge for a remnant of beings from a time long since past when chivalry and romance reigned.

The thunderstorm had not lasted long but had thrown down copious amounts of rain and rent the sky with violent flashes of lightning. Fey had taken shelter in a hollow tree somewhere in the southeastern part of the immense expanse of trees, rather than have her delicate gray dress of cobweb silk spoiled. She was not only vain but frugal. Such silk was costly, but worth it as it contrasted perfectly with her pale, lavender-hued skin. She fingered the fringed edge, which fell just above her knees. The tiny creature had nothing to fear from the approaching darkness. Faeries owned the night as well as the day—even more so, as magic took better hold under the moon and stars.

The dainty being, no taller than a tube of lipstick and delicate as a meadow blossom, waited patiently for the trees to finish dripping before venturing out into the approaching night. The oak tree was snug enough, in spite of the damp, and it smelled nicely of leaves and earth, a comforting scent to a child of the forest such as herself. She whiled away the time lost in thought.

Guiscard would be arriving in the meadow soon. She sighed at the thought of him, picturing his red-gold curls dusting his sturdy blue shoulders; his neat, well-trimmed beard; his amber eyes, alert and dancing with fun and mischief. Fey struck a pose to practice. She wanted to be there waiting when he arrived, but it had to appear accidental. He was used to being sought after, and she didn't want to seem too forward.

Oh, if only I had a mirror, she thought. She wanted to look just perfect for him. She smoothed her profusion of russet curls, which fell to just above her waist, and freshened her gossamer, peach-scented lip gloss in anticipation.

Guiscard was a great favorite among the faerie maidens. Thus far, however, he had not indicated a preference for any one lucky girl but was maddeningly solicitous to all. Perhaps he was keeping his options open. Perhaps he was just so kindhearted he couldn't help but shower all of his would-be soul mates with compliments and chivalrous attention.

"So complicated," Fey huffed to herself. The male gender was supposed to be simple, right? But perhaps that was where Guiscard's allure lay—he refused to fit convention.

Deep in thought, Fey swore she saw movement out of the corner of her eye. The contours of the hollow log flowed dark brown in some streaks, light brown in others, trailing down to the ground. She followed the patterns with her eyes but saw only stillness in the soft light. The storm had moved away, leaving the trees dripping and sparkling in the sun and a rainbow casting a bright ribbon over the sky above, but the air remained heavy and damp in the oak tree.

All of a sudden, she screamed in terror. An enormous black bat, hanging upside down right in front of her, stretched out its evil wings and bared its dagger teeth. She was only inches from its deadly fangs. Terrified, she shrieked and pasted herself against the opposite wall of the hollow oak as the horrible creature flapped its rubbery wings violently, glaring at her in a crazed and menacing fashion like a vision from a nightmare.

"Please spare me!" she cried, covering her face with her arms to shield herself from the terrifying sight. "If you do, I'll grant you a wish—anything you like," she begged. Fey was sure this monster would want nothing more than a fat rabbit to gorge itself on. Better to grant it a wish than have the life's blood sucked out of her by the odious beast.

Being young and having only rudimentary knowledge, she was not yet powerful enough to inspire the awe and fear that a more experienced faerie would; plus, it was obvious that the giant bat was a stranger to the forest, as she had never before encountered such a behemoth as she now faced. The treaty between the Fae and the other forest dwellers would not be binding to this intruder. She was as vulnerable as a cornered mouse before a hungry cat.

Fey slowly lowered her arms. The hideous creature was eating holes in her with its large black eyes but had not yet moved in for the kill. She had to think fast, or she would die right there; she was sure of it. In a voice small and timid with fear, she pleaded for her life.

The large, furry bat, who had taken shelter in the hollow oak as well, had just awakened after a satisfying sleep. He had spent the last full night of summer feasting on a banquet of fruits and berries until, completely sated, he had crawled into the inviting confines of the old, dead tree. He yawned and stretched with the complete lack of restraint that comes only with solitude. Usually, he was very reserved, being extremely shy by nature. A high-pitched shriek made his sensitive ears ring, and he cringed, feeling dizzy and startled. The shrill scream reverberated throughout the narrow space.

The bat, his ears still ringing, shook his head. *What on earth was that?* he asked himself. Coming to his senses, he peered into the dim light at the source of his auditory pain. A faerie! So tiny and beautiful! She cowered in the concaved fissure of the tree with her lavender skin and soft, wispy dress. Her brilliant coloring was visible to him, even though his world was usually a bland vision of black, white, and gray.

He could see that she was terrified of him, but he didn't know why. He meant her no harm. Drinking in the sight of her like refreshing water from a cool spring, he listened to the sound of her little voice, which tinkled like a cat's bell. She was begging him for mercy, strangely enough, and offered to grant him a wish. None of this made any sense to him. Transfixed, he continued to stare at the lovely vision before him.

"There must be something you want. I am small and would provide poor sustenance, but think of what I could give you," she coaxed in honeyed tones. "What is your heart's desire?"

My heart's desire? Why does this lovely creature want to know that? She was beautiful beyond anything the bat had ever seen, and having traveled a great distance from his homeland on a solitary journey, he was drawn to her in his loneliness. He sensed instinctively that she must be very good. He felt he could tell her anything.

No one had ever asked him about his thoughts, and it moved him to think someone would actually care. Among his own kind, it was assumed that everyone wanted the same things—the freshest, sweetest fruit; a healthy mate; and the companionship of the community, bats being generally social creatures—but he had seen that there was more in the world, and his longing to experience it was overpowering. That was why he found himself here, instead of in the company of his peers.

He watched as a ray of the setting sun illuminated the tiny, elegant figure. Her eyes flashed brilliant violet. Her long, curly hair, which appeared a gingery russet in the soft twilight, glowed with fiery highlights in the sunset. He was dazzled. Overcoming his usual shyness, he decided to answer her question, because he desperately wanted to talk to her.

The faerie continued to babble while her eyes darted restlessly about. "… a fat, juicy rabbit; a lovely she-bat; a farm full of plump, lazy chickens …" she prattled on, before petering out into nervous silence, squinting in the bright, blinding light.

The bat saw that this radiant little female creature was waiting for him to speak.

"Uh … I'm actually on a journey," he began hesitantly. "You see, I've heard that … somewhere to the north, exists a beautiful city of lights, and I'm trying to make my way there."

He wondered if the faerie was really paying attention to him, as her eyes became fixed on a spot to his left, where the light streamed in through the crack he had entered at dawn. She shifted, but he continued speaking, emboldened by his loneliness.

"That, lovely lady, is my heart's desire, to see the City of Lights. I wish I were human, so that I could enjoy its beauty all the more fully, but even just to see it would be enough."

He spoke softly, as she had moved to within an inch of his face. Being this close to her was intoxicating, especially as she smelled enticingly of sweet, fresh peaches. As he spoke, she lowered her eyelids and relaxed her tensed body like a marionette whose strings had been cut.

The bat watched, horrified, as the beautiful faerie fell into a dead faint. He let loose his foothold from his perch and swooped to catch her as she fell. He carried her outside and laid her gently on the damp ground.

The forest floor was mostly bare of vegetation, the canopy being particularly thick in this section. A few small plants struggled for survival here and there, and a few last peeks of fading sunlight danced over the brown, barren earth, which had been sprinkled with fallen leaves and twigs by the storm. A temporary stream flowed nearby, and the sound of the water created relaxing music for the minuet of dappled brilliance.

As night fell, he stood vigilantly by her, fretting and anxious. He had an unpleasant suspicion that he had somehow caused her distress and felt a responsibility to watch over her until she recovered, lest some rat or boar scoop her up as a prize. He sat patiently by his new friend as the moon rode across the sky. The air grew cool, but he was used to that. The soothing sounds of insects mingled with the more frightening tones of owls and other predators. Those latter noises caused his eyes to dart about anxiously. He could easily fly away, but he would not leave her side. In the hour before dawn, he began to nod off, heavy-lidded and hungry. He put one wing over her protectively and fell into a fitful sleep.

To her initial horror, Fey awoke under the bat's wing, lying on the damp ground. She scooted quickly away from its sheltering folds. Staring with revulsion at his sleeping form, she remembered with dismay the promise she had made. With a hard swallow of resignation, Fey held her breath and forced her hand to the face of the repulsive, unconscious animal, only to find the dream that played inside his mind was of a peaceful evening in Italy, where he perched in a tree above a striped awning, a banquet of fruit peeking out from underneath the expanse of canvas. His body may have been black as soot, but his soul was as pure as newly fallen snow. Transforming him, from that moment, was almost too easy.

She had been so close to him in the tree, she scolded herself as she watched his form undergo the dramatic transfiguration—the black fur of the beast giving way to bare pale skin, the foxlike snout and pointed ears transforming into a more familiar human type of visage. She could have easily read his aura of innocence, if only her fear hadn't blocked her from receiving it. Another fatal mistake.

The Fae could read the minds of humans and animals simply by touching their faces or hair, pulling out their thoughts as easily as one would pluck a ripe grape from a vine. Reading those of their own kind was usually more difficult, as they had developed the ability to shield their minds to protect their privacy, and it was considered exceedingly rude to take another faerie's thoughts without permission. To read someone's heart, the faerie had only to place his or her hand overtop as it beat to tell what love lay below the surface. To feel the emotions of another, faeries had only to draw close enough to feel their subject's aura.

Backing away to hover over him, Fey surveyed her handiwork. To be honest, she had been, initially, rather shocked. By all accounts, a vile, merciless predator such as he should have made a hideous human. According to her magic, the character of one transformed would be written in the countenance and frame.

Here lay no Quasimodo, however, but a peculiarly handsome young man. Yes, his nostrils were a bit too broad, and his ears were rather large, recalling what he had once been. His mouth was a thin, serious line—more thoughtful than sensual, she reflected. He was covered in soft black hair, even a little on the tops of his hands. Rather savage, that. Maybe he was a bit sensual, after all, she reconsidered.

Hmm, perhaps just a little bit of his former self, she mused, recalling the big, furry creature that had blocked her way. She couldn't tell for sure. His figure was sturdy and tall, like a peasant's. Still, he had a high brow, giving him a look of intelligence; pale skin with a hint of olive tones; and wavy brown-black hair that fell sweetly over his right eye, and he wore a look on his young face completely devoid of guile.

"I have misjudged him," she lamented. "He was nothing but a fruit bat and no danger to me."

Now her magic was spent and would not come back until he died. Fey knew that men could live to be eighty.

"Oh, I hope you were worth it," she scolded the sleeping man, as a tear slid down her cheek. She wished, now too late, that she had studied the arts of enchantment with more diligence. Perhaps then, she would have found another way to fulfill her honor-bound duty to grant the bat his wish that would not have expended all her frail powers, leaving her nothing. Instead, she had frittered her time away fashioning silly garments to array herself and her friends.

Such senseless frippery! she chided herself.

She thought of Guiscard with a heavy heart. He would not desire her now. She would be useless and dull for a long time. He would choose another, and who could blame him? She looked at her arm, seeing the lavender skin paled to a dull grayish-cream. She fingered her hair, which, she could see, had turned a flat, limp, mousey brown. Her beautiful silk dress was stained from the damp ground. She was … plain.

There was no time to cry though. That would have to wait. Fey needed to finish up before the now young man woke up. She laid everything she thought he would need in his new situation in a neat pile: a soft, wool overcoat in black merino; a pair of trousers in a dark-brown, lightweight wool/silk-blend fabric; a crisp, undyed linen shirt with shell buttons; a vest of chocolate-colored velvet; cashmere socks; well-oiled black leather boots; and, for underneath, garments of soft white cotton. A supple black leather wallet filled with euros, a belt, and an onyx ring completed the gift. She had given him the best of everything, sparing no expense.

There were other gifts she gave him as well, though these remained unseen. Knowledge, too, is a gift, and more precious than any material item. Pressing her face to his open palm, she willed him to receive her own thoughts. He sighed in his sleep, his finger twitching slightly, which startled her for a moment, causing her to jump up in alarm. Without meaning to, he could easily crush her if he clenched his hand. After he relaxed again, she continued, closing her eyes and concentrating. She hoped that which she imparted would be enough. She was, after all, not a man, not a human. She could only guess what it would be like. She hoped that he had received enough information to survive in the new, unfamiliar world to which he would awaken.

Fey may have been mistaken when she made her frantic offer, but she would not try to weasel out of her obligations. She had promised a wish and had made no stipulations as to what it could be. It would only bring her misfortune in the long run to go back on her promise. The code of honor among the Fae was quite clear on that. Besides, as she thought back, the bat had made no move to injure her. He seemed, actually, quite friendly.

"Oh, I am a fool!" she cried. She felt immensely sorry for herself, but also, watching the young man sleep, she pitied him, for although he seemed to be impressed with the accomplishments of mankind—too much so, in her estimation—she had the feeling he had seen nothing of its darker side. He was a pure innocent, full of idealism, and had a romantic, wandering spirit. Oh foolish youth! Why do we always want more than we have?

Fey kissed her new charge on the forehead, leaving a small tear, which glistened in a ray of the morning sun that played over his face, and flew sadly home. Yes, he was now her responsibility. It was part and parcel of changing a creature. They were now bound, soul deep, for the rest of their lives, though he, for his part, she thought, would probably never realize it.

2

Lemonade

When the tall, dark-haired man awakened in the forest late that morning, it was as if from some bizarre dream. What was real and what was not were confused, like he had downed a fifth of whiskey. There he was, lying beside a dead tree with not a stitch on, but with a neat pile of the most beautiful clothing left obviously with great care and consideration. He admired each piece, running his long fingers over the soft fabric before slipping into it—each one a perfect fit as if tailor-made just for him.

He then sat on a mossy rock, his lips slightly parted in wonder and confusion. The ring and wallet he held in his palm, studying them. He examined the ring. He admired the smooth onyx face for a moment before sliding it onto his finger and then clenched and unclenched his hand a few times. Next, he examined the wallet. The man opened it slowly. An exploration revealed bills and coins in its folds, but nothing else. No clues.

A small stream flowed nearby, having been fed by the recent rain. He splashed his face with the cool water to clear his mind of the muddled thoughts and then cupped his hands and drank deeply.

He remembered, as if in a dream, being upside down. It seemed preposterous now. A vision of a beautiful woman remained etched in his memory, but there was an air of unreality about her as well. The confused traveler raked his fingers through his hair and squeezed his eyes shut, furrowing his brows with the effort. He wheeled around and studied the hollow oak as if for the first time. He had a bizarre feeling that, somehow, he had been inside of it but knew that was impossible; there was no way he would ever have fit in there.

Hunger began to gnaw at his belly with persistence. He pushed his confusion aside to deal with the more pressing concern of finding food. Slinging the black coat over his shoulder, he began to walk through the woods, unsure which direction to take or where he was even headed.

After a while, he came upon a narrow, paved two-lane road. All roads lead to towns and people. He knew that he must find people. That was the start. After that, well, who knew? Walking along in silence, he eventually noted a sign that indicated a town was nearby. Printed on it was "Achères-la-Forêt, 2 km." It seemed the best way out of the endless wilderness.

He trudged along the road, his beautiful wool coat draped over his arm and vest unbuttoned. Trees surrounded him on both sides for as far as he could see in either direction, providing a familiar comfort in his confusion. A sheen of perspiration shone on his high forehead. His butter-soft boots were, by anyone's standards, sublimely comfortable, but even so, his feet grew swollen and sore, as if unused to treading such hard ground.

He did not recall ever having experienced the midday sun. The beauty of it was, literally, blinding. It scorched his dark hair, causing rivulets of sweat to trickle down his back. To add to his overall discomfort, he found the sheer weight of his own body oppressive. At almost six feet tall, with a sturdy build, he felt the force of gravity bearing down like a lead weight.

He walked along, deep in thought. The vision of the beautiful woman with skin the color of lavender and hair of flames hung just at the edge of his consciousness. He walked on, trying to remember who she was—and who he was, for that matter.

A dog barked in the distance. The forest soon gave way to open fields, and the blue sky expanded overhead. The heat became even more oppressive without the shelter of the trees and their offer of the occasional puff of cool, damp air. A small stone farmhouse rose from the soft, grassy fields like a beacon. An old European structure that spoke of centuries of use, it was set back from the road a good distance, as if it desired privacy from passersby. A large, old tree stood alone in the front yard, offering shade. A barn with a low enclosure constructed of matching stone backed up the house protectively, its rugged functionality lending a masculine air to complement the femininity of home and hearth. The tired wanderer stopped in front of the tree, surveying the marriage of structures, and finding himself overcome with shyness.

Shifting his weight from one sore foot to another, he was spared the agony of approaching the door and knocking by an old man who came up from behind with an empty bucket hanging from his gnarled hand. He was short, having lost several inches to the years, and his face was wrinkled from working long hours in the sun. He had bright, hazel eyes and a beaked nose that appeared somewhat oversized for his face. Overall, he projected an air of approachable friendliness.

"Young man?" he greeted the tall, dark-haired stranger in query.

The boyish-looking man turned, startled, to face him.

"Yes, sir?" he replied sheepishly.

"Ya look lost." The old man chuckled.

"That I am, sir," he replied gratefully. He smiled timidly, tilting his head downward, a sweaty lock of black hair falling over one eye, as if it could shelter him from scrutiny.

"Well then, come on and take a load off. We'll get you figured out," he said kindly, moving toward the house.

Just then, the dog he had heard barking earlier bounded up, letting loose two loud blasts of sound and wagging her tail. The newcomer cringed in terror, dropping his coat at his feet. Completely exhausted and faint from lack of food, he knew there was no way he could outrun it. Fearing for his life, he gulped and stood, rooted to the spot, fists clenched at his sides, as the yellow Labrador sniffed at his trousers and offered another loud bark. He flinched but remained stiffly in place, his head tucked down and teeth gritted as he eyed the dog warily.

The old man, seeing the look of terror on the young man's face, called the animal off as his visitor staggered backward, almost falling over.

"Sorry about that. Sophie takes her job a little too seriously sometimes," the old man apologized and picked the lovely coat up off of the ground. He gave it a shake and handed it back to him with a look of puzzlement. "You okay?"

"No, sir, not really," he answered honestly, taking a deep breath of relief. He wasn't referring to the dog, however, but his overall pervasive sense of disorientation.

"Well, come on then, before you keel over right here in my driveway."

He stumbled along behind, keeping one eye on the Labrador, who, her task completed, had claimed a patch of shade to commence her nap. The old man plunked the bucket on the step and motioned him inside.

"Name's Guillaume Paysanne, but my friends call me Guy," he offered, pulling out a chair in the small, bright kitchen and smacking the back of it with his open hand in invitation. The tall guest sank down gratefully, sighed loudly, and closed his eyes in relief. He dropped his black coat across his lap and surveyed his host with an expression of exhaustion on his pale face.

The traveler took in his surroundings with curiosity as he tried to remember his name, which, oddly enough, seemed to elude him. The kitchen was old-fashioned. The finish on the appliances and counters was worn, as if the polish had long been scrubbed off of them by countless cleanings. They all looked as if they had put in many years of service and were working well past their expected age of retirement. The table, crafted of sturdy oak, was clean and bare, save for a smattering of condiments left conveniently in the middle. A matched pair of salt and pepper shakers painted with yellow flowers hugged up against a glass cloche, which trapped a half-used chunk of butter on a wooden circle underneath. The chairs were small and unornamented. There was a sparse utilitarianism about everything, which appealed to the wanderer's intrinsic preference for simplicity. The decorating style, or lack thereof, indicated that the old farmer was a no-nonsense sort of man.

Then, the young man's mind found what it had been searching for, or was it a name he had heard in his travels? It was the only name he could think of, so it would have to do, for now.

"I'm Paolo. Pleased to meet you, Guy, and thank you for your kindness," he rasped, as a glass of lemonade was pushed toward him with a wink. Guy lifted his own sweaty glass in a mock toast and downed it quickly, as if he, too, were very thirsty.

Paolo lifted his own beverage more slowly and sipped at the lemonade like a wine expert at a tasting, appreciatively, yet critically. He rolled the flavor around on his tongue. Amazing. After one small sip, his parched throat felt refreshed. *Sweet, tangy …*

"Paolo, eh?" Guy reflected, his face expressing amusement as Paolo swirled the lemonade over his palate as if a review were forthcoming. "You don't sound like you're from around here. You have a bit of an accent."

"Oh, I came from Lombardia, in Italy. It's in the mountains. Very beautiful," Paolo explained.

At least, he thought that was where he had lived. He clearly remembered the beautiful mountains and breathtaking lake but was still completely muddled as to why he was here now in this man's kitchen and where his journey had actually started. Lombardia was the only other place his memory registered. Strangely, he felt a pervasive sense of happiness, in spite of his hunger and confusion. Here he was, sitting across from a very nice person, sharing the most amazing thing he had ever tasted. Guy was very kind; he could tell that. He knew he had been very lucky to have stumbled upon this place.

Paolo, looking away from his host to take another sip of his drink, spotted a small bowl of apples on the counter. He was so hungry he was tempted to take one, but he had a strong feeling that it would not be polite. As much as the lack of food pained him, he valued his sense of deportment more than satiating his hunger. At least the sugar from the lemonade had given him a little strength.

"Let me guess," Guy probed. "Your car broke down a few miles back. Do you need me to call a mechanic for you?"

"No, Guy, but thanks for asking. I don't have a car."

"Well, what are you doing all the way out here, dressed up like you're going to a job interview?"

"I don't know. I can't remember. Maybe I hit my head or something. I do feel very confused right now."

Shaking his head sympathetically, Guy clicked his tongue and concluded, "Well, I can't very well send you on your way in this condition, can I? You want me to take you to the hospital? Have you checked out for a concussion?"

"Uh, no thanks," Paolo answered, a prickling sensation stealing over him that he couldn't quite pin down.

"Okay. Let me know if you change your mind. I don't blame you, though. Never had much time for doctors, myself. Eighty-two and sound as a nut," he proclaimed proudly. "Without those pill pushers reaching their hands in my pockets."

Rising from his chair, Guy explained to Paolo that he had a few more things to take care of in the barn; he told him that he should make himself at home and rest up for a while in the living room. Grabbing an apple from the bowl and tossing one to his guest, he left to finish his daily work. Paolo, after he saw the kitchen door shut, sighed with relief and devoured the whole thing gratefully, leaving only the little brown stem.

Fey sat dejected in front of her full-length mirror, which hung inside her closet door. Faerie houses were, generally, earthen-colored dwellings, made to blend in with their surroundings. Fey's domicile was no exception. The walls and floor of her home were a deep, rich brown. Texture, rather than color, was the element of style. A soft rug of woven moss graced the floor, giving a greenish warmth to the room. The walls were lined with pinecone pieces, creating a herringbone pattern, which appealed to Fey, as it reminded her of fabric, her favorite medium of expression. The furniture had been crafted from delicate willow branches and twigs with seats of woven grasses, like rushes. The curtains were curled, dry oak leaves, which elegantly framed the windows with their crisp, swirled ornamentation. Dried flowers graced the walls in place of pictures. The hearth was constructed of river pebbles with a tiny slate mantel.

Turning first one way and then another, she noted with dismay that her sour expression made her dun looks even plainer. She had cried her eyes out and then depuffed them with a cucumber poultice. She had tied her dull hair up in a colorful silk scarf, but it only made her pallid skin look worse. Rows of bright garments, arrayed in order of color, like a textile rainbow, mocked her from their hiding place. She sadly shut the closet door, hiding the mirror and the clothing from view, and then left to find her friends, Fleur, Yasmine, and Arcenciel.

It didn't take her long to find them. She heard giggling coming from an outcropping of fungus on a large, old tree and flew to join them. She landed as light as a breeze on the brown, woody surface and sat down.

Fleur, a silky-haired blonde with skin the color of ferns and amber eyes flecked with specks of green, sat to one side. Arcenciel, a raven-haired beauty with heavy bangs and eyes the color of emeralds, perched between Fleur and Fey. Her skin was a luminous, pale silver, like mercury. Lastly, Yasmine, a bouncy, giddy blonde with bobbed curls that danced when she moved, stood beside them. Her eyes were sky blue and her skin a creamy alabaster.

"I swear, what a surprise it was to see him there!" Yasmine gasped. "He was definitely man-beautiful." She giggled naughtily. "I was going to play a trick on him and hide that pile of clothes," she went on, "but he woke up and I had to just scrap the idea."

"I'm glad you didn't have the chance," Fey said dryly. She was irritated that her friend had spied on her charge like that. She felt in her heart that it would have been embarrassing to him, if he had known. She sensed a poetic delicacy about him that was completely incongruous with his earthy, rustic exterior.

"But, why, Fey dear? Where is your sense of fun?" Yasmine scolded. "Fey, oh … what has happened to you?" Yasmine's tone went from giggly to somber in an instant as she turned and took in her friend's ravaged looks.

"He is mine, and, oh, I am in such trouble!" Fey broke down sobbing as her friends gathered around. She told them the story, with tears flowing anew, of her misunderstanding and hastily granted wish.

"Oh, but he should be punished," Arcenciel fumed, "for stealing such a gift!"

"You don't understand," Fey lamented. "He didn't even understand that he was taking anything from me. I think he believed we were just talking. He acted like he was starved for conversation and seemed to feel he could confide in me."

The three faeries looked puzzled. Pity for Fey shone in their lovely eyes.

"Well then, if he expected nothing but conversation, that's all he should have gotten." Arcenciel shrugged. "We can still fix this. Let's go find him and reverse everything."

"No, it's too late!" Fey wailed. "I have nothing left in me."

Again, the three beauties huddled around their ruined friend and offered her what comfort they could, but among themselves, they exchanged somber looks, as they knew Fey's life would be very different for a long, long time.

3

Friend

G uy offered Paolo a roof for the night. The young man accepted gratefully and begged his host to allow him to repay by helping him with his work on the farm. After all, he had nowhere pressing to go—as far as he could recall. The old farmer gratefully accepted his offer, telling Paolo he could find plenty of tasks to occupy his time.

As evening drew on, though, his host's attitude seemed to change, as if he were experiencing second thoughts on the idea.

"Paolo?" he asked, opening a can of beans.

"Yes, Guy?" he answered, standing awkwardly by the kitchen door, wishing he knew how to help with dinner. His host looked tired.

"I live alone here, but they know me in town. I have friends. We meet every week for cards and just to shoot the bull. They'd miss me, if I didn't show up. Y'know?" he said sharply, stirring the steaming contents of the saucepan and then emphatically banging the spoon against the lip of the pot.

Paolo shifted his weight uncomfortably and hugged the door frame, feeling the heat of scrutiny as Guy eyed him with a critical expression on his wizened face.

"I don't know what to say, sir. As I told you before, I can't remember how I got here or what it is I'm supposed to do. It's very frustrating," he replied, crossing his arms tightly, aggravation at his lapsed memory betrayed by his voice.

"No car, no suitcase, no nothin'. Heck, do you even have a toothbrush?"

Paolo shrugged, obviously uncomfortable. Guy shook his head, studying his guest with discernment.

"You a city boy?" he continued, judging him by his finely tailored, albeit sweaty, clothes.

"No … I mean, I'm not exactly sure right now." Paolo looked out the window, an expression of pained embarrassment on his face. He hung his head, looking perfectly miserable.

"Well, then, how about we sit down for some dinner now?" the old man suggested in a gruff, quiet voice, spooning a generous scoop of hot beans into each of the two bowls and placing a basket of baguette chunks in the middle of the table. "Maybe if you just relax for a bit, everything will come back to you."

He looked over at his host with gratitude and nodded. Paolo waited until Guy picked up his spoon and then eagerly dug into the fabulous meal that he had been offered, enjoying the uniquely blended sensation of heat and flavor. He could not, for all his effort, recall ever experiencing such a treat. He noted, between blissful bites, that Guy seemed to watch him with amusement twinkling in his hazel eyes.

"Ladies, what is all the commotion?" interrupted a fluid tenor voice.

The four friends turned to see Guiscard standing, arms akimbo, at the edge of their huddle. Fey hung her head. She wanted to hide. Here was the man she had longed for, and he was about to see her at her worst. Beautiful Guiscard, his amber eyes wide, approached them slowly, like one would a skittish rabbit.

"Fey … what happened to you?" he gasped.

Was she that hideous? She let her mousy hair cover her face. Her voice was blocked by a lump clogging her throat. No sound would come out. She could barely even breathe.

"She was tricked into granting an enormous wish," Arcenciel spat indignantly.

Arcenciel then proceeded to relate her version of Fey's story, which was much less sympathetic to Paolo than Fey would have been. Guiscard, deep in consideration, tilted his head to the side, listening thoughtfully. He then lifted Fey's chin in his cupped hand and met her miserable gaze with an intense expression in his gold eyes.

"You have done a fine and just thing. I have seen your young man walking toward the village this morning. His face speaks of a noble character, and, from his raiment, I can see that you have done your absolute best to honor our principles. It will all turn out well in the end. Fey, I am honored to be the friend of such a being as you."

Friend. Oh, Guiscard, I wanted so much more, she lamented silently as a lone tear trickled down her cheek.

Guiscard released her chin with a look of surprise. Fey realized, too late, that he had heard her unguarded thought. Oh, would her shame never end?

4

Nightmare

The evening progressed, the sun setting behind the trees, the air growing cool with the hint of early fall. Sitting on the porch swing, watching the glaring brilliance recede to a gentler light, Paolo began to grow restless, as if overcome by a sense of urgency. A few birds darted by overhead, and he stood up from his seat, as if he would follow them to their lofty climes. Standing with one arm on the porch rail, he watched as two bats flew by in the opposite direction. It was like a changing of the guard. The feeling of oneness with these airborne creatures was almost tangible to him. He stood for a long while, watching, until darkness overtook the landscape and Guy came to join him before retiring for the night.

Guy switched on the light in the guest room, and with a sweep of his upturned palm, he gestured to his guest to make himself at home. Paolo thanked him, feeling significantly refreshed after his meal. He heard the door shut and examined the space. A small dresser overlooked an antique, metal bed. Moving toward the furniture, he glimpsed another man in the room with him.

No, it was just his reflection. He looked intently at himself and found that his own features were completely unfamiliar. Running his hand over his chin, he gazed at his countenance with horrified fascination. How could he not know his own face? It brought back his earlier feeling of disorientation, staring at this stranger that was his reflection. He turned away, unable to look any longer. Instead, he laid his clothes over the small kitchen chair angled in the corner diagonal to the bed, crawled under the sheets, and closed his eyes, trying to will his thoughts to order.

Paolo flew beside the beautiful woman with the lavender skin and hair of fire. They soared effortlessly over the treetops beside a large lake, whose water was an inky black with ripples of white light on the surface; the moonlight illuminated everything with its gentle glow. He looked over at her and smiled with happiness at the thought of sharing the beauty of this night, this place, with her. To his horror, she fainted and fell from his sight. Suddenly, he realized that he was but a wingless man and followed her fall with his own.

Paolo woke both Guy and himself with a loud cry of terror.

"What in the devil, young man?" Guy shouted, switching on the light and appearing in the guest room door. "You about scared the soul out of me." Paolo saw his host's face soften as he looked at him and noticed his expression of confused panic.

"Sorry, Guy," he gasped, shuddering. *What in the world was that about?* he wondered. It had, as dreams often did, seemed very real, but it made absolutely no sense. His heart was racing, and he had broken out in a cold sweat. He took a few deep breaths, willing his composure to return.

"I'm okay, I'm okay," he protested as Guy reappeared, offering him a drink. "Sorry," he repeated, embarrassed.

"Hey, it's all right, kid," the older man said softly, proffering the glass. Paolo accepted it, took a quick swallow, and then exhaled sharply.

"What did you just give me?" He choked. "My throat is on fire."

"Just a little brandy. It'll calm you down. Give it a minute."

Guy shook his head, switched the lights back off, and then shuffled sleepily back to his room. Paolo flopped back on the bed, a comforting warmth stealing over him. It did feel very nice. He closed his eyes and let the brandy wash away the nightmare's ill effects. The vision of the woman, though, remained etched in his memory.

Early the next morning, Paolo put his sweaty clothes back on and stood at the top of the stairs. He could hear Guy in the kitchen fixing breakfast and wanted to join him, but the dog was blocking the way, staring up at him, her tail swishing languidly back and forth as she met his gaze. Again, he eyed her warily, his hand sliding hesitantly back and forth over the banister. He had been told that the dog wouldn't hurt him, and he sensed that his new friend thought his fear irrational. He wanted to trust Guy, as the man had shown him trust.

Slowly, he had made his way down the stairs, keeping his eyes fixed on the dog's face. Breathing somewhat heavily through his mouth, his heart beating quicker in his chest, he approached the bottom step. His face tensed. The dog sat down and lifted up her paw in front of him. Paolo, surprised, knelt slowly and put his palm under the rough pads, looking into her inscrutable eyes, a smile tugging at the corners of his mouth.

Truce.

Looking up, Paolo noticed Guy watching from the kitchen doorway with an expression of amusement. He gave his host a broad grin, and the old man chuckled before returning to the kitchen.

After enjoying a delicious breakfast of sweet, glazed bread and fruit, he sat on the sofa, wound in the bedsheet. Guy had taken all of Paolo's garments that didn't look like they needed dry cleaning and put them in the washer. Courteously, he had told Paolo that he didn't want him to have to accompany him dressed in dirty, stale-smelling clothes and that he was certain there was nothing that would fit the tall, broad-shouldered man in his own wardrobe. He had told his guest that he had to go into town for some groceries and invited him to come along and perhaps get himself some basic necessities, as well.

The living room was small but cozy. It held only a few pieces of furniture. A sofa, old, but in good shape, done up in a blue tweed flecked with earthy brown, faced a functional fireplace. A comfortable chair, in a coordinating plaid, sat closer to the hearth, an ottoman offering rest to the farmer's tired feet. An old coffee table and matching end tables, decorated with plain lamps, and a patterned wool rug completed the decor. Inexpensive, faded artwork graced the walls, and a picture of a young Guillaume with his wife, Marguerite, stood, a happy sentinel, on the mantel. A curved clock with a round face kept time in the middle.

Paolo sipped a mug of steaming coffee laced with milk and a hint of sugar. The flavor was complex—bittersweet and nutty. It seemed to cause a feeling of vitality to steal over him as he ingested it. The lemonade had been very tasty, but it was the mental clarity that the coffee induced that made it superior to the tangy, sweet beverage he had enjoyed the previous afternoon.

He felt bad that his host was out doing the morning work without him, but the old man had refused to let him help until he was properly dressed. Farming was dirty, messy work, Guy had told him, and had added that he didn't want Paolo's only set of clothes—nice ones at that—to end up torn and ruined. He had let him use his shower the night before and told his guest to help himself to whatever he needed. So he sat, clean and comfortable, enjoying a moment of leisure, grateful for the hospitality so freely given. Sophie lay at his feet, man and dog forming a tenuous bond of friendship.

He waited patiently for the farmer, who came in an hour later and handed him his clothes, nearly dry from hanging in the warm autumn sun. He thanked Guy and returned to his room to change. The two men then took off for town.

Paolo sat in the passenger seat of a rather worn, tan pickup, dressed again in what the older man now referred to as his "interview suit." He enjoyed the feeling of moving yet remaining still as the pickup swept along the narrow road to town. It was like flying, yet resting at the same time. Being borne along by a force not his own was unique and exhilarating to him. Strangely enough, it felt both new and familiar at the same time. He let the wind whip over his face as he gazed out at the passing landscape. Full enjoyment of the experience required a certain amount of trust, and occasionally, he would glance over at Guy, whose attention remained focused on the road in front of him. A smile stole over Paolo's face, and he leaned back against the seat and relaxed.

"What're you thinking about, Paolo?" Guy asked.

"Just enjoying the moment," he answered honestly.

"I can see you were meant to live off the land," Guy noted with admiration. "You seem to take such pleasure in the simplest things. Why, I never saw anyone enjoy a glass of lemonade like you." He chuckled.

Paolo turned toward Guy, taking in his amusement. He liked this old man. He could sense wisdom in the soft furrows on his face and in the knots on his hands. Was he brought here on purpose, or was it just luck? He would probably never know.

They pulled past the village square, Paolo taking in its weathered stone paving and carefully manicured public garden, graced with wooden benches so the villagers could sit and enjoy the efforts of the local horticulture club. Achères-la-Forêt was a small but prosperous village. A beautiful fountain stood at the center of the town square; the centerpiece of the round oasis of grass and flowers, traffic flowed around it like a metal river. Businesses lined the main street. The square and most of the alleyways were paved in cobblestone, creating a picturesque warmth. The village was steeped in its agricultural heritage and boasted a museum dedicated to its history. A large stone church, St. Fare, held court in the center, surrounded by its lesser minions.

Guy parked the truck in front of the grocery store.

"You coming?" he asked, as Paolo sat, lost in thought.

He looked over at his host, sincerity in his dark eyes. "It means a lot, that you decided to trust me," he told the farmer. "I can sense that you felt it was a risk, and I wouldn't have blamed you if you had decided not to."

Guy nodded. "Y'know," he offered, "you can stay for a little while, if you'd like, till your head clears a bit."

Paolo was grateful and felt profoundly relieved. He was, truth be told, afraid of what was to come. He was adrift, alone, and unsure why he was even there; the old man was a life raft in his sea of confusion.

The two men then left on their errands together, Guy giving his young friend a reassuring slap on the shoulder.

They stopped in at the grocery store, where Paolo followed Guy around. Bewildered by the overwhelming number of items, he numbly accepted the older man's help in picking out a few basic things to make up a simple toilette. Afterward, Paolo sat on a bench in the square, soaking in the gentle warmth of the autumn sun, Guy having gone to meet his friends for coffee and to "shoot the bull." He had invited his guest, who had demurred, not wanting to be a pesky tagalong.

A dark-haired preteen girl sat on a nearby bench, her nose in a book. Paolo studied her surreptitiously. He didn't want to make her uncomfortable, but he was curious. Her long, brunette hair was held back from her face by a thin black elastic band. She had a straight nose; sharp gray eyes; and thick, arched brows. Her lips were full and rosy and tended to pout more than they smiled. She wore a long-sleeved black T-shirt with some kind of writing on it, which looked foreign though the letters seemed familiar. Her skirt was long and gray, coming to the tops of her boots, which were military style, with thick soles and a low, rugged heel. She wore no makeup but was naturally pretty and wouldn't have needed it anyway. She glanced up, and he smiled unsurely. To his surprise, the girl snapped her book shut and approached him.

"I haven't seen you here before," she stated boldly, slipping onto the opposite end of the bench where he sat.

"Oh, well, I'm not from here, actually," he answered vaguely, hugging his own end of the bench.

"I can tell," she noted.

Paolo looked puzzled at that. Could she read minds, this girl?

"Your accent," she added in explanation.

He nodded, suddenly feeling silly for failing to note the obvious.

"What's that?" he asked, wanting the conversation to continue.

"Just a novel," she responded nonchalantly.

"Any good?" he asked, curious.

"Yeah," she admitted, handing it to him. Paolo studied the cover. It was *Les Miserables*, by Victor Hugo.

"You read it?" she asked.

"No, not yet," he admitted, embarrassed by his ignorance. He handed it back to the serious-faced girl with the hint of a smile. "Maybe you could loan it to me when you're done with it. If you think it's good, I'd like to read it."

"Borrow it yourself. I got it there." She motioned with her head to the medium-sized stone building opposite the church. It was the public library.

"I saw you with Guy Paysanne, didn't I?" she inquired. "You his grandkid or something?"

"Uh, I'm just kind of staying with him for a little while, but no, we're not related," he explained. "Oh, I'm Paolo," he added, remembering formalities.

"I'm Natalie," she introduced herself in return.

They smiled shyly at each other. Suddenly, she drew a sketch pad and pencil out of her backpack and asked in an excited voice, "Could I sketch you?"

Paolo's eyes widened, and he shook his head.

"Oh, no. I-I don't think I would feel comfortable with that." *Why would she want to do that? It's not like I'm interesting to look at.* Really, he was still very uncomfortable with the unfamiliarity of his own countenance. Watching Natalie outline its likeness on paper would only emphasize the strangeness of his blank memory with regard to even his own physical form.

Disappointed, she stuffed the pad and paper back into her bag but stayed in spite of his rebuff.

Guy sat with his buddies at an outdoor table at the crowded café, enjoying the beautiful, early fall weather and the companionship of good, old friends. They sipped strong coffee and smoked, the plumes drifting lazily out over the sidewalk. Usually, about six to eight of them, mostly farmers, would gather at around the same time every week. They met to catch up on the week's events, but for Guy, it was a chance just to talk to someone. His siblings and wife had all passed away, so his friends were all he had left.

The Little Penguin Café was across from the square. It was frequented by most of Achères's coffee-loving shoppers and merchants. The outdoor tables were always occupied until the snow began to fly. At that time, the indoor tables became a hard-won commodity. Claude Bessette, the owner, had an amazing ability not only to pick the finest coffee but also to brew the perfect espresso and the most bliss-inducing café au lait in town. The Ethiopian Yirgacheffe he served was sublime. The building was small—too small for the crowd that usually gathered there. Business had picked up significantly since the dark-haired, energetic man with warm brown eyes and curved nose who stood a mere five foot two had taken the place over. He was a passionate businessman and took his product, but not himself, seriously. He joked openly about being "vertically challenged" and about the difficulty of finding a suitable life partner in a small, rural village.

The tables were immaculately clean. The walls, whitewashed beadboard, were hung with photos of local scenery and Paris landmarks, taken by the proprietor, who, aside from his acumen with an espresso machine, was also a half-decent amateur photographer. The floor was worn golden wood; it was scratched by use but cleaned and polished on a regular basis. The counters were charcoal-colored granite, also skirted with whitewashed beadboard. It was simple and neat. People came for the excellent coffee, but the inviting atmosphere didn't hurt, either.

"Well, I'm just glad to have the help, for now," Guy went on, leaning back in his chair at the end of one of the wooden, outdoor tables. The other men nodded. A few of them were farmers too and understood the need to take advantage of the opportunity for any kind of assistance at this time of the year.

"Odd, though. He shows up dressed in some of the nicest clothes I've ever seen—like from a magazine or something—but has no car, no identification, nothing," he related, perplexed by the enigma Paolo presented.

"Strange," they agreed.

"You trust him?" asked a burly, middle-aged man to Guy's left with dark hair and shrewd blue-gray eyes that looked at him sharply. He was Vincent Durrand, one of the two law enforcement officers in town.

"Aw, I don't know." He shrugged. "My Marguerite used to say I was way too trusting of people. I guess I'm not a good judge of character. The kid has a nice way about him, though—really polite and genuine. Something happened to him, and he woke up in the forest, really far from the road. He says he can't remember anything. It's strange," Guy noted. "He seems so bright, but some things that anyone would know, he acts like he's never seen. You should've seen him in the grocery store. He was absolutely overwhelmed. I offered to take him to the hospital to get checked for a concussion or the like, but he didn't want to go. I just don't know what to make of him," Guy admitted, shaking his head.

"Want me to check around for you?" his friend offered. "I could run a profile for you. Make sure he doesn't match the description of someone they're looking for."

"Sure, thanks," Guy responded appreciatively, glad to have the onus of figuring out his houseguest's intentions off of himself. He scooted his chair back, left money on the table, and made ready to leave.

"Couldn't hurt, if he's got nothing to hide."

5

Mischief

Natalie lingered in the square with Paolo, chatting casually with him, until Guy beckoned. Turning to look back, he noted her watching him with her intense gray eyes as he receded. They made their way to the other side of the street, where the farmer helped Paolo pick out work boots, heavy leather gloves, and several shirts at the local men's outfitters. De Gaul and Son was an old, well-established business, whose owner, Jacques de Gaul, Guy shared, was a longtime friend.

Jacques had stepped out for an hour, but his son, Gilbert, was eager to help.

"So," he noted Paolo's clothing with professional discernment, "Ralph Lauren? I think I saw this outfit in the fall line. Very nice," he noted, approvingly.

Paolo looked at him with a confused expression. What was he talking about?

"Um, I'm not sure," he shook his head as Gilbert fingered the sleeve of his shirt.

"I'll bet your girlfriend bought it for you," he guessed smugly, giving it a tug.

Paolo laughed under his breath. It was possible. He did remember a woman from his past. If only he could get his brain to release the information. It was like it was dammed up inside of him, stubbornly refusing to reveal itself.

"You're probably right," he admitted humbly. He would have never picked out anything so fine for himself.

"What size do you wear?" the shopkeeper asked him matter-of-factly, his head tilted to the side in consideration.

"Ah, I'm ... I'm not sure, really," Paolo confessed, uncomfortably.

Guy flipped through a pile of work clothes, picking out an item and handing it to his new friend.

"Here, try these on for size, and we'll go from there."

Gilbert shook his head with a sneer of disapproval at the overalls Guy had chosen. After whipping out a measuring tape and precisely measuring his customer's waist and inseam, to Paolo's discomfort, he replaced them with a pair of jeans. He had a strong sense of personal space, but, obviously, the shopkeeper did not.

"Perfectly fitting clothing is an affirmation of the human form," Gilbert explained, noticing Paolo's reaction to his efforts. "But these things," he scoffed, holding the offensive garment up over his head, switching gears to a less poetic bend, "are a total chick-repellant."

Paolo laughed, nudging Guy, who proudly sported a similar pair.

"I had the best woman a man could ever want." Guy bristled. "And she never had a problem with my work pants. I'm a farmer, Gilbert. We're not into making fashion statements."

"You want your friend here to end up a lonely old bachelor?" Gilbert asked with sarcastic humor.

Guy just laughed, but he looked hurt by the salesman's barb. Paolo realized that the widower fit that description, for all intents and purposes.

"Don't ever take wardrobe advice from anyone over forty," the junior salesman admonished Paolo with a wink, oblivious to his gaffe.

The owner's son had a pleasant attentiveness about him. Immaculately dressed in a dark-navy suit, white shirt, and bright-yellow tie, he wore his light-brown hair swept elegantly back to one side. It shone with gold highlights when hit by the sun streaming in through the large, bowed display window. His eyes were the color of Caribbean water, and they were quick to betray a twinkle of mischief. Gilbert was small and neat compared with Paolo's bulk; he was a good three inches shorter with a leaner frame. His face possessed an unflawed masculine symmetry. He seemed to have an unshakeable confidence that Paolo found made him immediately likeable.

The business of "De Gaul and Son, Haberdashers," was large in size, stocking both work clothes for the farming community and formal, dress, and casual attire for businessmen. The shop looked prosperous and neat, the merchandise seemed conservative and classic. The clothing store, for some reason, was a more comfortable place for him than the grocery store, as if the fabrics themselves had soothing voices that spoke to him like old friends. The floors were dark, polished wood. The counters were old, well-cared-for mahogany. The walls were paneled in antique, well-preserved, dark wood, as well, and were lined with cubbies for merchandise. Everything was folded meticulously.

Holding court over the shop, just to the right of the door, a row of somber portraits hung near the ceiling, depicting the line of owners, from the scowling founder to the gentle, round-faced proprietor as he looked in his midtwenties. Giving his attention to the portraits, Paolo noted that, in the first one, the hostile eyes of the business's original owner seemed to follow him wherever he went. It was kind of unsettling.

"Pay him no mind," Gilbert stated, noting Paolo's discomfited study of the painting. "He's always in a bad mood, that one."

Paolo looked blankly at the salesman and then laughed under his breath, unsure what to make of the shopkeeper's sense of humor. He went to try on the jeans, as well as a few other items Gilbert had piled on top. He tried them on and was impressed to note that the man seemed to have a genuine knack for his job.

After handing the items back to Gilbert with a quiet nod of approval, he decided to poke around the shop. After neatly folding the items and wrapping them on the counter, the smartly dressed man asked Paolo if he needed anything else.

"Oh, I just would like to get something for Guy," he answered absently, his eyes roving in vain for something that would please his friend.

"Well, I know Guy," the young shopkeeper responded quietly with a glance at the old man, who was looking at the sale rack at the opposite end of the store and beckoned for Paolo to follow him. "I think I can help. He fishes with my dad, and last time they went, he said his waders were no good. They must've gotten a hole in them somewhere. Well," he said, showing Paolo a set of long, thigh-high rubber boots, "these should fit. What do you think?"

Paolo had no idea, really, but checked his wallet to make sure he had enough money left to pay for them. It had seemed a large sum at first, but he went home with very little left to thicken the billfold stuffed in his back pocket. He didn't really care. He liked the soft leather holder much more than the starchy paper inside anyway. The idea of money was confusing to him. He knew the denominations of the euros and their approximate worth almost, it seemed, in an abstract way, as one would know of a place he had never visited. But the need for it? The concept eluded him.

From her perch on the edge of the picture frame that encased the scowling visage of Jean Jacques de Gaul, Yasmine watched with delight as Fey's boy entered the shop, accompanied by a grizzled old man. She giggled as Paolo looked right at her, as if he could feel her gazing down upon him. Fey would be so jealous! Really, she was there to spy on Gilbert. She had taken him on as a challenge. He was getting to be just the right age to become hopelessly smitten with a girl. Trouble was he seemed to be more interested in the chase than the prize. Well, she would fix that, she vowed. She would help the handsome villager find his soul mate.

She observed as Gilbert picked the perfect outfit for the tall, luscious man, transforming him from Fey's vision of metropolitan elegance to rustic swain. The latter seemed, actually, to suit him better. Fey could learn something from this human about men's attire, she noted with admiration, watching as Gilbert wrapped up Paolo's purchases, made witty pleasantries, and sent him on his way with a friendly smile. As the door shut behind his customers, though, Yasmine's project looked up at the picture with a frown.

"Stop your staring, Grandpa," he scolded. "You're scaring my customers with your nasty scowl."

He pulled a suction-cup-tipped dart out of his pocket and flung it at the picture, his jaw twisted in concentration. Yasmine squealed and flew quickly to the side as it hit just below where her legs had been swinging.

"I swear, when I take over, that thing is going in the Dumpster," he muttered. "The bloody thing gives me the creeps."

Yasmine wondered if he sensed her presence or if it was the gloomy picture that bothered him. His humor restored, young de Gaul busied himself tidying up until the next customers arrived. The faerie flew out the open door as they came in, eager to tell her friends what she had seen.

Fey halfheartedly traipsed after Guiscard and Yasmine as they spied upon two lovers enjoying a picnic in the clearing. She was a dark-haired, natural beauty with gray eyes and full red lips. Her lover was handsome, with thick, auburn hair and sharp, light-brown eyes, but there was something thuggish about his expression, the morose faerie noted with distaste. His build was powerful, yet compact, and he held the reins in the relationship, that was clear.

"And thus, the haughty are brought low by my mighty hand," Guiscard laughed, as he shot a tiny, invisible arrow at the cocksure swain's chest. It hit the mark. He slapped and then scratched at his chest right where his heart should be. Fortunately, in his vanity, he had removed his shirt so that his lovely companion could admire his rippling abs, making Guiscard's task much easier.

"But I shall do thee mischief in the wood!" he quoted from his favorite play, *A Midsummer Night's Dream*, winking at Fey, who blushed at the innuendo.

Yasmine laughed in delight, clapping her little hands and jumping up and down with glee, making her blonde curls dance. She added her Helena to his Demetrius:

> We cannot fight for love, as men may do;
> We should be wood and were not made to woo.

"In a few hours' time, yon lover will be but a puling puppy at the lovely maid's feet," he boasted, looking over at Fey with a self-satisfied expression.

She, in turn, finished up the scene, but her words fell flat, spoiling the lighthearted moment.

> I'll follow thee and make a heaven of hell,
> To die upon the hand I love so well.

Yasmine folded her arms and shook her head. Guiscard coughed. Fey felt like a stodgy old spinster crashing a party of teenagers. She tried to swallow her melancholy, grateful that Guiscard still called her friend and sought her company. Oh, how worthy he was!

Not one to be kept in low spirits, Yasmine quickly tried to recover the levity of their outing. "Fey, do you think this young man's looks parallel your own black-haired boy's?"

"No, Yasmine, I don't," she replied, a tad too acidly. "His mannerisms are boorish, and his good looks are tainted by vapidity," she spat, arms crossed, looking down her nose at the subject of discussion.

Yasmine laughed a deep, throaty chuckle and looked knowingly at her friend, as if reading her like an open book. Uncomfortable, Fey looked away from her discerning gaze and resumed staring at the couple below. She had tried to look disinterested when her friend told her that "her boy" was living with a local farmer and that it looked like he might just decide to stay on for a while, but Yasmine was canny, being a skilled matchmaker, in spite of her outward silliness.

"I find him sorely lacking in chivalry," Guiscard agreed.

"I wonder which one the woman would choose," Yasmine mused, narrowing her almond-shaped eyes in contemplation and twirling a lock of hair around her finger, "if she was given the opportunity?"

Fey studied her friend suspiciously, feeling suddenly protective of her charge, but Guiscard interrupted, clapping his hands together with finality. "Well, a fine day's work. Fair ladies, hie we to imbibe sweet nectar at my loft."

Fair ladies? Fey lamented. *He must have been imbibing already to include me in that statement.*

After unloading the truck with Paolo, Guy went to fix dinner. By the time the food was ready, the young man had put away his new clothes, left the gift for his host in the living room, and set the table.

The first night, Paolo had enjoyed Guy's cooking, finding it simple and satisfying. That night, though, it smelled of dead, charred animal flesh. He could already feel his stomach growing uneasy.

"Steak dinner tonight!" Guy proclaimed proudly, setting a platter with two juicy strips of beef on the table between them. He speared the smaller piece with obvious glee and then generously motioned for his young guest to have the larger share.

Reluctantly, Paolo imitated his host, slowly spearing the piece of seared flesh and dropping it onto his plate with unmitigated disgust, which he tried valiantly to hide. Guy did not deserve his kindness repaid with ingratitude.

Guy lopped off a hefty chunk, chewing contentedly on the savory treat. Paolo pared as small a sliver as possible and brought it to his lips.

Oh, I can't do this, he thought, closing his eyes.

"Good stuff, eh?" Guy asked with self-satisfaction.

Paolo smiled weakly, choking down the glob of masticated corpse with a large gulp of water. He broke out into a cold sweat. His insides began to churn.

No, no, no, he pleaded with his uncooperative digestive system and ran, gagging, from the house. He leaned, retching, over the porch rail. His stomach recoiled, unrelenting, until all that was left inside of him was the burned lining of his esophagus.

Guy caught up with him and handed him a glass of water. "Paolo, what's the matter? Are you sick? Maybe you do have a concussion, after all. One of the symptoms is nausea, they say. We should take you to the hospital," he said with concern, seeing the violence of his reaction.

He shook his head, wiping his face on the towel Guy tossed him. Cringing with embarrassment, he explained himself. "Um, I hate to seem ungrateful. Sorry, sir," he apologized, "but I don't think I can eat that."

"You a vegetarian?" he guessed.

"I think maybe I am," Paolo responded. How would he know? He could barely remember his first name. Still, the very thought of eating another living creature filled him with revulsion. Something about it seemed barbaric. He would never try again.

"Well, why didn't you just tell me in the first place?" he scolded. "I wouldn't have cared. Lots of people are nowadays," he assured him. "You're cheaper to feed that way, anyway," he joked.

Paolo gave a self-deprecating laugh, downing the proffered water in a few gulps. Guy went back to finish his dinner, but unable to bear the smell, Paolo sat on the porch swing to wait for his well-meaning friend to finish.

Again, as evening drew on, the same feeling of restlessness stole over him, as if there was something else he should be doing, somewhere else he should be. As the sun set, again, he found his thoughts borne aloft over the fields, as though they would take flight and carry him away. This time, instead of giving in to the feeling, he changed into the new work clothes he had purchased and helped Guy with a few chores, the feeling of usefulness replacing the hunger to flee.

Fey lounged languidly on Guiscard's comfortable chaise. He, himself, was perched atop a three-legged stool, an acorn mug of nectar in his hands. His loft was decorated in the same earthy colors as Fey's hideaway, to blend in with its surroundings. His furniture was made of carved wood, with clever owl heads on the chair tops, wings swooping down the sides. The table sported intricate designs engraved on the edge. Moons, stars, and suns wound their way around the circumference. The walls were of beautiful white birch bark, unornamented.

A shelf that ran around the perimeter of the room near the ceiling was lined with vials full of potential actions. Guiscard, unlike Fey, had studied enchantments carefully. He was definitely the one they all went to when in need of a spell or powder. Among their clan, only Arcenciel could compete with his knowledge.

A slate hearth fronted a pebbled fireplace, which blazed merrily with tiny twigs. The window ledges were of rough, mossy bark. It was a cheery place and bespoke a being of station in their world. Yasmine hovered beside him, her arm draped cozily over his shoulder. She was on her second cupful of nectar—and feeling it.

"I think Fey has a crush on her Paaahwlow," she drawled, giggling. "See how her face lights up when I even just say his name?"

Fey scowled at her friend. "Nonsense," she protested, but her pallid skin betrayed a blush, which she attempted to hide behind a long draft of nectar. She noted Guiscard had looked her way, and she hoped he had not caught her flushed complexion before she had had a chance to conceal it. He was too perceptive to be fooled by her weak protest, she knew. Yasmine was a matchmaker and, even in her cups, would be able to discern feelings of love between a man and woman.

"Y'know what *I* think?" her half-inebriated friend slurred. Fey just looked at her in anxious silence, wishing she knew how to stop her before she went on.

"I think that Fey doesn't *want* to change him back. I think she wants to keep her sweet, lovely boy as a pet," she opined, adding in a seductive, throaty purr, "He certainly is delicious."

Fey looked over at Guiscard, mortified by Yasmine's candid observation. She must have been mistaken, but she thought she saw hurt written on Guiscard's face. Was the object of her affections so self-absorbed that he required all the faerie maidens' complete adoration—even ugly old Fey's?

After exchanging a loaded glance with Guiscard, she watched as Yasmine slipped her free hand in the sheath of love arrows still hanging from his back. The drunken matchmaker delicately slid two out with a smirk, tucking them in her belt. She held one finger to her lips and winked. Fey's eyes widened at her friend's audacity, but she said nothing. In their world, deception was never rewarded. No action was necessary on her part to ensure it. Fey realized, with some concern, that her knowledge of Yasmine's theft made her an accomplice.

"Well then, my friends," the matchmaker crooned, giving Fey an air-kiss on each cheek and Guiscard a real one on his lips, "I really must be off then. Thank you so much for the lovely day." Making her way out, she brushed past him, caressing his shoulder as she left.

An awkward silence ensued after Yasmine had swept gracefully into the night. Both Fey and Guiscard attempted to break it at the same time, resulting in an even longer pause. Fey rose up and looked into her adored friend's beautiful golden eyes. She took his hands in her own.

"I know how I look," she began. "I just want you to know how grateful I am that you still count me as your friend and include me in your endeavors."

She dropped his hands and flew off into the night before he could respond.

6

Stolen Arrow

Weeks went by, and still, Paolo remembered nothing of his life before Achères. Guy was growing used to his presence and began to hope his young guest would stay on. His new apprentice learned quickly and was fast taking over the heavier chores, which had become so difficult for the stubbornly independent octogenarian. Many tasks the old farmer had neglected, because he lacked the physical strength to do them had been tackled by his willing young helper, whose pale skin had, at first, burned and then lightly tanned before autumn set in.

The farmer tried to encourage his young charge to seek the company of those his own age, maybe get a girlfriend. Paolo would grow quiet, his introversion taking over. The messy mop of black hair would drop down like camouflage. He would nod, smile guiltily, agree with everything Guy said—and do nothing.

It had become their normal Saturday routine. The pickup rolled along slowly on its way to town on a chilly morning in November. The frost graced the trees and fields, and it gave a sparkly coating to everything as the sun glowed gently, warming the night-cooled landscape. Guy parked in his usual spot in front of the grocery store. Today though, he gave Paolo a few errands to do while he went to join his buddies at the Little Penguin. Despite the chill, the regulars sat outside, so they could smoke.

"Hey, Guy." Vincent Durrand pulled up a chair at the outdoor seating of the café and joined them. He nodded to the group in general as a greeting and then continued, "I found nothing amiss on your hired hand. Fact is, I found nothing on him at all."

"He's a good person, Vin," Guy argued.

"Just be careful," Vincent cautioned, taking a slow sip of hot black coffee. "Con men can weasel their way in, earn your trust, and then wipe out your life savings," he went on, emphatically slapping his hand on the table.

Guy snorted. "He's worked with me for almost two months, and I had to beg him to take his pay," he told the officer. Guy had loved the new waders he had been surprised with but felt terribly guilty that this penniless boy would spend his last bit of money on him. Touched by his selfless generosity, he had vowed to pay Paolo well for his hard work from the wheat profits of last year's crop. "No, Vin, I think Paolo's just a nice young man who ran into some bad luck."

Yasmine bided her time, waiting for her chance. She would stir up some fun before this old year ended—she would. She followed Paolo as he strode through town, dressed in the beautiful clothing Fey had given him, in just the direction she had hoped he would take. She had been doing this for several weeks with no success, but perhaps today would be different. It was too perfect! He opened the door to the Achères Herb and Natural Foods Store, which sold natural remedies and organic health foods, and, after glancing around unsurely, ducked inside. Yasmine whizzed by just before the door shut and perched among the bottles and boxes on the top shelf.

The shop was small but cheerful, the aisles close. Shelves ran from floor to ceiling, neatly stacked with plastic bottles filled with herbal supplements and bins of bulk nuts and grains. A bowed window in the front of the shop displayed merchandise and specials, the business name printed in gold-leaf lettering on the panes of glass. Toward the back of the store, refrigerated cases held organic produce, most of it locally grown. The atmosphere of the shop was utilitarian and simple, and the employees, all women, dressed casually in denim skirts, jeans, and T-shirts.

Just below where Yasmine had perched herself, the dark-haired beauty she had seen in the clearing that day with Fey and Guiscard was bent over a display, putting out new stock. Yasmine took the stolen arrow from her belt and nocked it in her bow. As Paolo turned to ask the woman for assistance, she stretched the bowstring taut and let the arrow fly. She danced and giggled as it hit the mark, her jaunty curls bouncing. Oh, how she wished Fleur was here to share the moment! He brushed the front of his vest and caught the woman's gaze.

"Uh, hi," he greeted her quietly, looking loath to bother her.

"May I help you?" she replied with a friendly, detached smile.

"Ah, yes, um, my friend, he has, uh, really bad arthritis in his hands and he, uh, he sent me here to …" Paolo trailed off, at a strange loss for words. He stared at the woman with a dazed look for a moment, as if he were in a stupor.

"Right here," she instructed and beckoned, as he followed her down the aisle. Yasmine chuckled knowingly as she noted her subject breathing in the woman's vanilla-scented shampoo like an aphrodisiac. The old, wooden floorboards protested noisily as the two proceeded down the aisle.

"This product works really well with few side effects," she offered. "Is he on any other medications?"

"No—I mean, I don't think so," he answered hesitantly, as if he were struggling to pay attention.

"Well, make sure he checks with his doctor before he takes it," she admonished with a serious look on her pretty face.

"Oh, sure, sure."

Yasmine rolled her eyes. This was going nowhere. She took a small vial from around her neck and sprinkled the contents over the top of Paolo's head. Just then, however, the door opened as another customer entered, blowing the powder in the girl's direction.

"*Zut alors!*" the faerie fussed. "That was courage. I should have screwed it to the sticking place," she joked, availing herself of any opportunity to quote the

Bard. Oh, she could crack herself up all right. But now what would happen? With the love arrow firmly nestled in Paolo's breast and the courage to act wasted on the silly girl, she waited with bated breath to find out. Paolo looked like he was locked in an inner conflict. Yasmine imagined love and shyness dueling for dominance in his embattled psyche. Flying over his head, she sought to tip the balance in Eros's favor. Turning the empty vial upside down, right above his head, she smacked it hard three times.

"Oh, I just need a little bit," she fretted, giving it a hearty shake. A few flakes drifted lazily down before he moved away. Would it be enough? She might not get another chance like this.

They returned with a white bottle to the register. *It's now or never,* Yasmine thought nervously. Paolo swallowed hard and gave the beautiful girl in front of him a sideways glance, saying softly, "So, would you like to go to a movie or something … after you get off work, I mean? I just got paid. We could go the Denis à Achères for dinner. I heard they have great eggplant parmigiana," he rambled on.

"Michelle!" a loud voice interrupted.

It was the arrogant punk from the meadow. Yasmine recognized him immediately. The love arrow must not have hit the mark, because his cocksure swagger had been replaced with a frightening, dangerous possessiveness. Funny, it had seemed a direct hit at the time. Guiscard was an excellent archer. How could he have missed?

Michelle swirled around defiantly to face her bullying boyfriend. The courage dust had hit her square on.

"Excuse me?" she threw back, tossing her dark mane of hair. Paolo watched, entranced, as her silky brunette tresses danced enticingly in front of him.

"Who's this loser?" he bristled, shoving Paolo aside to get closer to Michelle, hoping to intimidate her with his physical strength.

"It just so happens," Michelle retorted, "that … this person …"

"Paolo," he introduced himself, smiling broadly at her.

"Paolo," she nodded toward him, "is taking me to a movie this evening, and dinner."

She quickly rang up his purchase and completed the transaction, looking him purposefully in the eye while saying, "I'm done at six."

Paolo smiled at her but shot a nervous glance at the brutish stranger, who glared daggers at him as he left.

"Oh, this is not good," Yasmine fretted, shaking her head. "I have a very bad feeling about this, and Fey is not going to be happy."

7

Date

*P*aolo's heart soared as he flew through the rest of Guy's errands. He stopped by the flower shop, where he mulled over the roses, freesias, and daisies before settling on a single pink rose—perfect for the first blush of love he felt for his beautiful Michelle. Then he crossed over to the library to see if Natalie was finished with her book. If such a bright person thought it was worth reading, it had to be good.

No, it was still out. Well, it did look pretty thick. Paolo pictured himself leafing slowly through the pages on a Sunday afternoon. He turned to leave and almost bumped right into Natalie, who was just coming in. This was not surprising. He seemed to run into her almost every time he came to town.

"Oh, hi, Natalie," he said, genuinely glad to see her.

"Hey, Paolo. You look happy today," she noted, taking in his undisguised glow.

"Yes," he answered, dropping his head to mask the feeling of exuberance he felt.

"What're you doing here?"

"Oh, I came to see if you were done with your book, yet."

"Sorry, it's really long, and I have other stuff I have to study. I promise you I'll let you know when I'm finished, though. I really am enjoying it. I think it's my absolute favorite book ever," she shared with genuine enthusiasm.

She stood before him, her sketchbook in hand, craning her neck to inspect the packages he was balancing in his arms. She spied the rose peeking out from the waxed paper wrapping, and her face again grew serious.

"Date?" she asked archly.

"Yeah, her name is Michelle. I just met her today. She is so gorgeous. I can't believe she said yes," he gushed.

"She wouldn't happen to work at the herb store?" Natalie asked, her gaze flitting from the white pill bottle he clutched in his hand back to his face; her eyebrow rose, and her lips pressed themselves into a pout.

"You know her?" he asked excitedly. He hoped Natalie could tell him a little more about her beforehand.

"She's my sister," she sneered and stomped off to the stacks in a huff.

Paolo stared after her for a minute, unsure what to make of this peculiar, unpredictable little girl.

Natalie found a quiet spot in the library stacks, sat down cross-legged on the floor, and opened her sketchbook—ferns, the fountain in the town square, a dog sleeping in the sun, and then Paolo, deep in thought. She ran her pencil lightly over the shoulder she had sketched. She had been instantly drawn to him from the first time they had sat together in the square and had been finding every opportunity to run into him when he came to the village on weekends. She, who had been so badly hurt by the evil of another's intentions, instinctively recognized the innocence of his spirit and wanted to be close to him.

She had followed him one day. He and Guy went to Mass at St. Fare every Sunday. She had slipped in quietly as the liturgy was beginning and easily found a seat in the half-empty, vaulted hall. She had chosen her spot carefully.

A well-placed pillar both hid her from sight and gave her a clear view of her subject, bathed in rosy light from the stained-glass windows.

The church was fairly large for a village as small as Achères and was well maintained. Its walls were of grayish stone, which was freshly whitewashed on the inside. Fluted pillars with classic acanthus leaf ornamentation at the top lined themselves up on both sides of the aisles, somber sentries to the atmosphere of reverence. Stained-glass windows, depicting St. Fare and various other worthies, lined the walls from front to rear, with a small rose window facing the nave. A round dome graced the front, directly above the altar. The interior of its concave surface was frescoed with images of the four evangelists, looking, to Natalie, way too old to be realistic, unless people aged really fast back in those "ancient" times. They were just boring, judgmental old men who had nothing to do with her or her life. No wonder the place had been half empty.

What had he been thinking about? He hadn't seemed focused on the homily, which had been insufferably dull, in her estimation, but had let his eyes wander over the beautiful, colored glass that had adorned the openings in the stone walls for centuries. Guy had sat beside him, back straight, eyes forward, a real old-school Catholic.

Natalie hated God. He had abandoned her even as she cried out for Him to save her. She guessed she would go to hell for this, but she didn't care. She didn't want to go to heaven anyway. From what she could see, it was a place for Goody Two-shoes who didn't question anything and wore their precious purity on their backs in the form of silly, white, baggy choir robes. She didn't want to go to hell either, though. She felt she had suffered enough already. *Just snuff me out when You're done with me, please,* she would request of God, sarcastically. After all, she hadn't asked to be born.

She pulled out her pencil and began to sketch.

Gilbert leaned on the front counter by the cash register, bored. He hated working every Saturday and longed to have weekends off, like normal people did. The shop bell rang, and he looked up. It was that Italian guy staying with old man Paysanne. People had been talking about him. It seemed he was quite a mystery.

Well, this should be interesting, he thought, his aspect brightening.

"Hey, new kid in town," he greeted his customer with a cheerful smile, lifting his elbows from the counter and walking over toward him.

"Hey, yourself," Paolo returned cheerfully.

"What brings you in?" Gilbert asked. "Need some new overalls?"

Paolo laughed as Gilbert pulled out the largest pair he had and waved them in front of him, making them dance.

"No, thanks." He shook his head.

"Well then, since I'm not a mind reader ..." he joked. He would never have done this with his older customers, but he could get away with it with the younger set, as long as his father was not around.

"I got a date." Paolo beamed. "And I don't really have much to wear, besides my work clothes."

"Girl in town?" Gilbert asked, his eyes growing wider, hungry for some new gossip.

"Yes ... as a matter of fact, she works at that natural foods store on the next block."

"Jacqueline?" Gilbert guessed. She was okay, but not exactly amazing. Not bad for a first try, though, he conceded.

"No, her name is Michelle," he answered, pronouncing her name like a poem.

Gilbert shook his head and gave Paolo a dubious look. "Man, her boyfriend is a real jerk. I'd steer clear of her if I were you," he warned, his brow furrowed for emphasis.

"She can go out with anyone she wants," Paolo countered, his chin lifted in defiance. "Besides, I didn't exactly have to twist her arm," he added proudly.

"Still, you don't want to go looking for trouble," Gilbert cautioned, his liquid blue eyes expressing genuine concern. He folded the giant overalls with the perfect efficiency of a practiced shopkeeper, placing them back on their shelf. "Don't say I didn't warn you."

Truth be told, if he could have bagged a date with Michelle, he would have done it a long time ago. He still carried a torch for her that went way back to high school and was a bit jealous of Paolo at the moment. It seemed to be true that you always wanted the most what you couldn't have. At the present, though, she seemed hung up on that muscle-bound mechanic she dated.

The two young men took their time deciding what the best look would be. Gilbert chose a black oxford shirt and black wool dress pants, as if guessing, on some intuitive level, that it was the customer's natural palette. Paolo preferred a white shirt and charcoal tie, since his coat was black. Plus, it would look better for Mass on Sundays, he argued. Gilbert nodded approvingly, and the two shook hands.

"Good luck, man," Gilbert offered, a note of concern still lingering in his voice.

"Thanks," Paolo called back over his shoulder as he hurried out the door.

The shop began to fill up with the Saturday rush, and Gilbert was soon occupied with his duties. His father joined him to handle the flow of customers.

"I was about to send out a search party for you," groused Guy, as Paolo threw his bundles in the back of the pickup and climbed up into the passenger seat.

"I got a date!" he exclaimed, his face lit up with a slightly manic glow.

"No, sir!" Guy chuckled. "Who's the lucky lady?"

"Her name is Michelle. She works at that shop you sent me to. Oh, by the way, here's the stuff you sent me to get," he added as an afterthought, handing the driver a large plastic bottle of tablets.

"Thanks," Guy replied, tossing them on the seat.

The passing countryside looked twice as beautiful on the ride home, the midautumn sun illuminating the drowsy landscape with its gentle warmth. It was a feeling like no other, the excitement of meeting someone with whom he just might fall in love, and Paolo drank it in with all the enthusiasm of his inexperienced heart.

8

Black Onyx

Yasmine sat in the branches of a nearby tree, whose leaves had almost all dropped. She looked, of all the faeries, the most human, with her creamy skin; riot of blonde, bobbed curls, which showed the curve of her neck enticingly; and almond-shaped, baby-blue eyes. Her dress was a frothy pink creation of Fey's, made of milkweed threads and thistledown. She shivered as the air changed from cool to cold, waiting for the appointed time. She felt the cold, but it, alone, was no threat to her.

She spotted a young man ducking out of the alley beside the haberdashery at about ten minutes to six, a guilty look on his face. He cast his gaze about as if looking for someone, pulled his collar up against the cold, and hurried away. It was Gilbert, closing shop ten minutes early. Yasmine smiled at his naughtiness, her coquettish dimple appearing on her cheek as she narrowed her eyes and shook her head. She would love to have spied on him, but she had other fish to fry this evening.

She saw Fey's boy walking purposefully up the sidewalk toward her.

"Now the fun begins," she said aloud to herself, rubbing her hands together, both in glee and to warm them as she followed him up the dark street.

Paolo stood in front of the Achères Herb and Natural Foods Store nervously waiting for Michelle. Yasmine watched from her perch in a nearby tree, as anxious as her subject. At six o'clock, Michelle emerged from the darkened building, locked the door, and pocketed the key. She turned, only to see Paolo standing there, one hand in his coat pocket, the other behind his back, a hint of an unsure smile playing at the corners of his mouth. Yasmine thought she looked startled to see him standing there waiting for her.

Paolo didn't seem to notice, though, and pulled his hand from behind his back, offering her the waxed paper bundle.

"Oh, how sweet," she cooed, taking the rose with obvious delight.

Yasmine, warmed by the scene below, forgot about the cold. She could almost feel the heat of passion burning beneath her. She clapped with delight as Michelle held the rose like it was a sleeping child.

"I made dinner reservations at Denis à Achères, if that's okay, and I found out what movies are playing, so you can pick what we go see," he stated with happy pride. He took her arm in his and led her down the street.

She smiled up at him nervously and then glanced behind them.

"You okay?" he asked, sensing her discomfort.

"Sure," she responded nervously. "Let's go."

Yasmine trailed them as they made their way to their trysting spot.

What had gotten into her? Michelle felt a gnawing anxiety growing in the pit of her stomach. This was not going to end well, she was sure. And yet, here she was, with this adorable, charming guy, though he was not her usual type. She went for a touch of danger in a man, a "bad boy." Yet, it was refreshing to be treated like a lady, she thought, as he pulled her chair out for her at the table they were led to in the restaurant. She noted that he had changed from the outfit he had worn earlier in the day. Suddenly, she felt underdressed.

"I wish I had had time to go home and change," she lamented. "You look so nice."

"You look fine," he assured her with an appreciative smile. Her outfit consisted of a belted cream sweater, which fit her curvy figure rather nicely; a denim skirt that fell to just above her knees; and brown leather boots with a high, wedge heel. Her clothing, earthy and intelligent, suggested an approachable confidence. There was nothing pretentious about Michelle.

Denis à Achères was the only nice restaurant in the village. It had achieved one Michelin star, to which it clung tenuously. Still, the locals relied on it for anniversaries, birthdays, and any other noteworthy occasion where dropping a substantial amount of money on dinner was required. It was a fairly large facility and boasted a banquet room for small wedding receptions. The exterior was light stone; the interior had whitewashed, smooth walls decorated by decent artwork with an idyllic flair. White-robed tables, surrounded with skirted parsons chairs done up in burgundy silk adorned the dining room. An excess of silverware was laid out to confuse the more rudimentary diner. The wine list was extensive and expensive—overpriced, an ungenerous patron might say. Michelle had been there once or twice, but never with René le Roux. The place just wasn't his style.

In the colder months, as on this particular evening, a cheery fire burned in the large, river-stone hearth at the far end of the dining room, lending a casual note to the overall impression of elegance the establishment attempted to portray. Patterned carpeting gave warmth to the decor. Quiet jazz music in the background completed the atmosphere.

The host frowned as Paolo eagerly jumped in on his attempt to seat Michelle, as if his moment to impress her had been stolen away, she noted with amusement. The waiter arrived and recited the wine suggestions and the specials.

"The veal osso bucco is very good tonight," he suggested.

"Ah, I'm a vegetarian," Paolo responded automatically. Michelle saw him shoot her a nervous glance, as if aware that he had made a gaffe by professing his own preferences before even finding out hers.

Her face had brightened, however, and she looked at Paolo, exclaiming, "Me too! What a coincidence!"

He beamed at her and lowered his head shyly, his dark hair falling over his right eye as if trained to do so, relief clearly written on his features. Michelle smiled, which made him blush. René never blushed. She thought it was absolutely adorable.

From that moment on, the conversation flowed like a mountain spring. Michelle forgot her anxieties, and, for a while, she laughed, flirted, and was happy. Paolo glowed under her attention. He leaned forward in his chair and seemed to hang on her every word, which was very flattering. René always wanted to talk about himself and grew bored when she tried to tell him anything about something she found interesting. Paolo told her of his desire to travel, of the beauty of Lombardia, and about the places he still wished to explore. She spoke of her love of nature, both animals and plants, and of her special knowledge of the healing properties of foods and herbs. He jokingly quizzed her on their meal, asking her what salubrious benefits lay below the tasty sauces. She proudly impressed him by actually giving serious responses to his lighthearted queries.

She told him of her dream of traveling to the rain forest to study the beautiful, mysterious plants that grew there, to see them in person, in their natural setting. The conversation then turned to dreams in general. She told him, hesitantly, that she kept having a recurring dream about a rat. He listened attentively, but she suddenly felt sorry she had told him.

"Sorry, not very appropriate dinner talk," she apologized. It was strange, though. The rat would show up in her bedroom, at work, even in her car once. It always scared her. She never talked about it with Natalie. This guy, though, she felt she could tell him things, and he would understand.

"Don't worry about it. I think it's kind of interesting," he responded, not seeming offended, but intrigued. "You're going to think this is really strange," he said, blushing.

"What's that?" Michelle laughed, her eyes sparkling. It seemed that she was right. He did understand.

"I, uh, I keep having dreams about bats," he shared, smiling self-consciously. "At least you can jump on a chair in your dream to get away from it. Mine are all flying around my head sometimes, in my dream." He gestured for emphasis, as if he were shooing the imaginary pests away.

Michelle laughed until her stomach hurt at the thought of it, and Paolo joined in.

The dinner crowd changed from early to late diners, and Paolo gasped, "What time is it?"

"Why?" she asked, her face clouding over. "Do you have to leave?" Her voice expressed genuine disappointment.

"No, it's just that … I promised you a movie," he explained.

"Oh, I'd rather just talk," she replied, not wanting to break the spell that hung over their table.

The waiter, however, brought the check and gave the couple a pointed look that clearly said, "Your time is up. There are others waiting for this very good table."

Paolo pulled out his wallet and paid the bill, leaving a generous tip, she noted. So, he wasn't stingy. Another feather for his cap.

I wonder if he has any flaws at all, she mused with admiration, becoming more and more attracted to him by the moment.

The tiny faerie hid in a potted plant, as near to the—obviously—enrapt couple as possible. She couldn't quite make out what they were saying, but she didn't really have to. She watched Michelle's face light up with the first blush of love as Fey's charge smiled at her shyly, his brown-black hair falling delectably over his sweet face.

"Oh, Fey, he is divine," she whispered. "It's really too bad he didn't wish to join with the Fae," she pouted, licking her lips with delight. "He'd give old Guiscard a run for his money."

The evening seemed to fly by as Yasmine enjoyed the vicarious adventure. Paolo was all too soon helping Michelle into her coat as they made ready to leave.

"What next?" the tiny spy wondered, following them out into the dark street.

"Well, what now?" Paolo asked, as the couple stood in the November chill outside of the restaurant.

"How about we stop in at the pub for a drink?" Michelle suggested.

"Sure," he agreed cheerfully.

Yasmine put her hand to her heart and rolled her eyes in bliss as Michelle's fingers sought his. Their hands locked together comfortably. As they strolled through the night, he would occasionally glance at his date with a hint of an unsure smile when she happened to meet his eyes.

Only too soon, they reached the door of the pub. He opened it and held it back to let her enter. She gazed cautiously around the room, her eyes alighting on a spot toward the back.

"Too smoky in there," Michelle complained, backing out quickly.

Yasmine had almost tried to duck into the pub with the couple. She spied, peeking over the tops of their heads, the reason for the woman's quick retreat. Sitting at a table in the back, littered with empty green bottles, sat that brutish René, ready to spoil everything.

"Oh, toadwarts!" she huffed. Yasmine saw his dark glance as the door shut, blocking the unattractive scene from view. Had the boorish oaf seen them? She wasn't sure, but her intuition set off an alarm in her head.

She looked up to see Paolo watching Michelle with fierce intensity. In an instant, Yasmine felt the mood of the evening shift as the man and woman gazed at each other for a moment in the shaft of light escaping from the pub. She flowed around him, not turning her back. He followed her with his eyes and took the hand she offered him. They drew away from the doorway in a graceful dance as the ray of light evaporated in the night.

Michelle led the way down the darkened streets to her door, the streetlights offering little oases of luminescence in the night-darkened village. Her own entry was obscured between two of the widely spaced lamps, and they stood in the darkness in front of her narrow townhouse. Paolo folded his hands over hers, the black onyx ring flashing in the moon's bright light.

Yasmine watched with amazement herself, as the woman stared down in surprise at the strange, unexpected sight before her, for when the moonbeam hit the stone just so, the outline of a bat with outstretched wings appeared on the surface, glowing with the fiery intensity of an Australian opal.

"Neat, huh?" Paolo smiled, noticing her awestruck expression. "It only shows up in the moonlight."

"It's like magic," she breathed, twisting his hand gently back and forth to watch the effect.

Yasmine purred her throaty laugh. "You have no idea," she commented.

"Paolo?" Michelle asked, looking suddenly serious.

He waited for her question with patient attentiveness.

"I really like you," she went on.

He looked suddenly as serious as she, Yasmine noted. The faerie, too, found her stomach in a knot. This was the defining moment. Would the woman choose the powerful, domineering le Roux or the gentle, shy Italian? *I know which knight would sport my garland,* she noted to herself.

"I want to see you again, but René …"

"He doesn't want to lose you," Paolo finished.

"He's not like you. He's mean and selfish and …" She gulped. "I'm afraid of him," she finished in a whisper.

"You are free to choose, Michelle," he said simply, "and I hope you'll choose me."

Pulling her in close, he buried his face in her hair. She leaned on his shoulder, closing her eyes. Stepping back from her, he let his hands slide slowly, slowly down her arms, barely touching her until the tips of his fingers rested lightly just underneath hers. His head tilted slightly to the side, a look of thoughtful seriousness on his face. Yasmine felt sure he would kiss her, but no, he let her hands gently drop and turned, albeit reluctantly, to go.

"Oh, if only I hadn't wasted all of that courage powder," she lamented, crossing her arms sternly and frowning. "I'd make him kiss her, I would!"

Well, she had done the best she could, and at least Fey's boy was on his way to having some semblance of a social life. In opening up his heart to love, she just hoped she hadn't opened up Pandora's Box, along with it.

9

Dark Alley

*M*ichelle unlocked her front door and entered her dwelling. It was a neat, brick structure with two narrow windows facing the street from the second floor, a larger window and front door on the first, and an herb garden in back. The modest house was wedged closely between others much like it. The downstairs boasted an eat-in kitchen and a small, cramped living room with a nonfunctional fireplace and furniture that had seen better days but was still serviceable. It was decorated with pictures painted and drawn by Natalie in various stages of her artistic development, from a blue elephant, drawn in crayon at age five, to a somber self-portrait, larger than life, executed in charcoal and framed in thin black metal. The portrait hung over the back of the sofa, looming menacingly over all who dared to sit there. The upstairs, equally parsimonious in size, consisted of two bedrooms that were just large enough to contain the necessary furnishings, and a bath. It was, however, enough for the two of them and was all they had ever known. It was home.

Michelle heard the artist, herself, busy in the kitchen, banging the dishes noisily into submission. She had called her earlier, telling her not to wait for her for dinner. Upon hearing her arrival though, Natalie appeared in the doorway to the small living room, arms crossed, a scowl on her face.

"Have a nice *date*?" she asked, acid sarcasm permeating her voice. "You're back kind of early." She almost sounded pleased as she shot out the latter comment.

Michelle ignored Natalie's tone, replying with a satisfied smile, pulling out the rose from where she had tucked it inside her coat and holding it thoughtfully to her nose, "Yes, yes, I did, actually. Oh, Bug, he's so sweet. Romantic, funny, interesting, and even kind of sexy when he hits you with that 'eat you up' stare he has going on," she gushed. "He's even a vegetarian."

Natalie flopped down angrily on the sofa, propping her feet on the edge of the coffee table.

"What's wrong?" Michelle asked, finally noticing her sibling's disapproval. "I thought you didn't like René anyway."

"You know, I met Paolo way before you did," she answered defensively, staring her sister down. "I consider him a friend."

Michelle shook her head, a look of sympathy on her pretty face. "Oh, Bug, honey, you're twelve years old, and Paolo, well, he has to be somewhere around twenty at least, though I forgot to ask. You can't mean to have him for yourself, that way." She snorted. "He'd be run out of town or arrested as a pervert."

"Don't ever use that word about him!" she yelled, her face on fire. "Save that one for your precious, Neanderthal, scumbag boyfriend."

"I'm breaking up with him," Michelle stated with a look of firm decision. "You obviously can't stand him. He's driving all of my friends away, and, honestly," she admitted, "he has recently gotten way out of hand."

"Well, it's about time," Natalie agreed, her tone softening. She reached over and gave Michelle a hug, which was gratefully returned. They had to stick together. Their parents had been taken from them by a drunk driver two years prior. Fortunately, Michelle had been old enough to get custody of her younger sister.

They smiled at each other. Michelle found she couldn't hide the happy glow she felt—a feeling she hadn't had in a long time—and Natalie picked right up on it.

"So, did he kiss you?" she teased, wrinkling her nose.

"No, he didn't," Michelle admitted, shaking her head with slightly furrowed brows. "He looked like he wanted to, though. I'm not sure why he held back. It was perfectly obvious that I really liked him."

"I get the feeling he's kind of shy around girls," Natalie observed.

"I think you're right," Michelle replied with a pensive smile. "Well, I guess next time, I'll just have to kiss him first!" She giggled.

Yasmine followed Paolo as he made his way home through the darkened streets. He stopped briefly to look in the window of the shop where he had spoken with Gilbert. He studied the front window, with its old-fashioned, gold-leaf lettering. It read "J. de Gaul and Son," in an arch and then underneath, "Haberdashers," curving the opposite way, forming the outline of an open oval. In the middle of the letters, in straight font, was etched "Est. 1835." He stared at it for a moment, as though deep in thought.

Yasmine began to grow anxious. She wished Paolo would just hurry up and get home. She had had a bad feeling all day, and her worry seemed to be growing, rather than receding. She felt a responsibility toward Fey to see that her boy got home safely. She gasped to see three figures approaching.

"Stupid, stupid, stupid!" she chastised herself, so caught up in Michelle and Paolo's romance that she hadn't been sufficiently attentive to her surroundings. Being a matchmaker, she was armed only with the enchantments of love. As for helping Paolo, she was about as useful as an umbrella in a house fire.

It was too late to do anything now. They were on top of him before she could even think. Before he could shout, a thick band of duct tape was wrapped around his head, covering his mouth.

"Who do you think you are?" René glared at Paolo, inches from his face. "You knew Michelle was mine, but you thought you could just walk right up to her and take her for yourself. It doesn't work that way, farm boy," he fumed. "Besides, she doesn't really like you, anyway. She only went out with you to make me jealous. Well, guess what? It worked."

Yasmine bit her fist as the thugs dragged Fey's sweet boy into the alley and proceeded to beat him senseless. The attack was swift and brutal. From the first punch, she could see that he would not be able to free himself and quickly recognized that his life was truly in danger.

Oh, if only Guiscard were here, he would know what to do, she wished, panic clouding her thoughts. But their chivalrous ringleader was not, and she knew that the responsibility for this fiasco rested on her slender shoulders.

She covered her mouth in terror as Paolo fought to free himself from the restraining arms. René lashed out with his hard fists, raining punches at Paolo with lightning speed and such force that the first one seemed to knock the wind completely out of him. She thought she heard a cracking sound as René launched a particularly vicious jab, and she swore she could feel Paolo's panic filling the alley.

The barrage went on and on until Paolo ceased to struggle and slumped in his captors' arms. Still, they did not let go. Yasmine screamed as René picked up an abandoned brick lying in the corner of the alley and bashed it against the side of his head. Then, the two men who were holding Paolo finally dropped him to the ground, shooting an anxious look at René and then at each other. They took off at a run, leaving the merciless assailant to launch one final, savage kick at the unconscious figure sprawled on the pavement. Paolo did not even flinch.

Before turning to leave, she watched with furious anger as René reached into Paolo's back pocket and pulled out his wallet. He grinned with avarice at the large wad of folded bills that it contained. Tossing the empty leather container in a corner behind the Dumpster, he dragged his victim by the foot to the darkest part of the alley and stalked off, leaving him to live or die as fate would choose.

10

Tripped Up

After making sure Paolo was still alive, Yasmine darted forth, searching desperately for someone, anyone, who could help. She canvassed the square in vain. Everyone seemed to have, unpropitiously, vanished. Only a skinny tabby cat strode through, looking for a meal. Yasmine began to despair but knew that she couldn't give up. As she was flying through the cold, dark streets, her eyes alighted upon the same pub that Michelle had narrowly avoided. She noted that three healthy-looking young men stood milling about in front, puffing on cigarettes, their breath mingling with the gray smoke that floated up to the streetlight.

"So, want to check out that new club, or just go back inside and be bored some more?" the tallest of the three asked impatiently.

"Wait right here," offered his companion in a light, pleasant tone. "I'll go get my car. I left it in front of the shop."

Yasmine couldn't believe her luck. It was Gilbert. He finished his cigarette and flung the butt in the street as he hurried in the direction of the clothing store.

She raced on ahead, growing breathless with the exertion. When she reached the alley, she saw that it was deserted. Fortunately, René and his accomplices had left. To her dismay, as she illuminated the scene with a sprinkle of twinkling stardust, she spotted Paolo sprawled ungracefully on the ground, his mouth covered with a gray band of some kind. A trickle of blood made its way down the pavement, coming from just underneath his head.

Her stomach lurched to see Fey's boy like this. She had teased her about it but knew her friend's affection for the young man was deep and genuine. He lay very still. She wasn't even sure if he was still breathing but did not have time to check. She had to find a way to get Gilbert to go down the alley, but how? His car was parked in the street.

A flash of inspiration hit her just in time. She whizzed around front, squeezed through the mail slot, tearing her dress in her hurry, and made her way to the electrical box in the back room. She knew exactly where it was, because she often came in to spy on her favorite project. She began flipping switches furiously. The store was soon bathed in light. She finished in time to see Gilbert fumbling with his keys at the front door and raced to beat him there.

"Oh no, you don't," she scolded, turning the deadbolt at the exact same moment he twisted the key to the bottom lock.

Gilbert rattled the key in the lock, frustrated with this tedious delay to his plans.

Oh, that's right, he remembered, as the knob turned but the door remained stubbornly shut. *I came out the back door so I could take out the trash. I probably locked the deadbolt from the inside. I could've sworn I shut off all the lights, though. Boy, am I glad I came back. Dad would've been furious if I had left them on all night.*

He strode in a leisurely fashion around the side of the building, jingling the keys in his hand. Maybe tonight he would get lucky and some gorgeous girl from Fontainebleau wearing one of those little nothing dresses they bought in Paris, the kind that made you wonder why girls bothered wearing clothes at all, would—

He'd tripped on something in the darkness and fell scraping the heels of his hands on the rough pavement. Gilbert swore and picked himself up, dusting his burning hands on the front of his jacket.

"What the ... what was that?" he asked out loud.

Squinting, he snapped open his cell phone to use as a flashlight and peered into the blackness. The dim light illuminated the face of a man, his mouth covered with duct tape. Gilbert dropped his cell phone with a clatter, backing away with a shout.

"God, no!" he exclaimed. It was Paolo, the guy he had waited on that afternoon. Gilbert scrambled to retrieve his phone, nervously punching in 112, the emergency number, his hands shaking. Not wanting to move him, just in case he had a back injury, Gilbert put his ear to the unconscious man's nose, to see if he was still breathing. He wasn't sure.

He shouted into the phone as the emergency operator calmly picked up. He was almost hysterical. She tried to calm him down, giving him instructions to follow as the minutes ticked away with agonizing slowness. Gilbert reached into his jacket for the pocket knife he always carried. Switching open the blade, he tried to slide it gently under the tape covering Paolo's mouth. He was afraid the poor guy would suffocate before the ambulance arrived. He sawed carefully at the tape, but his fingers felt like clay, and he gashed Paolo's cheek.

"Sorry," he whispered.

A bead of blood appeared on the cut and trickled down his neck. Pulling the tape away, Gilbert heard him gasp lightly.

"Oh, you are alive! Thank God!"

Taking Paolo's hand, Gilbert found it to be icy cold. He quickly removed his own coat, laying it gently over the still figure, hoping that the warmth it contained would be of some help in keeping him alive. Oh, this was not his thing. He felt so unequal to all of this. The emergency worker continued to talk with him as he bit the flesh of his index finger, shivering in the November cold.

Relief flooded him when he heard a siren approaching at a distance.

Gilbert backed gratefully away as the emergency workers took over and then phoned his father, who took an inordinately long time to pick up.

"Dad?" Gilbert whimpered into the phone, still flooded with panic.

"What is it, Gilbert?" Jacques answered, sounding profoundly irritated. "You aren't drunk already, are you? Did you wreck your car?" Then, a note of worry replacing his annoyance, he added, "Are you all right?"

"No, no. I'm fine," Gilbert answered in a trembling voice, ignoring his father's disapproval for the moment. "It's that guy that your friend took in. Somebody tried to kill him. I found him in the alley behind the store. Oh, Dad, I think I know who did it," Gilbert continued nervously, taking comfort in the anchoring presence of his father.

"I'll be right over," Jacques answered. "You'll have to stay there. I'm sure the police will want to talk to you."

Gilbert leaned against the back wall of the shop, lit a cigarette, and inhaled the soothing smoke deeply. He was still shivering from fear as well as from the cold. He could hear the shouts of the ambulance workers. Things didn't look so good for Paolo, who lay oblivious to the ministrations being performed on him.

The team of medical technicians worked valiantly to save him. The comments he overheard sounded dire though. He watched helplessly as his new acquaintance was strapped to a stretcher and whisked away. Oh, if only Guy's friend had listened to him. He had seen René in the pub that evening, and he had looked dangerous. Sometime after Gilbert and his friends had arrived, le Roux had just about stormed out of the place with his posse, a black look on his face. Gilbert hadn't put things together at the time, having been focused on his own affairs. Besides, to him, René always looked like a jerk.

Jacques arrived. Seeing his son shivering against the wall, he asked him, "Where's your coat?"

Gilbert shrugged, too much in shock to care. Jacques ducked into the shop and brought him one from the merchandise. Gilbert looked up gratefully at his father as he draped the coat around his shoulders. He knew that his dad thought he was a major screw-up, but the fact that he could count on his old man to be there for him meant a lot. Jacques stayed with Gilbert as he spoke with the police and then called Guy to let him know what had happened. They never bothered to turn off the shop lights. His friends, he noted, must have gotten tired of waiting and left without him, taking one of their own cars, oblivious to the horrible event in which he had become entangled.

Manifestations of Loss

The police left. Father and son remained alone in front of their business.

"I have to pick up Guy," Jacques explained to Gilbert, who still felt shaken by what he had seen, "To take him to the hospital to be with his friend. You going to be okay?"

"Sure, Dad," Gilbert answered, in an unconvincing tone. He didn't want his father to see how badly unnerved he was. It made him feel inferior. His dad always seemed to have his act together. As much of a comfort as this was when he needed his parent's strong presence, it also made him feel inadequate that he, himself, was so weak in a crisis. He could feel the panic rising inside of him, ready to send him over the edge, and folded his arms across his chest, hunching over involuntarily.

"Can I drop you off at your apartment?" Jacques offered, frowning in concern.

"Thanks," he answered in a choked voice, fighting the black tide that loomed.

Jacques clapped him on the shoulder, pride in his offspring evident on his face. For once, Gilbert noted bitterly, he seemed to have met his father's expectations.

He made it up to his apartment just in time. It had happened to him before, but this episode was the worst he had ever experienced. He collapsed onto the bed, gripping his sides as his heart raced, feeling the sweat trickle down his brow. He lay, groaning, his teeth gritted, as fear overpowered him. Every muscle in his body was tensed, and he had the terrifying feeling that he was dying. Dark thoughts crept through his mind, overpowering his reason.

The feelings of abandonment that he kept carefully closeted, barred by a fierce determination to find happiness, broke through and tortured him. Some of this was his own fault, as he pushed away any woman to whom he began to feel too strong an attachment, for fear she would hurt him by leaving, as his mother had done. He tried to convince himself that his father would always be there for him, but he couldn't make himself believe it. Gilbert knew he had become increasingly frustrated with his bad behavior and would eventually wash his hands of him as well. It was only a matter of time before he found out everything he was hiding.

He kept the wastebasket nearby and was glad he had thought to do so. After voiding his stomach, he began to breathe heavily, his fingers going completely numb. To keep from passing out, he held his breath and squeezed his eyes shut. Shuddering, he felt the wave of pain and terror pass over him, only to be replaced by a feeling of complete exhaustion.

Dragging himself wearily off of the bed, he made his way, trembling from the exertion, over to the sideboard in the living room and poured a generous amount of straight scotch from the cut-crystal decanter into the glass he kept next to it, a gift from one of their suppliers. He took a quick swallow of the strong, amber liquid and let the warmth wash over him. Slumping heavily down onto the sofa, he closed his eyes. Willing the unsettling scene he had witnessed that evening to recede from his brain, he downed shots until the oblivion he desired set in.

Guy had offered to wait in the pub until the boy was finished with his date, but Paolo had stubbornly insisted on walking home, not wanting to create an inconvenience. As the months wore on, the newcomer had toughened up significantly. He worked hard and rarely complained. So, in the end, Guy had shrugged as if to say, "Okay, have it your way," and then went to sit at home and worry. He wished he could have taught his apprentice to drive, but he was still working on getting his missing documentation straightened out. The fact that he was, of his own admission, not French made it more difficult. Jacques was helping him with this, and in the end, his fishing buddy wound up spending many hours and shelling out a fair amount of cash, both under and over the table, to make sure Paolo could legally stay, for which Guy was immensely grateful.

The old farmer had fallen asleep in his chair, waiting for his young friend to return, worried that he was walking so far in the dark by himself. The phone rang. He awoke with a start. He sputtered and snorted and then reached over to pick up the receiver with a weight inside his chest. A phone call this late at night was never a good thing.

"Hello?" he asked, groggily.

"Guy? This is Jacques. I'm afraid I have some bad news about that boy of yours."

His mouth went dry, and he leaned forward in his chair, tensing. "What happened? Is he okay?"

"I'm afraid they're not sure," Jacques said gravely. He briefly explained to him how his son had found him, as well as what Gilbert suspected had happened, and then suggested, "Let me come pick you up, and we'll drive over to the hospital together."

"Thanks," Guy rasped over a lump in his throat.

The two men said hasty good-byes, and Guy threw on his coat. He couldn't understand how this had happened. Paolo was not the kind of person who looked for trouble. Oh, why hadn't he insisted on driving him home? He should've listened to his gut. Guy stepped out onto the porch to watch for Jacques's approaching headlights.

He had come to love this funny kid who came out of nowhere to relieve the oppressive loneliness of his long days. For Paolo, everything seemed new and exciting. He had a childlike quality about him that was both endearing and disarming. Yet, at other times, he would come up with something so profound and poetic, he sounded wise beyond his twenty-odd years.

He had to be okay. Guy knew it would kill him if he wasn't.

Fey sat with Arcenciel at the painted dining table in her own hideaway, playing cards and sipping nectar cocktails. Arcenciel had proved to be a true friend, treating her no differently after her transformation than before. This put her at ease, and some of her old sparkle returned, at least on the inside. Arcenciel herself looked as darkly beautiful as ever. Her silky, raven hair hung to her waist. Emerald eyes and silver skin gave her a gothic allure that was unique compared to her more conventional friends. It suited her more serious nature. She usually wore clothing in shades of maroon, gray, and black, which complemented her rare coloring. As a result, she could be intimidating when she chose.

"I win again!" Fey squealed, drawing the dried corn kernels they were using as chips to her pile, which had grown disproportionately large compared to her friend's. "Hmm." She scowled, darting an accusing look at her companion. "You aren't, by any chance, letting me win, are you?"

Arcenciel did not have a chance to respond. She had stood up abruptly with a look of shock on her face, knocking the chair over behind her.

"What is it?" Fey asked nervously, glancing over her shoulder to find out what had startled her companion so badly. The look on her face was frightening.

Arcenciel walked around the table slowly, took Fey by the shoulders, and steered her to her closet. She then turned the knob, and the door swung open, revealing the mirror hanging on the inside.

"Paolo, no!" she screamed.

"We have to go find Guiscard. He'll know what to do," Arcenciel determined, hugging Fey in a tight embrace.

What the faded faerie saw in the mirror shook her to the core, for staring back at her was her former self, all loveliness and light—her russet hair falling over her shoulders like a soft halo, her lavender skin glowing, her violet eyes wide with terror. Arcenciel took her by the hand, and the two friends flew off into the night. They both knew Guiscard's favorite haunts but stopped first at his empty loft before heading to Fleur's abode, which also stood empty.

On the third try, they found him in the clearing where he had shot René with a love arrow. He was sitting on a large, flat rock with Fleur snuggled up beside him. They were admiring the moon shining down through the bare branches and murmuring softly to each other.

"We have a problem," Arcenciel stated sharply, drawing Fey forward, a lovely, trembling mess.

Guiscard jumped up from his cozy spot and studied Fey with astonishment. The dainty fern-colored faerie who had been sitting beside him rose gracefully and ran over to Fey, smoothing her hands over the faerie's sumptuous curls.

"Oh, Fey, darling, your looks have come back. How wonderful!" she crooned.

"No, Fleur, this is not wonderful at all. Don't you see, this means that something terrible has happened to Paolo," he corrected, in a tone of irritation at her thoughtlessness.

Fleur stepped back, chastened. Guiscard took charge, as Arcenciel knew he would.

"We must go to my loft," he ordered. "Hurry, we may already be too late."

At his loft, the three anxious female faeries watched as Guiscard carefully mixed a warm drink for Fey. The glow of tapers danced over the scene as he carefully measured ingredients into a glass vial, focusing intently to ensure it attained the proper color before pouring it into a beautifully carved wooden goblet.

"You have to go to him," he ordered her. "If, that is, he is still with us."

Tears spilled down Fey's cheeks as he voiced the awful possibility.

"How? I don't even know where he is."

"Drink this," he commanded.

"What is it, Guiscard?" Fey asked hesitantly. "And how will it help me to find Paolo?"

"It is something I have been working on, with Arcenciel's help," he explained. "I call it the Dream Travel potion. It allows lovers to meet in their dreams and, if it works correctly, will allow both you and him to share thoughts and feelings with no walls between your souls."

"But we aren't lovers," she protested.

Guiscard looked pointedly at Fey, disagreement written on his very countenance. She could feel herself blush at his wry expression of disbelief. Without another word, he held the cup of warm liquid to her lips, while his other arm braced her back. He tilted the cup gently as Fey gulped it down. She sagged into Guiscard's grasp the moment it hit her stomach.

Abduction

*M*ichelle lay on the sofa watching a movie, but lost in a romantic reverie, she would not have been able to tell you what it was about. Her gaze was fixed on the images on the screen, but it was Paolo's face she saw before her.

The front door of the girls' row house burst open, and René strode in. She whirled her head around quickly, chiding herself for forgetting to lock the front door when she had returned home from her date. René stood before her, hands on his hips, a look of smug satisfaction on his chiseled face.

"What are you doing here?" Michelle asked nervously, her last bit of courage deserting her as she realized that she was alone with a very angry and jealous man. A thought of her younger sister sleeping above them flashed through her mind. She had to be careful. It was not fair to get Natalie involved in her problems.

"We have to talk," she stated.

"Go right ahead," he shot back with a thrust of his chin, folding his arms across his chest.

"Not here," she replied. If things got too heated, Natalie would wake up and have to deal with the quarrel she could see brewing. "Let's go to the pub. We can talk over drinks."

"Fine," he agreed in a tense, controlled tone. Then, motioning with his head toward the door, he added, arms still folded defensively, "My car is just outside."

Maybe he wasn't as angry as she had feared he would be. Perhaps, seeing that she, too, could show some backbone had taught him to treat her with a little more respect. She slipped nervously into the passenger seat of René's old red Fiat and closed the door firmly. Sandwich wrappers and empty soda bottles littered the floor. The car looked like it hadn't been vacuumed in several years and smelled strongly of stale cigarette smoke.

Glancing over at her boyfriend, she was relieved to see that he actually appeared somewhat calm. He gripped the gear shift and put the car in first, and they sped down the dark streets. They passed the pub, and Michelle shot him an anxious look.

"Relax," he told her. "I don't want to go to the pub. It's too crowded there. Saturday night," he explained.

Michelle nodded, panic rising inside of her like yellow bile.

"Well, where are we going then?" she asked, trying to mask her fear with mock irritation.

René remained silent, speeding on out of town.

"I think we should see other people," she blurted out after a long, uncomfortable silence.

"You mean that worthless farmhand you picked up at work today?" René sneered. "Scraping bottom, are we, my dear?" he goaded her sarcastically. "Oh, don't worry about him. He won't be bothering you anymore. I saw to that."

Michelle's eyes grew wide as she stared at René, seeing him for the monster he had become.

"What have you done to him?" she shouted, fear gripping her. She believed him capable of about anything at this point.

René stopped the car on a lonely stretch of road, pulled the parking brake, which ratcheted noisily, and gave her his full attention, the smugness again evident on his face.

"Y'know," he taunted her, "he never even threw one punch. Nice choice, Michelle. Nice choice."

"You animal!" she screamed, pounding him uselessly with her fists.

René grabbed Michelle by the hair and pulled her close. Her heart raced in terror as she struggled to escape his iron grasp.

"Now listen," he growled, his lips close to her ear, "there's only one way you and I are going to break up."

He whipped out a switchblade, slicing Michelle's throat with a quick, hard thrust. The scream escaping from her turned into a strangled gurgle.

Her last thought was of her sister, who still lay sleeping peacefully in her bed. Natalie would be alone now, with no one to protect her. Then her body slumped forward onto René's chest, and she was gone.

Natalie jolted in her sleep, awakening with a start. She could've sworn she heard a loud noise. She lay there for a moment, but no further sound intruded upon the stillness, except the soft babbling of the television, which was still on in the living room. She slipped out of bed and headed to the bathroom, noting on the way that the door to her sister's bedroom was ajar, the bed still made.

"Michelle?" she called down the stairs quietly. "You still up?"

Silence answered her. She made her way down to the living room see if her sister had fallen asleep on the sofa. A light had been left on, and Natalie could clearly see that no one was there. Strange. Where could she be? Everything looked normal. A half-eaten bowl of popcorn sat on the end table, along with half a glass of watered-down, flat soda.

Natalie searched the house and then called Michelle's cell phone, which rang until her voice mail kicked in. She began to feel sick in the pit of her stomach. Opening the front door, she peered outside into the night. Nothing. She hugged her arms to herself after she shut and bolted the door. She sat down on the sofa, halfheartedly picking at the remaining popcorn, washing it down with the flat soda, worry growing like a tumor as the night wore on.

Michelle slumped against René as she fell unconscious, bleeding profusely all over the front of his shirt and jacket. He grew horrified at the sight, almost as if he had witnessed, rather than committed, her murder. His stomach wrenched as he felt the weight of her dead form on his, and he fought against a rising nausea and revulsion.

Extricating himself from the car, he pulled her out roughly after him, noting with disgust that there was blood all over the front seat. It continued to seep from the savage wound on her neck, and his eyes grew wild with terror as he realized the enormity of what he had done. The alcohol had worn off, leaving him feeling sick and sober. How he had managed to get there without wrecking the car was a mystery to him. He couldn't remember driving. All he could remember was beating the crap out of that loser Michelle had picked up at work to try to make him jealous and arguing with her about it. He shook his head in frustration, still holding her in his arms, her eyes wide and staring.

He dragged Michelle's body into the woods as far as possible. It was then that he discovered what they meant by the term *dead weight*. As he pulled her along carelessly, her clothing ripped on the brush and her skin scraped against the rocks and twigs scattered on the ground. Sweating in spite of the cold, he heaved her lifeless, battered corpse into a small ravine, raining down rocks, leaves, sticks, and whatever else he could find to cover her with. There was no shovel in his car, so he had had to use his bare hands, as best he could, to conceal her ravaged form, breathing heavily with the effort.

He worked furiously for over an hour, and his hands began to bleed from the rough stones and twigs he handled. It was very dark, with only the moon for light as it shone through the bare tree branches. He tripped in the dark several times as he searched for things to throw onto the body to conceal it, scraping his knees and tearing up his clothing in the process. Panic had completely replaced the consuming rage he had felt earlier in the evening, and he had to fight the eerie feeling that he was being watched. René staggered back to his car, skidding away in the dark night, covered with dirt and blood, Paolo's hard-earned money in his pocket.

Lilith watched in fury as the body of the slain woman was thrown like so much rubbish into the cold ravine. Would men never cease to afflict the weaker sex? She had witnessed their violence against them for centuries and was heartily sick of it. She observed the villain with disgust as he pelted the beautiful, lifeless form with rocks and dirt, obscuring her pale face from the light of the witnessing moon.

An aura of eerie beauty surrounded the tall, elegant figure, swathed in a full-length, black, hooded cloak lined in red, cobweb satin. Her long black hair glistened in the moonlight, her eyes glowing like brilliant rubies in the night. Her skin was pale alabaster, cold and creamy against her black robe; her long nails were painted crimson. As a daughter of the Fae who had mastered the rare and difficult feat of changing her form at will, the few men to whom she had appeared were both fascinated and terror stricken by her at the same time, as if she were an irresistible poison that they would gladly drink before they died.

René would know this delicious torture, she had decided. Among the Fae, an evil deed would come to its deserved reward as a matter of consequence, with no further action required. They had no need of police, soldiers, or courts. But sometimes among humans, she thought, narrowing her eyes as he cast an anxious gaze about him, as if he could feel her malevolent scrutiny, Justice needed some prodding to work out her goal to its rightful conclusion.

13

Lovers' Tryst

Fey lay as still as death on Guiscard's chaise. He would not let anyone in the loft but Arcenciel, who was a quiet comfort to him. It was too hard to watch her lying there, knowing that she was with another , whom she loved more than she did him. He wished he had made his choice earlier, but he had failed to see past her sparkly, vain exterior to the surpassing beauty within. Now it was too late. She had given her heart to Paolo. Guiscard knew she would not return until her charge was out of danger and waited patiently with Arcenciel, who laid her hand over his on the table, sympathy showing on her silvery face.

Yasmine alighted on the doorstep in the hours before dawn. Arcenciel held her finger to her lips to hush the excited babbling that was ready to rush forth from the golden-haired faerie. Yasmine stopped, her mouth open, and then peeked around, following Arcenciel's finger, which had moved from her lips to point in the direction of the chaise.

"Oh," she mouthed silently and then beckoned the pair, with a frantic motion of her hand, to follow her outside so they could talk. She stood on a pine bough nearby, wringing her slim fingers. Arcenciel and Guiscard settled lightly next to her.

"What a disaster I have created!" Yasmine wailed, holding her hands over her face in shame.

Arcenciel and Guiscard exchanged a loaded glance before turning back to face her.

"I have a confession to make," she stated, pulling her hands slowly away, eyes downcast, a guilty look clouding her bright features. "Guiscard …" She looked him meekly in the eye, her shoulders slumped. "I stole one of your love arrows and shot Paolo with it."

Guiscard became enraged. "Foolish creature!" he roared. "Do you realize that the boy lies closer to death than life and that Fey is heartbroken? She loves the lad more than her own soul and has gone to be with him by an untried potion until his fate is known—a dangerous journey, even for our kind."

He looked the shamefaced faerie up and down with overwhelming disgust, his nostrils flaring, brows knitted in fury.

Arcenciel, being of a cooler disposition, interjected, "What, exactly, happened?"

Yasmine sat down daintily on the branch, gesturing for the others to do the same. She launched in to tell her story, attempting to give as much detail as possible. When she described René's consuming jealousy and rage, Guiscard looked baffled.

"But the love arrow is a gentling spell. It creates a yielding spirit. It is as if the lover becomes a cloak. He is willing to spread himself over the mud for his lady to tread upon. I thought it would even things out between them," he explained, a puzzled look on his face. In their world, the balance of masculine and feminine was very important. It created harmony in their relationships and the optimal use of each gender's unique talents.

Arcenciel, who was quite erudite, offered her thoughts. "I have read that if the lover has a defect of character, the spell can go awry. Also, if it hits the spleen instead of the heart, a similar reaction can occur."

Guiscard accepted the lecture with humility. He felt that he had been more at fault than Yasmine, who had simply tried to help open the heart of Fey's shy charge to the possibilities of romantic love. He, himself, had been selfishly playing the showoff in front of the admiring ladies.

"I apologize, Yasmine. I should have seen the brutish edge to René's character and stayed my arrow. I'm only glad that Fey sleeps on. It would be too much for her to bear to know that her dearest friends would take such foolish risks with the man she loves."

As Dawn began to make her presence felt in the east, lightening the sky with a faint hint of color, a tiny figure flew through the town, stopping to peer in the top window above the back of the flower shop. Yasmine peeked into Gilbert's bedroom, through a crack in the blind. He was not in bed. Flying around to the front of the building, she looked through the half-drawn shutters and saw him sprawled on the sofa, sleeping with his mouth half open, an empty, cut-crystal glass lying beside him on the cushion. He looked an exhausted mess.

"Oh, fie!" she declared. "I can't be here to take care of you all the time, now, can I?" she scolded the sleeping figure.

She flew down to the apartment door to the right of the shop, squeezed through the mail slot, and continued up the dark, winding staircase. At the top, she glided under the crack between the bottom of the door and the old, polished floorboards, just able to fit. She was glad he hadn't sealed it against the draft. Dusting herself off, she flew into the living room, tsking as she saw the pathetic mess on the leather sofa. The room reeked of scotch and sweat.

Still, in spite of her scorn, she felt torn that she had had to leave him in such a state as he was in the night before, but Paolo had been of more pressing concern. She vowed she would make it up to her favorite human, though.

"It's not good for you to live like this, all alone," she scolded. "I'll find you a girl you just can't resist," she vowed. "I'll make you love her, I will!" she declared emphatically to the unconscious drunk on the sofa.

She untied a floral-scented, lace pomander from around her waist and fastened it to the pull chain on the mica-shaded lamp on the end table. It was a Love Wish, a charm to help the recipient find that perfect, special someone who was right for him. A gentle charm, it needed to be repeated frequently to work. But that was just fine by Yasmine. She liked visiting her pet project. He looked like one of the Fae, with his bright-blue eyes and perfect features. Well, usually. That night, he just looked like a pathetic sot.

Taking a packet of powder from her pocket, she sprinkled a relaxing blend of enchanted herb dust over his sleeping face. He reached up and rubbed his nose with the back of his hand, as if the particles tickled. Then he tucked his feet up on the sofa and folded his arms across his chest. His features immediately looked more peaceful. The empty glass dropped silently onto the rug. She left and flew home then, completely spent. What a dreadful night it had been!

René hastily returned to his apartment and changed out of his bloody clothes, which he stuffed into a garbage bag and took with him. He then drove all night, carefully obeying all traffic laws, trying not to call attention to himself. He wanted to put as much distance as possible between himself and Achères. Fortunately, it was Sunday, so he wouldn't be missed at work. Monday, he would call and say his mother was in the hospital in Calais. That way, they would be uncertain as to whether he was even still in the country, as he might have squeaked through the Tunnel to England. As to where he was headed, he drove south, as far south as he could go. He pulled off in a commuter parking lot just before dawn and fell asleep in a sea of automobiles, safe, for the moment, in the crowd of empty cars.

The sun shone brightly on his face as René took the cup of coffee Michelle handed him with a smile. She placed a plate of bacon and eggs in front of him and sat down in the opposite chair. Just the two of them, he noted with satisfaction. They were in their own house, enjoying the life he had always wanted.

He sliced open the egg and watched the yellow insides run in a puddle onto the plate. Somehow, the sight of it was off-putting, and he looked up at Michelle to ask her to bring him scrambled eggs instead.

His eyes grew wide with terror, however, as he gazed at the gory figure of his girlfriend, who now appeared as she had that awful night, yellow blood streaming down her neck, covering her chest, flowing all over their table, and pouring onto him as he struggled, unsuccessfully, to flee. Looking over in the doorway, he noted a beautiful, black-haired woman with red eyes, frightening and mesmerizing at the same time. She was laughing at him. He lunged for her to shut her up.

Awakening with a jolt, René found himself in his bloodstained car, the sunlight streaming in the front windshield, illuminating the remains of carnage that the previous night had complicitly concealed.

Fey remained under Guiscard's spell for three nights. Their minds and spirits were at peace. They were able to share thoughts and feelings as only her people could. As a result, she guarded and directed her mind to spare him the full knowledge of the truth, as he was clinging so tenuously to life. She saw, with wistful joy, that his thoughts had taken him to their meeting place at the dead oak tree, deep in the forest of Fontainebleau.

She sat with his head in her lap, combing through his thick, dark hair with her delicate fingers, gazing adoringly at his face and taking in his thoughts and his love for her. The beauty of his innocent spirit dazzled her, in much the same way as he had been by the lovely vision of her in the shaft of sunlight at their first meeting. She wondered how she could ever have been afraid of this gentle, kindhearted being and vowed never again to make snap judgments such as she had with him.

Paolo relaxed under her touch. He still could not move, but Fey noted that the bone-chilling cold that had overtaken him had receded. She noticed that his skin had lost its bluish cast but still remained ashen pale. Every now and then, he would glance up at her, and she would smile down at him. Then he would shut his eyes and wait.

She passed the time by telling him the stories of her people—stories of love and chivalry, of jealousy and revenge, of mythical creatures and magic. The words she spoke appealed to his poetic nature. She knew he heard her and searched her brain for every last tale she could think of to keep his attention—and to keep him from asking about his past.

Fey told the old story of a beautiful faerie who disguised herself as an ugly old woman. She went begging to the Haberdasher of Achères for a length of wool to fashion warm clothing for winter. She really had no need of it, as the Fae possessed far superior fabrics than scratchy sheep's hair. She knew, however, that he was a mean, selfish man who beat his wife, causing her to lose the baby girl she had carried in her womb and wanted to avenge the death of the poor babe, who would never see the light of the warm sun.

As he turned her away with a look of sour disdain, which she fully expected to happen, she revealed herself as a beautiful creature with eyes of ruby hue. She cursed the cowering villain, telling him that neither he, nor his descendants, would ever be blessed with a beautiful girl to grace their home, since he had chosen to abuse the woman who had given her heart to him and slain the child with which her love had blessed them.

"I saw his picture in the shop. That's a shame. I think they are very nice people, now," Paolo uttered quietly.

"Such is the way of curses and blessings," Fey explained. "The actions of parents, for good or ill, do ultimately affect their children."

"Hmm," Paolo agreed.

She recited sonnets from memory, ones that Yasmine had taught her. She gave him the language of the Bard and knowledge of his poems, as a gift to help ease his pain. He listened attentively, silently.

He had no more strength to talk, and every now and then, she would sense him slipping away to the sleep that lay beyond dreams. She would call him back then, her panic scarcely veiled. "Stay with me, Paolo. Stay with me," she would beg, patting his face with her hand. He would make a valiant effort to comply, knitting his brow and frowning.

Fey was torn between not wanting to see his suffering drawn out and not wanting this precious time with him to end. She was consumed with love for her beautiful, dark-eyed boy. But as the third dawn approached, she sensed a change. Her heart wrenched with loss as he slipped back into consciousness.

14

Walking through Fire

The morning sun shone brightly through the overgrown shrubs that surrounded the well-hidden house. Natalie sat with her book in the garden of Valjean's Paris hideaway, impatiently waiting for Marius to arrive. The atmosphere was heavy with mist, the long grass bending and wet and the sunlight illuminating the watery air around her. She arranged the folds of her long, cream-colored silk dress on the bench, which resembled the seating in the town square of Achères. When he slipped through the concealing bushes to join her, she saw that Marius, to her great joy, was really Paolo.

Natalie awakened to find herself not in bed, but lying on the sofa, the remains of the bowl of popcorn spilled on the rug. She jumped up and ran to the stairs, making a beeline for her sister's room. Empty. Natalie's stomach clenched as she stared into the vacant room; the bed was still made. Maybe Michelle's girlfriends had finally called to take her to a late feature or to drive to a club. She wished her sister had left a note.

She threw on her clothes and left the house, at a loss for what to do. It was early morning, and the sun shone brightly, painting the earthy warmth of the village in brilliant relief against a cool blue background. She ran first to the herb shop, which, of course, was closed. Her footsteps sounded twice as loud in the empty hush of dawn. The lights were off except for a dim bulb in the front window. A ray of morning light looked in with her to aid in the search. Still, Natalie rapped on the glass, hoping that maybe someone was in the back room.

Receiving no response to her repeated pounding, she wandered toward the center of town. The bells were tolling for early Mass, and Natalie got an idea. She knew that Paolo attended the second service with Guy just about every week. He would help her.

She sat on a bench in front of the weathered steps leading up to the entrance to the stone church and waited, glancing around anxiously. A few old people passed by, the women's little head veils looking, according to Natalie, completely ridiculous, like those filigreed paper circles that bakers put under cakes. She sneered disrespectfully as they passed by, feeling superior. She could hear snatches of their conversation and shamelessly eavesdropped.

"Yeah, it was Guy's boy, you know, the one he took in a few months ago. Found him near dead in the alley behind the de Gauls' shop last night. I heard it from Jacques this morning when I went to pick up a paper."

Natalie gasped and jumped off of the bench. She ran over to the beefy, white-haired man and stood in front of him, her facial muscles working.

"Excuse me," she interrupted, looking up at him. "Did you just say that something happened to Paolo last night? You see, he's a friend of mine, and …" She added as an afterthought, her voice reduced to a squeak, "… he's dating my big sister."

"Oh, honey, I'm so sorry," the old man offered solicitously, his face expressing compassion and concern. He put his hand on her shoulder and told her what he knew—that Paolo had been found by Gilbert de Gaul late Saturday night, lying beaten and bloodied in the alley behind his shop.

Natalie's face twisted, and she tilted her head upward to hold back her tears. Then, suddenly, she sprinted away. She ran until her lungs burned and her side was stabbed with sharp pains. She coursed through the nearly empty streets until she reached her house, where she threw the front door open and stamped up the steps to her room.

She lay on her bed and wept, her tears leaving a large, wet spot on her bedspread. Her nose streamed, and she could barely breathe through her gasping and hiccupping. She had never felt so alone in her life. Her parents had been taken from her, her sister was missing, and her only friend was lying in some stupid hospital somewhere—maybe even dead.

Then, her deepest pain surfaced. Something else had been taken from her as well. She would not do it for herself, but for Michelle and Paolo, she would walk through fire. She reached under her bed and pulled out a plastic garbage bag that had lain there like a boogeyman for months. Slowly, like on an execution march, she shuffled down the stairs and out the front door of her house, the bag hanging from her tensely clutched hand.

The big bear of a man who acted as Achères's head cop sat back in his chair as Natalie plunked the white, plastic trash bag on his desk. She looked at him with a sidelong glance, briefly taking in his military-short, silvering, dark hair and icy blue-gray eyes that would have been attractive in someone who didn't look like he hibernated for the winter.

She glanced more carefully around his office, which was contained within a nondescript, brick building next to the pub, conveniently enough. No need to haul the drunks more than a few steps to their overnight accommodations. A front desk, a few holding cells, and several offices were all that were needed in their boring village. Metal desks and filing cabinets, along with sparingly cushioned, metal chairs, constituted the furnishings. Cheap and cheesy, she noted. Paneled walls of dehydrated, light-colored wood were hung with documentation that no one would ever read and the occasional piece of uninspiring artwork that made her eyes hurt to look at. Maybe that was part of the punishment for being there.

The grizzly opened the bag and reached inside to withdraw the contents.

"It's evidence," she explained dryly, her eyes staring somewhere off to his right, her full lips turned slightly downward. She noticed he had removed his hand from the bag without touching the contents. Instead, he peered in to see a pile of clothes crumpled inside. His eyes grew heavy with sadness, which made him look like a person, instead of a cop, and his bottom lip puckered as his brow lowered in a frown. She found, to her discomfort, that his display of compassion made her want to cry.

"You okay, sweetie?" he asked.

"No," she replied adamantly, meeting his eyes with her own brimming with tears, "I'm not."

Durrand asked Natalie politely to give him a minute. She heard him in the hallway, calling his wife. She could tell it was his wife because he called her "Dear." He returned in about a minute and explained that his wife was a licensed counselor. Natalie couldn't have cared less if she were the Easter Bunny. All she wanted was to get this over with.

Mrs. Grizzly arrived shortly after her husband's call, her heels clicking on the hard tiles as she walked briskly down the hallway. She slowed as she approached her husband's desk and gave Natalie a reassuring smile.

"Hi, Natalie, I'm Marie Durrand," she said warmly. "You can call me Mrs. Durrand or just Marie, whatever makes you feel more comfortable." She was a small woman, with warm brown eyes and short, dark hair, styled in a practical cut. Her figure was plump and matronly, and she wore a tailored bouclé suit that emphasized that fact. Natalie thought they looked mismatched in size but perfectly matched in dowdy, middle-aged blandness.

"Well, I'll give you both some privacy," Vincent Durrand offered tactfully, backing out the door.

"No, please," Natalie pleaded. "Please. I need you to stay."

Husband and wife looked at each other in surprise. Natalie explained herself, noticing their silent communication.

"This is about more than me," she said, her face expressing a deep seriousness. "This is about my sister, Michelle, and my friend Paolo."

Vincent sat down and leaned forward in his chair, keeping himself at an angle where Natalie could see him but could focus her conversation on his wife, like she might be afraid of him. Well, she was not. Anything she could possibly be afraid of had already happened.

Natalie first described her sister's relationship with René le Roux. The big cop began to jot down notes. Marie had switched on an audio recorder to capture her testimony. Natalie didn't care, not even glancing at the device. She described how René had started off all sunshine and roses, but, over time, things began to turn ugly. He would call the house all the time, just to make sure Michelle went straight home from work. He became possessive and violent, striking out at her physically if she stepped out of line and then apologizing, promising her he didn't mean it and that it would never, ever happen again. This last fact she delivered in a voice dripping with bitter sarcasm.

"He got really scary toward the end," she shared in a somber tone. "Michelle's friends all stopped visiting and asking her to do things with them because he would treat them really rude. If she wanted to go out with her girlfriends, he would get mad, saying she just wanted to go clubbing so she could ..." she trailed off, holding back a fresh wave of tears.

Marie put her hand over Natalie's, which only succeeded in making her cry harder, and handed her a tissue. She dabbed at her swollen eyelids and continued with sheer force of will.

"One day," she said, her face twisting with inner agony, "I was home waiting for Michelle to come home so we could have dinner together. That pig came right into my room. He was strung out or something. He asked where Michelle was, and I told him she was at work."

Her face crumpled, turning red with shame and rage. "He said," she gulped, "he said, 'Well, you'll do then, little sister,' and he pinned me down on my bed with his body. He had one hand over my mouth so I couldn't scream. Oh, God, it was awful!" she wailed.

Marie reached forward, scooping Natalie into her arms. Her pent-up grief and shame burst like a boil, and she began to sob. Natalie let her tears come, this time. It felt so good to tell someone, even if it was these two people she didn't even know. They really did, she felt, care. That made her feel better, as well.

Vincent, she observed, brushed a tear away and poured a glass of water from a plastic bottle that had been sitting on his shelf. He handed it to his wife, who passed it to Natalie, like he wanted to pretend he was invisible, which was ridiculous, because he took up about half the room. She gulped it down, setting the empty glass on the desk. They both seemed very patient, waiting until she was ready to continue, not rushing her or saying stupid stuff to fill the silence.

"Do I have to tell you what he did to me?" she asked Marie, her face red and wet with tears.

"Are you sure you don't want me to leave?" Vincent asked.

"No, please stay. You'll see why I asked you soon," she replied. She regained her composure and dried her face with a tissue.

Natalie took a deep breath and closed her eyes. Marie took both of her warm, moist hands in her own and tightened her grip gently for reassurance. Then Natalie launched forth, holding nothing back. She laid out every disgusting, revolting detail. She did not open her eyes but held on to Marie's hands as if they were the safety bar on a roller coaster.

When she was done, she opened her eyes and shuddered, looking blankly around the room as if she had just awakened from an evil trance. The cop looked down at his hands. Marie eyed Natalie with compassion.

"I never told her," Natalie whispered. "I never told anyone until today. It was too horrible, too disgusting," she spat, her face again tightening.

"There's more you want to say, isn't there?" Marie prodded gently, giving her hands another gentle squeeze before letting them go.

"Yes," she agreed, glad to be moving away from her own personal hell on earth. "Like I said, Paolo and I are friends. We always run into each other in town, like at the library or at the square. Saturday, he met my sister at work, and, well, he must've really liked her, because he asked her out. You see, he's pretty shy. She was getting really sick of René's bullying, so she said yes. They went out that night and had a really great time."

Her voice changed in an instant, becoming strained and panicked. "Now, my sister is gone and Paolo is maybe dead and I have no one left—no one," she cried, her voice trailing off to a hoarse whisper.

Durrand looked at his wife, his mind working, and then addressed Natalie in a pensive tone. "I actually knocked on your door last night, after talking to de Gaul, just to check on her, but no one answered. You must've been sound asleep. It was pretty late, after all. Gilbert thinks this le Roux is involved, as well," he noted. "Looked in the front window but didn't see any signs of a struggle, so I left." It sounded to Natalie like he was thinking out loud, putting the pieces together.

"Please, please find Michelle," she begged. "Please find my sister. She's all I have," she pleaded, looking directly at him with desperation in her brimming eyes.

Guy sat vigil by Paolo's bedside. When he had first walked in after the surgery, Guy had hardly recognized him. The mass of lush, dark hair was shorn away, a white bandage wound around his head. There was a nasty gash on his face, and he was hooked up to an IV and a heart monitor. It was hard to look at him, remembering how happy the boy had been the last time he had seen him. Guy reached out and placed his rough hand over Paolo's. It was still and cool to his touch.

The doctor, a petite, middle-aged woman with short, dark hair; light-brown complexion; and compassionate brown eyes had spoken with Guy, as no family members could be found, telling him how her patient had flatlined and then recovered. Fluid on the brain was a concern, and the bruised organs, internal bleeding, broken ribs, and a collapsed lung complicated things further.

"He was a mess," she said wryly, shooting her patient a sympathetic glance, "but he fought hard to stay with us. I'm not sure how he made it, to be honest, but I'm so glad he did."

The old farmer thanked the doctor for her efforts and then sat down in the hard chair next to the bed. He kept his vigil in silence, praying the Rosary over and over. Paolo lay still as stone, a look of absolute serenity on his face.

Marie drove Natalie to the hospital to see her friend later that Sunday morning. They walked down the Spartan, linoleum hallway, the counselor's arm draped around her shoulder. They slowed up as they approached Paolo's room. Natalie noticed Guy sitting in an uncomfortable-looking chair by the bed. He glanced up, seeming surprised to see visitors, but apparently recognizing Marie, he rose and shuffled out of the room.

"Thanks for coming," he said gruffly, his voice ragged with fatigue.

Marie gave Guy a hug and suggested they both go down and have a cup of coffee. Natalie watched as the old man glanced back into the room at the still figure on the bed, like he was afraid that he would expire if he left.

"I'll stay with him until you get back," Natalie offered. "You look like you could use a break. Go get something to eat."

Guy nodded his thanks, and the two adults walked away, murmuring quietly. Natalie slipped into the room, pulling the curtain halfway shut to conceal her, afraid that the nurses would kick her out for being too young.

The stark hospital room was bright but far from cheerful. The white walls were graced with a single picture of flowers in a vase, just in case no one had brought any, for real. Jesus hung in agony on the wall to the right, as if to remind the patients that someone had suffered worse than they were. A clock showed mockingly that they were wasting their time being sick, while healthy people got to spend theirs having fun. A television bolted to the top of the left corner strove for a sense of normalcy, like an uncle who told randy jokes at a funeral luncheon, and a decent-sized window off to the left of the bed streaming sunlight onto the adjacent wall reminded the sick person that life was going on without him. It was silent, save for the beeping coming from the monitor by the bed and the occasional jarring sound of voices and movement coming from the hallway, like an out-of-place intrusion to the stillness in the curtained chamber.

The somber girl moved stealthily over to the bed. Paolo lay so still, he barely looked alive. If not for the heart monitor indicating otherwise, she would have thought he was a corpse. She studied his face, having been given the opportunity to look closely without being perceived as rude or making her shy friend uncomfortable with her scrutiny. Of all the subjects she sketched, the human face held the most captivation for her, and for one so young, she was amazingly adept at reading what lay beneath its surface.

Delicately, she brushed her fingers over the soft black hair covering his forearm. She thought it looked beautiful, like shiny threads of silk. He did not stir. She then grasped his cool fingers in her own warm hands and held them until they had lost their chill. With an artist's discernment, she thought to herself that his hands were his best feature, strong, graceful, and elegant. Laying his fingers back carefully on the blanket, she moved in close to his face, pulling the edge of her sleeve tight with her fingertips. She reached out and slowly, gently wiped off the stream of saliva that had escaped from the corner of his mouth. The fabric scraped on the rough, dark stubble that had appeared on his face, an uncomfortable reminder of how much older than she he was.

Then, leaning in, she pressed her lips to his forehead. He smelled strangely antiseptic. Resting her forehead against his, her hair falling like a canopy over their two faces, she pleaded with him in a soft whisper.

"Please come back, Paolo. I love you so much. Please don't leave me."

15

Awakenings

G uy walked back into the hospital room just after dawn on the Tuesday morning after that fateful weekend. He had gone home the night before and had stood under the steaming shower for a long time, hoping to wash away the bone-deep tiredness he felt. Then, exhausted, he had collapsed onto his bed, not even bothering to pull down the covers. Paolo's comatose state was beginning to take its toll on him. He wasn't sure how much longer he could bear it, sitting there for hours on end with no change. It was starting to seem hopeless.

He approached the bed and sighed. Paolo looked just the same. Guy began to despair that he would ever regain consciousness. He slumped into the chair, shoulders sagging. After a while, he began to doze, and his Rosary beads slipped from his relaxed fingers to the floor.

He roused himself when the nurse bustled in. She performed her ministrations on Paolo quickly and efficiently with detached professionalism, checking his lines and taking his blood pressure and temperature. Lifting his eyelid, she shone a light directly at the pupil in an attempt to elicit a response. "How are we doing today, Paolo?" she asked him brightly. "Ready to wake up yet?"

Guy felt she made too much noise. He had grown used to the silence, which was disturbed only by the consistent beeping of the monitoring devices.

She bustled back out after greeting him with dispassionate cheerfulness. He reached down to scoop up his Rosary beads, which lay coiled at his feet. As he rose back up, he heard a soft groan.

Paolo felt completely disoriented. His head throbbed painfully, and his chest seemed tight. The last thing he remembered was being held by men he couldn't see. He recalled that Michelle's angry friend had wrapped duct tape around his mouth. Was he still in the alley behind Gilbert's shop? No, he was warm, and the air was still.

Opening his eyes, he saw Guy standing over him, a smile lighting his face, which otherwise looked drawn and anxious.

"So you finally decided to wake up," the old man teased.

Paolo tried to respond, but he was confused. Words seemed to elude him, and he could only grunt in reply, which sent a stab of pain shooting through his chest. He closed his eyes, furrowing his brow, causing his brain to throb. Groaning softly, he shifted, and the grip of agony wound itself around him in constricting bands. He began to breathe heavily, which made his ribs and lungs protest sharply. Tears squeezed out of the corners of his eyes. Every movement, every breath brought suffering. He couldn't find anything that didn't hurt and continued to writhe in desperation, trying to escape the vice grip that kept getting tighter and tighter.

Guy pressed a buzzer by the side of the bed in three fast taps. A nurse arrived quickly, and after observing him, she took a needle, slid it into his IV, and drained a light-brown liquid into it as he watched. She made no move to tell him what it was.

"It's okay, Paolo," she said in a soothing tone of voice. "You'll feel better in a minute. Hang in there." She got a damp towel, blotted away his tears, and then pressed it to his forehead to calm him.

"Calm down, buddy," Guy admonished, patting Paolo's arm with his rough, gnarled hand, as he squirmed, groaning softly, his face contorted with the effort. "Keep still. You're okay now," he crooned in a raspy voice.

Paolo made a sincere effort to relax, aided by the mysterious substance she had given him. He sensed that he was making his friend anxious. He shuddered, closed his eyes, and took a few shallow breaths, afraid even to inhale too deeply. The nurse took his hand, giving it a reassuring squeeze, and he looked up at her in confusion, wanting her to explain.

"That's good, Paolo. Don't try to breathe too deeply. Take it easy," the woman coached him. His expression went from pained to relaxed as the substance took hold. He thought it kind that she waited until he calmed down, holding on to his hand to comfort him, before she left. The touch and concern of another person seemed to help as much as the potion she had injected into him.

"Y'know, young man," Guy joked, "you really should be more careful who you hang around with."

Paolo appreciated the humor, and the corners of his mouth turned up in a weak attempt at a smile. He gave a little laugh, which sent sharp spikes of pain through his chest. His brows again squeezed tight as he groaned softly in protest. The old man sat back down, picking up his hand as the nurse had done. Paolo looked over at him. His gaze, through half-closed eyes, projected the wordless gratitude he felt.

"Paolo," he said quietly, "I haven't known you that long, but in the short time you've been with me, I have come to see that you are an exceptional human being." He nodded his head for emphasis. "Now, my Marguerite and I, we were never able to have any kids, though we had planned on about a half dozen." He chuckled sadly. "But, if we had been blessed with a son, I would have hoped he would've turned out like you," he finished.

Paolo looked away for a minute, the farmer's kindly thoughts sinking into his battered spirit like a balm. *"An exceptional human being."* Guy could not possibly fathom the deep meaning those words held for him, as he strove to live his life with purpose. He looked back at his good friend again, wishing he had the strength to thank him.

"I have no idea where you came from, whether you have family anywhere that you haven't told me about for whatever reason, but I want you to know," he said solemnly, squeezing Paolo's hand, "that if you need someone to look to, like a father, I would be honored to be that person."

Paolo shut his half-closed eyes and tightened his fingers around the gnarled hand he held in response. Then he drifted off to sleep to escape the prison of pain in which he was locked.

Fey lay on the chaise in Guiscard's loft for three long nights. She looked beautiful and peaceful. He studied her sadly, racked with guilt. Arcenciel had curled up on his bed, worn out from her long vigil. As the sun rose over the bare trees, he looked up from the book he had been staring at, but not reading, to see Fey's beauty fading. It was as if the sun were setting on her, yet rising on everything else. Guiscard rejoiced at the sight. Fey's boy was alive. He would never have been able to meet her gaze had this not been so. He still blamed himself more than Yasmine for this tragedy. He was more advanced in study and should have known better. He hoped they had both learned a stern lesson from what had transpired.

He scooted his chair from the table, strode quickly to the chaise, and perched himself on the edge. Arcenciel, hearing him stir, looked in their direction and covered her mouth with her hands to keep from shouting out her joy. She jumped up, ran lightly over, and placed her arm gently over Guiscard's shoulder, giving him a half-hug.

Fey slept on for some time but began to move about. She was making the journey home. In a burst of nervous energy, Arcenciel began to make breakfast, brewing bergamot tea and mixing up a porridge of stewed grains and fruits sprinkled with walnuts. She poured a generous amount of honey in both the tea and the porridge, tasting as she stirred. Now that the danger had passed, the two vigilant friends found that they were both famished.

Guiscard watched with concern, relief, and remorse as Fey finally opened her eyes. She sat up, swung her feet over the side of the chaise, and braced her hands on the edge. Her shoulders began to shake, and Arcenciel rushed over to comfort her as she dissolved into tears.

René awoke on the sofa in his friend's apartment in Marseille. It wasn't much, just a one-bedroom flat with a pullout sofa in the living room, facing a television, and a cramped kitchenette, littered with small appliances. The single window looked out over the narrow street, which was crowded with similar, humble dwellings of the blue-collar set. The walls were old, bumpy plaster and the carpet a dirty, faded brown. Music posters hung on the walls in lieu of pictures, the edges curled and torn. The curtains on the window were thin, cheap, and stained. A hookah pipe held court on the coffee table with a dirty, plastic ashtray and a pile of unopened mail.

He hadn't fully explained why he was there, but his friend seemed to have a feeling that there was trouble. He had left for work, asking only that René clean up after himself. René, sensing his friend's hesitancy, vowed to get on with what he had come to do and be gone as soon as possible.

Sitting with his elbows propped on his knees, he contemplated the ill-fated night that had brought him there. How the hell had everything gone so wrong? He had loved Michelle and wanted her to move in with him. What had gotten into her? Everything had been going just fine and then that stammering farmhand showed up and she went crazy. Seeing how much money he had been loaded with, René was sure the filthy vagrant had stolen from the old man. It was shameless, how he acted so dumb and innocent and then took advantage of the old fool. A real con artist, that one. Typical Roma—and René was dead certain at this point that the Italian stranger was just that. It only made sense.

If not for the burden of her bratty younger sister, Michelle and René would have moved in together a long time ago. He couldn't understand why the little monster hated him so. He had never done anything to her and treated both her and her sister pretty well, he thought. Such a shame that Michelle had been saddled with her. She always put Natalie first, which irritated him, and she had spent way too much time with her useless set of high school friends, who treated him coldly. If you were going to have friends as part of a couple, they should treat the other person in the relationship with some respect.

The car was the first order of business. He cleaned the blood off of it and then set about finding a chop shop to ditch it at, which was not as easy as it might, at first, appear, since he was so far from home and didn't really know many people in Marseille. After he had spent three exhausting days digging up what he was looking for, it hadn't panned out. The owner of the shop just looked at René in silence, studying his face. He then told him he had a bad feeling about the whole thing and refused to take the car. René, frustrated beyond belief, abandoned the Fiat in a public parking lot, sanded off the VIN numbers, and removed anything that might tie the vehicle to him. He moved on to Paris, where he had more connections.

16

Storm

Rain pelted dismally against Gilbert's collar before running down his neck as he dashed into the hospital. He never seemed to be able to remember his umbrella, which sat, warm and dry, in the coatrack at his apartment. After stopping to ask for directions at the front desk, he made his way through the maze of corridors to his destination. The soggy salesman, in his soaked black leather jacket, peered uneasily into the room. The light from the gloomy sky cast a dim glow over the plain white space. Guy sat by the bed, a book in his hands, reading aloud in a quiet voice as Paolo listened and watched him with quiet attentiveness through half-shut eyes.

Gilbert grabbed his collar with both hands, shaking loose the remaining raindrops on his shoulders and timidly entered with feigned cheerfulness.

"Hey, Paolo!" he announced brightly, to mask his discomfiture. "You're awake. That's great."

Paolo gave a listless wave but did not speak. Gilbert approached, stuffing his hands awkwardly in his jacket pockets, his brown hair darkened from the damp, falling in uncharacteristic messiness over his face. Unsure what to do with himself, he stood stiffly beside the bed. He noticed the gash on his new acquaintance's face had been mended with surgical tape. Boy, he really had been clumsy! He felt bad about that. It would leave a nasty scar. He didn't feel comfortable saying anything about it and just tried to put it out of his mind, biting his lower lip.

The last time he had seen him, Paolo had been sprawled in the alley behind the shop. He felt a responsibility to stop by and check up on him, having been the one to discover his unconscious form that night. Weird, how things worked out. If he hadn't forgotten to shut off the lights, if he hadn't twisted the deadbolt on the front door before leaving for the night, this nice guy, who seemed like he would actually be pretty cool to hang out with, would probably be dead right now.

Guy stood up and shook hands with Paolo's visitor.

"Gilbert," he stated warmly, "I'm so grateful for what you've done. Without you, Paolo wouldn't be here."

"It's nothing." He shrugged. "Anyone would have done the same thing."

"Thanks for coming," Paolo said softly.

"Hey, I had to make sure you were okay," he answered cheerily. Paolo nodded but didn't say anything more. Gilbert grew kind of uncomfortable. He shifted his weight, searching for something to fill the silence. His usual nonchalance had fled. Hospitals really knew how to suck the confidence out of a person.

"Sorry about Michelle," he blurted out, for lack of anything better coming to mind. "I sure hope they find her soon. I hear Vin Durrand is pulling in every favor he can to try and locate her."

Paolo's eyes blazed. "What do you mean?" he asked, panic sweeping over his face. His gaze darted pleadingly to Guy, who looked abashed and shot Gilbert a disapproving glance for letting this slip. *Oops.*

Paolo looked horrified. "No, no, no," he lamented hoarsely as Guy put his hand on his shoulder to calm him. "Not Michelle. No."

He snapped. Ripping the IV tube from his arm, he tried to heave himself out of bed.

"I've got to find her."

Blanching, he collapsed as the blood rushed from his head. Gilbert helped the old man catch him before he hit the floor, trying to bear the lion's share of the tall, broad Italian's weight.

The nurse rushed in, righteous anger flashing on her face. "You!" She pointed to the horrified, well-meaning miscreant. "… are leaving right now—and don't try coming back!" she added, hostility etched on her rigid features.

They hoisted the limp body gently back onto the bed, with the help of the angry nurse. Gilbert shot an apologetic glance at Guy, who didn't notice. His attention was focused on Paolo. He backed out of the room and punched his fists against the wall in the hallway as the nurse muttered to herself in a furious growl.

"And he was doing so well today. Now I've got to reattach his IV, make sure he didn't hurt himself … probably have to shoot the poor kid full of morphine again. What an idiot!"

"Aw, well. Some people just aren't comfortable in hospitals. He didn't mean for this to happen."

Gilbert listened in humiliation to their commentary, covering his burning face with his hands, still leaning against the wall. How could he have been so stupid? Any moron knows that you don't talk about things that might be upsetting to a critically ill person. Mortified, he slunk out of the hospital, determined to be a better friend to this quirky but likeable character.

Guiscard stood remorsefully observing as Arcenciel comforted their friend, who sat trembling and weeping in her arms. It seemed that after a heavy dose of the potion, it would take the recipient several days to recover, a flaw Guiscard wasn't sure how to correct. He wondered, though, if Fey weren't suffering more from sincere lovesickness than the aftereffects of the Dream Travel potion. He looked on, shame and guilt struggling on his face.

"Oh, Arcenciel," she cried, "it was awful—the hardest thing I have ever had to do!"

She raised her eyes from her friend's damp shoulder.

"He was almost blue from cold, and in so much pain," Fey lamented.

"You could feel this?" Guiscard asked. It seemed that the briny concoction had achieved the desired effect of allowing the two souls unfettered access to each other's thoughts and feelings. Fey ignored his question, though, and went on with her story.

"He acted so brave, but I knew that he was in agony," she shared. "But the hardest thing of all—the thing that ripped the heart right out of my chest— was when he left. Oh," she groaned. "I may never get to be with him again." Fey's body was again racked with sobs.

Guiscard looked on uncomfortably at the consequences of his thoughtless lark as the cold rain lashed at the window, scolding him for his foolishness. Any pride he might have enjoyed in the success of his new potion was completely eclipsed by his sense of guilt for necessitating its use.

The rain continued all afternoon, noisily pelting the front window of J. de Gaul and Son. Jacques stared out at the dismal square, the damp, chill air sending a shiver over him as he gazed through the reverse side of the gold-leaf lettering on the window. His eyes were drawn to a barely visible scratch on the glass, after the word "Son," where Jacques had scraped an "s" off with a razor blade, with tears in his eyes. He had done this after Gilbert had left one evening, a few years back, wanting to spare him the ache that he, by himself, endured. It was too hard to look at, but just as hard to scrape the flakes of gold from the pane. The scratch remained, a permanent reminder of what had been, like a scar formed over a wound. It seemed there was no way to escape the pain of losing his child.

The rain continued to pelt. The shop bell rang, and he looked up to see his son skulking in, with a sheepish air that made Jacques wonder what trouble he had gotten into this time.

"Your hair is soaked. Where's your umbrella?" Jacques groused. "You're going to catch a cold."

"I'm fine. I'm fine," Gilbert protested curtly, pulling a tissue from behind the counter and blowing his nose vigorously. He looked upset and shaken, but Jacques let it go. Gilbert hated how emotional he always got. Better to ignore it. He would only snap at him if he asked what the matter was.

"How's Guy's friend?" he asked, instead.

"Oh, well, you know," Gilbert floundered, his face flushed. He looked out the window as he raked his hand through his sopping wet hair. "He's awake, anyway," he muttered, donning his coat and tie like a suit of armor, his tell-all eyes betraying a storm within.

Buried Sins

*P*aolo reached for the book Guy had brought to read. It lay on the bed beside him. His friend had stepped out for some air and a cup of coffee with Vin. He was not surprised to see it was a Bible. Guy was very religious and actually tried to live out his faith. Paolo thought that maybe that was why he had been so open to helping him, a stranger with nothing to offer. It was just one manifestation of his genuine belief.

The cover of the book was very worn. It had obviously been read quite a bit, and Paolo felt that if the man who had so kindly offered to be both father and mentor to him thought it worth studying, he should do likewise. Paolo flipped casually, as most people did, to chapter one. At any rate, it might help get his mind off of Michelle, whose unknown plight filled him with both fear and guilt. There was, unfortunately, little he could do for her, at the moment.

The story was beautiful and appealed to his romantic view of the world. When Guy returned though, the book was open, facedown, on the bed and Paolo lay with a dejected look on his face.

"What's the matter, Son?" he asked. "Is it Michelle?"

Paolo raised his eyes to the ceiling and sighed. "I can't stop thinking about her. I sit here, useless, while she may be in danger. I want so badly to find her, but I can't even take care of myself or even go to the bathroom on my own," he explained huskily, "and I feel so very humiliated by this."

"It bothers you, that the nurses have to take care of you, doesn't it?" Guy perceived.

Paolo nodded, looking down at the book. Completely unused to human contact, he recoiled instinctively, as he had from the approach of Sophie, Guy's dog. He hated how they would whip back his coverings like they owned him, pressing their cool hands onto his abdomen to check for swelling, or, even worse, to sponge him down. They thought nothing of this, but he found it almost unbearable, hating to be touched and physically exposed this way without any say.

"Paolo, they have to. It's their job. They don't think anything of it. And you need help right now. You need to stop being so squeamish and just focus on getting better. I thought that kind of modesty died out in Europe long before the twentieth century expired," Guy joked. "One would certainly think so, from the stuff they show on television nowadays."

Paolo looked up at Guy, taking the chastisement in, his large eyes wide with despondency. He would do what he was told, but he didn't have to like it.

"And then I read this story about Adam and Eve in the garden," he continued, steeped in melancholy, his fingers dusting over the cover of the book that lay next to him. "They were naked but weren't ashamed because they didn't sin, and I thought, well, I must have sinned, that I feel such shame over this."

Guy thought for a moment and then gave a characteristic answer. "It's called original sin," he explained. "And we all bear the same burden of it, the moment we're born."

It made it easier to bear, knowing he was not alone in his suffering, but he didn't want to be in a state of sin. It made him uncomfortable thinking about it. "How do I get rid of it, if I haven't committed it and it just appears? How can I confess this sin and make it go away?" he asked, rubbing his hands tensely over his arms, feeling frustrated. Maybe if he could, he thought simplistically, then his uncomfortable feelings of shame would be expunged, as well.

"Oh, it's forgiven when you get baptized."

"But I don't remember getting baptized. Maybe that's the problem," he realized, nervously.

"We'll look into it when you get better. I promise," Guy assured him.

Paolo nodded gratefully, but this would eat at him until it was taken care of.

"But for now, Paolo, just do the best you can, every day, to do what's right. Nobody's perfect. You can't spend all day beating yourself up over things," he explained in a somewhat scolding tone, adding with a grin, "Somebody already took care of that for you."

Paolo lowered his head and smiled, but the messy mop of black hair that used to fall over his eyes was conspicuously missing and the smile was now tainted with sadness.

René stood over the ravine where he had buried Michelle's body. The moon filtered through the bare branches of the trees. He surveyed his handiwork critically. No, he could still see the pale, bloody fingers of her right hand reaching out from under the pile of rocks and debris he had poured over top of her like a cairn, as if she were trying to reemerge from her grave. Sick and panicky, he began to search the area for more loose rocks, leaves, twigs—anything that would finally conceal her rotting form. Reaching down to pick up a particularly large rock, he started when he noticed a figure watching him. It was a cloaked woman, like an ancient pagan sorceress. She possessed an eerie beauty, but it was her eyes that struck terror into his heart. They glowed, fierce and red, and were glaring at him, full of fury. He could hear sirens in the distance and knew they were coming for him. Rooted to the spot by the forest spirit's mesmerizing stare, René was powerless to run as the police closed in on him.

"It's her fault. She made me do it!" he exclaimed.

He awoke to the sound of a police cruiser blaring by outside the hotel in Paris where he had temporarily holed up. Sweating profusely, he held his breath until the noise receded, but the image of the fiery-eyed sorceress remained long after the silence returned, a recurring dream, or rather, an alluring nightmare.

A striped awning fluttered in the breeze as the setting sun played over the shopfront. A mouthwatering banquet of fresh fruit peeked out from under the undulating canopy. Everything appeared in shades of gray.

"Ciao, Paolo! Come stai?" a voice called out.

"Molto Bene! Venuto a comprare un po' di frutta? Se non, ti hanno di dare al mio amico nascosto in un albero," Paolo replied, as if it were someone else, not he, responding.

Suddenly, thunder ripped through the forest, and Paolo found himself in a damp, hollow tree, far away from the sunny, warm fruit stand.

The dreamer awoke to the sound of a gurney making its way noisily down the hallway. He lay still, holding fast to the receding images, as if to an ephemeral treasure. Had he been a fruit vendor, then, in his past life? He certainly did like fruit more than anything else he ate, needing to have a bit of it with every meal, it seemed, before he could truly feel satisfied. Where was this stall? This village? Frustrated, he racked his brain until his head began to hurt and then gave up and fell back to sleep.

18

Love Wish

*P*aolo, after what had seemed an eternity to him, was finally released from the hospital. The ride home was not pleasant. He had always enjoyed riding in the truck as Guy steered it over the winding roads that led to the farm, but at that moment, all he wanted to do was lie down. The pain medication they had given him made him queasy, which only added to the discomfort he felt as the truck moved along the road like a boat riding over swells. A cold mist cloaked the bare fields, sucking every bit of warmth from whatever it touched.

The truck pulled into the gravel drive to the farm. Paolo opened the passenger door to the pickup and managed to climb out unassisted, hanging onto it for support. He looked wearily at Guy, who hurried over to help him. His head throbbed, making his vision blurry. Guy had him drape his arm across his back for support, and the two men made their way toward the house, Paolo shivering in the cold, damp air. With every step, more of what little strength he had left fled. When they arrived at the porch steps, the newly released patient looked up hopelessly, as if he were facing a mountain. Too tired to move, he sank down on the stair, leaned back, and closed his eyes.

"Just let me rest for a minute," he requested.

He didn't get back up. Guy sighed and shuffled wearily into the house.

Gilbert crouched in the changing room, arms crossed, his eyes squeezed closed with effort. His chest felt tight, and he could feel his heart racing. His armpits were drenched with sweat in spite of his antiperspirant, and he felt dizzy and nauseous. He could hear that there were customers in the store, but there was no way he was going out there feeling like this. He wished they would just go away and leave him to suffer in peace.

Gripping his hair in his hands and groaning softly, he held his breath, willing himself to calm down. He found that this usually worked to stave off his tendency to hyperventilate. He had been through this before. Usually, he would be okay in, say, five minutes—not even enough time for his dad to notice that he was missing. Today, though, he knew that he had already been hiding for about twenty minutes, and that thought really scared him.

Exhaling sharply, he looked up to see his father standing before him, looking at him with, not anger, but concern on his face.

"Son, what's wrong?" Jacques asked, reaching over to help Gilbert up off the floor. The sudden movement made his stomach churn.

He avoided his father's gaze but instead caught his reflection in the mirror. He noted with embarrassment that he looked absolutely terrible. His hair was a mess. His face looked ashen and strained. Turning away from the unwelcome sight, he darted over to the wastebasket beside the changing room door and vomited into it with the uncomfortable knowledge that his perceptive parent was watching.

Gilbert felt absolutely humiliated. He wouldn't even look at his father. His heart rate began to slow, and the feeling of dizziness faded. "I think I must've eaten something bad. I'm okay," he muttered, running his hand through his hair. His jaw tensed defensively, and he averted his gaze to the floor.

"Let me take you home," Jacques offered, sounding unconvinced.

He nodded, the feeling of tightness slowly draining away from his chest as he let himself be led out, feeling very shaky. He stood awkwardly against the wall as his dad asked the customers to please excuse them; he explained that there had been a family emergency and he had to close for about an hour. Thinking that Jacques was referring to him, he protested, "Really, Dad, I'm okay. I'll just get back to work. I don't want to put you out." He felt sweaty and beyond tired, but having his father become suspicious about his problem was much worse.

"No, Gilbert," his father clarified, "I just got a call from Guy. Paolo was released from the hospital today, and he needs some help getting him settled. That's why I came to find you. If you want, I can take you home first and then drive over to the farm. You don't look so good."

"Oh," he replied. Then, seeing an opportunity to deflect attention from himself, he offered, "I'll go along to help."

"Are you sure you're up to it?" he asked quietly, his head lowered in concern.

"Sure, Dad. Let's go," he returned, trying desperately to act more energetic than he felt. He watched passively as his father turned the sign and locked the door and then spent the brief car ride silently staring out the window, avoiding his father's scrutinizing glances in his direction. He noted with relief that, as soon as the car stopped in front of the farmhouse, the focus shifted to his new friend, who lay sprawled on the damp steps to the porch.

Between the three of them, they managed to haul Paolo into the house and up the stairs to bed. Gilbert could feel his shoulder blades poking sharply through the fabric of his jacket. He did look to Gilbert as if he had lost weight in the hospital. The food was probably awful there, he mused. Paolo awoke as they carried him in but seemed somewhat incoherent. He protested numbly that he was okay and didn't need to be carried.

"Put me down, please," he begged.

"Aw, c'mon," Gilbert teased, in a tone of voice one would use with a baby. "I came over just to tuck you in and read you a story."

Paolo glared at him, and Jacques and Guy both laughed.

"They just hustle a body out of the hospital, whether he can stand up or not," Guy growled.

"That's just the way it is," Jacques shrugged resignedly, puffing with the effort.

Gilbert, as promised, tucked his new friend in himself; he even took his shoes off and placed them neatly below the bed. After casting one last reassuring smile at the barely conscious figure, he closed the door and leaned against it with a sigh of relief, his own last bit of strength wrung out by sheer force of will. He vowed silently to return when both Paolo and he were doing better. He felt protective, having been the one to find him that terrible night. This guy was nothing like his other friends—he was a lamb in the woods, who had had the misfortune to stumble upon the wolf.

After leaving the Paysanne farm, Jacques took Gilbert, not to his own flat, but to the family home at the edge of town. He wanted to keep an eye on him that night, being just as unnerved by this incident as his son was. He felt helpless as he watched him self-destruct. He noticed subtle personality changes. Gilbert definitely had a shorter fuse. He ate very little, had lost weight, and was prone to showing up late for work. It was disturbing, but he didn't know what he could do about it. His son was an adult. If he became too overbearing, he was afraid he would push him away, and Gilbert was all he had.

He knew that he had, and continued to, overindulge his only remaining child. The trouble with him had started after his wife had left them for a man she had met on a shopping trip to Paris—paid with her husband's money. He had buried his hurt by focusing on teaching Tristan the business, letting Gilbert have a few more years of freedom before he would begin his tutelage.

His youngest son went wild after his mother left. Gilbert ran with his friends, smoked, drank up his father's liquor, and started chasing after girls rather obsessively. Whereas before, the two brothers had gotten along very well, things grew tense. Gilbert would goad Tristan, intentionally making him angry. He acted like he was jealous of his older brother. Jacques couldn't fathom why. Gilbert definitely had it easier. He was better looking as he favored his mother, smarter, and had less responsibility but just as many privileges as Tristan.

Jacques felt that, in some way, Tristan had been glad to get away during his military service. Now, his oldest boy was gone, an early casualty of the French involvement in Afghanistan, and he held on to his younger son by a tenuous thread.

A messy, disorganized array of dried flowers spilled over the tabletop in Yasmine's hideaway. Pretty, starched lace hung over the edge of her fluffy sofa, which was upholstered in pink-dyed cobweb silk. A clutter of pretty garments hung on pegs on the wall and over the bedstead in the corner. A birch vanity held a vast array of tiny pots, brushes, feathers, combs, and assorted toiletries, which vied for attention in front of an oval mirror. The walls of clean, cheerful birch bark were lined all about with shelves full to overflowing with spell books, love potions, and powders, all grouped by project, each one representing an attempt by the matchmaker to assist one of her own kind or the human sort to find his or her one true love or to rekindle a fresh flame from long-burning embers.

The orchestrator of the chaos that Love made of the heart snipped lengths of lace, filling them carefully with a precise mix of natural and supernatural elements as her apprentice watched with admiration.

> Red petals of one rose, Love's own sweet breath.
> Forget-me-nots to seal the heart's pure troth.
> Fair lily, such that Love be true till death.
> Bound in lace, white as the wingéd moth.
>
> > Off we fly into the chill, dark night
> > The burning flames of passion to ignite.

After sprinkling a sparkling powder over her creations, Yasmine strung the freshly made pomanders on pink satin cords and tied them to her waist.

"And that," she instructed Fleur, "is how you fashion a Love Wish. They are also fun to deliver, as you never know in what state you will find the recipient," she went on in an edifying tone, with a twinkle in her eye. "Why, once, I slipped into a faerie bower, only to find that my services were no longer needed."

The matchmaker and her student both giggled conspiratorially as they made ready to leave on their mission to help their forest-dwelling kin and the humans of Achères to find the perfect, special someone to make their lives complete.

"Whither do we fly?" Fleur asked.

"First to our friend, Guiscard," she noted thoughtfully. "He is ready to make his decision, and, love him as we all do, he must make the right choice."

She, herself, had been mildly interested in the leader of their small clan and had thought they would make a good couple, as being a matchmaker would place her in high status among her people, as well, but she was, above all, a professional and would never use her skills to manipulate his heart in her favor. To do so would bring misfortune, not happiness.

"Next," she went on, "The purveyor of the humans' morning brew. He is a challenging case, as he is enamored of men, and Achères has not proven to be fertile ground for such a hunt," she shared as Fleur nodded, listening attentively.

"Next, a woman disappointed in love, who, her own ambitions crushed by a thoughtless being who should have appreciated a kindred spirit, has forsaken him and now awaits new love with a hungry heart."

"But you have four pomanders," Fleur noted.

Yasmine raised an eyebrow and smirked. "This last one is for my own pet project, which I have known since he was a babe. His heart yearns to be loved, yet he pushes away all who would cling to him. With this Love Wish, I have included an extra dose of *poussiere d'amour*."

"What does it do?" Fleur asked.

"It stirs the flames of passion. He will not be able to push his next conquest away so easily. She will, I do attest, worm her way into his heart."

The matchmakers donned their cloaks and flew off to deliver their charms to the unsuspecting benefactors.

Dreamers

ey lounged on the chaise in Guiscard's loft, pondering her options aloud as he listened in attentive silence.

"If I visit him in a dream, we can talk," she thought aloud. "But if I do that, he might ask me questions regarding whence he came, and I find it difficult to keep my thoughts from betraying what I know he couldn't handle," she argued with herself, as Guiscard stood, chin cradled between his thumb and forefinger. "If I steal into his room, I might see how he fares, yet not disturb his tranquility with my presence."

"You must decide on your own. The Dream Travel potion has exceeded even my own expectations, giving lovers such intimacy that their thoughts and feelings mingle like a dram of wine mixed within a goblet of water, clarity and color inseparably combined. I owe you much gratitude, Fey, for testing it."

"I would stray to the edge of death, for him who holds my heart," she vowed with downcast gaze, tracing her finger across the brocade fabric.

Unwitting, you did, Guiscard noted silently.

The next day, Paolo lay on the sofa as Guy busied himself with his daily chores. He stared out the front window, drinking in the familiar scene. Oh, it felt so good to be home. He had no recollection of what had happened to him after he lost consciousness on the porch. He had awakened, the next morning, in his own bed, unable to recall how he'd gotten there.

Sometime later, feeling sleepy, he slowly made his way up to his room to take a nap. The journal that Guy had given Paolo after their conversation on Genesis, chapter one, lay on his dresser, his gold ring resting on top. Guy's thought was to give him a way to sort out the sometimes bizarre and confusing thoughts that popped up in his head. Paolo had been pleased with the gift, immediately taking to writing down his musings. It did seem to help him.

He slipped appreciatively under the handmade throw Marie had left lying across the bed and dozed.

The striped awning fluttered in the breeze, an array of fruit peering out from beneath. A man in a white shirt, long apron, and dark trousers swept the walkway in front of the outdoor display, singing in Italian. He looked to be about thirty-five, with dark hair and a pleasant face, thick black brows, and a hint of beard that no razor could defeat.

A beautiful woman sauntered up with supernatural grace. She was radiant and lovely, her skin the color of lilacs in springtime. She stood and looked up at the tree beside the fruit stand.

"Come down and speak with me, Paolo," she called up to the branches.

The aproned man ignored her and, his chore done, disappeared under the striped canopy.

Paolo descended from the branches with a swoop, as if he had no weight at all.

"I came to see how you fare," the beautiful woman told him. "I was worried about you."

Her fiery hair hung in profuse glory all around her shoulders, and her eyes were bright and sparkling. Beside her, all the world seemed trapped in muted shades of gray.

"Um, it's been hard," he stated truthfully.

"I know, my love," she sympathized, reaching out and pressing her hand to his face.

Suddenly, he felt himself falling …

Marie's car pulled into the drive. She came crunching up the gravel, led by Natalie, who scooted out before the car was even placed in park. After much debate in the Durrands' living room, the grizzly, his wife, and the social services worker all came to an agreement that Natalie would be safest at their house, since René had still not been found. Her aunt Yvette had begged to take her to her home in St. Quentin, but Natalie had protested, pretending she was afraid she would be a sitting duck without Officer Durrand to protect her. Really, she wanted to be close, just in case Michelle turned up. She was still sick with worry over her sister's absence and thought that maybe, if she could get away from René, who probably had her under his thumb while he hid from the police, she would make a beeline for home. She knew the brutish pig hated her and was probably glad he had her sister all to himself.

The counselor had a casserole in her hands, while Natalie carried a small, square package. Old man Paysanne hurried up from the barn to meet them, shuffling in what probably, to him, was a sprint, Natalie noted condescendingly. He welcomed them inside, expressed appreciation for the cooked dinner, and indicated that they should be quiet in case Paolo had fallen asleep on the sofa. They noticed upon entering the living room, however, that he wasn't there.

"Maybe he went upstairs to lie down then," Guy wondered aloud.

"May I go see?" Natalie offered, clutching her package. She could talk to Paolo about Michelle. He would understand how badly she missed her, how she hated that René had such control over her that she couldn't even let her know she was okay, how she waited each day for a call, even keeping her cell phone on in school. Marie always offered to talk every time she started to get upset, but with her, it always felt like a "session."

"Okay, but try not to wake him up. He seems to be doing pretty well today, and I think rest is the best medicine," he warned her.

Natalie slipped her shoes off before padding up the stairs. She peeked beyond the half-opened door. Paolo lay asleep on the bed. She slipped into the room, sweeping it with her glance. It was as bare as a monk's cell, save for a bad piece of mass-produced artwork on the wall that didn't look like it had been moved for, say, thirty years. A small dresser hugged the wall opposite the bed. A wooden chair that looked like it had once been meant for the kitchen sat angled in the corner beside it. She slid the small package onto the dresser and caught sight of his ring. She had seen it on his finger and was curious, so she picked it up and studied it. It was a plain, flat black onyx encased in gold—simple and elegant. She turned it in her fingers, perceptively noticing an inscription on the inside of the band:

Prends soin de mon Coeur

Take care of my heart. What did that mean? It seemed kind of romantic. She wondered, jealously, who had given it to him.

She looked over at him as he slept. He looked very pale and thin, and she could see that he had dark circles under his eyes. A bright red slash marred the left side of his face. She missed his thick, wavy hair. Now, he wore a knitted cap to keep his shorn head warm. He slept soundly, not moving at all.

Her gaze swept over the book upon which the ring had rested. She fingered the cover. It was brushed leather the color of milk chocolate. A leather cord attached by a hole in the spine sealed it. A small, wooden bead pulled the two ends of cord tight. She turned to look over her shoulder—yes, he was still sleeping soundly—picked the book off of the dresser, and sat down on the room's single chair, sliding the wooden toggle loose. She opened it and began to read.

The City of Lights
And thus my journey starts. I search alone
For that fair City far off to the North,
Where Knowledge, Beauty, Love all find their throne.
Despite the Solitude, I must press forth.
Found, amidst the forest's peaceful hush
Awake, to find that all my thoughts hath fled
Fall is in her lovely maiden blush
To this idyll, fair, she hath me led.
City of Lights, thou art so very close,
Yet here my heart doth stop and bid me stay
To bide my time with those that I love most.

> *The journey's end will come another day.*
>   *Suffering hath mixed a potent brew*
>   *To taint the sweetness of the peace I knew.*

Paris, Natalie thought. He had made it sound like the Emerald City of Oz. She thought she recognized the style of poem but was more interested in the content, which she had to review three times before it made any sense to her. She read, with no small amount of happiness, that he planned to stay in Achères, putting off his travels indefinitely. Drinking in the otherworldly feel of the writing, she turned to look over at her friend, whose features were slack and relaxed in sleep.

He always pretends he's so ignorant, she thought with irritation, *and then he writes this.* He never spoke English and had claimed never to have studied it, but the poem was written in that language. She would make sure not to take him at his word when he started in on his self-effacement next time. Natalie turned the page and read on. This time, the passage was in prose, written in everyday French.

> *I sit at Mass with Guy. Every Sunday, we go to witness the beautiful sacrifice that was made for us, filthy sinners that we are. I love to hear the readings, served like small slices of cake to savor. The priest, though a good, kind man, sometimes loses my attention when he speaks. My own thoughts keep crowding in, drowning him out.*
>
> *I stare up into the faces of the saints and angels, reflected in the rich colors of the glass, and wonder if I, like them, have a soul. I have a vague feeling that I am somehow different from all of them. Is it a necessary part of being human? Is it something I have to earn? Or is this something beyond my reach. Having been blessed with so much, am I guilty of greed for wanting even more?*
>
> *It seems that, no matter what I have, I always seem to find something else that I don't. Perhaps this is the buried sin I was looking for but couldn't find as I lay in the hospital, so full of shame. There is no way to be sure.*

What's he talking about? Natalie wondered. *You either believe that people have souls, or you don't.* How could he sit there and think that he wasn't good enough to have what he assumed was given freely to all of those other self-righteous, pious fakes whose smug images graced the walls and windows of the church? He was better than the whole lot of them thrown together, in her mind.

She sat and fumed, thinking of how they cherished their precious purity like a treasure, while God had let hers be ripped away from her as she screamed silently for Him to save her.

Brushing back a tear, Natalie turned to the next entry.

I am thinking of the day I first met Natalie.

She straightened up, her eyes glistening, heart beating faster.

> *She was the first girl I had met. She is very young, a pretty child with a quick mind, who makes me fear I will say something stupid. There is a great sadness in her eyes, which pains me to look upon.*

She didn't like that he referred to her as a child. She certainly didn't feel like one, after what she had been through. But then, he had no way of knowing that, though she could see here that he sensed it.

> *I see her often about town and like to think of her as a friend. She sometimes swallows her pain down deep, and then she makes me laugh, poking fun at me in an easy, lighthearted kind of way.*

She smiled to think that he considered her to be his friend. She hadn't been sure how he felt about her. Was he just being nice, as adults sometimes were, by giving her a little attention? No, he seemed to really like her, and that thought gave her a thrill.

> *It is difficult to imagine how she feels now, with her sister still missing. Fear for Michelle eats at me like a gnawing hunger.*

Tears again spilled from Natalie's eyes. His words were beginning to rub her emotions raw. He did understand; he did feel the same way. The thought was comforting, even as it brought a fresh flow of grief. Sighing, she again turned the page. There was another poem, written, as the first, in a strange kind of English that she found difficult to understand.

Embracing the Fall
As Autumn's dawn throughout the forest grows,
Her hand hath taken all my thoughts away.
Every corner of my mind she knows,
Hath given me a gift I can't repay.
She grants the wish that I, unwitting, made.
Her lovely hand she presses to my face.
I lay before her, naked and afraid,

And bid adieu the state of Perfect Grace.
She stands above, behold my lovely Eve.
While I lay, shameless Adam, at her feet,
The proffered apple gladly didst receive,
The sting of loss too soon be forced to meet.
    In my mind, a vision of her face.
    The downfall from my Eden I embrace.

Natalie stopped, her cheeks flushed, the enormity of her prying revealed in the subtle intimacy of this entry. She was shocked at the veiled sensuality it contained, as Paolo always seemed to her a bit prudish. Maybe he just hid this side of himself, she speculated. Also, who was this "Eve"? Was it the same woman who had given him the onyx ring? She was eaten up with curiosity.

Natalie heard him jolt in his sleep, as if having a dream. She looked up to see Paolo glaring at her, outrage and hurt written on his features. She gasped and snapped the book shut. "Oh, Paolo, I'm so sorry," she pleaded with genuine contrition in her voice.

"S'okay," he muttered sourly, turning his face to the opposite wall, his mouth working in a furious frown.

"No, it's not," she disagreed, noting with a sick feeling in her stomach how angry she had made him. "I promise I won't do it again," she said penitently, sliding the wooden toggle over the leather straps to tighten them. She placed the book back on the dresser.

"How much did you read?" he asked, swinging his long legs over the side of the bed, the flush of embarrassment on his cheeks matching her own. He did not look at her as he asked this but kept his face turned downward, his palms rubbing the thighs of his pants.

"Not much," she lied, looking out the door of the bedroom, "Maybe two or three entries."

"Did you find what you were looking for?" he asked sarcastically.

"Yes, I did," she admitted honestly. "I saw inside the mind of a beautiful person that I don't deserve to have as a friend."

"Oh, Natalie," he protested. "How can you say that?"

"I may as well tell you now," she said sadly, "because you're going to find out anyway. You say you have sin buried in you?" She snorted dismissively. "Well, my soul is a filthy black cesspool. René has violated me," she admitted to him, her lower lip trembling, eyes red and brimming. "He came into my bedroom and raped me. He stole both my sister and my purity, and I am consumed with hate." This last statement was made with venomous ardor, through gritted teeth, her features reflecting her rage.

Paolo patted the bed beside him. Natalie hesitantly stepped over and slid up next to him. He pulled her close and held her in his arms, her head leaning into his shoulder.

"I miss her so much," she sobbed. "If only she would just call me, just let me know she's okay."

Natalie let Paolo hold her while she cried. Her body shook with deep, uncontrollable sobs. She made no attempt to stem her tears. Her strangely angelic friend was the perfect bowl to pour them into as he held her comfortably to his chest. He felt warm from his nap, and she could hear his heart beating softly. She was surprised that he, who represented all things pure and good to her, would want to touch her, knowing that she was completely his opposite. For a moment, the constant terror she felt lay just beyond the confines of their embrace. She eventually relaxed in his arms, falling asleep against him, escaping in the oblivion of sleep.

Natalie stood in the dark, winding sewer. She squealed as a rat darted between her legs, scurrying away around the bend. From the dark recesses of the winding maze of tunnels, she heard a loud scream and knew without a doubt that it had come from her sister.

"Michelle!" she shouted into the echoing space.

She ran toward the sound, her feet dragging like clay. As she turned the corner down the same tunnel that the rat had taken, she saw René glaring at her, blocking her way.

"Michelle's not here," he told her as her heart pounded in terror. "Looks like you'll have to do, then, little sister. It's time to go ..."

"Natalie!" a voice called out in an angry whisper. "It's time to leave."

Natalie heard herself whimper as Marie shook her shoulder to wake her up. She gazed into her guardian's furious face and noticed that Paolo had his arm wrapped around her as he lay, sound asleep, cuddled up against her. She gently slid from his comforting embrace, so as not to awaken him and obediently left, casting a last glance at her only friend.

"What?" Paolo shouted petulantly. "Was I supposed to just ignore her, as she sat there crying? Her sister is missing, she's beside herself with worry, and ..." he went on, before petering out into silence.

Guy knew Paolo had meant no harm, but sometimes this grown man acted like he had been born yesterday. They were in the living room. Paolo sat slumped on the sofa. Guy was standing over him, trying unsuccessfully to reason with him.

"Paolo, please," he argued. "I know you didn't intend anything wrong, but Natalie is just a kid. It's not normal for a grown man to have a twelve-year-old girl as a friend. It just looks bad, especially after what she's been through. Marie is very protective of her, and with good reason."

"She thinks Michelle is with him, that she's going to come back," Paolo said grimly, his temper calming.

"What do you think?" Guy asked him.

Paolo went over and looked out the window. "I never believed such hate possible, as was directed at me that night," he shared shoving his hands in the pockets of his blue jogging pants, his profile pensive and gloomy. "I'd believe René capable of about anything."

The two men stood in somber silence for a moment. Then, Paolo turned to face him.

"Do you really want me to give up being her friend?" he asked, looking at Guy with his dark eyes full of sadness.

Guy had not expected him to give in so far, realizing the boy didn't even understand that he had done anything wrong. It was touching to see the respect that Paolo held for him, that he would sacrifice his friendship with

Natalie if asked to do so. It was obvious to him, though, that the two young people needed each other, having formed a strong bond in their mutual grief. He would not be the one to take that away from them, whether it seemed odd to people or not.

"No," he decided. "Please, just be careful with her. She's been hurt enough already. Even I can see she has a big schoolgirl crush on you."

Paolo looked at Guy with surprise, shaking his head in denial. "No, Dad, you can't be right. She's … she's so young and smart, and I'm, well … I'm just a nobody, a farmhand with no education, no money."

"That's not what she sees, nor do I," Guy disagreed. "Think about it, Son, and, like I said, be careful."

Black Hole

It was one of those drizzly, drippy Sunday afternoons in February that actually made you long for the weekend to be over. Natalie's thirteenth birthday had passed the day before, with no call from Michelle. She had closed her eyes and wished as hard as she could for news, any news at all, of her sister as she blew out the candles on the beautiful chocolate cake Marie had bought at the bakery, but night had fallen and eventually, her temporary guardian had gently suggested she go to bed after she fell asleep on the sofa, her cell phone waiting silently beside her on the end table.

Now, she sat snuggled up next to Paolo on the sofa, his arm around her shoulder, watching an old black-and-white romance about a girl and a guy who looked way too old for her, flirting with each other in some exotic African town. Bored with it, she shut the volume off and began to make up her own dialogue to the sappy love story, just to make Paolo laugh, to pretend she was all right, even though her stomach felt heavy and tight inside of her.

Guy, who sat in his favorite chair, peeked over the edge of his newspaper and chuckled. The old man was all right, really. He had offered to chaperone Natalie's visits to the farm, as if she were on a date and might take Paolo out to the barn and make out or something. Like that would ever happen. It would be like kissing her brother, if she had had one.

The telephone rang, and Guy growled as he reached to answer it, like he was annoyed at the intrusion into their privacy. He turned to face the view of the field in front of the house as he picked up the receiver. Paolo and Natalie ignored the interruption but hushed their giggling to be polite. Guy spoke briefly to the fields, filled with wet, slushy snow, and then hung up the phone.

Paolo looked at his "dad" with mild curiosity. He had started calling him this in the hospital, Natalie noted. She could empathize, as she still missed her own parents so badly sometimes. After they had died, she sometimes felt like she was the parent in their house, instead of Michelle. That was probably the main reason she found Marie and Vin so difficult to deal with, she realized. She was long past needing someone to tell her what to do.

"That was Marie," Guy shared. "She and Vin asked if they could stop in for a few minutes."

Well, speak of the devil, and he appears, Natalie thought. "I thought you were taking me back, Uncle Guy. I wanted to stay for dinner." Natalie frowned.

Guy shrugged, looking disappointed. "Guess I'll have to cook for myself, tonight."

Natalie heard the car pull in. Guy met Mr. and Mrs. Grizzly at the door and ushered them in. She thought he seemed anxious. Then, she suddenly felt guilty for trying to forget, for a moment, what a hell she was living in. Her stomach knotted up. The look they cast her was full of bleak sympathy, like the way you might look at someone who just told you he had cancer. She remembered the wish she had made the day before and longed to take it back.

Natalie hugged herself up against Paolo, as if he could protect her from what they had come to say. Paolo, for his own part, shrank back, huddling in the corner of the sofa. Ever since that day Marie had caught Paolo spooned together with her on the bed "like a pair of lovers," as she had scolded, Natalie noticed that he felt uncomfortable around the counselor, as if he felt guilty for something he hadn't even done. She hated how Marie could make him cringe that way. He didn't deserve it. Natalie just looked up at them both with scorn.

"Natalie," Vin began softly, looking like he wanted to be anywhere but there in that moment. He perched lightly on the edge of the sofa, his big, bear face looking profoundly sad, his icy blue-gray eyes watery. "We found your sister's body. I'm so sorry, sweetheart."

She buried her face in Paolo's shirt. She heard herself wail, but it was as if she were detached, like she was deep inside of herself, not even feeling anything. She felt strong but gentle arms surround her, support her lest she fall into the black pit that tried to swallow her up completely. She abandoned herself to them and just let her body face what her mind could not even begin to comprehend.

Never in her life, not even while she lay pinned underneath René's filthy, vile body, did she ever feel such complete annihilation. A beautiful angel held her fast in his arms, supporting her as she hovered over the abyss, which waited eagerly to swallow her while God, in his mercilessness, tortured her to her very last bit of strength. She cried out in rage and grief, struggling against his strong hold on her, wanting the oblivion to take her, but he held stubbornly fast. As she sagged in his grasp, sobbing, the angel spoke, bravely defying God's requirement that she suffer to the depths of her soul until it ceased to struggle against Him.

"Natalie, I know that no one, no one could ever take the place of your amazing, beautiful sister, but I want to tell you," he stated with quiet strength as God listened jealously to words that she already knew deep in her heart were true, "I love you, and I will always be here for you. God willing, I will never leave you."

Natalie insisted that Paolo sit next to her at the funeral. Guy took the seat on his opposite side. Distant relatives, hearing about the brutal murder in the newspapers and on the evening news, sat scattered throughout the church. Natalie tried to avoid them, as their expressions of sympathy were odious to her. She hardly ever saw them and was not in the mood to be sociable with people she barely knew, who pretended to care. All of Michelle's friends came, probably feeling guilty that they had not done more to help her, ashamed that they had let themselves be pushed away by such a ruthless monster.

During the Mass, Natalie clung to Paolo's hand. He was her only beacon in the darkness of her soul. She seethed with hatred for God, who showed her no mercy at all. She absolutely despised being in this stupid church and would only sit through the meaningless ritual for Michelle.

To add to her suffering, her aunt Yvette had pleaded with Marie to ask social services to allow her to take her away to her home in St. Quentin, arguing that her current arrangement was meant to be temporary and that Natalie needed to be with family. They promised that they would take precautions to ensure her safety. That, to Natalie, meant she would be watched around the clock. Plus, Aunt Yvette had two bratty little boys, Phillip and Gerard, who annoyed her to the core, making noise and chasing each other around her house with their mindless plastic toys. There was no way at all that she was going to be packed off to her dad's sister's house to act as an unpaid babysitter to those two vile savages. She would rather kill herself first.

After letting Marie know this, in no uncertain terms, Natalie had refused to eat, vowing to continue her fast until she was allowed to go live with Guy and Paolo. Marie had held out for a few days, thinking that Natalie would eventually wear down, but after she passed out from hunger, Mrs. Grizzly reluctantly gave in to her demands and made arrangements with social services, she and Vincent vouching for Guy's character as a longstanding member of the community and old friend, with the understanding that Yvette would act as a backup in case the old farmer's health should decline. Aunt Yvette gave in reluctantly but offered to come at any time, should Natalie change her mind. Natalie wanted to tell her not to hold her breath but bit her tongue instead, thanking her aunt with a quietly muttered *merci*.

Everyone else finally left. Guy walked out of the cemetery, flanked by Marie and Vin. The air hung, cold and damp. Wet, graying snow melted into the ground. Winter was enjoying her chilly embrace of the sleeping earth. Paolo stared at the unfinished grave, Natalie at his side. Enclosed in a low, stone border, the engraved markers of Michelle's new neighbors held vigil with the two mourners. They would keep watch when the frail, warm beings fled to their necessary comforts. Bare trees, blackened by the damp, sent up their arms to the heavens in supplication as if they, too, recognized the tragedy of this loss. The wet grass wept its tears on their shoes.

From inside his new black wool dress coat, he pulled out a single pink rose. Holding it to his lips, he closed his eyes. Then, ripping the petals off, he scattered them into the open pit, tossing the thorns away. Turning back to Natalie, he reached out his arms to her and pulled her close. She clung to him tightly, sobs racking her body.

That evening, just after six o'clock, Paolo returned to the cemetery. Gilbert, just having closed up shop for the evening, caught sight of him making his way there. He was supposed to meet up with his friends but was fascinated by the eccentric loner and followed him at a distance instead. Paolo entered the cemetery. The ground was still wet and cold, the frost beginning to form on the tips of the pale green blades that shivered in their places. The air had lightened with the fading day, growing clearer with the decreasing temperature. The tall, black-garbed man made his way over to the grave, mounded with turned earth and flowers. Now, alone, he sank to his knees in the wet grass, where he beat his fists into the soft earthen mound and raked his fingers violently through his hair, an agonized moan coming from deep within. He pressed his forehead into the dirt and closed his eyes.

He called out her name as Gilbert listened, feeling sadness and sympathy. He, too, had had feelings for the beautiful, unattainable Michelle. He watched as Paolo held his hands over his head, his face pressed to the earth. He seemed, in his poetic expression of sentiment, to belong to another time, and he wondered where the wanderer had come from, before he had stumbled into Achères.

He stood behind a tree, waiting. He vowed to do better this time, after his total humiliation at the hospital. Allowing Paolo to spend out his grief in privacy, he waited and then approached him slowly, offering his hand, his features set with a look of compassion. Paolo looked up, quite dazed, his face covered with dirt, and slowly reached out his own hand in return. Gilbert pulled him back up from the wet ground, and the two left in silence.

Gilbert had kept his promise to himself, managing not to stick his foot in his mouth at the cemetery by not saying anything at all. His silence hadn't seemed to matter to Paolo, who accepted the ride home that his new friend offered with gratitude, wiping his dirty face on a towel Gilbert kept in his car to clean off the windows.

21

Moving On

*L*ife settled into a new routine. Guy had taken on yet another responsibility with open arms, Paolo noted with admiration. Natalie was quiet and helpful, the grief she felt subduing her normally fiery spirit. When not studying, she vacuumed, dusted, did the laundry, and cooked. She did joke that it was weird living with a bunch of dudes, after she and Michelle had been on their own for so long, and said she felt like she had wandered into a monastery. The comparison was pretty accurate, Paolo noted. He thought, in his heart, that no other woman could come close to Michelle and had no desire at all to ask another girl out after what had happened.

Guy taught Paolo the business of running the farm. The latter couldn't understand why this was important for him to know but respectfully did his best to learn what was being taught. If Guy thought it was necessary, well then, it must be so. He disliked the cold abstraction of numbers. They evoked no feelings, unlike the more physically demanding chores. He would rather breathe in the earthy smell as the fields were plowed, which brought satisfaction and a restful tiredness at the end of the day. Writing out bills and balancing the checkbook were dry and uninspiring tasks. It was only out of love and respect for his kind mentor that he tolerated the mind-numbing boredom it brought.

The farmer also dug into the perplexing problem of Paolo's lack of official identity. He offered to adopt him legally, in order to give him a last name. Paolo was deeply touched that this kind man would share something so meaningful with him. He thought of the de Gaul family and the continuity their name provided them in business and as members of the community and realized what a powerful thing a last name could be. Paysanne suited him well, being a name that hearkened back to a connection with the earth.

He despaired of ever regaining his past, as every time he made an effort to do so when awake, it made his head pound with the effort, and when he dreamed, the bizarre things that combined in his subconscious seemed too outlandish to constitute any sort of reality. Instead, he clung to this old man, who had given him so much. He was both family and moral anchor to Paolo. He obeyed him without question in all things, not trusting his own judgment, which was often confused and unsure and had almost brought him to his end.

Driving lessons commenced. Paolo enjoyed them with unabashed delight, glancing over at Guy once in a while to see if he had any input and cringing apologetically as he ground the gears on the truck or hit a pothole with too much force. His teacher was patient and just rolled his eyes or chuckled when he made a mistake. He frequently assured his young charge that everyone went through the same thing when learning this necessary skill.

Being a farmer was much more complex than he ever imagined. It was not just a simple matter of planting wheat each year, watching it grow, harvesting it, and taking it to market. Wheat couldn't be grown in the same field year after year, for fear that the soil would become contaminated with a fungus, ruining it for years afterward. After about two or three years, you had to rotate the crops, or the yield would be poor. Guy always tried to have about three or four different types of crops at the same time. Each crop had its own cycle of growth and harvest, its own use to mankind, its own method of making its way to market.

It was quite intricate, this full and fascinating life he was experiencing, but oh, so worth the occasional feeling of being overwhelmed and confused by the sheer amount of tasks that needed to be juggled. How had Guy done all of this on his own for so many years? He looked at the old man with increased respect. His dad made everything look so easy as he glided through life at a steady, unruffled pace.

Guiscard stopped in to visit Fey. He had news that he wanted her to find out from him, before it became generally known. She busied herself sewing, not the flashy, bird-of-paradise finery that had so suited her before, but a smoke-colored shift, which shimmered subtly as the fabric moved. She appeared as one seen under the moon—colorless, yet still illuminated in reflected light. He found it mystically attractive. It gave her an ethereal quality, which was unique and compelling.

"Fey," he caught her attention, approaching the table upon which she worked, "I am going to be joined with Arcenciel."

Fey dropped her head, letting her gaze fall to the puddle of luminous fabric on the table.

Guiscard looked down. He realized that this was not going to be easy on Fey. He knew that, before her change, she had vied fiercely for his attentions. His words would in no way be enough to ease the disappointment in her heart. Now, she could have neither the man she admired, nor the man she loved.

"I had hoped to find a soul mate," he explained to her, his gaze seeking shelter in the bare branches outside the window, "a noble soul whose lofty ideals matched my own. I found her, but it was too late. She had given her heart to another."

Guiscard had decided that since he could not have his soul mate, he would settle for the next best thing. Arcenciel would act as his helpmate. Her knowledge, which surpassed his own, would keep him from performing rash, uninformed acts in the future. He turned back to Fey, who met his eyes, her own filled with sadness.

"I wish you all the happiness in the world," she told him magnanimously, sadness dripping like February rain from her voice.

Checking his wallet, René noted with alarm that only a few euros stood between him and eviction. He had moved from Marseille to Paris after only a few days' time, putting a deposit on a horrible, one-room garret apartment, where he froze every night and could look forward to baking all summer. If he didn't find work soon, he would have to start breaking into houses to get money, which was risky.

That morning, he had purchased fresh hair dye to touch up his roots. He had gone dark brown to hide his conspicuous auburn hair, which he had grown out from its original, short, clipped style to a longer cut. He shaved every day, as he didn't want to have to dye his beard, as well.

He was an auto mechanic by trade, but being on the run, he had difficulty finding steady work. He had fought it until now, but taking a long, hard look at the reality of his situation, he had come to the unpleasant conclusion that he was going to have to take a nontraditional job.

Flowing down into the bowels of Paris with the evening commuters, René caught the metro to Pigalle, the section of the city famed for its night scene. Several tempting prostitutes approached him, but he didn't have any money to spare on that sort of thing—at the moment. He walked purposefully through the darkened streets to a narrow, nondescript apartment building and rang the bell, two long and then five short taps on the buzzer. A light came on in the foyer, and he moved on to the next chapter of his life.

22

Initiation

Walking with Guy in town a little over a month after Michelle's funeral, Paolo caught sight of Gilbert jogging across the street to catch up with him. The impeccably dressed shopkeeper asked eagerly if he would like to join him and his group that night. They had begun to frequent the club that Gilbert had missed checking out the night that Paolo had had the crap beaten out of him, he explained with cheeky good humor, and wondered if he might like to give it a try. Paolo looked hesitantly at Guy. Gilbert stood by, hopeful, hugging his arms to his side in the chilly March air as he hadn't bothered to don an overcoat.

"Go on, boy," he almost ordered. "You need to get out more. Also, I'm getting a little tired of babysitting you every Saturday night," he teased.

Paolo nodded at Gilbert, smiling hesitantly. He really liked this confident, clever young man, but it was hard for him to be around people his own age. It made him uncomfortably aware of how unlike them he was. With Guy's friends and with Natalie, it didn't matter. He was different because they were not the same age, so there were no uncomfortable comparisons. Guy was right, though; he did need to get past his fear and shyness. Like his introduction to Sophie, the worst part would be approaching the situation. Generally, people were kind if you gave them a chance.

128

"Thanks," he responded quietly, pulling his canvas barn coat tight against the cold.

The young clothier winked impishly, punched him on the arm, and then hurried back to work, deftly dodging the puddles of slush that threatened his immaculate dress shoes. The rest of the afternoon, Paolo fretted anxiously about the coming evening, both dreading and anticipating his first social outing with peers.

That night, after the skies had completely darkened, he heard a car crunch up the gravel lane. The sound of two sharp blasts on the horn had him scampering from the sofa. He grabbed his coat from the rack beside the door and turned to see Natalie standing in the kitchen doorway scowling, her arms folded across her chest. He gave her an apologetic shrug and sped off down the front steps.

And now, here he was, wedged in the cramped backseat of the silver BMW, introducing himself to Gilbert's two good friends. Overall, Paolo decided that he liked the lively, fun-loving young men. He enjoyed their easy camaraderie. They talked about sports, cars, their jobs, and girls. It was a different kind of conversation than went on between Guy and his set. It was edgier, more humorous, and definitely a lot crasser. Still, he accepted this, as everyone was so good-natured. They even poked fun at Paolo, including him in their innuendos, though steering widely around his disastrous date with Michelle.

He noticed that Gilbert had changed out of his work clothes and wore a black leather jacket and jeans. The others were dressed similarly. He suddenly felt overdressed and took off his tie, stuffing it in his coat pocket. No one seemed to notice, though, for which he was grateful.

Latif Nasiri was a few inches shorter than Gilbert; he was stocky with beautiful, cinnamon-colored skin; short, thick black hair; a friendly, round face; and large eyes as dark as Paolo's. He and Gilbert had been roommates in college, Latif told him. The Parisian native had a good-natured, easygoing way about him and seemed to possess a more mature mind-set than the others. Paolo knew that he liked him right away.

Luc Flambert was more abrasive. Most of the randier comments came from him, and he was a bit too loud. Paolo thought he was an attention seeker. He, personally, tried to draw attention away from himself. At over six feet tall, plus an inch of brown, spiky hair, with his strong, chevaline features, Luc would've been hard to miss anyway.

Paolo blushed at their suggestive comments about him as they compared the French and Pakistani men to the Italians. He smiled uncomfortably and hung his head, his short, curly hair doing nothing to mask his discomfiture. Paolo noticed Gilbert sneaking a glance at him in the rearview mirror and then laughing heartily at his embarrassment.

"We'll get you loosened up," he warned. "Just wait and see."

The club was louder than anything Paolo had ever heard. He sensed a manic air about the place. The dance floor was crowded with people, and those who were not dancing were huddled around the bar and the small, high tables, drinking and flirting. Several couples had found refuge in various corners, displaying way too much intimacy, as far as Paolo was concerned. The others just ignored it as if the trysting couples didn't even exist.

The pulsing music hurt his ears. Gilbert, seeing him wince, handed him a pair of clear, silicone earplugs and indicated to his friend to use them. They, at least, made the throbbing bass that leaked through a little more bearable. Paolo knew that even without the earplugs, he wouldn't have been able to hear conversation anyway. He would never in his life have believed that noise this loud existed. Still, the muffled music that filtered in had an appealing primal quality about it.

He began to relax as Gilbert handed him a glass full of beautiful, sea-blue liquid. He smiled in thanks and sipped appreciatively. Rolling the elegant-looking stuff around on his tongue, he could not, at first, decide whether he liked it or not. After a few cautious sips, he decided that maybe, in some strange way, it was rather good. Gilbert, sipping his own drink, took in his reaction with undisguised amusement; his own blue eyes twinkled with mischief over the rim of his glass.

The night wore on. Paolo sprang for a round of drinks himself, not wanting to appear to be a mooch. Guy had insisted on giving him some money. Paolo had protested, admitting it was his own fault he was so broke. He shouldn't have been carrying all of his money with him the night he had been robbed. Guy had countered by stating that if he wanted him to treat him like a son, he had to let him have the luxury of a few kindnesses once in a while.

He noted that Gilbert ordered a Coke, though he looked longingly at the drinks the waitress brought the rest of them. *Why does he not order what he wants?* Paolo wondered. He, himself, had tasted a Coke in town one day, and it was good, but the cocktails were much better, he thought. Gilbert did not explain himself, so Paolo just chocked his confusion up to his general

Ignorance of All Things Culturally Relevant and sipped the next round with increasing pleasure, beginning to grow deliciously relaxed.

He watched the dancing with interest and hesitancy. Then, after he had consumed a few—he wasn't sure how many—of the lovely blue beverages, they dragged him into the crowded mosh pit, everyone gyrating with joyful, reckless abandon.

Gilbert ordered another Coke and dug his fingernails into his palms as the dealer walked by, catching his eye with a questioning look.

Focus, he told himself and turned away. This was not his night, but Paolo's. Turning back to check on his charge, he raised an eyebrow in surprise as a beautiful girl approached Paolo on the dance floor. He watched, envious, as the lovely blonde vision came on to him, no holds barred, and his envy turned to incredulity as Paolo had reacted with something akin to revulsion. Was he crazy? The girl was amazing. Well, not one to let a good thing go to waste, he ordered an extra Coke and, taking the initiative, went over to her table, where she sat sulking with her two friends.

"Hey, sorry about my friend," Gilbert yelled over the loud music, placing the drinks on the table with his most charming smile. "He was raised by nuns. They would beat him with a ruler every time he looked at a girl," he said with a mischievous smirk. She laughed, her dark eyes shining, and then looked down at the drinks before her.

"It's just soda. I'm the DD," he explained with an apologetic shrug, motioning for her to choose which glass to take, so she wouldn't think he had drugged it. "I'd be glad to order you a real drink, if you'd let me," he offered. She looked mollified by his attentions. She took one of the proffered glasses and motioned for him to take the empty seat next to her. They introduced themselves and made small talk, leaning in close to each other in order to hear. Gilbert, who craved physical contact of any kind, loved how close you could get to a girl at the noisy club, whether you knew her or not. He found it absolutely intoxicating—better than a shot of really good scotch.

He divided his attentions between his new prospective girlfriend and his increasingly incoherent inductee for the rest of the evening; he was so busy between the two that he forgot to feel sorry for himself and remember that it was "his turn." After setting up a dinner date for Friday night, he left Marie-David with one kiss, which he made sure communicated the depth of lust he felt for her but at the same time, would leave her to be the one wanting more. She leaned toward him as he pulled slowly away. It was like hooking a fish. He stared into her eyes for a moment with a hint of a smile and then told her sadly, running his fingers longingly over the top of her hand with his best puppy-dog face, that he had to leave.

"Man, Paolo, you really know how to bust a move," Gilbert teased, as he drove his friends home.

"Yeah, and he didn't have any trouble finding someone to dance with," Luc noted, elbowing Paolo playfully. "He had a couple of girls go after him. Did you see that blonde he was with? She was all over him," he leered. "Did you get her number?" he asked.

Paolo shook his head.

"He's too wasted to speak!" Luc laughed, the rest of them, including Paolo, joining in.

At this point, Gilbert raised his cell phone above his head, the carful of admirers roaring their approval. He was definitely better at this game than any of them. He sat, calm and satisfied, in the driver's seat, laughing out loud at his success in transforming Paolo from a shy, quiet newcomer to one of the guys. He wanted his friends to like him, hoping they would want to spend more time with him as much as he did. Paolo was different, and Gilbert felt that there was something about him that he needed in his life, kind of a balancing force to counteract all of the excesses to which he was prone.

His turn to let loose would come next time. Tonight was Paolo's initiation into their circle, and he watched him abandon his usual restraint, pleased to see him laughing and having fun. His conscience was eased, and he had the prospect of making love to Marie-David to look forward to, besides. Maybe it was his night, after all.

After dropping everyone off, he returned home to his apartment and slipped into bed just before 4:00 a.m. Feeling too excited to sleep, he closed his eyes with a deep sigh and pictured the beautiful brown-eyed girl he had left just a few hours before, looking forward to holding her in his arms. Just before he dozed off, as dawn began to lighten the sky, he thought he smelled something girly and sweet, roses and jasmine. It was nice, living above a flower shop ...

23

Consequences

Guy had heard the car pull up. He looked over at the clock on his nightstand. Five minutes till three. The boys must've had fun, because they were making more noise than a herd of cattle as they shouted their good-byes to Paolo and skidded out of the drive. A few minutes passed, and he still hadn't heard the front door open. Sighing, he trudged downstairs. He opened the door to see Paolo sitting dazed and disoriented on the top step of the porch.

"What's the matter, Son?" he asked. "Why don't you just come on in out of the cold and go get some sleep?"

"Los' my keys," Paolo slurred, his voice even deeper than normal.

Guy frowned disapprovingly. "C'mon, let's go," he ordered gruffly, struggling to help the clumsy, confused drunk to his feet. He led Paolo up the stairs, dumped him onto his bed, and closed the bedroom door. Shaking his head, he made his way back to his own room. This was definitely not what he had expected.

The next morning, the farmer left his bedroom, neat as a pin, in an outdated, yet immaculate suit. Paolo rushed past him in the upstairs hallway, making a beeline for the bathroom. He retched over the toilet in misery. Guy just frowned and descended the stairs; he had to leave for Mass. He would deal with the boy later.

Guy drove to St. Fare alone, leaving Paolo to sleep and Natalie to do whatever it was little girls did on a Sunday morning. She refused to attend with them and always made sure an especially enticing lunch awaited their return. A kind of bribe, he thought disapprovingly.

When he entered the living room upon his return, Paolo lay on the sofa, curled up with Sophie, and Natalie hovered with a cold cloth, which she placed carefully over his forehead. She looked pointedly at Guy, as if to say, *Well? So? He got hammered. What are you going to do about it?*

Guy walked into the room slowly and sat down on his chair, surveying Paolo with a mixture of compassion and judgment. Natalie retreated to the kitchen.

The old man reflected back upon his own youth, remembering fondly how he had sown his wild oats many years ago. Still, there was Natalie to consider, and she was so impressionable. Paolo could do no wrong in her eyes, he could see. Such high regard was a big responsibility.

Paolo lifted the soothing covering from over his eyes and sat up, eyes downcast. Sophie laid her head on his lap.

"Son," Guy began gently, "I was young once myself, and I am glad you have finally found some nice young fellows to hang out with, but you have to remember that you have, by choice, taken on Natalie as your responsibility. You have set a very poor example for her here. She loves you so much, forgiving you for your stupidity even before you ask."

Paolo hung his head and closed his eyes. "I'm so sorry, Dad," he rasped, his head still bowed in shame. "I don't know how it happened. We were all having such a good time; then it's like my mind disappeared into this fog and … and I don't remember anything else," he admitted. "I'm so very confused." Paolo put his head in his hands and shuddered.

It was all pretty clear to Guy. "Paolo?" he asked gently.

Paolo looked up at Guy, his big, dark eyes full of contrition.

"How much did you have to drink?"

"Uh, I can't remember, but the color of it was like the sea," he answered in his usual poetic fashion.

Guy snorted, amusement mixing with his irritation. Paolo was really difficult to stay angry at. He could be such a child sometimes.

"Gilbert was so nice; he just kept buying me these beautiful drinks, and I didn't want to be rude ..." Paolo trailed off, rubbing his temples with his hand.

"Please keep it to one or two next time, okay?" he suggested. "Then everything will be all right. Remember, all things in moderation."

"'Kay, Dad," he promised.

Natalie listened carefully from behind the door. Gilbert could be such a jerk. She had no idea what Paolo saw in him as a friend. He was so naive, it was unreal. She wondered how he had been raised; he didn't seem to know anything that guys usually did.

She was a little disappointed that the discussion between the two men hadn't become more heated. Paolo listened to Guy like he actually had to obey him. It was strange to her, as she, herself, found any authority to be abrasive. She knew that Paolo was completely unworldly and suspected that maybe he didn't trust his own judgment. Well, from what her sister had told her about Gilbert, that would probably change pretty quickly if he kept hanging out with him.

It had been almost too easy. René laughed to himself as he returned to his new employer's abode in Pigalle, enough cash in his jacket to keep him hidden for a year, if he hadn't had to give most of it back. Still, it would be enough to let him move out of his current apartment into someplace better, eat well, and maybe invite one of those girls from the Bois over once in a while. Plus, he got to hang out in clubs every weekend, enjoying the scene. It wasn't a bad life.

He returned, for now, to his chilly apartment and fell asleep across the unmade bed.

A beautiful girl in a short, tight leather skirt handed him a drink. René smiled and invited her to sit on the sofa in his apartment, which looked out over the Bois du Boulogne. It was night, and he could see the other prostitutes walking along under the bare trees, hoping to get as lucky as this girl. Taking a sip of his drink, he turned back to the unnamed woman to start to enjoy her, only to see Michelle sitting by his side.

"But you're dead," he told her.

"Yes, you would know that, wouldn't you?" she asked.

Suddenly, Michelle's eyes appeared as red as blood, her skin as pale as the moon in the night sky. He let the drink in his hand drop to the floor and tried to flee but found he had no power to escape. The liquid in the glass spilled across the white rug, spreading a wet red stain across the immaculate surface. He looked down to find his shirt covered in blood ...

René awoke in a cold sweat. Opening his nightstand drawer, he reached for a bottle of pills. He popped one into his mouth and swallowed it with a sip of the whiskey he had stashed there, as well. He fell back asleep, this time in a dreamless oblivion that lasted until the middle of the afternoon.

24

Dilemma

Spring returned. Fey kept herself busy to help cope with her disappointment and grew accustomed to her plain looks and limp, mousy hair. Losing her magic was not of much consequence to her, as the art of fashioning garments was more about creativity than magic, but losing the possibility of a life with Guiscard, that caused her no small amount of emptiness in the pit of her stomach. He had read her correctly, though. She was hopelessly in love with her newly human charge.

She had begun to take lessons from Arcenciel, learning as much as she could from her intelligent friend about the properties of herbs and plants and their effects as healers and instruments of change in the spirit. Somehow, it was just too difficult to look at the brightly colored fabrics that she used to take such delight in as she created beautiful works of art in cloth for both herself and her lovely friends. Besides, who was she trying to attract? She gave all of her old wardrobe to Fleur, who gushed her thanks and then disappeared, for the most part, from Fey's life.

Arcenciel was an enthusiastic teacher. She willingly discussed her favorite subject, and Fey, stripped of all her former vanity, began to show herself as a person of great seriousness and intelligence. The two of them went off to canvass the forest, looking for yarrow, which Arcenciel described as a useful plant capable of relieving everything from headaches to digestive ailments, along with its astringent and sanguinary uses. She proudly shared with Fey that France boasted the oldest known painted images of healing plants on the walls of a cave in Lascoux. The art of herbal healing went back fifteen to twenty-five thousand years among the humans of their land, and even longer among the Fae.

Immersed in the fascinating world her friend had opened up to her, Fey pushed her loneliness to the back of her mind, filling it, instead, with knowledge of a completely new kind. She tried not to think about Guiscard or Paolo. What use would it be? They were both unattainable dreams. She would find strength in knowledge and in standing on her own delicate feet.

It was a Saturday morning, around seven. The sun streamed in through the window of Marie-David's bedroom, which was littered with an orgy of discarded garments, but otherwise neat enough and smelled nicely of Shalimar. Gilbert quietly slipped on his clothes, casting a glance at the young woman, her tousled blonde hair looking, to him, absolutely enticing. Add to her beautiful curls and lovely brown eyes the fact that she was Jewish, and you had a combination that he found irresistibly exotic. It was not love, but an attachment was definitely brewing, which he found to be exciting, but frightening, at the same time.

He always loved how a girl looked in the morning, her face soft in sleep, her hair a tangled mess. It made him want to crawl back into bed and snuggle up against her, but he didn't have time. She slept, as all girls did, on the very edge of the bed. Gilbert often wondered why all women seemed to do this, but, like many things about them, it would remain a mystery.

Looking over at her as he buttoned his shirt, he idly wondered what it would be like to make love to a woman with whom he was actually in love. Would it be better than what he had experienced last night, or was he just starting to turn sentimental from hanging out with Paolo? The idea of love was enticing, but the reality, not so much. Anyway, it hadn't worked out too well for his poor father. All his mother had to do was say what she wanted, and Jacques would make it happen, no questions asked. His dad had loved her without reservation, and look where it had gotten him. He was now a lonely, middle-aged man with no life to speak of. Not very inspiring. There was no way he was going to end up like that, he thought bitterly, slipping into his shoes.

Quietly scooping up his car keys, he made ready to leave, dropping a note on the dresser explaining that he had to be at work, so she wouldn't feel hurt or angry and make a scene. Maybe he could keep this going a little while, anyway. She was, after all, so affectionate and fun and really seemed to like him. Still, he guarded his heart, not letting himself give in too much to his feelings. It was too risky. Love was indeed a trap, one which he would avoid at all costs.

Paolo continued to frequent the club scene with his new friends. Natalie always sulked as he prepared to leave, but he tried to make his absences up to her on Sunday afternoons, when they would spend hours hiking, picnicking, and, on rainy days, playing board games and cards and watching old movies.

He had offered to be the weekly designated driver for his group, as he had just gotten his driver's license. He had promised Guy that he wouldn't have more than one or two drinks, anyway, so he might as well help out, since they all seemed to like to get themselves smashed every week. This thrilled his new friends, who never looked forward to their turn. They thanked Paolo by always buying the single drink he would enjoy, surprising him each time with some new and interesting concoction. Gilbert always tried to pick the drinks with the raunchiest names, so they could all have a good laugh together over it to get the fun started.

That night, on their weekly drive to the club, Latif sat in front with Paolo. Luc and Gilbert were occupied in the backseat with something that seemed to annoy the usually easygoing Parisian. Latif lectured Gilbert sternly, telling him that if he were in his shoes, with the world being handed to him on a silver platter, there was no way he would be doing that. He swore for emphasis.

Gilbert turned uncharacteristically nasty, telling Latif in very crass terms that he should mind his own business. Paolo glanced back to see what the fuss was about, but Gilbert snapped at him as well.

"Eyes on the road!" he barked.

He turned his attention back to his driving but was disturbed by this unusually aggressive outburst. Neither Latif nor Gilbert normally acted this way. He just brushed it off, though. There was nothing he could do about it, and a short while later, Gilbert had mellowed significantly. He and Luc were singing and laughing like fools in the backseat, the former in his horrendously off-key voice. Latif still seemed annoyed and sat scowling, arms folded across his chest, in the front passenger seat.

Paolo fell asleep late that night, after puzzling over his friends' confusing behavior.

The air was cool and dark; a gentle breeze was blowing through the treetops. A voice spoke quietly in the darkness, but it was a voice like no other he had ever heard.

"It is time," the voice told him, in words that were not words. "You can do it."

He knew what the meaning was, without further explanation, and let go of his grip, falling first, and then reaching out and swooping effortlessly upward, his first flight.

Suddenly, the Lavender Lady was there, by his side. She smiled at him, and they flew over the water, the moon shining down in splendor, turning the surface into a thousand sparkling lights, so that if he looked up or down, all was aglitter. Still, the light that shone in her lovely eyes was more mesmerizing to him than all of nature. He wanted so badly to touch her, but when he reached out, he fell toward the black, inky depths below …

The Sunday morning after the incident between Latif and Gilbert, Paolo mentioned their tiff to Guy. Natalie, listening in, interrupted with her own interpretation.

"Gosh, Paolo!" She rolled her eyes. "You can be so dumb sometimes."

He looked over at her, visibly offended. "Well, since you obviously know everything, maybe you can enlighten me."

"They were *obviously* getting high on something," she explained. "Y'know," she added, "there's such a thing as enabling, big brother. Did you ever think of that?"

"Uh, I'm not sure what you're talking about," he admitted, abashed that she honestly seemed to know so much more than he did. That always made him uncomfortable around her.

"Well," she continued, her tone condescending, "let's see. Every week, you drive your friends to a club, so they can all get drunk, high, laid, and whatever else it is you all do. I wouldn't know," she added sarcastically. "What does that make you?" she asked, looking at his troubled face.

"Hey," he scolded, still feeling the sting of her words, "you better watch your mouth, Natalie."

Guy nodded in agreement.

"Oh, like you haven't heard worse," she countered. "I just hate the way Gilbert uses you. He's sneaky, Paolo. Did you know he asked my sister out?"

Paolo shook his head. Gilbert had never mentioned it.

"Oh, yeah, he had a big thing going for her in high school, but she could see what a selfish jerk he was, even back then. He'd drop a girl as soon as he could get her to go all the way with him. Of course, she said no. That made him want her all the more. That spoiled daddy's boy gets everything he wants."

Paolo began to get angry. He didn't like her talking about his best friend that way. Gilbert had been very kind to him. He saw him differently.

"He's not like you say," Paolo disagreed. "He's been nothing but a good friend to me. I am the one who offered to drive everyone each week. They always would take turns before. I did it so that I wouldn't be tempted to break my promise to Dad."

Guy looked over at Paolo with pride.

"You have nothing to be ashamed of, Son," he assured him. "Being a designated driver is a very good thing and could save somebody's life. I would think that you, of all people, would appreciate that," he admonished Natalie, who had backed off upon hearing Paolo's side of the story.

She went over to him and gave him a hug. "Let's not fight," she pleaded, as he returned her embrace. "I just have this really bad habit of saying whatever comes to my mind, without filtering it first. You know how much I care about you," she finished, backing away to meet his eyes.

Paolo nodded, taking in her thoughts. They would trouble him for some time. It was a dilemma. He needed his friends, and, as Guy had said, being a designated driver was a good thing. But being an enabler meant that he was giving them free rein to do things they shouldn't. Guy had given his opinion, but this time, it wasn't so simple.

A short time later, Paolo sat at Mass, listening to the homily. He had begun to borrow Guy's Bible, but the more he read, the less sense any of it made to him. For example, he had just started reading the story of David and Saul. Now Saul, he could see, was a classic villain. As for David though, Paolo couldn't figure out why he had been celebrated as one of the great heroes of the Bible. His accomplishments seemed to consist mostly of killing people and pillaging what didn't belong to him to impress his overlord, who probably already had plenty—not to mention the women he went after.

Owning next to nothing himself, Paolo couldn't understand people's desire to acquire vast amounts of property. It seemed pointless. Other than his ring, the notebook Guy had given him, and the few remaining clothes he had arrived with, material things did not matter to him. His room was as bare now as when he had first moved to the farm; the drawers in the small dresser remained half empty.

He wondered why God hadn't chosen Jonathan to lead the people instead. He was an admirable, noble young man with whom Paolo could find no fault. He shot a nervous glance at Guy. He wished he could speak to him about his thoughts but was afraid he was being disrespectful for questioning one whom centuries of human beings had held up as a hero. Was he the only one who found all of this so confusing? His friends never talked about such things, nor did Natalie. Guy seemed to have it all figured out, as he sat calmly in the pew next to him. His mentor, seeing the somber look on Paolo's face, gave him an amused smile in return and patted his arm indulgently. Paolo returned a hint of an absent smile and then looked away, lost again in his thoughts.

Above all, he wondered why everything that other people took for granted seemed so unfamiliar to him. He couldn't recall ever hearing these stories before, even though they seemed pervasive to the culture, not only of France, but Italy, and pretty much all of Europe. It was assumed that, even if you hadn't read the Bible, you at least knew who Adam and Eve, David, and Jesus were. To Paolo, they were all strangers, to whose stories he had only just been introduced.

Shakespeare was different. He had been reading through his plays after catching *Henry V* on the television one Sunday afternoon. A spark of memory had struck as the actors recited their lines, which had driven him wild with the feeling that he was on to something. He wondered if his people were actors. Every play he read sounded familiar, and, he swore, several of the sonnets he could practically recite by heart before he even looked at them. The story of Titania and her changeling struck him as especially familiar, leaving him with a prickling sensation that, unfortunately, had also given him a pounding headache. It seemed that, whenever he tried too hard to delve into the depths of his subconscious, his brain would shut him down with a violent protest. It was frustrating beyond belief.

All of a sudden, everyone stood up. He had been daydreaming again, he noted. He never could get through the homily without wandering away. It seemed that even his mind was a restless vagrant.

25

Jogging

It was a cool, clear night in mid-April. Yasmine had prepared a fresh Love Wish for Gilbert, including a sprig of fragrant lilac in the pretty pomander. Slipping out of the mail slot into the night air, she hovered, open-mouthed with shock, as her pet project opened the passenger door to a strange car in front of the flower shop. It was not Marie-David, but someone else, whom he pressed up against the door as he pushed the key into the lock. He was kissing her with a vengeance, so it would seem. As the door swung open, they stumbled in, laughing and giggling. She watched incredulously as he put his arm familiarly around this woman, who seemed at least five years younger than he, but a perfect match in maturity level. The door slammed in her face.

"Oh, I don't know why I even bother with you!" she scolded the closed door. In a huff, she flew on to her next stop.

Several weeks after that very enjoyable evening, Gilbert laced up his running shoes and grabbed his keys. Heading quickly down the stairs, he stepped out into the predawn chill. A peaceful hush lay over Achères as he performed a few quick stretches, taking deep breaths of cold air to wake himself up. Heading off into the darkness, he began the grueling first few miles of his run. His body kept telling him to go back to bed, but his mind needed the release that would come later. His heart rate increased, but fatigue dragged at him as he pounded over the empty streets.

For some reason, Tuesdays were especially hard for him, in spite of the fact that it was his weekday off. In fact, his father had intentionally made the schedule that way, grousing that he was basically worthless on most Tuesdays—"moody as a girl with PMS" was the way he had rudely put it.

This particular one was especially depressing. Marie-David had broken it off with him a few days ago, on his birthday, to add insult to injury, leaving him a quick voice mail that said what all the others did. Basically, that he was a really nice guy, but she didn't think it would work out between them.

What she meant to say was, "I think you are really hot, and I love how you spend all your money on me, but I can't handle how immature and selfish you are," he thought bitterly.

Well, he was what he was and would not change for her, or anyone else, for that matter. It was a shame. He had grown very fond of her.

And that, he thought glumly, as he pounded over the blacktop, *is why I am never going to fall in love.*

Had she found out about Jocelyn? The whole thing had meant nothing to him. It was just a casual hookup, no strings attached. He didn't even know her last name. Anyway, he had never made any promise of exclusivity to Marie-David, nor she to him.

He ran past his father's house as the sun rose, casting a soft glow over the trees. Still feeling fatigued, and morose, he continued on, out of town, past the fields, the road beckoning toward the forest, which stretched on infinitely before him on either side. As the air began to warm, his mind grew clear. The rosy glow of the sunrise playing through the trees spoke to him like poetry. All his thoughts were swept away, and he felt a rare moment of peace. At this point, he felt he could run forever, thinking nothing, feeling nothing.

Tuesday evening, Gilbert lay in bed thinking about Marie-David. He missed their Friday-night dates. He missed waking up next to her, and, of course, he missed having sex with her. But it was more than that. He just missed her, plain and simple. All of a sudden, he realized he hated being alone. Was that the trade-off? You got your heart smashed eventually, but in the meantime, you got to have someone to cuddle up next to at night, to wake up with, and to have coffee with in the morning?

Why does life have to be so hard? he wondered.

Thursday rolled around. It was time to close for the day. Gilbert watched as Jacques turned the sign on the door and went to switch off the lights. He stood patiently by the counter, waiting to speak with his father. He usually took off as soon as he was given leave, without so much as a backward glance, but tonight, he had a favor to ask.

"What's up?" Jacques asked him. "You can go now. We're closed, and the banking is taken care of."

"Oh, ah, I thought we could have dinner together tonight, if that's okay."

He could see his dad scrutinizing him, reading him like the open book he was to his old man. It made him blush, which he hated, and he looked away.

"Chinese?" Jacques offered.

"Sure." Gilbert smiled, rubbing his hand absently behind his ear.

"Why aren't you going out with your girlfriend?" Jacques probed.

"She broke up with me," he admitted with genuine sadness, slipping his necktie off, rolling it neatly up, and tucking it in his suit pocket, his typical after-work ritual.

"I'm sorry," Jacques told him, but it sounded insincere. He had already admitted to Gilbert that he thought she was a gold digger, but then, his dad thought all women were gold diggers, and who could blame him? Then he added, "Why?"

"Oh, well, you know," he stammered, unbuttoning his shirt collar, "we just didn't see eye to eye on certain things."

"Hmm," Jacques growled, crossing his arms. "In other words, you cheated on her, and she found out."

Gilbert looked over at Jacques with a sheepish expression before heading to the back room to shut off the lights.

De Gaul, Senior, left to pick up their dinner, while the junior partner went on ahead in his own car to set the table at the house. His dad returned home with the bags of takeout, and the two sat down to dinner in the elegant dining room, furnished with over a century's worth of family heirlooms. Neither of them paid much mind to the opulence they had both grown up with. Having always been there, the mahogany table, carved chairs and sideboard, and various Limoges vases were all but invisible to them. The oil paintings hung, unnoticed, on the papered walls. Gilbert resumed his usual, cheery mood.

"Dad, this is amazing," he gushed with feigned enthusiasm. "You make the best chicken teriyaki ever," he joked. "I think I saw your name in the Michelin guide with, ah, two stars next to it?"

His dad laughed. Gilbert knew his father never cooked but could always be counted on for some good takeout. He picked up one of the fortune cookies that lay on the table, unwrapped the cellophane, and snapped it open.

"This one is mine," he stated seriously. "It says … hmm, no, I can't read it out loud. Wouldn't want to embarrass you," he continued, looking playfully over at his father, who shook his head, smiling.

"Oh, you got one too," he continued enthusiastically. Gilbert unwrapped another cookie, broke it open, and put the tiny slip of paper on his lap so that his father couldn't see it. He scribbled the real reason for their dinner together, his features tensed in focus as he managed to print a brief message on the tiny paper, and handed it to his father.

"Remember, Dad," he told him solemnly, "fortune cookies never lie, and it's bad luck to disobey them."

He made a wry face as he took the paper from Gilbert's fingers. Gilbert raised an eyebrow, trying to look serious, but not succeeding, his irrepressible smirk appearing as he watched his father take the bit of paper. Jacques squinted at the almost microscopic print and then slid his reading glasses on.

"It is a wise father who gives his son a Saturday off."

Gilbert looked on, his face bright and hopeful. "I could get Latif to help you for the day," he offered. "He's always whining about not having any money."

"What do you have planned?" Jacques asked suspiciously.

"Well …" Gilbert's tone became more genuinely serious, "my friend Paolo can't remember anything from before that day he came to Achères, except being in Lombardy, and some weird dreams about Italy and bats. I thought it might be nice to take him there. You know, see if it would help jog his memory."

"Oh, that's very thoughtful of you, Son. Of course. Take the day and go. Latif is more than welcome to come and help. He's a nice young man and might be a good addition for the long term, if he wants some part-time hours."

Gilbert, who really needed the break himself thanked him with his most winning smile. His dad was such a pushover.

"Italy and bats, eh?" Jacques snorted in amusement, pinching another bite of chicken in his chopsticks with practiced skill, a master of takeout dining.

Late that night, Fleur and Yasmine made ready to deliver fresh enchantments to the objects of their ministrations. They were dressed in delicate rose-petal skirts, with shimmering corsets of dragonfly wing, some of Fey's cast-off finery.

"Have you something special for your haberdasher?" Fleur teased.

"No, certainly not." Yasmine scowled. "I am finished with him. I have tried everything to help, but his heart is cold and stubborn. I should have given him pink larkspur instead of lilac in that last pomander, so fickle he is. He is doomed to be a lonely bachelor," she proclaimed bitterly. "After much careful study, I am returning my attentions to Fey's lovely boy, who at least is open to love."

"Won't Fey be angry, if she finds out?" Fleur asked.

"My dear," Yasmine condescended, "I am a matchmaker. It is my calling, and I can't abandon it. Our hearts were meant to love and be loved in return," she instructed as they flew off into the spring night.

Fleur was going to point out that her teacher seemed to have abandoned her most needy subject, but she held her tongue. Yasmine was touchy about him. Perhaps a bit of professional ego over her frustrating failure.

Reflection

riving with Gilbert was very different from riding in Guy's truck. With his dad, Paolo felt relaxed as the wind caressed his hair and the landscape passed slowly by. With his friend, it was pure adrenaline as he raced over the smooth highway, engine roaring, radio blasting American pop music, to which Gilbert sang along, obliviously off-key. Paolo looked back upon his first trip into Achères with Guy. It seemed like nothing now, as he let Gilbert take out his inner frustrations on his BMW and the tarmac before them.

He had been touched that his friend wanted to help him remember his life before he had wandered up to the stone farmhouse, hungry, confused, and exhausted. Guy hadn't pressed him too much. It seemed enough for him that Paolo was there and that they truly cared about each other. Gilbert, though, continued to badger him for answers that he didn't have. To him, it was a mystery to be solved. It could prove annoying sometimes as, without meaning to, Gilbert's stressful probing sometimes made his head ache with the effort. It wasn't his fault though, Paolo magnanimously concluded. He was just trying to help.

Now, as the two drove on to Lombardy, Gilbert dug into a fresh interrogation.

"If you remember being in Bellano, then why don't you think that's where you're from?"

"I don't know. Just a feeling that I was maybe just passing through," he replied, his brow furrowing with his effort to remember. "I can't be sure. I was traveling, remember?"

"Yes, to Paris, your own personal Mecca," Gilbert recalled, adding with sarcastic disbelief, "And here you are, less than an hour's drive away, yet you now seem content to hang out in our little backwater and cool your heels."

"Paris will still be there," Paolo noted defensively. He felt, in his heart, that Guy needed him, and even more so, he needed his dad's guidance to help him understand his own life and its complexities. He knew that he wasn't ready to take on his dream just yet.

"You say you might have hit your head, but you didn't have a bump or a headache, or anything?"

"No, that's right," Paolo agreed, becoming annoyed by his friend's persistence. He now had headaches constantly, but that was after René had bashed his head with a brick. That didn't count, so he refrained from mentioning it.

"Well then, I think that, in my humble opinion, as your unofficial shrink, that you didn't get knocked upside the head. You are, rather, repressing some deeply traumatic personal event. It's not that you *can't* remember," he challenged, pointing his index finger for emphasis. "You don't *want* to remember."

That was an interesting thought. He took off his sunglasses and studied the driver intently. Catching his brooding stare, Gilbert asked, "What're you thinking about, my friend?"

Paolo was not sure if he was ready to trust him with his deeper thoughts. He wanted someone to talk to about these things, but it was difficult to let the protective wall down. Other than in his journal, they remained locked up inside of him. Perhaps that was why he couldn't remember anything. He looked down and bit his lip, trying to decide whether to speak.

"Hey, I won't say anything. You can tell me," Gilbert coaxed, a little too eagerly, in Paolo's opinion.

He looked over at his friend again, wanting so badly to trust him, yet feeling vulnerable. Paolo felt the car slow down. Was Gilbert trying to help him relax or to get his guard down? He took a deep breath.

"There is this woman," he admitted, half sorry as soon as the words came out of his mouth.

Gilbert's attention was immediately piqued. He glanced over at Paolo like a dog spotting a squirrel, and Paolo caught the eager intensity on his face, only half hidden behind the wraparound sunglasses. Gilbert looked back at the road, as if he were only half listening, but Paolo knew better. He wished he had remained silent, but now, it seemed, it was too late.

"I dream of her about every night. In my mind, I am so much in love with her, but I can't even tell you what her name is. She's so beautiful. I can see her face before me—her gorgeous red-brown hair all curled down her back; her eyes, kind of a deep blue, almost indigo. It's weird, but …"

"Go on," he prodded, taking peeks over at Paolo's face every few seconds.

Paolo laughed in a wry snort, too embarrassed to continue. "I can't," he demurred. "It's too strange."

"I won't laugh," Gilbert promised sincerely but eagerly.

"Ah, now this is just the way I keep dreaming about it. I'm sure it's not real, but …" he stumbled on, not wanting to share.

"Oh, come on, Paolo. Just tell me!" he begged.

"Well, her skin was this beautiful shade of lavender," he added with some embarrassment. It was too odd. He shouldn't have even said anything.

Gilbert looked surprised. He stared out the window to compose himself, pretending to read the road sign they had just passed. To Paolo's discomfiture, he could see Gilbert struggling to suppress the laugher that threatened to overtake him; his shoulders were shaking with the effort.

"Well," he finally exclaimed, taking a deep breath and gesturing with one hand, the other on the wheel, "maybe she was wearing that color, and it got all mixed up when you dreamed about her. That can happen, you know."

"Yeah, I guess," Paolo hesitantly agreed, relieved that he hadn't gotten called out for his craziness. There was more, but he wasn't going in any deeper. It was too strange, even for him to fathom.

"Do you think she broke up with you, and that's why you left?"

"I don't even know if she's real. I mean, it feels like she is, but I can't be sure. I can tell you this, though, if she is real, she would never hurt me like that. She is so good and knows me better than anyone else, to the depths of my soul."

Paolo was, at this point, talking aloud to himself. He then stopped and sat, lost in thought, his face reflecting a distant pensiveness that Gilbert was tactful enough not to disturb. Paolo looked over at his friend after a while, to make sure of his reaction. He received a reassuring nod—not the usual smirk, but a look of sincerity. It was at that moment that their friendship cemented into a permanent bond of trust. The rest of the ride went on in peaceful silence, except for the familiar sound of French pop music playing quietly on the radio, after the driver had grown fickle and switched stations. Gilbert, he was thankful to see, seemed content with merely humming along for a while.

Several hours later, the BMW pulled into the parking lot of a beautiful, old hotel in Bellano.

"Paolo, this is so beautiful!" Gilbert exclaimed as they looked out over Lake Como. Forested, snowcapped mountains towered in splendor in the distance. The hotel itself looked like an ancient fort and was full of the essence of time.

"This is just what I needed right now." Gilbert sighed. He plunked his overnight bag on the ground and admired the view, stretching his arms over his head.

Paolo looked sheepish and distracted. He felt decidedly withdrawn, having shared so much personal information that day. It was too much for him. Gilbert sensed his unease and after checking in, took him to an outdoor café to have a few beers and relax. They sat at a filigreed, metal table on cushioned, matching iron chairs. The flagged patio overlooked the lake, a low, stone wall separating the establishment from the shoreline. Umbrellas lent useless protection against the setting sun, which slanted its fiery orange glow over the diners.

Taking a long drag on his cigarette, Gilbert studied Paolo, who was noticeably uneasy, narrowing his sensitive eyes against the strong light.

"I made you uncomfortable, didn't I?" he guessed astutely, his piercing blue eyes studying Paolo intently.

Paolo looked out over the water, his hands playing with the glass of amber-colored beer, not wanting to admit Gilbert was spot-on in his observation.

"You came here to get in touch with your past. Well," he shared with a frown, "I came here to get away from mine. Marie-David broke up with me."

"I'm sorry," Paolo offered, not a bit surprised by this revelation. He looked over at his friend, who lit another cigarette and took a deep inhalation.

Gilbert shrugged, breathing out a cloud of gray smoke, undisguised hurt written on his face.

"Maybe you're looking for what you want in the wrong place," Paolo suggested, recalling his experiences with the half-drunk girls at the club.

"Well, where do I go, then? Remember, I work in a men's clothing store. It's not like Ms. Perfect is going to just walk right in and introduce herself," he said in a dramatic voice laced with sarcasm, sweeping his arm to the side. "The only women who come into the store are married and are shopping for their husbands, who are too lazy to do it for themselves. And don't even mention church," he went on, folding his arms across his chest. "I'd like someone under eighty, thank you very much."

Paolo laughed. It was true. It was difficult to find someone. He had gotten lucky in meeting Michelle but could think of no words of wisdom to share. He certainly was no expert himself. He made no mention of what Natalie had told him about Gilbert being in love with Michelle. It was in the past now, and reminding his friend of that could bring no good at all.

The last hint of sun caressed the distant mountaintops, kissing them with one final, warm embrace before retiring for the night. Gilbert relaxed as the glaring light ceased to accost his vision. The sky began to darken slowly. Candles were lit on the tables, both for the ambiance and to keep insects at bay.

As Gilbert began to grow tipsy, he shared with Paolo some suspicions about his origins.

"Luc thinks you're Roma," he blurted out. He finished his drink and motioned the waiter over to get him a refill.

"Uh, I'm not sure what you mean." Paolo was genuinely confused. He spoke Italian and French. What else would he be?

"Well, you do look Roma, though you're a bit tall for the stereotype. There are Roma in Southern Italy, you know."

Paolo had watched the news. He knew the Roma were *persona non grata* in France, among many other places. He eyed Gilbert with fear.

"Don't worry, Lambie. I'll still be your friend, even if you are Roma. In fact, if all Roma are like you, I want to be one, too."

Paolo laughed and took a small swallow of his beer, which he had been sipping for about an hour. He had gotten used to nursing a drink, being the designated driver for his friends every weekend.

"Do you know any gypsy magic?" Gilbert asked hopefully, beginning to grow silly.

"Ah, I don't think so," he responded. Then, remembering the ring, he rose from his seat, beckoning his friend to follow until they were out of the range of the electric lights, under the soft glow of the moon, which, overcoming her shyness, had arisen from her hiding place behind the mountains and was sending a soft glow over the lake.

"Watch this," he ordered, tilting his hand back and forth under the moonbeam.

Gilbert stared in fascination as the ring revealed its secret. "Oh, Paolo, that's amazing!" he exclaimed breathlessly, grabbing his hand to get a closer look. "Where did you get this?"

"I think the woman I told you about gave it to me," he explained, omitting the part about the inscription.

"Well, I think we know who you are, now," Gilbert ascertained, looking up at him with admiration.

Paolo looked a lot less cheerful about this verdict on his origins. He would have to tell Guy. It was the only honest thing to do. He didn't want this man, whom he truly loved like a father, to get in trouble over his presence. He would rather leave than have that happen.

The two men sat at their outdoor table for hours. They ordered a late dinner, which Paolo consumed with the hearty appetite of one who worked outdoors. Gilbert picked at his own meal but drank like a fish that evening, switching from beer to whiskey, ending up completely soused. He began to grow maudlin, and as Paolo steered him toward their hotel room, he started to spew his drunken sentiments.

"I'm so sorry, about how I make you so uncomf'able sometimes, Lambie," he apologized, leaning into Paolo for support.

"S'okay," Paolo grunted, as he struggled to keep his drunken friend upright.

"No, no, no," he protested. "Issnot. I'm a'ways so rude to you. I'm such a jerk," he lamented. "Do you still love me?" he hiccupped, leaning against Paolo's chest, looking up at him with anxiety.

"Yes, my friend, now save the snuggling for your girlfriend." Paolo frowned, pushing him away.

"She lef' me, remember?" he reminded Paolo sadly, sagging as the sober man struggled to keep him moving.

"It's your fault, Gilbert; you cheated on her. She probably found out. Girls talk, you know."

"I'm never, never going to cheat on a girl again," he promised. "I miss Marie-David," he began to cry, wiping his tears on his shirt sleeve.

Paolo hoped his friend wouldn't puke all over the hotel room. He didn't want to have to clean up vomit in the middle of the night.

"Are you going to leave me, too? Go to Par's an' live out your dream?" Gilbert asked fearfully, grabbing his friend's arm.

"No, Gilbert, I'm here to stay," he assured his overwrought companion. "My life is in Achères now. Guy wants me to stay, and I do, too." *As long as I'm still welcome,* he added to himself, morosely.

"My mom said she love me, too, an' she still lef', to go live in Par's," he mumbled softly. "My dad doesn' love me, but him," he said pointedly, stopping to meet Paolo's eyes, "him, I can always count on."

"Why would you say your father doesn't love you?" Paolo asked, offended but still moving him along. "He spoils you rotten, gives you everything you want, and is pretty indulgent, if you ask me."

"He never tells me, an' he always criticizens everything I do," he complained, sniffling.

"He's not the let's-talk-about-our-feelings kind of guy," Paolo tried to explain to him. "He shows you he cares by what he does for you, not what he says, and he's trying to teach you things you need to know, but you're too pigheaded to listen. Oh, I don't even know why I'm trying to explain this to you!" Paolo exclaimed, growing exasperated, "You aren't even going to remember any of this tomorrow, anyway."

Finally, they arrived at their room. Paolo unlocked the door with a sense of relief. Gilbert was now babbling about how he was done with women and was going to join a monastery. Paolo just rolled his eyes and steered him to the bed. He took off his drunken friend's shoes and shut off the light. Stepping back outside, he made his way to the water's edge, sat down under a tree, and watched the moon rise high over the lake, owning the sky with bright victory. Later, when he returned to the room, where Gilbert lay sleeping soundly, he took out his journal and began to write.

> *As I sat by the shore of Lake Como, bathed in soft moonlight, then,*
> *in my heart, I truly felt at rest. Strange, though, as I gazed out over*
> *the water, which reflected the silver light like an undulating mirror, I*
> *pictured the scene from above, like a vivid dream. My thoughts soared*
> *over the trees in such a way that I could clearly see it. But, even more*
> *poignant than the sensation of weightless movement was the feeling*
> *of peaceful emptiness, as if nothing could disturb the tranquility of*
> *my soul. I began to long for this feeling so deeply that it was actually*
> *a physical pain in my chest. Such a perfect state of mind, I know, can*
> *never exist as I am now. Was it a gift of my effaced childhood or a*
> *vision given to me of what is to come at the end of my journey?*

The prose set his thoughts loose, and a sonnet began to take form in Paolo's mind. Turning to the next blank page, he sat for a moment, biting the end of his pencil, and then started to write again.

Reflection
The Lake's dark waters like a mirror see
The Moon, above, reflected in her face
Adam, fallen, sits beneath the tree
Pondering, alone, his loss of grace.
The Mountains in the background whisper soft.
The Trees caress the hills about the Lake.
My battered soul, released, is borne aloft,
Wouldst of past tranquility partake.
The pain of loss so strong my heart doth sting

Recalling such a perfect state of mind
Wondering, indeed, if such a thing
Is something that, alas, I'll never find.
    O, that I with what I seek be blessed,
    Then my soul couldst find, at last, its rest.

The moon peered, curious, into Fey's window, the only companion who had stopped by to visit her. Sighing, she snapped shut the text on herbal lore she had borrowed from Arcenciel. Somehow, it was more fun studying with her friend than poring over a dusty, old book by herself. It was the touch and smell of the plants and the conversation she desired more than anything.

Well, she noted brightly, pulling herself out of her mopey mood, which had become all too characteristic lately, *I'll just have to pay a visit to my tutor, then.*

She took off for Arcenciel's hideaway, which lay close by in a sturdy beech tree. The night was cool, yet pleasant; the breeze ruffled her simple, undyed cobweb shift and her limp, straight hair. She alighted at her good friend's door and swung it open with the surety that she would be welcome.

She stood, abashed, in the doorway. To her shock and mortification, she found that she had interrupted a lovers' tryst. Arcenciel and Guiscard sat, wrapped in each other's arms in relative dishabille, blue skin entwined with silver. The very aura of the room was filled with passion. A beautiful picture, certainly, but not one she was supposed to have seen. They both looked over at her in surprise, Arcenciel's raven mane swishing as she moved.

"Oh, f-forgive me!" Fey stuttered, backing away and fleeing. Her luminous companion followed her home, and the night air caressed the heat from her cheeks, aided by tears of humiliation and loneliness.

René squeezed a palm full of hair coloring from the plastic bottle and bent over the bathroom sink to touch up his auburn roots with the dark brown he had chosen. He also went over his eyebrows, which were beginning to revert to their natural, reddish tint as well. He was careful to use skin lighteners and concealing creams to fight his tendency to freckle and stayed out of the sun—easy, as he worked at night. Overall, his look had become decidedly more urbane, as had his lifestyle in general. *Ironic,* he thought.

He was grateful to have moved out of that attic apartment before summer had set in. That would have been unbearable. Now, his living room window looked out over the Bois de Boulogne; a pleasant, spring breeze caressed the sheer curtains. The walls were smooth, painted in a soft slate. Black-and-white photos hung in spare white frames throughout. He had hired a professional decorator, recommended by his new boss, to fix the place up. It felt like someone else's flat, so sparse and modern—certainly very different than his messy bachelor digs in Achères, which were cluttered with hand-me-downs that didn't match.

Rubbing the coloring vigorously into his scalp, he stopped as if frozen for, behind him, staring into his eyes in the reflection, was Michelle.

He whipped around and stared at the gray wall, on which hung a photo of bare trees bathed in mist. Goose bumps prickled his arm, and his eyes grew wide with fright. When he turned back to the mirror, he saw only his own horrified reflection, made even more ghastly by the smears of dark dye, which enveloped his brows and forehead.

27

Protest

Church bells tolled early the next morning. Paolo awoke with the sun and looked over at his companion, who still slept soundly. After performing his morning ablutions quickly, he left a brief note, in the remote chance Gilbert would actually awaken before noon, and took off to explore on his own.

The first place he searched for was the fruit stand he had dreamed about. The striped canvas awning, the tree, the street, all were foggy in his mind, but he was sure he would know it if he saw it. He loped through the early cool of morning, passing a few elderly faithful on their way to Mass. He felt guilty about not attending, but he needed answers and he only had a few hours to search.

Every time he saw a door open, a car drive by, or a figure pass by a window, he looked, as well, for her. Did she live in Bellano? He recalled, so clearly, the lovely figure sauntering like a vision from paradise up to the edge of the awning, calling to him. Did he live above the shop? Did he work there?

Suddenly, he stopped in the middle of the nondescript street down which he had wandered. There it was! He was sure of it. He jogged up to the entrance and stared—the tree, the buildings, and the awning, which was torn from neglect. The shop was shuttered, and dried leaves huddled in front of the door.

The crates that he had seen in his mind, full of nature's bounty, were now full of fallen leaves and debris instead. A sign for a real estate agent was tacked to the front post, reading "For Rent" in Italian, with a phone number.

Angrily, he picked up a pebble and tossed it at the disappointing sight. It ricocheted off of the green, peeling wooden window covering and dropped like a reproach at his feet. Sighing in frustration, he punched the realtor's phone number into his cell phone, saved it, and then copied the address as well. Turning to go, he stopped in his tracks and then darted around the side of the building, glancing about as he did to make sure he had not been seen. He tried the back door and then the window, which resisted before giving way. Rejoicing at his good fortune, he entered the empty shop.

His boots echoed on the dusty floors. Everything had been cleared out. Even the back office was pretty much empty. Odd, as familiar as the shopfront seemed to be, the interior appeared completely foreign. Maybe the upstairs apartment would bring back some memories.

Climbing the stairs brought no fresh recollections. He was grateful to find the second floor was also unoccupied, and he wandered through the empty rooms. Nothing he saw stirred a clue in his mind. Looking out the front window, however, he gazed across the street, and his heart leapt to see the streetscape from above. He clearly recalled sunny, summer days, watching passersby from overhead. Switching eagerly to the side window, he looked out at the tree beside the building and, strangely enough, felt it call to him as to an old friend. Looking down, he saw the Dumpster, which stood open and empty, but he saw it full in his mind—though not with refuse but, rather, with delicious food.

He wondered if he had been so down on his luck that he would be Dumpster diving. It made no sense, because when he had awakened in the forest near Achères, he had found his wallet full of money, and he had been wearing clothes that even impressed his persnickety friend. Had he robbed someone, rather than been robbed? Was that the thought he couldn't face? Was he a murderer on the run? Was his quest to see Paris no more than a desire to lose himself in a crowd of people?

A quote from Hamlet ran through his mind, unbidden: "The lady doth protest too much, methinks." Was he an overcompensating villain, with his regular churchgoing, weekly confession, and abhorrence for all things sinful? The thought made him sick to the core, and he left quickly.

That afternoon, Paolo drove back to Achères. It was, for the most part, a quiet ride, as he remained mired in his gloomy thoughts and Gilbert nursed his hangover. As they made their way out of Bellano though, Gilbert grabbed Paolo's hand from the wheel and once again examined the ring, which appeared a smooth black surface encased in gold.

"Hey," Paolo protested, "you're going to cause an accident!"

Gilbert ignored him, furrowing his brow.

"It looked different last night, didn't it?" he asked, his usually light tenor voice gruff and hoarse.

Paolo just cast him a wary, sidelong glance before pulling his hand away and turning his eyes back to the road. He was relieved his friend didn't seem to remember something he never should have showed him.

Gilbert soon fell asleep in the passenger seat. Paolo thought he didn't look so good. He seemed to be getting too thin and was beginning to get dark circles under his eyes that didn't go away. He thought again about what Natalie had said, about him being an enabler to Gilbert's tendency to drink too much. She was also right about him getting involved in drugs. Paolo wondered what he should do. Should he talk to Guy about this or to Gilbert's father? He wasn't sure.

It was late when Paolo climbed the front steps to the house. The ride back had taken much longer, as he drove more cautiously than Gilbert. Paolo stood hesitantly on the porch, filled with gloomy thoughts—of his possible connection to a despised race of people, fear of Guy's reaction upon hearing it—and worry over his best friend, whose behavior seemed to be growing more and more out of control. He slumped on the porch swing, not wanting to disturb Guy or Natalie with his melancholy, and put his aching head in his hands. The sounds of summer insects sang insouciantly in the fields.

He looked up to see Guy standing over him.

"Ah, hi." He sighed.

Guy sat down next to him with a sigh. "Things didn't go well, then?" he asked, perching on the end of the swing. He turned toward Paolo with his arm set comfortably on the edge.

Paolo shook his head, not sure where to begin.

"Gilbert thinks I'm Roma." He frowned, casting a concerned look at his mentor. "I'm not sure, but he might possibly be right."

"I'd heard that rumor," Guy admitted.

"Why didn't you tell me?" Paolo asked in a mildly exasperated tone. Then, he added, "I won't stay, if it would make trouble for you."

"Paolo, I adopted you. You are a Paysanne now. I'm not going to take back what I've said or done because of some rumor that may or may not be true. I don't care one way or the other."

Paolo exhaled in relief and looked over at his adoptive father with immense gratitude, a thoughtful expression on his face. "Thank you, sir," he said softly.

Guy frowned to hear himself addressed so formally.

"You can still call me 'Dad,'" he assured Paolo, who looked miserable.

Paolo laughed under his breath. "'Kay, Dad." The mood finally lifted, and he smiled. Guy patted him on the shoulder and then rose to go back into the house.

"C'mon, Son. Go get some sleep. We have work to do in the morning."

A dark-clad figure crouched in the alley beside the fruit stand. The stars gave off a feeble light, vainly attempting to reveal his intentions. A man in a white shirt and long, dark apron whistled as he carried a box of overripe fruit and decaying vegetables to the Dumpster. He lifted the box up over the top and let it fall. He was cut short, midway through his carefree tune, as a red slash appeared on his neck. The blackened figure lifted the limp vendor high and hurled him, with a grunt, into the Dumpster. He shut the lid and then stole underneath the awning and disappeared.

Paolo started awake, his eyes wide. It had felt eerily real. Had he witnessed a murder and fled for his life, or had he committed one? He lay there, heart pounding, trying to figure it out.

Rash

I t was summer. The two men were very busy with the harvest of winter wheat, which had been about half completed. The farmer, himself, was at work in the barn, changing the oil in the tractor. Paolo pored over the bills, making a glum effort to concentrate on the papers in front of him. He would much rather have traded places with his dad, taking on the more physical task, but Guy had insisted he tackle the bills instead, explaining that he needed more practice at bookkeeping than equipment maintenance.

He had learned so much. Guy had even taught him how the crop was taken to market. Paolo drank in the knowledge. He loved farming, and wheat was such a beautiful crop, so biblically significant and poetic. It fed the body and the soul.

Natalie moved noisily about the kitchen. She yelled loudly for Paolo, asking him to go to the barn and tell Uncle Guy that dinner was almost ready. Relieved for the break from his least favorite chore, Paolo gladly took off in search of him. The air outside was heavy with humidity. The sun shone almost too brightly. He trudged, unhurried, over the coarse gravel, inhaling the perfume of the fields, a trickle of sweat immediately making its way down his spine, leaving a damp streak on his T-shirt.

As the barn door swung open, a shaft of brilliant light invaded the relatively cool, dim interior. Dust swirled gracefully in the golden glow of the sunbeam, creating an effect of almost magical beauty. He stopped for a second, mesmerized, to admire it.

"Hey, Dad!" he called loudly, still watching the swirling bits of light.

Greeted by silence, he peered into the dim interior. Maybe he had gone to the chicken coop to feed the hens, since Natalie was busy cooking. Before turning to leave, he spotted, at the edge of the shaft of sunlight, an upturned palm, lying on the straw.

Paolo and Natalie clung to each other like passengers on a sinking ship. After the graveside service, Vin and Marie drove them to their house for a late lunch, having invited the small contingent of fellow mourners to join them. Guy's family had, for the most part, all passed away. Some local farmers and a few close friends were all that he had left. The two young people ate very little and sat quietly on the sofa, sorrow and dread mixing inside of them.

Gilbert tried to talk to Paolo, appearing sincerely sympathetic to his loss, but he had nothing to say. He felt rude, but he couldn't help it. He was mired in sadness. After the last guests had left, they drove to the farm, Natalie sitting gloomy and silent beside him in the backseat, her hand lying lightly over his. He appreciated the comfort of her presence but stared out the window to hold himself together.

The four entered the empty house. Natalie went to fix coffee. Paolo flopped down on the sofa, indicating to Vin and Marie to do the same. Marie sat down at the opposite end. Vin stood behind her, his hand resting on the back of the seat. Guy's chair remained conspicuously empty.

"Paolo," Marie began softly.

"I know," he said huskily. "She can't stay. It wouldn't look right."

He pressed his lips together, willing himself to keep calm, lifting his eyes to the ceiling to hold back the flood of grief that he didn't want Natalie to see.

"Could you please give us a little time together, to say good-bye," Natalie asked them, appearing from the kitchen, where the coffeepot was sending out a comforting smell.

"Of course, dear, and we'll make sure you get to visit each other," Marie promised vaguely.

Natalie's guardians gave her time to pack up her things. They told her they would be back in an hour to take her with them to their house, where she would stay until more permanent arrangements could be made. They both watched from the front window as the car pulled away, Paolo sadly, Natalie full of scorn.

Then he turned to her and sat down on the arm of the sofa, pulling her toward him until his forehead rested against hers.

"Natalie, I would do anything for you, but please don't make me stay here and watch you leave. I don't know if I could stand to see you drive away," he admitted.

He stood up and studied her face one last time to store it in his memory, and then he left the house, taking off down the drive at a quick walk. He turned onto the road in the direction that led away from town.

Natalie watched Paolo go anxiously. He seemed a little crazy, and she feared the look of desperation in his eyes. Throwing a few sodas and a couple of apples quickly into her schoolbag, she took off after him. The Durrands could just screw themselves, for all she cared. Paolo was all she had left in the world, and she had to make sure he didn't do anything rash.

She had a difficult time keeping up with him, as he was so much taller than she was. He walked purposefully, as if driven from within.

Oh, Paolo, where are you going? she wondered as she struggled to stay with him, yet remain hidden.

He was dressed in the clothes he had worn for the funeral, not having bothered to change, and had the suit coat he had just bought from the de Gauls slung over his shoulder. Natalie knew that Paolo did not have much of a wardrobe, and she pitied his poverty. She had never seen someone who owned less.

The black-clad man had stopped, she noticed thankfully, and was loosening his tie. He looked around as if searching for something and then took off into the woods. Natalie swore softly. What was he doing? It felt like they had been walking for hours, and her feet had begun to hurt in her stupid dress shoes.

It was much more difficult to follow him in the woods. Although it was easier to conceal herself, there were branches and things everywhere that echoed with a loud snap when she stepped on them. He turned back in her direction a few times, as if sensing he was being watched. Natalie, though, was careful to keep out of direct sight, her dark clothing helping to camouflage her.

He stopped by a small stream, overcome with thirst. After drinking deeply from his cupped hands, he bathed his sweaty face and neck in the cool water. Natalie longed to do likewise but feared he would see her, or worse, that she would lose him as he strode on. His pace finally slowed. Paolo looked about, trying hard, she could see, to remember the exact spot he was looking for.

She knew he had found it when, sinking roughly to his knees, he dropped his forehead to the ground and cried out—a loud, heart-rending groan that punched Natalie right in the gut.

Standing up, he pleaded loudly, his voice echoing through the empty forest.

"I can't do this anymore!" he shouted at the top of his lungs. "My heart is breaking. Please take me back."

Leaning up against a dead tree, he sank slowly down and hugged his knees; laying his head atop them, he sobbed violently.

Oh, Paolo! she thought bitterly. *I've been where you are, and unfortunately, I can tell you,* she lamented silently, *that God won't answer you.*

Guiscard had spied the two dark-clad people hurrying through the woods. He recognized Fey's boy and followed him. He had a strong feeling he knew where Paolo was headed and was not surprised when he dropped to his knees in front of the hollow oak tree where he had first met Fey. He listened, his heart welling up with guilt as Paolo's agonized plea ripped through the forest like thunder.

He had put it off long enough. The time had come to make amends for his rashness.

Shooting Star

*P*aolo looked up, feeling a slight pressure on his right shoulder. His eyes were red and streaming. His lips parted in shock. For there stood Natalie above him, her head tilted to the side, her lovely dark hair framing the right side of her face like a silken waterfall. She looked like a somber angel in her simple black, long-sleeved dress and tights.

"Oh, Natalie," he groaned, "I am so sorry you had to hear that. It was so selfish of me to run off like I did," he lamented, regretting his loss of composure. Of course she would be thinking she didn't matter to him, that he would give up so easily. After all, she had been through just as much as he and had borne it with more strength. His features tensed in humiliation as he looked away.

"I was really worried about you. You looked a little crazy when you left," she answered.

He snorted. "Yeah, I was, actually."

She reached into her backpack and handed him a packet of tissues to dry his face. He mopped at his eyes and nose and then leaned back against the dead oak, knees pulled forward, eyes closed. He took a slow, deep breath.

"We all say things we don't mean, when we're upset," she explained, sitting down next to him in a mirrored posture.

"I don't even know why I said it," he admitted. After having visited Bellano, his dreams of peace and tranquility from his past life had since become tainted with the bloody scene in that distant alley. To deal with the trauma of loss and suffering he had known in Achères or to long for a past where conflicting ideas of who he was vied for space in his mind—it seemed there was no escape for him.

She leaned up against him, and they sat for a while, resting, drinking in the peaceful quiet of the summer forest.

"This is where you woke up, the day you first came to Achères," Natalie guessed.

"Yes, it is."

"Paolo?"

He looked at her, remembering that day in his mind.

"What happened to you?"

"I don't know." He sighed.

She opened her backpack again and pulled out the apples and warm soda.

"Not my usual gourmet dinner," she joked, handing him his share, "but I didn't exactly have time to pack a picnic lunch."

Neither one of them had eaten all day. She devoured the simple snack and then looked vainly in her backpack for a stray candy bar or pack of crackers to supplement it. Paolo ate halfheartedly, to please her. His throat felt tight, and it was hard to swallow. He washed the apple down with the warm soda.

Tossing the core aside, he asked, "Do you have paper and a pencil in there?"

"Sure," she answered and pulled out a composition notebook and a stub of thoughtfully chewed pencil.

He took the proffered implements and went over to sit on a fallen log.

"What are you doing?" she asked, curious.

"Oh, Guy taught me to do this," he explained. "When my thoughts get too bottled up, he told me that it would help to write them down. That's how I started my journal. It was a gift from him, as I lay in the hospital," he finished, opening the notebook and lowering his gaze.

Paolo began to write. Natalie took out her sketchbook and began to study him. He paid her no mind, rapt in his own thoughts. She began to tickle the paper lightly with her pencil. He didn't ask her what she was sketching, because he did not want to share his thoughts with her in return.

For a long while, the only sounds were those of the forest. Poet and artist created in silence as the birds trilled their incongruous joy overhead and the occasional breeze rustled the leafy canopy with a teasing puff of air. The sky began to darken, and the air grew cool. Night would soon be upon them. Paolo finished with the sonnet he had composed, tore the page out of the notebook, and folded it twice before sliding it into the pocket of his suit coat. He would copy it to his journal when he returned home. The restlessness he always felt at twilight stirred him from his reverie.

"We'll never make it out of here by dark," he suddenly realized, looking concerned. "We're really far from the road, let alone home. I'm afraid we'll get lost."

He had lost track of time, engrossed in his thoughts.

"That's okay," she assured him. "We'll just stay here till it's light again."

"What about Vin and Marie?" he fretted.

"They can stuff it, for all I care," she spat dismissively.

"Natalie, they really care about you," he admonished her.

"Well, they have a funny way of showing it."

"I don't want you to go, but you have to," he ordered her gently.

"I know. I think, deep down, Marie thinks you are some escaped child molester or something," she joked.

"I don't want to be thought of that way," he answered her nervously, a knot of anxiety growing inside of him. Marie, as a professional counselor, seemed a good judge of people. Did she see things in him that he, himself, failed to notice? The thought filled him with renewed fear.

"I think that she and Vin have both seen too much bad stuff, with their jobs and all," she admitted, zipping her bag shut and plunking it on the ground beside her.

He nodded noncommittally and then lapsed into silence for a while.

Paolo took his beautiful, new Italian suit coat and laid it on the ground. He patted it lightly, and Natalie settled comfortably back, her lovely tresses forming a dark halo around her sweet face. He lay on the ground next to her, one arm curled behind his head, the other draped across his chest, watching the night sky. The two of them lay side by side in companionable silence for some time. Then, as they began to grow drowsy, a shooting star darted across the space between the trees, directly over their heads. Paolo closed his eyes, sure his dad had just sent him a sign that, his long journey over, he was doing just fine.

Natalie watched until she was sure Paolo was asleep and then switched her cell phone on and set it to silent. Using its light, she pulled the folded paper out of his coat pocket and began to read.

Reluctant Lover
As Summer's sun upon my face doth gaze,
Bleak clouds upon the far horizon rise.
Happiness is numbered in her days.
Dark Solitude toward me, now, she flies.
Jealous of the love I bear my friends,
She wouldst take place of them in my abode.
All too soon the beauty of life ends;
Death and Loss my idyll, sweet, corrode.
Age and Wisdom, first, Death's hand doth seek,
Then Youth and Beauty, Loss doth look upon.
Solitude my company doth keep;
In her embrace, no wish to carry on.
*   Reluctant lover! Wouldst that I could trade,*
*   For she who once my life didst kindly save.*

She knew right away that he referred to the woman who had given him the onyx ring. Who was she, that when he could remember nothing else from his past, he thought of her so obsessively? How had she saved his life? She was eaten up with curiosity. First, she copied the sonnet into her sketchbook, and then, after refolding the paper, she replaced it in his coat pocket and lay down, studying his sleeping face in the dim light.

She had promised not to read his journal, but the pull of it was too strong, as they lived together under the same roof. Many times, upon returning home from school, she would steal up to his room and read, knowing that she had about an hour's time before he would return from the fields or the barn. Many of the sonnets she had copied into her sketchbook, making a companion illustration for each. It was her way of making a secret connection to him, to tie their work together in a soul-deep way.

Growing cold in the night chill, she snuggled up next to him as he slept. He reflexively moved closer, draping his arm over her. She fell asleep, feeling safer than if she were tucked in her own bed.

Hunger gnawed at his belly as a loud noise broke through the silence of predawn darkness. The scrape of metal on metal resounded through the alley as the Dumpster tilted upward, its sweet burden of perfumed fruit tumbling into the yawning chasm that would consume it. The lifeless body of the grocer lay partially obscured by his discarded wares, lit by the moon overhead. Slowly, the strange sight and the accompanying noise receded from view.

30

Avenging Angels

*G*uiscard watched over the sleeping figures throughout the night, protecting them from anything that would harm or disturb them. He felt sure that he was the cause of their misery. His own pervasive happiness at joining with Arcenciel only made his sense of guilt sting more strongly. Recognizing the miniature version of Michelle that Natalie presented, he could see the strong bond the two young people had forged through their shared suffering.

He nodded approvingly as Paolo spread his expensive coat on the dusty ground for Natalie. He lay on the hard forest floor.

Ah, he too has a chivalrous heart, Guiscard thought. He could see why Fey loved him. Just from observing him for a brief time, he had seen Paolo shelve his own grief to spare the little girl's feelings, eat just to please her, though it seemed almost to choke him to do so, and make an unpleasant decision because it was the right thing to do.

He would have done it for Fey alone, as it tore at him to see her so filled with hopelessness, but he was very pleased that the immense sacrifice he was about to make would also be expended on a worthy and noble soul. As dawn brightened the east, Guiscard made his way wearily home, casting one last glance back at his sleeping rival, uncomfortably aware that he had been vanquished in the battle for Fey's heart by the better man.

Paolo and Natalie made their way slowly back to Guy's house the next morning, tired, hungry, and sore from sleeping on the cold ground. Neither one of them wanted to hurry. What awaited was going to be very unpleasant. Paolo, especially, was filled with dread. The Durrands had made it quite obvious how they disapproved of his bizarre friendship with Natalie, and they were sure to judge him harshly. It looked very bad. His face was tensed with anxiety. As soon as he arrived home, he phoned them.

"She's here," he said simply, as Vincent picked up. He hung up before the officer could respond.

Slumping down on the sofa, Paolo exhaled loudly. He leaned back, brows knit, stomach in a knot. Natalie stood anxiously, wringing her hands, her eyes wide, her rosy lips pulled down at the edges.

Shortly afterward, the Durrands' car almost skidded into the drive. Paolo pushed down into the sofa, wishing he could disappear. He felt sick—from anxiety and from not having eaten practically anything for the past twenty-four hours. A headache lurked, waiting to snare him in its grasp. Natalie hovered protectively behind him, ready to face the brewing storm.

The couple entered without knocking and strode into the living room.

"Just what were you thinking?" the big man bellowed at Paolo's reclined form. "Or," he added sarcastically, his hands on his hips, "let me guess. You weren't thinking at all. I have a mind to take you in right now on child abduction charges."

Paolo closed his eyes and bit back a retort, a look of pain on his face. Conflicted as he now felt about his past, he was in no position to claim the high ground.

Natalie looked at him, waiting for him to respond. He remained stubbornly silent, so she let her own thoughts spill out.

"I am sick and tired of you treating Paolo like he's some kind of pervert!" she screamed at the couple, who stood like avenging angels ready to strike him down. "He has been nothing but thoughtful and kind to everyone since he came here, and neither one of you can find it in your filthy black hearts to say one nice thing about him. *I* followed *him* yesterday, to make sure he was okay. By the time he even knew I was there, it was late and we were God knows where in the woods."

Hazarding a glance at the police chief and his wife, he noted that the look of righteous indignation had fled their faces, but Natalie was not finished yet.

"Did you even care about him yesterday? No. You just think you could yank me out and leave him all alone in this empty house in the middle of nowhere and, well, he can just suck it up."

They looked at Paolo, who sat with his arm on the edge of the sofa, his hand draped across his mouth, literally containing his own thoughts. Disheveled and dirty, wearing yesterday's dress clothes, he sat in silence.

Natalie's final barb had stung them like acid. Red-faced shame rose up like a sinister tide on Vin's face.

"You want to see a pervert? You find René. How you coming with *that*, anyway?" she finished, stomping off into the kitchen as they watched abashed.

After an extremely awkward silence, Vin backed away from Paolo, staring out the front window. "I did," he stated softly, tucking his hands in his pockets, "actually get a lead. Le Roux's car's been found in a parking lot in Marseille."

Jacques hired Latif to work part-time at the shop. The young man made it clear that he needed the money, and he was a respectful and diligent worker. Gilbert's inconsistencies concerned him, and he didn't want to be shorthanded for the fall season because his son was going through a difficult period.

He was getting burned out. His best friend was gone, and his own son was no support to him at all, but, rather, an emotional drain. At this point, life was no pleasure, just a grind. The monotonous routine of work, followed by lonely evenings at home, was not enough to satisfy him. Jacques was a very giving person, but he, too, had needs. He continued to meet with the crowd Guy had hung out with at the café on Saturday mornings, but the talk was superficial and dull. He missed having a woman in his life, but with the way his son was acting, he had no time to go looking for someone. He had to keep the business running smoothly. That and Gilbert were all he had right now. He thought about visiting his brother in Normandy but couldn't trust the shop to Gilbert for the time it would take him to go. Feeling trapped and frustrated, he began to grow depressed.

31

Making Amends

After Paolo returned home from the oak tree to face his tryst with solitude, Natalie in tow, Guiscard went directly to Fey's hideaway. He was glad to see that Arcenciel was there—after Fey had chanced upon his intimate moment with his betrothed, things had gotten decidedly uncomfortable between them. The two faerie scholars sat poring over a book, with samples of herbs, leaves, and bark they had collected lying in a pile in front of them. They both looked up as he entered the room. His beautiful Emerald was dressed in a gossamer sheath of black, which, when she moved, showed glimmers of iridescent green. Her hair hung in raven splendor to her waist, her lips shone red and full. Fey, on the other hand, sat garbed in matte, autumn-leaf-colored swirls, her dull hair cut in a page boy, tucked behind her ears. Her sallow skin was a stark contrast to Arcenciel's shimmering silver.

Looking directly at Arcenciel, he declared, "The time has come for me to make amends to Fey and Paolo for my misdeed."

Fey looked confused. "What could you have possibly done to feel that you must make up to me, and why would you need to make anything up to Paolo? It was sad, what happened to him, but surely not your fault," she assured him. "You are being too hard on yourself."

Seeing her confusion, Guiscard sat down heavily on the chair and explained himself. Arcenciel looked on with a serious expression gracing her cool silver face.

"With no thought but to show off my bowmanship in front of my friends, I shot a man that, had I been more careful, I would have seen as seriously flawed and dangerous. Love arrows can prove a potent danger in one so filled with negative sensibilities."

"I don't understand," Fey puzzled. "If René was as dangerous as you say, why would Paolo have dared to ask Michelle for her attentions?"

Guiscard cleared his throat, uncomfortable with revealing Yasmine's part in the fiasco. Frowning at the uncomfortable moment of silence, he reluctantly continued, "It seems that Yasmine stole one of my love arrows and used it to open his heart to the possibility of romantic love. After all," he admitted toying with a dish of dried mushroom bits on the table, "she is a matchmaker."

Fey's aspect clouded, and Guiscard thought she looked angry for a moment.

"I think our dear friend was playing a game of her own," she disagreed. "I saw her take the arrow, Guiscard," she admitted. "And by my complicit silence, not only have I been punished, but my charge and those he cares for have, as well."

"She has expressed remorse for her actions," Guiscard informed her.

"I foresee much trouble in her future," Arcenciel shared. "Our code is clear, Fey. She will not escape the game of love unscathed, on her own part. As she has caused mayhem to beset your beloved charge, so shall another afflict her own heart. She will, before it is all over, regret ever setting her sights on the one with whom she joins."

"I wish her no ill," Fey protested. "She is still my friend, misguided as she can sometimes be in her ministrations."

"I know that," Arcenciel concurred, "but it will happen. It is her fate."

"As for myself, Fey, please let me make amends for my share of your misfortune. I wish to absolve myself of this and to make things right for you and your young man."

"Guiscard," she addressed him, "I judge your intentions, and they were good, but there is nothing you can do to bring Michelle back. I would gladly have endured what I did for Paolo a thousand times over, so you have nothing to make up for my sake. As for he who holds my heart, I accept the fact that I can never have him. I will live alone; the little time we did have will comfort me over the long years ahead, and I will cherish it."

He took her hand in his, looking into her face. "I will send you to him, make you human as you did for him. It's the only way to pay for my recklessness and set everything right."

Arcenciel looked at Guiscard with surprise, but she remained silent.

"No, Guiscard! The cost is too great. Think what you would be giving up. Why, just look at me!" Fey exclaimed with disgust.

His betrothed looked pointedly at Fey and then at him, as if in agreement.

"I have looked upon the man you love and seen that he possesses a trait which I am sorely lacking," Guiscard admitted, addressing Arcenciel as much as Fey. "He is humble and self-effacing, where I am full of vainglory and hubris. This has been my downfall. Unless I repent of it, I will be cursed with it forever. Please, Fey. I want to do this."

Their code of conduct was clear. Failure to follow his conscience would only lead to his ruin. To sacrifice, though, brought growth to the spirit. He, through his self-denial, would become even more powerful, earning a position of high esteem. Yes, his motives were mixed, but that could not be helped. Also blended in, though he said nothing of it, was the love for her that would always burn in the back of his heart. Arcenciel knew of this, as the Fae could not keep such a secret, sharing thoughts and feelings as they did, but she accepted it. Love, when acted upon honorably, was never a bad thing.

"Thank you, my friend," she whispered, her eyes glistening with unshed tears.

Arcenciel went and stood behind him. She placed her silvery arm around his back. He could feel her love and support flow through him at her touch. He was truly a fortunate being.

An oppressive solitude took over the farm. Paolo coped as best he could. He finished the harvest on his own and had Gilbert help him with selling it at market, as he was afraid to go on his own. His friend didn't really know anything about the process, but his confident business sense gave the new landowner the moral support he needed. Paolo had been absolutely floored to learn that Guy had changed his will, leaving him everything, and he felt a strong sense of responsibility to be a good steward of this incredible gift. Guy revealed in his will that he felt God himself had led this young man to his door and he had been blessed in much the same way that Abraham was by the late arrival of Isaac. Leaving Paolo his farm was an expression of his trust in God's personal plan for his life.

The recipient of his benevolence worked hard every day, the physical exertion helping him to sleep at night. It did nothing to ease the heaviness of his thoughts, however, as he wondered what the future would bring and agonized over the dreams that his visit to Bellano had awakened. The only relief he received was his weekly excursion to the club with his friends and a brief, weekly call from Natalie, for whom Marie had procured a full scholarship to a Catholic girls' boarding school.

During the day, his mind would wander as he worked. The physical labor awakened his thoughts, and he would ponder all sorts of things that came, unbidden, to his conscience. Natalie's admonishment against his activities with his friends troubled him, but he still continued to drive them every week, feeling guilty as he watched Gilbert slip further and further into the grip of the dark subculture they frequented. Confusing questions over what he read in Guy's Bible also came to mind. The loneliness he felt was eased, however, by the beauty of the landscape. Breathing in the scent of turned earth and ripe wheat was comforting, and that was when he felt the presence of his beloved mentor most strongly.

He missed Natalie intensely and could only imagine how she felt, in a strange place, never to see her sister again. He had had only had one date with Michelle and found her permanently written on his heart. The love he had felt for her that night mingled with strong feelings of guilt over his stubborn pursuit of her attentions, in spite of his best friend's clear warning.

In addition to talking to Natalie on the phone every week, he visited her as often as he could, but the visits were supervised by one of the nuns, and they couldn't really converse freely as they used to. Natalie's eyes would always be full of unspoken words, few of which came out while other ears were listening. Did she have nightmares, as he did? With what she had been through, he had no doubt.

The evenings, which were long and lonely, he spent reading, with Sophie, the Labrador, curled up next to him. He tried to read a variety of things—publications on organic farming, a tedious text on accounting principles, and the works of the great theologians, such as the St. Teresa of Avila's *Interior Castles* and *Dark Night of the Soul* by St. John of the Cross. It was comforting to know that troublesome thoughts and doubts, similar to those that plagued him over the existence of his soul were shared by others more worthy than he.

Gilbert stopped by on a regular basis to help Paolo with his bookkeeping, which tended to be sloppy. He bought a computer bookkeeping package and set it up, scoffing at Guy's handwritten journals.

One afternoon, the shopkeeper sat with focused attention dressed in jeans and a T-shirt, working on a piece of gum and drumming his leg restlessly as he straightened out the mess the young farmer had made of his books.

The clothier was explaining, in painstaking detail, how to post invoices. Paolo sat, eyes glazed, staring out the window.

"I'm not boring you, am I?" Gilbert asked sarcastically.

Paolo turned back to his friend with a guilty expression. "Oh, uh, sorry. I, ah, I was just thinking about something else."

Gilbert raised an eyebrow and then got that inquisitive look on his face that Paolo had begun to dread. "Let's have it. After all, you owe me. I gave up my whole afternoon to straighten out this disaster."

Paolo looked at his friend with wariness. Then, he remembered how he had told him about his dream of the Lavender Lady. Maybe he could trust Gilbert.

"I've been having these weird dreams," he admitted.

Gilbert leaned forward in his chair, his eyes growing wider with interest. Why did Natalie and Gilbert always manage to make him feel like such a curiosity?

"Go on," he encouraged.

"I, uh, I keep dreaming about that fruit stand I told you about in Bellano. I keep dreaming that the shopkeeper was named Paolo, like me."

"Was?" Gilbert noted.

"Yeah, was," Paolo concurred. "I keep dreaming that ..."

Gilbert made a circular motion with his hand to pull out the information that Paolo suddenly wished he had had the strength not to mention. Why did he keep giving in to Gilbert, anyway? His friend seemed to be able to extract information like a member of the KGB.

"I, um, I keep seeing that this guy was murdered and then thrown into the Dumpster behind his store. It's like I'm seeing it, but not doing it. Odd, though. Nobody else is around. I'm afraid, Gilbert. What if I killed this guy and don't remember? You said it yourself, that I might be repressing something. What if I'm really this awful person that killed some guy and stole his money?"

Gilbert snorted, waving his hand dismissively. "Don't you know, Paolo? Dreams never mean what they are on the surface. Let's find out what this means."

He pulled up the Internet and began typing furiously on the computer as Paolo watched dubiously. "Here!" he exclaimed. "You dreamed you killed this guy, right?"

"Um, I guess so," he answered. He really wasn't sure.

"This makes perfect sense," Gilbert explained. "It says here that if you dream you killed someone, it could symbolize that you are angry with someone who has no morals. Can you think of who that might be?"

"René." That was obvious.

"So, you see? It doesn't mean you literally killed someone, but that you have repressed anger against someone who completely deserves it. Satisfied?"

"Um, yeah, I guess," Paolo stammered. It certainly seemed a better thought than taking the dream at its face value.

"But why did I dream the victim was named Paolo?"

Gilbert thought for a moment.

"Maybe you have some self-loathing issues going on, something you feel you need to make amends for," he then assessed.

Paolo looked into his friend's ingenuous, round eyes and wondered if he might not have made a good psychotherapist. Was he that transparent? Was the guilt he felt over his part in Michelle's death that evident?

"I dream that I go to work naked all the time, which is weird, because I'm surrounded by clothes all day," Gilbert shared, leaning back in his chair. "They say it's a fear of rejection or of having your secrets exposed. Then," he added with a smirk, "this gorgeous girl walks up to me, and she's naked too, and then …"

"Okay, okay, I get it," Paolo laughed, cutting him off.

The two of them both had a good chuckle before they dug back into the accounting. Paolo was relieved that his dream was just that, a dream.

All was quiet in the darkened street. The Dumpster lay empty and open, hungry for food, which did not appear. The awning flapped angrily against the rainstorm that accosted it. Paolo lay in wait for the unfailing bounty to appear beneath him. His belly growled in protest as he watched the rain slam down in sheets, racing across the street in a pattering riot.

Below him, he spotted a wiry, reddish-haired man and a beautiful woman. The woman called out his name, looking upward as she did so.

"Paolo?"

The man, incensed, took a glinting, steel knife from his pocket and slashed furiously at her throat as she screamed.

"Michelle!" Paolo shouted. But there was no one to hear him. Gilbert had left, and it seemed that he had fallen asleep on the sofa, tired out from the exertion of trying to learn the new bookkeeping system. He lay still, listening to the patter of the rain on the porch roof.

Gilbert was right, he mused. *Dreams are much too confusing to take literally.*

Fey watched nervously as Guiscard made the final preparations for her journey. Arcenciel bore silent witness to his sacrifice. They had chosen the last day of summer for her travel, since it held such romantic significance to Paolo and her. Once she set out, there would be no going back. They went to his loft, where he consulted his library and his store of mysterious, multicolored bottles that lined the top of his walls.

"What if he doesn't recognize me?" she asked nervously, wringing her hands.

"That, too, is a risk," he replied honestly.

That would leave Fey stranded in a world not her own with no one to lean upon for help. She would be unable to return until Paolo died, at which time, her magical ability would be restored.

"And what of you, Guiscard? How long must you suffer for my happiness?" she fretted as he focused on mixing up a batch of sleeping draft.

"Have no fears for me. I will return to my present state when your human form expires, as will you, should you choose to stay until that moment," he commented casually, swirling the vial above a beeswax taper. "I would advise it, as you will return to the Fae with your full powers restored, if you wait until then."

Fey nodded, listening. Their time was long, compared with the paltry lifespan of a human. This would be just one adventure, among many, in their world. So then, it would turn out well for the both of them, and Paolo would get a much longer life as a human than as a fruit bat, a gift that she was more than willing he should have.

"I have done everything I can think of to prepare for this moment," he assured her, handing her the warm sleeping draft. "You know the lad's heart better than I. What say you?"

Fey nodded her head, resigned herself to whatever would happen, and then kissed her best friend, who stood beside Guiscard. Arcenciel wrapped her in a tight hug, squeezing her eyes shut. "Fey, I am going to miss you so!"

Next, Fey took one long, last look into Guiscard's brilliant, amber eyes and downed the draft. She awakened a few hours later to find the sun shining down through the branches of the trees overhead, feeling refreshed, as if she had just had the best sleep of her life. The breeze swayed the treetops, making them sing in their percussive tone, like a South American rain stick. She noted with delight that her body stood firm against its pull. She was no longer so insubstantial that it would push her about like a puff of milkweed down. She had always hated that.

Rising up from the cool earth, she noted the creamy glow of her skin. Her dun pallor was gone. Of course, as she was human, Guiscard had not been able to return her skin to its beautiful shade of French lavender, but this was just as nice. She fingered her hair, pulling a lock before her and exclaiming in delight that her reddish-brown curls had returned in all their splendor, thick and heavy, hanging almost to her waist. The color and texture had not changed at all from the day Paolo had first admired it.

"Oh, Guiscard!" she shouted joyfully. "It's wonderful. How can I ever thank you?"

Fey proceeded to admire the generous array of gifts that Guiscard had left for her, opening the beautifully crafted suitcase, admiring the contents with an artist's discerning appreciation. She dressed carefully, choosing jeans and a T-shirt for the long walk and donning the sturdy hiking boots, which had been considerately left for the long walk ahead. Neatening up her curls and slicking on some strawberry lip gloss, after sniffing the half-dozen flavors that had been tucked in her makeup bag, she stowed the rest of her things neatly in the suitcase and set off for a stroll through the familiar forest, making her way confidently toward the village of Achères-la-Forêt, heady with the excitement of a new adventure and the prospect of reunification with her beloved Paolo.

Fey's benefactor kept watch over her from a nearby branch, looking pleased with her delighted reaction to her beauty and his gifts. As she left, he spoke to her quietly, knowing that she couldn't hear or see him anymore. "Find your beloved, dearest Fey, and may happiness flourish."

It was actually a mercy that she couldn't. It would have pained her to see his brilliance dulled. His hair was limp and faded to a lifeless straw color, his skin a grayish tone the shade of the moon on a cold night. His amber eyes had turned a dull, murky shade that was difficult to describe but resembled the shell of a tortoise as it emerged from a cooling bath of mud.

Not one for vanity, he shrugged the change off with manly dignity. Guiscard's pride lay in his chivalry, more than anything else. Pride, though, had turned out to be a showy garment he strongly wished to discard.

Taking one last, wistful look at the happy, radiant figure on the ground, Guiscard flew off to begin his long decades of obscurity, during which he would study and learn. The door to his carefree youth firmly shut, he had moved on to a new seriousness.

"Yet now farewell, and farewell life with thee!" he quoted from *Henry VI* and flew off to his loft as the lovely human trudged through the woods in the opposite direction.

That afternoon, Paolo sat alone, poring over the confusing mess on the rolltop desk in the living room, wishing nothing more than to slam the louvered top shut and to lie down on the sofa and close his eyes; he could feel another headache threatening. He lifted his head from his work upon hearing the noisy crunch of an approaching car on the long drive. Pulling back the sheer curtain at the front window with the pencil he was using, he watched as a woman stepped out of a cab, handed something to the driver, and waved him away. Unhurried, she walked gracefully up the gravel with mincing steps. Her dress was a beautiful shade of lavender and fluttered in the light breeze as she walked. Her hair, an earthy russet brown, blazed with red-gold highlights in the midday sun. It hung in glorious profusion all the way to her waist. She looked like a princess from a fable.

Strong feelings worked their way to the surface as he watched her slow, elegant approach. Before he fully realized what was happening, his pulse had quickened and a sheen of perspiration had appeared on his brow. Shadows of a recurring dream played across his consciousness as he dropped the pencil and made his way to the front door.

PART TWO

Temptation

Ye have heard that it was said by them of old time, Thou shalt not commit adultery: But I say unto you, That whosoever looketh on a woman to lust after her hath committed adultery with her already in his heart.

—Matthew 5:27–28

32

Cinnamon and Salt

*F*ey slipped out of the cab and stood, staring down the gravel drive of the stone farmhouse. Everything was neat and tidy. Weathered, terra-cotta pots containing geraniums lined the steps, bright red in the summer sun. A large, light-buff-colored Labrador dozed on the porch. She lifted her head as Fey's cream-colored Prada heels crunched the gravel and then stood and bayed a greeting/warning, wagging her tail gently.

And then, there he was at the door, looking out at her as she approached. Her heart skipped a beat at the sight of him. He stepped slowly out onto the porch, as if sighting a wild animal that could easily be frightened away by a sudden, sharp movement.

She minced her way up the walk, her wispy, lavender silk dress swaying slightly in the breeze. Would he recognize her? She had thrown every caution to the wind for him. She stopped at the foot of the stairs. He leaned his forearm against the porch post and stared, much as he had the first time he had seen her. His beautiful, innocent face was now tainted with a hint of sadness. Faint, dark circles showed under his eyes. She could see that he had been suffering, and this pulled at her heart, which was already so full of love for him.

He broke the silence first. Pulling his arm down from the post, he slowly descended the few steps, looking shaky.

"You *are* real," he almost whispered, standing before her.

She stepped up onto the bottom tread of the stairs in order to even out their height. He gazed into her eyes with that same primal feel, which had, at first meeting, so terrified her. He reached out, so slowly, to touch her flaming russet hair, like he was afraid she would disappear. His hand tangled gently in her curls, and then slid very lightly down her back to her waist, barely touching her.

He drew in close, his face inches from hers. He looked at her with such intensity. She knew what he wanted and would not make him ask. She knew he had never kissed anyone. She had seen it when they spent those three long nights together as he lay so close to death. Closing her eyes, she gave him his first kiss. He didn't return it, but she heard him sigh. Again, she closed her eyes and kissed him.

He then made his first tentative attempt. Soft as a whisper, he pulled her lips to his own. It was very gentle, yet the feelings it stirred between them were intensely powerful. She had never imagined such love possible. Her heart felt full to bursting. She clasped her cool, slim hands behind his neck and held him there. A thought went through her mind that she couldn't suppress, and she felt a little guilty about it, but she was glad it was her and not Michelle who had shared this with him. She knew it was terribly selfish of her, but as he pressed his lips lightly to her own, she knew that this was incredibly special. Was that why she hadn't shared this knowledge with him? she wondered. The Fae often had premonitions. Did she, deep in her heart, know that he was hers alone?

He backed away and again met her gaze. He looked like he was about to faint, she realized with amusement.

"Um, I have to take care of something ... in the barn. Could you ... ah ... just give me a second?" he asked her hesitantly, backing away with a dazed look on his face.

"Sure." She smiled.

It was completely unfair, she knew, taking him by surprise this way. He had the classic deer-in-the-headlights look. He nodded gratefully and made a hasty exit, rubbing his temples with the tips of his middle fingers as he strode quickly away.

Fey leaned on the porch post, watching his receding form, rejoicing in the knowledge that he knew her and loved her as she had believed he would.

Paolo leaned against the dark, old wood of the barn, his heart beating rapidly inside his chest. His emotions were wreaking havoc on his mind. It had been surreal, seeing those vivid indigo eyes, which he had pictured so many times in his mind as he slept. And that kiss, it was so much more than he had ever imagined. Her lips had tasted sweet, like cinnamon, mixed with a wet, salty tear that had trickled down her cheek to join them. As if in affirmation that he had not been hallucinating, he licked the spicy sweetness from his mouth and sighed, letting the tide of emotion wash over him, effacing the aching loneliness of the long nights he had endured.

The headache was pounding so fiercely that he saw spots in front of his eyes. Humiliated at his hasty retreat, he sought some sort of equilibrium. It was such a curse, being shy. He would give anything to trade places with his confident friend, who seemed to be master of his emotions at all times. What must she be thinking, this beautiful, self-assured woman, who had dropped everything to come and find him? What could she possibly see in him anyway? It didn't seem possible that she could be his girlfriend. She looked way too pretty and worldly to be attracted to him.

He held his face in his hands and shuddered with pain, fighting against the concussion's vice grip on his brain and the debilitating self-doubt that bound him as tightly as the embrace of solitude ever had.

He stayed in the barn for as long as he dared, popping a few aspirin and allowing the familiarity of the quiet darkness to calm him, and then he made his way back to the house. She wasn't on the porch. Had she gone inside to wait for him, or worse—he thought with dread—left? Stepping inside, he smelled a delicious aroma of cooking food. Paolo sheepishly appeared in the kitchen doorway.

"I'm sorry. I'm not usually so impolite," he begged her forgiveness miserably, his mouth watering as the luscious scent awakened his appetite.

"Hey, it's okay." She smiled. "I should have given you some warning that I was coming, but I wanted to surprise you."

He sneaked a curious glance, still visibly uncomfortable.

Dio, but she's gorgeous!

Fey was pleased to see that Paolo had finally returned. She vowed to be patient, as this had to be a complete shock to him. She, too, felt dizzy with the strangeness of it. He wiped his palms on the front of his jeans and took the seat at the table she motioned to. He sat penitently, lips slightly parted, hair falling over his face, his body still tensed.

"I made supper," she offered casually, placing a heaping plate of fried potatoes, peppers, and onions in front of him.

"Oh, that's wonderful," he exclaimed. Paolo waited for her to take the first bite before he tasted the plate of steaming food, which she noted with pleasure. Chivalry in a man was always attractive.

"This is really good!" he exclaimed, giving her an appreciative smile. "I love to eat, but I can't seem to get the hang of cooking. I buy the stuff and try to make it, but it always turns out so badly that I end up tossing it out and just opening a can of soup."

Fey laughed, delighted that his tongue was loosening up. Maybe it was true, that old saying that the way to a man's heart was through his stomach. She noted with pleasure that he finished the whole plateful and then went back to the skillet, scraping out what was left as a second helping. He offered her more first to be polite, but she hadn't even finished what little she had put on her own plate. Being with him gave her butterflies, making it hard to eat.

"Ah, I don't know how to ask you this. Please don't be mad at me, but …" he trailed off, not wanting to finish. His face expressed fear and guilt.

"Ask me anything you like, Paolo," she urged him gently, a look of tenderness on her face.

He sighed, gathering the courage. "I hate to admit it," he went on, his features cringing in embarrassment, "but I don't know your name."

She had never told him, she realized.

"Fey," she answered.

"You're not angry with me?" he asked with incredulous surprise.

She shook her head and smiled reassuringly, and he let out a loud sigh of relief. He repeated her name and returned her smile with a happy grin that went straight to her heart.

She watched him clean up after dinner, drinking in the sight of him. Every now and then, he would glance over at her as she sat at the kitchen table, as if just to make sure she was, indeed, still there, a look of pure disbelief on his face. They spent the time quietly, needing no conversation to fill the silence.

Later, they sat on the porch swing together, looking out over the fields as the sun set on the last day of summer. Fey kicked off her shoes, tucking her feet up under her silk skirt. As they rocked gently, letting the orange glow of the sun wash over them, the many questions he had about himself and about her eventually came spilling out.

"You seem to understand, Fey, why I didn't know your name, but that I still love you with all my heart. I, on the other hand, am very confused about all this. Did something happen to me? Why can't I remember? And how is it that you came to me when I was so close to the end? I know you saved my life. Were you really there, or did I dream all of that?"

She wondered what she should tell him and what she should hold back. She wanted him to live in the present. He was already so different from the rest of humanity. To add this burden to him would make it even harder for him to fit in. Also, she knew he suffered from scruples and didn't want to make his condition worse by adding the bizarre story of how he came to be here to his already overloaded mind. She would tell him enough of the truth to fend off his queries.

"So many questions!" she said and laughed.

He looked hopefully at her, waiting for answers.

"We met in the forest, at the hollow tree where you returned the day of your adoptive father's death. I was, at first, terrified of you, because you're so much bigger than me and we were alone. And you do have a habit of looking so intently at a person," she explained. "It can be kind of scary when someone doesn't know you."

Paolo turned away, letting out an embarrassed laugh. "Sorry about that," he mumbled.

"I soon saw, though, what a good person you are and fell in love with you, though I had no hopes that we could be together. You had undergone a trauma that, yes, robbed you of memory, but you seem to remember all that is really important: how much I love you, where you came from, and where you were going. If it's meant to be, it will all come back to you. Lastly, yes, I remember every moment of being with you when you lay dying, and when I came to know that your last conscious thought was of me, I was consumed with so much love for you, I thought that I would die too."

Fey noted that he looked disappointed that she hadn't told him more, but he refrained from pressuring her further, to her relief.

He leaned over and kissed her softly. It was the first time he had touched her since their first encounter earlier that afternoon. She responded with great restraint. He seemed so unused to physical contact that it was difficult for him to take, like a child whose palate is much more sensitive to taste than his parents'. It would take some getting used to, as her nature was openly sensuous.

His expression became troubled as he looked at her.

"What?" she asked, pulling his question out, since she could see he didn't want to ask.

"Uh … no, never mind." He shook his head and turned away. He pressed his lips together.

"Please, Paolo, what's bothering you?" She noticed him trying to hold back the words that would come out.

He turned back to gauge her expression. She returned his assessing gaze with an expression of compassion and openness. He sighed and dove in with it, reluctantly.

"Why didn't you come with me? It would've been so much easier if you had been here, especially after what happened to me."

"Oh, Paolo, I would have loved that, but believe me, it was impossible. Can't it be enough that I'm here with you now, and that I'll stay as long as you need me?"

He looked like he wanted to say something in response, but instead, he just nodded, lacing her fingers with his.

"We're not like other people, you and I, are we?" he observed.

"Yes and no." She didn't want to emphasize this, as it would cause him endless rumination.

The sun had set. They sat there for hours, their hands entwined companionably, watching as the moon illuminated the shorn fields. She leaned into him and rested her head against his shoulder. Neither one of them wanted to move.

"It's getting late," Fey finally conceded.

Paolo suddenly grew tense, as if he feared where the conversation might lead them.

"Were we lovers?" he asked her and then cringed.

"We didn't really get a chance to be," she replied comfortably, the look on her face saying, without words, that he hadn't been too far off.

His palms were starting to sweat, she could tell, because he drew them roughly over his thighs. His aspect grew increasingly uncomfortable. Fey realized that, as much as they both loved each other, he would not feel comfortable moving too quickly. The old farmer had ingrained a strong sense of morality in his mind, and as an honor-bound daughter of the Fae, she herself would never ask another to betray his own inner voice.

"I'm staying at Natalie's house," she told him, with a reassuring smile to his panicked look. "A friend of mine contacted her at school to make the arrangements."

Paolo rose from the porch swing with relief.

"Wait right here," he requested. "I have to get the keys to the truck and, ah, something else."

He strode quickly inside, slamming the screen door in his hurry. He returned, not even a minute later and pressed a well-used leather-bound notebook into her hands. He smiled hesitantly as he handed it to her.

"So you can see what's happened to me, since we were last together," he explained.

Fey, thumbing through its leaves as the dim light from the living room window illuminated the pages, knew that she held not just a book, but his heart in her hands.

Just before midnight, a tiny messenger squeezed through the mail slot to the apartment beside the flower shop, but it was not Yasmine. Fleur, her fledgling apprentice, had decided to pick up her teacher's abandoned project. She glided up the stairwell in the darkness, flowing through the wide crack under the apartment door.

All was quiet in the small, neat flat as she rounded the corner and flew to the human's bedroom. He lay still and motionless in a ray of moonlight, his face an enigmatic mask as he slept. Quietly, Fleur tied a fresh Love Wish to his bedpost and then sped off to rejoin the head matchmaker, who was busy spying on her old friend in the midst of a delightful tryst that would surely become the stuff of legends among the Fae.

33

Temptation

I t was after midnight when Paolo reluctantly drove Fey back to Natalie's house in Guy's pickup. Dropping her off at the door, he leaned in for one more kiss, addicted to the feelings it brought forth. He buried his face in her hair, inhaling deeply of the perfume of the forest that clung to her. To him, she smelled of ferns, leaves, and cool water, with a hint of lavender. It recalled to him the past he couldn't quite pin down, and he found it as maddeningly compelling as the sweet taste of her lips.

Backing away, he held her at arm's length, with a look so fierce it would have made anyone else afraid, but Fey, who knew him to the depths of his heart, just smiled. It took every ounce of self-control he could muster to turn and walk away from her. Oh, how every fiber in him longed to stay. He left quickly but couldn't resist taking one final look over his shoulder. She stood watching him, the book pressed firmly to her chest.

The next day, Fey returned to the farm. Paolo walked up to the porch just after four o'clock, covered with sweat and dirt. As much as he wanted to spend every minute with her, he had to get the work done. It was getting close to the time Guy had taught him was ideal for planting the winter wheat, which grew so well in their region, and he had never had to do everything on his own. It made him anxious. He didn't feel ready for the load of responsibility with which he had been entrusted.

"I'm all sweaty," he protested, as Fey approached like they were opposing magnets. He looked, to her, absolutely beautiful. She was attired in a frothy confection of raspberry silk, which fluttered seductively when she moved, accentuating the curve of her hips. He didn't even want to get near her, lest he smudge the image of feminine perfection she presented.

"Let me taste," she coaxed, leaning in to kiss the salt from his lips. "Mmm, better than hot buttered popcorn."

He looked down at her with a hint of a smile, a little embarrassed that she should see him looking so disheveled. He couldn't understand what she saw in him. To Paolo, she was so refined and lovely, while he saw himself as hopelessly awkward, not particularly good-looking, and lacking in any outstanding qualities whatsoever.

"Oh, you've been reading, I see," he commented, noting the journal in her hands.

There was no embarrassment in this, as there had been when Natalie had taken it upon herself to read his private thoughts. It was different with Fey. Before his beautiful Eve, he would always be Adam, without shame, yet full of temptation, seething always just below the surface.

The shop had closed a while ago. Gilbert had taken off, at a little before six, eager to be gone. Jacques sat on the soft, burgundy leather sofa to the right of the mahogany desk, rolling a small cylinder between his fingers. Black thoughts wrapped themselves like an evil fog around his troubled mind.

He stared at the picture of Tristan in his army uniform that stood in a simple wooden frame on the desktop, lit by the green-shaded banker's lamp to its side in the otherwise darkened room. His features were not so regular as those of his younger son, but Tristan was no less pleasing to look at, with his thick, dark hair; soft brown eyes; and round, gentle face. Truth be told, he was almost the image of Jacques at that age. He had had a boyish sweetness about him and had been full of curiosity and wanderlust.

The stab of pain was almost physical as he recalled with regret how the two of them would spend hours together, fishing, walking, or just watching sports on the television. Gilbert was usually off with his friends; he was no less welcome but always occupied elsewhere. Tristan, too, had had friends but had always wanted time with his father as well. He seemed to be able to balance his life so much better than his younger brother, who was a study in excess.

The loss of his oldest son had definitely taken away much of life's sweetness, even more so than his ex-wife's abandonment. Add to that the death of his friend and confidante and the rejection he felt from Gilbert.

He had begun to wish for an end. As he lay down at the end of the day, waiting for sleep to come, his meditations had taken on a sinister tone. Imagining the scenarios in which he could get out from under the weight of it all had become his new relaxation exercise. Perhaps, knowing he could, at any time, was enough for him to relax and escape into the temporary release of sleep.

A car was always an easy way to go. You could just shut the door to the garage, lean back in your seat, and wait, listening to the radio as you did. No one would be hurt by that. He rejected the idea of driving off the edge of the road. Too risky. You could end up paralyzed or brain dead. Not an option. It had to be a sure thing. Too bad, because the violence of it was appealing.

The cylinder in his hand was obtained legally and contained powerful painkillers for a recently healed back injury. He had hardly taken any of them, and they lay in his desk drawer, tempting him. He should just throw them away, but he found himself hanging on to them, hoarding them, kind of a reverse life preserver, just in case.

But his favorite thought, the one that always helped sleep to come, was the thought of a simple free fall—the rush of air, the feeling of complete release followed by instant blackness. To feel intensely and then not feel at all—that was what he wanted.

Some days, the only thing holding him back was Gilbert. No matter what his son's feelings for him, he loved him more than he hated his own inner pain, and he would be there for him in whatever way his boy would let him. They were all they had to each other, and he was not a selfish man. He would just have to tough it out and trust that God had a better plan for him than he could, as yet, see.

Jacques sighed, vowing to call his physician in the morning. He needed help.

Arcenciel approached as Yasmine sat, her arms wrapped around her knees, head resting atop. She looked so sad. She could feel her friend's melancholy reaching out into the night. She was perched on a branch outside of her hideaway, watching the moon rise over the forest.

"What's wrong, Yasmine?" she asked, putting her hand on her shoulders.

Her normally bubbly girlfriend remained silent. Her words were choked up by the tears she held back.

Arcenciel handed her a handkerchief, and sat down next to her, waiting for Yasmine to regain her voice. They sat for a long while, Arcenciel patiently biding her time.

The delicate, golden-haired faerie finally looked over at her, drying her eyes. "You and Fey are so lucky," she said enviously. "You both get to be with the men you love, while I am beside myself, watching the one I love to distraction destroy himself because he feels so empty inside. I'm really worried about him." Tears again slid down her face.

"Who is it?" Arcenciel asked. She honestly had no idea. Yasmine had flirted with Guiscard, as they all had, but had hardly seemed to see him as anything more than a friend.

"Paolo's friend, Gilbert, the young haberdasher," she answered, to Arcenciel's great surprise. "I know. I know. It's hopeless to even think about him. But, Arcenciel, I've known him practically my whole life."

Arcenciel just looked dubious, listening with pity to hear that her friend had become entangled emotionally with a human. It was foolishness, but the heart does not always obey the dictates of wisdom. No wonder she had foreseen trouble in her future.

"I've been traveling to Achères to watch him," Yasmine admitted, rolling her sky-blue eyes, knowing how ridiculous she must seem. "I even caught his attention when he was young enough to actually see me with the eyes of his soul, though I'm sure he wouldn't remember, or if he does, he'd think it was just a dream."

"Why would you do such a thing?" Arcenciel scolded gently. To set oneself up for heartache seemed a foolish thing to do.

"I meant to help him find love," Yasmine justified her actions. "But every girl he met, he would end up pushing away out of fear, or she would grow tired of him. I thought that the lovely Marie-David was the one, but, well, he managed to botch that up about right. Ugh!" she exclaimed in frustration. "Why do humans insist on denying themselves the only thing that truly would make them happy?"

"They can be maddeningly contradictory," Arcenciel agreed. "And that," she lectured, "is why we don't set our own sights on them."

"Oh, what kind of matchmaker am I?" Yasmine wailed. "I broke the most cardinal rule of professional conduct!"

Arcenciel folded her arms and gave Yasmine a condescending I-told-you-so look.

Yasmine buried her face in her hands and muttered, "Never, never, never get personally involved with your clients."

34

Shopping

The bell to the shop gave a ring. Gilbert chewed absently on a piece of gum as he concentrated on his text message from Luc and then looked up guiltily, shoving his phone in his pocket. His dad thought it looked unprofessional to be texting on the job and would have been angry to see him sneaking it in during business hours.

Oh, it was just Paolo. *Hmm, he looks like he's in one of those moods of his. I wonder what's up,* he thought, flashing him a smile, relieved to have someone to talk to in person.

He hated when the shop was slow. It made the afternoons drag. Latif was off that day, which made it even worse.

"Hey, man, what's eating you?" He laughed, as Paolo leaned on the counter, a look of intense brooding on his tanned face. The sun stared in the front window, casting a cheery rectangle of brightness over the two friends.

"The great love of my life has come back to me," he stated in full-blown poetic fashion. "I thought I could never have her, and now, here she is, and I am consumed. I want to marry her, Gilbert."

His manner was so serious, Gilbert wanted to laugh. His new friend was such a kick. He was like someone from one of those nineteenth-century novels he had had to read in high school.

Wow, that one came out of the blue, he thought with amusement. One thing about Paolo, he was never predictable.

"Whoa, slow down there," he admonished, chuckling. "When you fall for a girl, you dive right into the deep end. You don't want to go rushing into some rebound relationship. Why, you still aren't over Michelle yet. Give yourself a little more time," he lectured.

His friend was way too impulsive. Someone had to rein him in, or he would end up making a huge mistake. There seemed to be no middle ground with this guy. It was either complete revulsion or love at first sight. Heck, Gilbert hadn't even seen this girl yet, and here Paolo was talking about marrying her. It was just insane.

"You don't understand," he corrected. "I never would have asked Michelle out if I knew that there was even the possibility that I could be with Fey. Then," he added with great regret, "none of this mess would have happened in the first place, and Michelle wouldn't be …" he trailed off, a look of pain on his face.

"Don't you dare go blaming yourself for that," Gilbert scolded. "You played the game fair, and I've known you long enough to see that you were too dumb to realize that you were pulling the tiger's tail."

Paolo snorted and then nodded thoughtfully.

"So," he brightened, "will you come with me and shop for a ring?"

"You're not kidding, are you?" he asked. It would have been hard to believe if it had been anyone else.

"One hundred percent serious."

Gilbert sighed indulgently. "Let me go ask my dad. He's in the office going over invoices." Gilbert was hesitant. He rarely asked his father for an afternoon off. Boy, he hoped the old man was in a good mood. He'd already pushed his luck taking that Saturday not too long ago.

"I'll ask him for you," Paolo offered. "I'd like to say hello to him anyway. I hardly see him anymore."

Gilbert pocketed his keys. He knew that his father liked Paolo and would be willing to grant him this favor.

He was right. The two friends set off in the silver BMW, full of high spirits. The beautiful weather of early fall made the occasion seem even more festive.

"So," Gilbert began his interrogation, "who is this mystery lady anyway?"

"As I said, her name is Fey," he shared enthusiastically, "and I fell in love with her the moment I set my eyes on her."

Gilbert had no doubt about that. When Paolo fell in love, it was no holds barred.

"Well then, how long have you known her?" He had always been immensely curious about Paolo's life before his arrival in Achères and was even more so now. Paolo was not quite the monk he had assumed.

"Hmm, a little over a year ... I think," he answered.

"But you've been here pretty much the whole time. What have you been doing, sneaking off to meet her?" He was, to be honest, somewhat disappointed that Paolo had held out on him. He had hoped that they would become close, and this kind of thing was the important stuff that best friends shared with each other.

"No, but she came to me after René attacked me. I think she helped me to hold on until the doctors could fix me up. She stayed for a long time. I think it was difficult for her." His face grew serious and thoughtful, as if the topic brought back all the pain of that awful time.

Gilbert was profoundly confused. She certainly wasn't at the crime scene, nor could she have been present in the operating room, unless she was a nurse or doctor, maybe.

"Oh, so she works at the hospital—took one look at the good-looking half-dead guy on the operating table and says to herself, 'I gotta save this one. He's just what I've been looking for!'" he stated dramatically.

Paolo laughed out loud, Gilbert joining in. "No, no. It wasn't like that at all."

Gilbert wasn't done with him yet. "I'll bet she took a peek under that hospital gown, just to check and make sure you were worth the bother."

Paolo didn't laugh at that. "Could you please find another hobby, other than trying to humiliate me?" he asked with undisguised irritation.

Gilbert realized he had touched a nerve and felt badly about it. He had managed to stick his foot in his mouth yet again. Sometimes, he didn't know when to quit, he admitted to himself.

"Look, Lambie, I'm sorry," he apologized. "It's just the way I am. I can't help it."

Paolo cast him a brooding, sidelong glance. "S'okay," he muttered irritably.

"So, that's it?" Gilbert asked, angry at himself for causing Paolo to clam up with his abrasive sense of humor.

Paolo stared out the window. It was obvious he wasn't going to clarify the situation, which made no sense at all. Gilbert would just have to wait until he met the woman to find out the real story from her. He threw his hands in the air in surrender and drove on to their first stop in the hunt for the perfect engagement ring.

The two friends canvassed the jewelry stores, looking for "The Ring." After a while, they all began to look the same, and they retreated to a café to take a break. Gilbert immediately lit up a cigarette. He offered one to Paolo, who held up his palm and shook his head. He shrugged and put the pack away. They sat quietly for a few moments, drinking iced lattes and relaxing.

"Man, you are making this way too hard," Gilbert criticized. "Just pick the biggest diamond you can afford, and be done with it."

"I'm sorry, but this is really important to me, and it has to be just right," Paolo explained, also growing frustrated.

Gilbert shook his head and took a long drag on his cigarette. The clothier then snuffed out the stub on the sidewalk and flicked it to the gutter, where it joined several others. The two men resumed their search, though Gilbert was beginning to despair of a positive outcome.

"Paolo, we only have two places left to go. You'd better find something soon," he warned.

Paolo stopped in front of the display window of their next destination, a look on his face that sent waves of relief through Gilbert. Finally! It was a beautiful heart-shaped stone, deep blue with a hint of purple.

"How perfect!" Paolo mused, breathlessly. "It's the exact color of her eyes. I don't care what it costs. This is the ring I've been looking for."

Gilbert eagerly pushed open the shop door, ushering his friend in with a wave of his hand.

"It's a tanzanite," the polished-looking man behind the jewelry counter explained upon hearing his customer's interest in the piece they had spotted. "Very good quality, and quite an unusual cut."

Paolo was ready to empty his savings account, but Gilbert took him by the arm with a firm squeeze and a raised eyebrow—a nonverbal *"tais toi"*—and took over the price negotiations for his lamb-in-the-woods friend. Mission accomplished, the two proceeded to the local pub, where they raised a toast to love, to the beauty of a woman's eyes, and to their own friendship.

Gilbert reentered the shop at half past four, tightening his necktie. Yasmine and Arcenciel sat atop the picture of Jean-Jacques de Gaul, which with his constantly roving eyes, constituted the perfect camouflage for that uncanny feeling the humans always seemed to have that they were being watched.

Jacques looked up from his customers, and the younger man smiled cheerfully. His father gave an understated nod and went on with his work.

"So, he's the one, is he?" Arcenciel noted.

He certainly had a puckish air about him that seemed a perfect match for her silly friend. They giggled as he made faces at the stodgy old customer behind his back, mimicking how he stroked his beard and frowned while considering his outfit in the mirror. Jacques shot a menacing scowl at his unruly offspring. Gilbert sneered disdainfully, shaking his head in disapproval as Jacques glowered at him, a nonverbal warning to behave. He held up a finger and darted away. He rifled through the merchandise with a purpose and then returned with a few items. The customer took them from the young salesman, who wore a look of obsequious pleasantness on his face, and went to change.

Jacques jutted his chin out but looked on in humble silence, arms folded. The customer emerged, looking ten pounds slimmer and five years younger.

Gilbert haughtily raised an eyebrow in victory. Jacques nodded in approval and gave his son a pat on the shoulder.

Arcenciel looked over at Yasmine, who sat mesmerized by her beloved, her blue eyes glistening with a light that she had never before seen. Yes, the matchmaker was in love, her own enchantments having ensnared her in life's oldest game.

She grew sad for a moment, looking at the two of them. Life would knock them both around pretty soundly before it was through with them. Still, their fate was written, whether she would intervene or not. Did she wish to help Yasmine to extract revenge for her foolishness, which had brought not only Fey's Paolo, but her beloved Guiscard, low? Did she want to share his lot, both his suffering and the eventual rewards of his sacrifice? Or was her motivation merely to bring together two souls who, in spite of the struggles to come, were matched for each other perfectly? Perhaps a bit of each, but help them she would. Right then and there, Arcenciel vowed that she would share Guiscard's lot. She would use her magic to send Yasmine to her human.

35

Serpent

*P*aolo opened the hinged, velvet box and admired the glittering stone it contained. He was so happy to be able to give Fey something special, as he had been given the onyx ring with its beautiful inscription so many months ago. Based on what Fey had told him, he was under the impression that they had known each other quite well before he had arrived in Achères, and she said nothing to dispel his assumption.

So, not even letting a week pass, he chose a well-reputed restaurant in Arbonne-la-Forêt, on the other side of the forest, as the setting for his proposal. It seemed a good choice. The establishment was cozy, and the staff was friendly. Elegant, mahogany chairs clustered in intimate groups around burgundy-swathed tables. Candle flames hovered overtop the red oases, creating a magical warmth. Waiters in long black aprons bustled quietly about as *tafelmusik* contentedly accepted its role as background noise. The host had reserved the best table for the couple, as Paolo had bravely explained the importance of the evening when he had called to make reservations.

All through dinner, he waited for the perfect time to remove the small box from his pocket. He hoped he would know when it had arrived. He sat looking at Fey with quiet intensity, eating very little. He thought she looked absolutely magical in the lavender dress she had worn when she had surprised him with her presence and felt impossibly inferior to his confident, sparkly dinner companion.

"Paolo, what's the matter?" she asked him.

"Ah, nothing," he answered vaguely, looking vacantly toward the back of the restaurant, his expression tense and anxious, until the waiter caught his eye, thinking he wanted something. Paolo quickly averted his gaze to his untouched dinner plate, his hair falling forward.

"You're not eating," she noted. "Are you sure you're not coming down with something?"

Palo laughed uncomfortably, trying to snap out of his mood. He began to ask her questions about herself that had come to mind after their first conversation on the front porch, where they had, to his later embarrassment, talked mostly about him. He was surprised she didn't think him self-centered.

"So," he began, "we met in the forest. What were you doing there, all by yourself?" he asked, truly as perplexed by her as by his own strange circumstances, taking a perfunctory bite of eggplant parmesan.

Fey bit her lower lip.

"I was hiking," she answered.

"That's not too smart for a pretty girl to go hiking in the woods, all by herself. That tree is really far in. I had a lot of trouble finding it again, and I think I have a good sense of direction," he assessed.

"You're right," she admitted. "I promise I won't do that again. You really scared me, like I said."

"You're lucky it was me that found you, and not someone truly dangerous," he scolded her. He had learned the hard way that the world was a dangerous place and that Fey, being physically small and delicate, would be most vulnerable to evil intentions.

"I am very lucky it was you who found me," she said, putting her hand over his. He looked down shyly, enjoying the compliment, knowing it came without fishing. He continued to try to steer the conversation toward her, asking about her family, where she grew up, where she went to school, but she, oddly enough, tried to redirect their conversation back to the present, asking him questions about the farm, his friends, and his beloved mentor. It was like a game, he thought, with each of them trying to dodge the other.

Dinner over, the couple left the restaurant. Paolo was frustrated with himself but still reveled in Fey's company. He gave her a slow, light kiss as he helped her into the truck. Tonight, he thought with wonder, her lips tasted deliciously of fresh strawberries. Was this true of all women, or was this something special about Fey? It certainly drove him crazy, making it difficult to back off.

She leaned on his shoulder as he drove her home. He relaxed just a little then, enjoying her warmth against his side. She always seemed so calm. It helped put him at ease, as well.

When they arrived at Natalie's house, he looked at her sadly, disappointment evident in his expression. She invited him in, switching on the light as she entered, drawing him inside with her other hand. Paolo could no longer stand the suspense. He walked Fey over to the stairs, leading her onto the bottom step. Slipping the ring out of its velvet-lined box, he slid it onto her finger, as she watched with joyous surprise.

"J'ai pris tres tendre soin de ton Coeur," he promised her softly, referring to the inscription on his onyx ring. Looking down at her hand, which he held in his palm, he offered, *"Ici, je te donne le mien."*

She admired the dazzling stone he had chosen for her. She looked from the ring to his face, and he thought to himself how well the stone matched her fascinating indigo eyes. He stood, so serious, taking in her reaction to his gift. He then drew very close, his face brushing hers, his arms loosely draped around her waist.

"Please marry me."

He spoke the words so quietly, his voice was almost a whisper, as if he were still in disbelief that she could possibly say yes. He gently kissed the soft skin at her pulse, caressing her neck with a warm exhalation.

"Yes," she answered quietly as he pressed his lips to the soft skin behind her ear. The sound of her whispered response sent a shudder of desire through him.

"Oh, Fey, I want you so badly," he admitted, desperation sounding in his voice.

His hands slid lightly up her back, and he pulled her close. Unexpectedly, he pressed his lips firmly to hers. She returned his kiss with matching intensity, until, taking a ragged breath, he backed away from her with the same look of fear as he'd had the first time they had kissed.

He turned his gaze away from hers for just a second, conflicted thoughts racing through his mind. Looking back to her with an expression of pained apology on his face, he shook his head as if denying himself permission and then fled into the darkness to escape the passion, which threatened to strike him like a serpent.

Hurrying away into the darkness, he climbed into the pickup and slammed the door. He leaned his arm against the steering wheel and rested his forehead against it, taking a deep breath to cleanse the lust from his thoughts.

Why, he thought with exasperation, *is it so difficult to do what is right?*

Everything had been so easy, in the beginning. It was only after his date with Michelle that he had begun to be plagued by his own impurity. He knew Fey understood, but he hated how confusing he must seem to her.

As he had pressed his lips to hers, thoughts of justification had raced through is mind, effacing his resolve.

Why wait? he had wondered. *She's made it clear she wants to be with me. I've made my commitment to her. What more is needed?*

He was painfully aware that they were but a few steps away from where he wanted to be, and he knew she would willingly comply. He had glanced up the stairs for a second and then looked back to meet her gaze. It was she who changed his mind. Fey stood there, looking at him with such trust. It was one thing to choose sin, but quite another to drag someone else down with you. He couldn't do it to her. He loved her too much.

He started the truck, shifted into gear, and headed home, sure he wouldn't be able to sleep. Instead, he sat on the sofa all night, reading the words of St. Paul and scribbling reflections in his journal to try to make sense of what he had read and done.

> *I read the words of Paul, whose name I bear. We are so very different, he and I, but are also the same in some ways. He, too, admits to being tormented by what he calls "a thorn in the flesh."*
>
> *What he said that feels so true to me is this:*

For I have the desire to do good, but I cannot carry it out. For what I do is not the good I want to do, no, the evil I do not want to do—this I keep on doing.

This, I think, is the fallen nature of man that my dad tried to warn me about, but I was too naive to see it.

I read of the love between husband and wife, as my dearest Fey has said yes to me, and realize that my actions no longer affect me alone.

When I think that I have almost led her into my sinfulness, and that she, so trusting, would follow, I am filled with shame. I pray that God will help me to do better, for myself and for the woman I love.

Then, as was his way, he began to form his thoughts into a sonnet. Pretty well exhausted, he dashed it off casually, not reworking the wording as much as usual. The title and the couplet were what he meant to emphasize. The former was a plea to Fey, who would read it later, the latter, an expression of his love and gratitude for her.

Patience

Eve hath chased dark Solitude away,
Pulled me gladly from her stern embrace.
Hath come to me upon this summer day,
Doth all my tortured loneliness efface.
I stand before her, wanting, yet unsure.
She doth see inside my heart's desire.
Bestows a kiss that leaves me wanting more;
Hath lit within me passion's burning fire.
Chaste Patience doth bid me to bide my time,
Wouldst not have me lead my Love astray.
Points me back to Virtue's path sublime;
Fulfillment of my thoughts she wouldst delay.
    'Tis thou, the one hath made my joy complete.
    Life saved and life worth living in thee meet.

He fell asleep on the sofa at dawn. Sophie lay snuggled up against his legs, her face resting on his hip. He dreamed he was back in the forests of Lombardia, unstained, yet unfulfilled.

His cell phone woke him up midmorning.

"Hello?" he grunted, half asleep.

"I hate it here!"

Natalie. He roused himself, sitting up. "I'm sorry, Natalie, but you know I'm not allowed to be your guardian. Believe me, if social services would let you, I would be glad to have you stay here."

"It's so stupid!" she shouted. "I hate how they act like you are just like René. It's so unfair," she went on. "I'm so lonely and bored. The girls are all stupid, giggling airheads here. Nobody likes me."

Sophie waited patiently at the door. He let her out and then stood at the window, gazing vacantly over the fields.

"Want me to come and visit you?" he offered.

"They spy on us so that we can't even have a decent conversation," she lamented. "I'm so sick of it all. I just want …" she trailed off.

"Michelle," he finished.

She didn't answer but sobbed into the phone. He stayed on, listening to her tears, which spoke for them both.

36

Smoke

The new girl in town was hard to miss. Dressed in a beautiful, multicolored peasant dress, she looked exotic and just a little bit "big city." Her long, curly ginger hair was a dead giveaway. Gilbert casually followed her. If the shop happened to open a few minutes late, then so be it. He had to find out more about her. The curiosity was eating at him like an ulcer.

She turned into the coffee shop, where she ordered an herbal tea. He watched with delight as Paolo's ring flashed on her hand when she went to grasp the steaming cup.

Wow, he didn't wait long to pop the question, he thought with admiration.

He came up right behind her and waited for her to turn around. She almost bumped into him as she turned to leave the counter and excused herself as she had almost spilled her tea all over him. Fey looked up, noting his expression with surprise.

Gilbert, dressed in his typical dark-suit-white-shirt-plain-silk-tie-too-much-cologne uniform, stood not three inches from the lovely, colorful, russet-haired vision; he was wearing, in addition, a smile the Cheshire cat would have been proud of.

"What?" she asked, a little uncomfortably, but smiling nonetheless, as if drawn to a kindred spirit.

"You're Paolo's girl, aren't you?" he asked, a sparkle of mischief lighting up his face.

Man, she's gorgeous. How did he pull it off? Gilbert wondered. He saw his friend as being hopelessly awkward and wondered how he had managed to attract so many beautiful women: Michelle, Marie-David, and now, the amazing, exotic Fey. It was incredible.

"Most definitely," she replied proudly. "And you would be?"

"Gilbert de Gaul," he replied, bowing with mock seriousness over her hand. "So pleased to meet Paolo's lady love."

She laughed, playing along.

"Actually," he continued, not letting go of her fingers, "I helped your precious Lambie pick this out not too long ago. So, do you like it?"

"Yes, very much," she replied as comfortably as if they were old friends.

He finally let go of her hand, reluctantly, and quickly turned to order a coffee for himself. Claude, the owner of the coffee shop, handed him his favorite beverage with a wink. Gilbert shook his finger at him in admonishment, worried that she had seen. The short, dark-haired man behind the counter, recognizing a bit of androgyny in Gilbert, had harbored hopes of swaying him into a relationship. The latter, though, had made it quite clear that, even though he was not as bluntly macho as his friend Luc, he had no interest in an alternative lifestyle. He couldn't help it; he had been born into the clothing business and looked uncomfortably like his mother. He wished he didn't. He despised her.

Still, he had been raised by his father, who had a generous spirit, to be open-minded, so he harbored no ill will against Claude. The coffee vendor was, in his own quirky way, a rather attractive man. He wore his dark hair, receding on both sides of his temples, neatly back and pulled into a short, glossy ponytail at the nape of his neck. A sturdy, square build, laughing eyes framed with thick black lashes, and strong, well-groomed brows bespoke a surety in his position as the Figaro of Achères. His humble domain was, indeed, the factotum of the village.

"My friend, you just have to stop flirting with me," he told him in a voice dripping with sympathy. "It just wouldn't work out. I would only cheat on you, the first time a pretty girl looked my way," he joked.

Claude laughed, retorting, "Sure, sure, de Gaul. You reject me, yet you have managed to have quite a bromance with the Italian boy who wandered into town not too long ago."

"That's different, Claude," he argued, flushing a hint at the inference, pulling a few euros out of his pocket with a frown. "He lets me pursue my real interests in unencumbered style. It's all purely platonic, I assure you," he dissembled as he placed them on the counter.

"No need to be jealous," he added playfully, toying with his admirer, taking a slow sip of his café au lait. "Now, as for me," he mused, just to finish up the conversation, pouting his lower lip thoughtfully, "I much prefer the art of Georgia O'Keefe to that of Michelangelo, if you get my meaning. As for you, though …"

He scribbled an e-mail address on a slip of paper and pushed it toward his besotted acquaintance. Claude, looking somewhat surprised, took the slip of paper and stared intently at Gilbert, who nodded encouragingly. An old college pal with whom he had kept in touch online, Matthieu Petit, had expressed interest in initiating a relationship with the desirable-looking coffee-shop owner.

"Call him," Gilbert ordered his fellow businessman. "You can thank me later," he called as he hurried to catch up with Fey.

He hoped things would go well for the two of them. As it was, if Luc and Latif caught wind of how Claude kept coming on to him, he'd never live it down. He could only imagine the fun they would have torturing him over it.

Gilbert caught up with Fey, coffee in hand.

"So, you are friends with my Paolo?" she asked, as they sat down at one of the prized outdoor tables, which seemed to open up for her like magic, for a chat.

"Yes. Actually, I was the one who found him after René tried to turn him into hamburger," he bragged, lighting up a cigarette.

Fey laughed. "Oh, that wasn't funny," she scolded.

Gilbert, unrepentant, just shrugged, breathing out a plume of smoke.

"So, how did my shy-to-a-fault friend, who starts stammering within ten feet of a girl, manage to ensnare such beauty," he pried and flirted at the same time.

She lowered her eyes, pondering carefully what to say.

"I fell in love with the goodness of his heart," she answered with simple honesty.

"Yeah, he's one of a kind, isn't he?" Gilbert agreed, looking suddenly thoughtful and sincere. "I think we visited every jewelry store between here and Lyons looking for that little bauble of yours," he joked. "And I'm sure he would have mortgaged the farm to buy it for you, if he had to. Fortunately, his best friend is a master negotiator," he bragged, looking at her with a smug but inviting smile.

Fey nodded, looking down with liquid eyes at the sparkling stone, which mimicked their indigo splendor to perfection.

Realizing that this was his chance to really get the scoop on Paolo's background, Gilbert availed himself of the opportunity. "So, would you like to meet your fiancé's other friends, as well?" he offered excitedly. "Have some fun too? We can't have you stuck watching movies on television in that dull old farmhouse. Come to the club tonight with us. Besides, if you steal our designated driver, I won't be able to get lit. You wouldn't want to be responsible for my having a boring time, would you?" he joked with a pleading look on his face. If she said no, Paolo would not budge; he was sure of that. He finished his cigarette, snuffing out the stub on the sidewalk.

"Certainly not," she replied with enthusiasm. "It would be fun to see how Paolo spends his weekends and to meet his friends. I'm in."

Gilbert smiled, chuckling with delight, and squeezed her hands in his own. Then, he kissed her on both cheeks, apologizing that he had to leave, and rushed off to open the shop.

Natalie despised being confined in the chapel with the other "inmates." To sit there and listen to this garbage about how "God loves us" and "God watches over us" just made her want to vomit. All God had done for her had been to take her parents, take her innocence, take her sister, and then, just to be certain He had taken everything, He made sure that the man who had claimed her as a sister was so far away that she could never see him. Oh, God was cruel, and she hated Him.

She sat glaring at the cheesy stained-glass window with the image of dear Saint Catherine Labouré, her virginal eyes upturned toward the God who gave her eternal sainthood and glory but gave Natalie only deprivation and, she was sure, damnation for her black heart.

Chapel had ended, but still Natalie stayed, full of loathing—for the Durrands, for condemning her to this torture chamber; for the other students, who avoided her like a pariah; for the sisters, who criticized her every honest word; and for smug, holy, virginal Catherine, who mocked her with her sickening, pious face.

Natalie grabbed one of the Bibles from the pew. With a primal snarl of rage, she flung it with every ounce of force she could muster directly at Catherine. The book hit the mark with a resounding crack, the sound of breaking glass mingling with the echo of her despair.

Gilbert drove on the way over to the club, so that Paolo could sit in back with Fey. Her fiancé pulled her close, a bit jealously. Luc sat, a little too admiring, on her other side.

Fey enjoyed the company of Paolo's fun-loving, slightly bawdy group. She noticed that, although he laughed at their naughty humor, and was often the butt of it, he was never the source. She also noted that he seemed especially close to Gilbert, who acted protectively toward him, as if he sensed his naïveté. She was glad he had had someone to watch over him since he had been left alone, after Guy had died. Gilbert definitely had some issues, she realized, but he was a good friend.

Fey was overwhelmed by the loud music at the club, just as Paolo had warned her he had been. He laughed at her look of shock and pain and pushed back her hair, pressing a pair of earplugs in. She sighed with relief at the muffled sound. She thanked him with a kiss, which he gratefully received, to the delight of his friends, who elbowed each other, laughing as if they were scandalized.

Luc ordered the first round of drinks and handed a glass filled with a very pretty blue liquid to Fey with a devious smile. He handed an identical one to Paolo. He lifted his glass in her direction and then downed it quickly. Luc eyed Fey with a mischievous look.

Paolo glared at him, seeming profoundly irritated.

Fey sipped at the seductive beverage, peering at her fiancé over the edge of the glass with large, round eyes. He took the drink from her hand, placed it down on the table, and led her out to the dance floor, pulling her close.

The three friends sat and drank in the rare sight of their shy, awkward friend embracing this tiny, but gorgeous, woman. Gilbert sipped his own drink, studying the couple with bemusement. Fey was not the kind of woman he would have expected to see Paolo end up with. She was very poised, dressed like a model, and possessed a knowing air that made her seem older than her humble fiancé. He guessed she had at least five years on him. She reminded Gilbert of what could only be described as a "flower child," not bound by common rules, but rather, guided only by her own inner compass.

If Paolo had not been his best friend, he would definitely have been tempted to steal her for himself, being immediately attracted to her confident sensuality, but that was out of the question. It was different with Marie-David. His friend had made it quite clear that he had no interest in her before Gilbert had moved in. No, Fey belonged to Paolo. He would just have to watch and admire from a distance. He took a gulp of whiskey to drown out his inappropriate thoughts and then glanced over at Latif, who was practically drooling as he watched her with unmitigated longing.

"When are you going to get a girlfriend?" he chided his persnickety college chum, who seemed to be turning into a confirmed bachelor.

"When I can get one like her," Latif exclaimed admiringly. "My dad keeps trying to set me up with these girls who can't even speak proper French and never had an original thought in their lives," he lamented.

"Who cares, as long as they're good in bed?" Gilbert teased, swirling the ice in his glass, his eyes laughing.

"I was a philosophy major in college. Remember?" Latif responded with exasperation. "Unlike you, I need a girl with a brain *and* a body," he stated firmly, watching the object of his desire seduce her man on the dance floor, oblivious to the scrutiny they were undergoing.

"I agree with Gilbert," Luc stated. "I want to be king of my castle."

Gilbert chuckled. Latif sneered at Luc and then turned back to watch the show on the floor.

Paolo wore a look of unrestrained longing, Fey, one of complete bliss. The three friends watched like a pack of wolves as they shared a long, slow kiss and then pulled in tightly together. Paolo seemed drawn to her like a sailor to the sirens. He looked, according to Gilbert's astute observation, completely tortured by his feelings for her.

"I say he takes her down right here," Luc wagered with a grin, shouting to be heard over the loud music.

"Nah!" Gilbert waved dismissively. "The old man put too much Catholic guilt in him. To be honest, I'm really surprised she even got a kiss out of him." He knew they weren't staying together. She had told him she was living in Natalie's house indefinitely.

"I think I see smoke!" Latif exclaimed.

They laughed until their sides hurt and ordered another round of drinks.

Sound pulsed loudly, drowning out virtually all other noise in the club. René was pretty much used to it, though, and had learned to read lips and body language. After all, it had become his livelihood. His past life fixing transmissions and changing oil was all but forgotten as he sat, dressed in expensive clothes from his favorite men's shop in the Faubourg St. Honoré. He had purchased, with cash, a beautiful black Ferrari; had a small but elegant apartment; and could buy whatever he wanted.

He noticed right away that a very pretty brunette was making eyes at him from the bar. She didn't look like a prostitute, and the look she was sending his way didn't speak of needing a hit. Maybe he wouldn't be going home alone this evening, after all.

Arcenciel and Yasmine exchanged a final embrace in the dark, predawn forest. The autumn air was damp and chill. The raven-haired faerie had just made preparations to give her lovesick friend an enormous gift, deciding to send her uniquely human-looking friend to make a play for Gilbert's affections.

Yasmine had protested, eyes wide with disbelief, as she made her offer, but Arcenciel had insisted that she wanted to share her mate's time of trial, which would last only the few decades of the human life span. Yasmine could not send herself, or she would never be able to return to her own world. Only a few faeries in the entire realm possessed such dark magic, and they were both feared and respected among their kind. It could, however, be bestowed as a gift to a lovelorn faerie and was performed only rarely, as the human world was considered an inferior realm that no faerie in her right mind would want to inhabit.

Yasmine would be able to return if she failed to capture the haberdasher's affections, her own magic being sufficient to transport her back if she desired. Either situation, in that case, would be bleak—stuck as a human for decades until her mortal form expired, with her beloved, for whom she had given up everything, showing no interest, or returned to the faerie realm, with a permanent loss of her magic and no love to call her own as, unlike with Fey, she had made no noble sacrifice that would earn her an easier passage back to her own world. She had to succeed.

"It will be as nothing," Arcenciel assured Yasmine. "And, of course, we shall emerge from our self-imposed sequestering as more powerful faeries than one could ever imagine."

So, with these reassurances, Yasmine gratefully accepted her friend's gift. She would, if all went well, enjoy life as a human with her beloved and upon the expiration of her ephemeral form, return to the realm of the Fae, restored to her youthful beauty for centuries to come. She vowed to herself that she would find a way to bring him with her, as well, when the time came. There had to be a way.

"The only thing that pains me is that I won't be here to witness your handfasting," Yasmine lamented as she hugged her friend tight. She had hoped to officiate their joining ceremony, as matchmaker. Now, though, she wouldn't even be able to attend.

"I'll send you there in a dream," Arcenciel promised with a smile.

"How?" Yasmine questioned. Her friend's powers would be severely curtailed by her leaving.

"Fleur has offered to learn how," Arcenciel told her.

Yasmine was pleased to see that the clan was beginning to have more respect for the matchmaker-in-training, who had stepped up to her new responsibilities with surprising maturity. *Sometimes,* she thought, *it's only the opportunity that is lacking, not the ability.* It was too late for her to win Guiscard's hand, but at least she would no longer be dismissed as a silly, worthless creature by even her closest friends.

Yasmine clapped her little hands, bouncing up and down on the branch with glee, not even shaking it, so light she was.

"Well then, I'm off!" she exclaimed with dizzy delight, giving Arcenciel a final set of air kisses on each cheek.

The day before, Yasmine had given her final love arrow to Fleur, with specific instructions on how it was to be used, this time with Guiscard's permission and approval. Fleur had promised to practice her archery carefully. She couldn't miss. There was no spare. The senior matchmaker explained how important it was to her that her target's heart be opened up to the possibility of love. She could see how miserable he was, and it filled her with pity for him. "Everyone deserves a chance at happiness," she explained to her pupil. By doing this, she was also passing the baton to her, as Achères's new official matchmaker. It was an important function, helping others find love.

Now, she made ready to leave. A sky-blue suitcase stuffed full of clothing lay propped against a tree, a satchel full of toiletries beside it. A red bicycle with a chrome shelf on the back and a wicker basket on the front to hold her belongings stood by, as well, a gift from her former student. Yasmine didn't know how Fey had managed to walk the whole way to Achères from deep within the woods, loaded down with a suitcase, but she, herself, was going to take an easier way. Arcenciel had chosen a well-hidden spot closer to town to leave her friend. The hollow oak belonged to Paolo and Fey alone.

Yasmine thanked her friend one final time, vowing never to forget her and her forest home. She had, in fact, chosen du Bois as her new last name. Downing the proffered sleeping draft, she sighed, smiled, and then fell asleep under a mushroom umbrella, to await her new beginning and dream of meeting her beloved face-to-face.

37

Guilty

The sun peeked over the building tops in Achères, greeting the early morning churchgoers on the last day of October, which had dawned crisp and cheerful. A woman in a red dress and black ballet flats, her head swathed in a silk scarf, pushed a cherry-colored bicycle up the street, a large suitcase balanced nimbly on its rear shelf. She made a pretty picture as she strolled, unhurried, past the town square.

Yasmine stopped upon seeing Gilbert's car drive by and donned her sunglasses. It was Paolo and Fey, returning her man's car after their Saturday night revels. Yes, he was her man. He didn't know that yet, but he would.

The village had one small, family-owned hotel, with just a few rooms. She hoped she wouldn't need to stay there long. She parked the bicycle out front and took a deep breath. Everything looked different. Smaller. Was this how her beloved saw the world?

She watched as Paolo held the church door for her old friend, who would receive quite a surprise at her appearance. She would wait to reveal herself, though. For now, she had business to attend to. Hoisting the suitcase off the bicycle with ease, despite its considerable heft, she turned to enter the hotel lobby.

After Mass, which Fey found to be a weekly exercise in tedium, she returned with Paolo to Natalie's and sat on the sofa, watching a movie. Fey thought he looked tired and guessed it was from staying up late. She had him lie down, his head in her lap. She ruffled his thick, dark hair, as they watched the story of Jean de Florette, who reminded Fey very much of her own dear boy, with his idealism combined with a love of the idyllic. Looking down, she saw that he had fallen asleep under her touch. Slowly, she slipped open the top buttons of his dress shirt and slid her hand just over his heart. She closed her eyes, feeling the peaceful beat pulsing under her fingers.

Fey knew that, as much as Paolo loved her, there was also fear. He saw her as the temptress, drawing him to his downfall from grace. This was not a role she wanted for herself, and she would never have touched him like this if he had been awake. It was difficult for her, because she was naturally affectionate and longed for physical contact with him, but even when they kissed, she could feel him tense, like a racehorse at the gate, holding back against the sensuality that had been awakened inside of him. She didn't want a wedge driven between them if it could be avoided.

Looking down at his sleeping face, she found that she wanted to be with him just as much as he longed for her. She would wait as long as he needed. She reflected upon what Yasmine had done to him, with her careless interference. He wasn't ready for all of this. It had been foisted upon him too quickly. She wished her friend had just left him alone. He would have come to understanding in his own good time. Now, though, he struggled with the feelings that, at times, overwhelmed him.

The bright light of the setting sun illuminated her glorious tresses, burnishing them with fiery highlights. Her lavender skin glowed in the magical light of the sunset. He could not recall seeing such a sight before. All else around him seemed to be in dull shades of black and gray. He saw fear in her brilliant, jewel-toned eyes and realized, to his dismay, that he, himself, inspired this fear in her. He had no wish to harm her though, only to drink in the sight of her, the likes of which he had never before encountered.

She reached out her slender arm, offering him an apple, which smelled as fresh and sweet as a summer peach. Wide-eyed with amazement, he took the apple from her beautiful hand and bit into it. To his horror, they both fell into the dark chasm of the hollow tree, which stretched on and on ...

Sometime later, Fey felt Paolo start, as if waking from a dream. She, too, had grown drowsy, comforted by the beat of his heart and their physical closeness.

"Can't keep your hands off me, I see," he teased her, stretching and taking a deep breath.

Recognizing a veiled admonishment in his words, she removed her hand from his chest and leaned down to kiss his forehead. He sat up, pushing back his messy waves of hair with one hand, stifling a yawn with the other.

"Hey, did Natalie call?" he asked absently, rubbing his eyes.

"No," she answered, tucking her feet up on the sofa.

"I'd better call her then. We always talk on Sunday afternoons."

He rose from the sofa to retrieve his cell phone, which lay on the end table.

"I worry about her," he admitted, punching in the number for the school dormitory on his speed dial. "She seems so miserable at that place."

Fey made a sympathetic face and then went to make coffee to help them both shake off their sleepiness. She heard him speaking into the phone and stopped to watch him.

"What do you mean, she's not allowed to talk to me?" he asked roughly. "Let me speak with Sister Phillipa, please."

Paolo flopped back on the sofa in frustration, waiting for the nun to pick up.

"Yes, this is her brother, Paolo," he answered. "What's going on, Sister? I'm starting to get a little worried, here."

Long silence. Paolo again raked his hand through his hair, listening.

"I need to come see you about this," he stated firmly. "Can you please meet with me tomorrow? No, I'm not her guardian, but I care very much about her."

His voice grew more resigned. "Yes, I'll call the Durrands. I understand. Yes, I'm sure they would come with me."

He looked very anxious, as Fey surveyed him from the kitchen doorway. She watched as he rubbed his forehead with one hand, the other still clutching the phone. She noticed that it meant nothing to him that he was not legally related to Natalie. He had promised to act as her brother, and that made it so, to him. He saw clearly that family was precious and clung to the relationships he had created.

"Yes, thank you," he answered into the phone. "And you too."

He turned to meet Fey's worried gaze.

"Uh, I have a problem to deal with."

"Do you want me to come with you?" she offered.

"No, please don't. This is not the way I want you to meet my little sister. I'll go with the Durrands," he decided firmly, burying his face in his hands in frustration.

The next morning, Paolo pulled up to the Durrands' house, his stomach a knot of anxiety. He was met at the front door by, not Marie, but Vincent. After he greeted the police officer with a respectful, "Good morning, sir," Vincent offered him a morsel of good news.

"We're closing in on le Roux," he shared with a steely glint in his blue-gray eyes. "The knife is in the evidence room; we found his Fiat, abandoned in a parking lot in Marseille, covered with blood and fingerprints, and he's been spotted on surveillance cameras in Paris, in spite of having changed his appearance. Natalie pretty much grills me about him every time I talk to her, but you've been more than patient," the officer admitted.

"I'm sure you're doing your best to find him," Paolo offered magnanimously.

Marie stepped out and gave her husband a peck on the cheek. She greeted Paolo with a sad smile, giving his hand a squeeze with both of hers. They took her car to Natalie's school. Her husband, busy with work, wasn't able to join them.

"I'm happy for you, Paolo, that you found someone to spend your life with," she said with genuine feeling. "I hope you know that Vincent and I really do care about you, though it must seem we have an odd way of showing it."

"I understand," he assured her, looking down at his hands. "I've come to realize that it's not just the way things are, but the way they look to others that we have to keep in mind when we act."

"She really did have a bad crush on you," Marie revealed.

"That's what Guy told me, but I wouldn't believe him," Paolo replied.

"Does she know about your engagement?" she asked, watching the road carefully.

"No, not yet. I really wanted to tell her in person," he explained. "Thanks for letting me come with you. I know I have no legal right to be here, but I do love Natalie like a sister and promised to be there for her."

"She needs you, dear."

They talked mostly about Natalie on the way over, Paolo expressing strong concerns about her well-being. She had forbidden either of them from telling anyone at the school about her rape, as she didn't want the other girls finding out and questioning her about it. They had respected her wishes on this, as Marie made frequent visits to check on her, but now, she admitted, she felt it had been a mistake. The two of them made little to no small talk. It just didn't seem appropriate under the circumstances.

They arrived at the school, and Marie pressed a buzzer to be let in. They were led to a bench outside Sister Phillipa's office by an older student. Paolo felt both anxious and fatigued. After what felt like a very long time, the nun beckoned them in with a warm greeting.

"So, you are Paolo." She beamed at him, shaking his hand lightly. "Natalie has told me about you."

"Pleased to meet you, Sister, and I'm sorry if I seemed brusque yesterday," he apologized.

She was a petite but stocky woman with thick glasses, dressed in a long, old-fashioned black habit and veil. The veil covered all of her hair, showing only her face, which shone with a benevolent inner light. Her overall appearance reminded Paolo of the pigeons that hung around the village square. He noticed that about a lot of people—that some animal or other often came to mind when he looked at them.

"No, no. I understand," she assured him. "You obviously care about Natalie, I can see." She then turned to Marie. "Mrs. Durrand, so nice to see you again." Sister Phillipa smiled, shaking her hand as well.

Glancing around nervously, he felt like he was on thin ice already, as his relationship with Natalie seemed to make him suspect in people's eyes. He brushed his palms reflexively against his trousers. His eyes roamed over the bookshelves in her office as if seeking escape. The room was plainly decorated, with a very old but well-cared-for desk, two straight-backed visitors' chairs in quartersawn oak facing it. Religious books lined the walls on either side of the entrance, and behind the desk, two large windows let in ample amounts of natural light. It was practical and no-nonsense, like the occupant.

They all sat down for what promised to be an unpleasant discussion. No amount of cheerfulness on the nun's part would disguise it. She took charge and laid her cards on the table.

"Usually, with this kind of offense," she warned, "we would recommend expulsion. Natalie has been, ah, difficult, from the time she arrived." She attempted to explain the situation diplomatically. "She makes no friends, pushes everyone away, and answers her teachers rudely, especially in religion class, where she is completely disrespectful. One thing I must say, though," she admitted with admiration. "She has a fine mind, but unfortunately, I'm going to have to revoke her scholarship, considering this incident."

What could he say to make her see the gravity of Natalie's situation? He felt like she was on the edge. Would the lifeline he brought today be enough, or would he fail to reach her? Sister Phillipa stood between them, a formidable obstacle. Oh, he felt so unequal to this. He looked anxiously over at Marie, glad she was there to help.

"Please, Sister," Paolo begged, "I'll pay for the window. Please give Natalie another chance. Let me talk to her. I'm sure I can make her see things differently." He felt her slipping deeper into darkness with every Sunday phone conversation, and now he wasn't even allowed to speak with her.

He rose from the hard wooden chair and turned his back to the nun, hugging his arms tightly across his chest, sure he had failed.

Marie stepped in, taking over. "Let us talk for a few minutes, Paolo," she requested of him. "Why don't you step outside and get some air?"

He turned halfway toward her, nodded obediently, and left the room, shutting the door quietly behind him. He was glad to have a moment to regain his composure.

He sat in the quiet, dark entryway for some time, listening to the low hum of their voices. If the discussion hadn't been so grave, he would have found the sound soothing. Both women were well trained in maintaining a calm exterior. He wished he were half as poised as they were.

"Paolo?" Sister Phillipa finally called, opening the door to her office.

He rose from the chair hesitantly.

"I will make sure Natalie receives the proper counseling for what certainly has been an overwhelming amount of personal trauma. As for you, I think it might be a good idea to arrange for expanded visitation rights, as you seem to be the only person she trusts right now," she conceded. "You do realize what a responsibility that is, do you not?"

"That's why I'm here, Sister." He sighed. "So, you'll give Natalie another chance?" he asked hopefully.

"Yes, considering what the poor girl has been through," she answered, her face reflecting kindness and sympathy.

Paolo rushed to take her hands in gratitude, a look of relief on his face.

Natalie threw herself into Paolo's arms, laughing and crying at the same time. The head jailor actually gave them some time alone in the common room, miraculously enough, inviting Marie for coffee in the faculty lounge. She was dressed in a hideous, generic schoolgirl uniform of knee-length plaid skirt and navy blazer that completely effaced who she really was.

"Oh, Paolo, I want to go home so badly, and I miss you terribly."

He held her close for a moment before pulling back so he could look at her. The look on his face was somber and serious, making him seem older and more grown up. She didn't like it at all. "That's not possible, Natalie. You would just end up living with your aunt Yvette, and you told me you didn't want to go there, either."

She rolled her eyes and let out a frustrated groan, hoping for some sympathy. Paolo, though, seemed different. Natalie sensed his irritation and was taken aback. The look on his face, his eyes flashing with anger—he had never shown this side of himself to her, and it left her feeling cowed.

He sighed, eyeing her with frustration. He dropped his arms to his sides. "Do you want to explain this to me?" he asked in an angry tone. "Because I really am having a hard time understanding what you have done."

"Oh, Paolo, please!" she begged him, hugging him as he remained stiffly somber. "Please don't be angry with me. I couldn't bear it." She needed a soft place to land, and suddenly, the last person in the world she could count on had gone parental on her. Was there no place for her to find comfort?

He looked up at the ceiling. "Why, Natalie, why did you do this? Do you know that Marie and I had to beg for them to let you stay? You almost lost your scholarship."

She let go of him, growing defensive. "You want to know why?" she retorted, balling her hands into fists. "Well then, I'll tell you. How can you sit at Mass, week after week, when God has made you an orphan, with no family at all? Then, when you finally find someone who loves you like a father and you get an amazing girlfriend, he takes them both from you in a matter of months. God is cruel, Paolo. I hate Him with all my heart!" she exclaimed with an angry scowl, venom dripping from her voice.

He sank down on the middle cushion of the sofa, as if the shock of her words was too much for him. Well, he did ask. Sometimes the truth wasn't pretty.

"That is not true at all!" he almost shouted back. "How can you think that way?"

"You really want to know? I'll tell you," she retorted bitterly, standing before him, crisply counting the blows the Almighty had dealt her on her fingers. "God has taken my parents, then my sister, then, to make sure I couldn't be with you, He took Guy. I have nothing left. Nothing," she finished breathlessly, waving her palms in front of her in a gesture of dismissal. "I truly hate Him."

"You want someone to blame for your sister's death?" he asked. "Blame me." He pounded his chest in a *mea culpa*, his nostrils flared in disgust.

"No, Paolo," she protested vehemently, putting her hand over his arm. "You did nothing wrong." He was the most innocent, blameless person she had ever met. There was no way she would let him pin himself with René's crime.

"Oh really?" he scoffed. "Well, if I hadn't been so self-absorbed, I would have seen the danger she was in. But no, I thought only of myself and how badly I wanted to be with her." He shook his head. "René looked right at me, when I asked her on that date. I saw his anger and ignored it," he admitted, his face displaying the guilt he felt.

He stood up, and she released her loose hold on his sleeve. "Gilbert tried to talk sense into me, but I wouldn't listen. No, I deserved what I got," he added, shaking his head in shame, his features twisted into a scowl of self-loathing. "If you want to hate anyone, hate me, not God. If I hadn't been so focused on my own selfish desires, Michelle would still be here. But she's not," he lamented in a shaky voice, his face flushed with shame. "She's gone, and my brazen play for her affections was the cause." He had walked over to the window and leaned against the deep white sill as she watched his profile, so full of remorse.

Natalie stopped for a moment at this unexpected turn in the conversation. She was not ready to give up, though, and came back with a rebuttal, rising to join him, crossing her arms defensively. "Well, what about Guy? God took him when we both needed him, without any warning at all."

He turned back to face her. "Natalie, he was, what? Eighty-four? I was lucky to have had him in my life at all." He shrugged, as if it was to be expected.

She saw, though, that his eyes looked wet. Yes, he missed that old man. So did she, really. He had been pretty cool.

"My parents weren't that old," she countered with a toss of her dark, glossy hair.

"God didn't take them either. From what you and Michelle have told me, it was the irresponsible actions of a drunk driver," he reasoned. "Even my friends, who drink way too much, know enough to have a designated driver when they go out."

He sniffed, and she handed him a tissue from her pocket. The only good thing about having bad allergies was you always had a tissue on hand. It seemed they needed them more than most people, as Fate, or God, or the Eternal Torturer would have it.

"Yes, you mean you," she quipped sarcastically, her mouth in a pout. She had always hated those nights, watching him drive away, only to come home at 3:00 a.m. exhausted and stinking of stale cigarette smoke.

"I really don't mind." He shrugged dismissively, wiping his nose as if he too just had allergies. "I didn't like how it felt, to drink too much, and I just want to spend time with them. We already went over that, didn't we? Yes, I do feel guilty about being an 'enabler,' as you call it, so again, I am guilty of sin." He looked absolutely agonized over this, leaning his head back against the white frame of the window and shutting his eyes as if in real pain.

"As for losing me," Paolo continued, his eyes meeting her own, "remember when you followed me into the woods, after Guy's funeral when the Durrands came to take you away from me?"

She nodded, wrapping his hand in her warm grasp.

"Yes," she replied, "you asked God to please take you back."

"I did," he admitted, his features softening into a more familiar expression. "Though I don't even know where *that* is." His gaze grew distant, as it always did when he tried to ponder his clouded origins. She watched him, fascinated by the mystery that refused to unravel itself.

"Do you know why I changed my mind?" he asked her. "Why I stayed here, living with such loneliness?"

She shook her head, her gray eyes large with feeling.

"Because you needed me," he responded for her.

Cupping her chin in his hand, he drew her face upward. Very tenderly, he continued, "Just as I need you. Please get better, Natalie, for me, if not for yourself. You are my family, my little sister."

He leaned in and placed a kiss on her forehead. He pulled her into a protective embrace. She leaned into him, enjoying the rare comfort of his presence, his scent of warm earth and autumn leaves, which she had missed so much.

"Michelle would want you to be happy."

The breeze rustled languidly through the tired trees, which shed their burden with each caress, ready for the sleep the coming winter would bring. Dressed in a simple, tan tunic and trousers, his limp hair pulled back by a leather cord, Guiscard flipped idly through the potion books for which he had traded Honoré, the potion maker of Arbonne, the formula of the Dream Travel potion. It was, in his estimation, a fair exchange, as he no longer possessed the magic to complete the newest concoction that had swept through the forest like savory gossip. It seemed everyone wanted to try the new beverage, which was now renowned for transporting lovers to the ultimate romantic tryst.

A shaft of sunlight appeared on the circular floor, ringed with the history of the tree's life. Guiscard looked up from his studies to see his beloved standing, framed by light, but dimmed in aspect, as if her spirit had escaped and hung in an aura around her instead. He stood up immediately and went to her, taking both her hands in his own.

"So, you have done it," he noted, feeling profoundly guilty that she should have felt such a longing to share his fate.

"Have no fears for me, Guiscard," she assured him cheerfully. "I am indeed at peace."

He noted with amazement that her eyes remained the same luminous shade of emerald green that they had always been. Her hair, though it had lost its raven undertone and shine, was still silky and black. It was as if some remnant of her magic had remained.

"Arcenciel," he proclaimed with awe, "you are truly the most powerful faerie of our clan. I am honored that you have chosen to join with me."

38

Playing to Win

*P*aolo watched with fascination as Luc and Gilbert battled it out on the tennis court. Tuesday was the latter's day off, and late in the afternoon, he would meet up with Luc to burn off some steam. It was unusually warm and sunny, a beautiful, early November day, and the two men were working up a sweat. He sat on the spectators' bench, mesmerized, as his funny, smooth-talking friend turned into a savage gladiator, like in the old movies he had watched with Natalie on Sunday afternoons.

Gilbert stood, shifting his weight, the lines of his face tight and hostile. Luc stood on the other side, ball in hand, trying to mask his intimidation. With his much greater height and broad reach, he had a definite physical advantage over his compact adversary, but Gilbert knew how to channel his energies with fierce intensity, making up for his smaller size, and moved with the easy agility his light frame allowed. As the ball came his way, Gilbert smashed it back with a savage snarl. Luc was hard pressed to keep up but seemed up for the challenge.

Paolo had the feeling that this was not just a game. He could see that something was being worked out in Gilbert's mind as he spent what seemed to be an enormous amount of energy chasing a fuzzy yellow ball around, slamming it back over the net as it came his way. He sensed that the ball was a target for some kind of frustration he was feeling. With Gilbert, though, Paolo reflected, there were so many issues fighting for attention in his psyche, it was hard to say which one was being smacked back to Luc on the other side of the net.

He wished he had a similar outlet for his own pent-up feelings. It was agonizing, waiting to be with Fey. Every time they were together, he felt tested. Each time they kissed, he wanted more but stopped before things got out of hand. She was so patient, always leaving the decision up to him. He almost wished she would push him away. It would be easier. He wouldn't tell her this, though. She would think him weak.

The game went on for some time. Gilbert was bathed in sweat but didn't let up on his intensity. Luc was beginning to tire, but valiantly kept up his effort. With a final growl, Gilbert smacked the ball over the net one last time. It bounced just out of Luc's reach, and the game was over.

Paolo was amused to see that his friend's face instantly relaxed, a peaceful smile replacing the angry scowl as he shook hands with Luc, who humbly bowed in mock submission to his small but mighty adversary. Gilbert just laughed, clapping him on his sweaty back.

"Sometimes, I think you're not quite right in the head," Luc observed. "I swear you make those crazy Jackie Chan noises just to throw my game off."

Gilbert just laughed and shrugged his shoulders. "Hey, I just play to win. Anyway, the game's over. No need to analyze it," he lectured. "There's only one thing you'll find digging into a pile of manure."

Luc laughed, seemingly mollified by his competitor's casual attitude to his win.

"So, Paolo, maybe next time you would like to play, hmm?" he asked his friend, who sat, his face suffused with admiration, on the spectators' bench.

"Uh, I don't think so, but thanks anyway. I get enough exercise with my work."

The victor just shrugged, giving him a humble, have-it-your-way smile, and headed to the showers, wiping his face on a clean white towel.

Yasmine trudged up the stairs with her suitcase. The small apartment she had procured was, according to the rather disinterested young real estate agent from Arbonne, the cheapest thing she could find. It was a steep, three flights of stairs above the grocery store. A bedroom too small to turn the bed the other way, a kitchen the size of a closet, and a bathroom that made the kitchen look spacious made up the bulk of the space, if that word could accurately be used.

It was all she needed, though. She had few possessions, and would not be spending much time in the tiny flat, anyway. She stuffed her clothes into the beat-up dresser and then went out into the fresh, fall air to get adjusted to her new human state.

She wondered what Fey's initial impressions were, as she walked through Achères for the first time. Had her feet clicking on the pavement sounded strange to her ears, after gliding noiselessly through the air? Had she enjoyed the feeling of standing firm against the wind? Had she found standing on the ground looking up as dizzying as she did, after spending so much time aloft?

She sauntered through the village. She made a stop at the market, where she purchased a large red apple and a delicious-looking sugar cookie but found she was too excited to eat, especially when she caught sight of her beloved making his way to the flower shop. Ducking into a doorway, she watched him unlock the door to his apartment and disappear inside.

It won't be long, my love, she told him silently. *I'm in this game to win.*

She spent the rest of the afternoon occupied with the more mundane tasks of being human, such as picking the right color for her cell phone and then finding a matching lipstick for her new dress. She rewarded herself for her accomplishments by reading *Much Ado about Nothing* in the library, where she sat curled up in the stacks, surreptitiously enjoying the novel taste of food as a human and daydreaming about the moment she would first gaze into her beloved's eyes.

"Your time is coming soon, le Roux!" a voice called out.

René searched the club with his gaze, the music sounding muffled and garbled. On the dance floor, in the midst of the pulsating crowd, a cloaked woman glided toward him, her red eyes full of malicious delight.

He rose quickly from his seat and tried to flee, but his arm was caught. Turning to free himself, he saw Michelle holding him fast in her grasp.

"Let me go!" he barked.

Michelle dug in deep with her fingernails, drawing blood, and René began to panic. The red-eyed vision drew closer ...

"Ouch, watch it!"

René woke up to find that he had punched his girlfriend in the face.

"Sorry," he apologized, though he couldn't really be held accountable for what he had done in his sleep, could he?

"You're crazy!" she exclaimed, ripping the sheets back and storming off to the bathroom.

He reached into his nightstand drawer, shook a few pills from a bottle, and then swallowed them without benefit of water. Manon had pulled on her clothes and had her purse in her hand.

"Wait!" he called.

She just shot him a black look and stormed out of the apartment. He flopped back onto the bed, covering his face with his hands.

39

Second Son

Yasmine stood outside of J. de Gaul and Son, breathing deeply to compose herself. After several days of gathering her courage and mulling over her approach, she had thought up the perfect plan to get Gilbert to go out with her. Checking her reflection one last time in the shop window as the last customers left—her blonde curls shining; sky-blue eyes sparkling with anticipation; pink-painted lips covered with sheer gloss; pearl drop earrings dancing—she turned to go in.

Well, here goes, she steeled herself, smoothing her pink silk, runched minidress. Stopping in the doorway, she looked nervously about to see where he was. He was in the midst of steaming some new suits. She watched his profile as he worked. He looked a little tired but just as polished as ever in a dark-blue pinstripe suit, white shirt, and pink silk tie. *Very classic,* she thought. He looked up to see her staring at him, shut the steaming tool off, and hung the steam nozzle over the metal hook.

She walked slowly over to where he stood, her heart pounding in her chest. He looked her up and down shamelessly, his eyes widening at her approach.

"Hello," he greeted her formally. "Is there something I can help you find?"

"Yes." She smiled, seeing by the look on his face that he was interested. He was so transparent it was funny. "I'm here to see you, actually," she told him, enjoying the expression on his face as it brightened. She had never been so close to him before, and it was making her crazy. He smelled deliciously spicy, and with his full lips parted just ever so slightly in surprise, she longed to reach over and kiss him, right then and there.

"Me?" he asked, all of a sudden becoming as unglued as Paolo the first time he spoke with Michelle. "Have we met?" he questioned her in a panic, his features tensing.

"No," she answered with a smile and a shake of her head. She was beginning to feel more confident, as he appeared to be the one struggling. Good. It would make things so much easier to manipulate.

He met her gaze, looking relieved, and waited for her to continue. She looked deep into his gorgeous marine-azul eyes and went on. "I'm a very good friend of Fey," she explained. "And I want to show up at her wedding. She doesn't know I'm here. The only way I can think of to go to the wedding and the reception without having her find out I'm in town or causing an inconvenience, since I obviously don't have an invitation, is for you to take me as your date and not tell them who I am ahead of time. Just say you're bringing a date, and leave it at that. It'll be fun and such a surprise for Fey." She giggled, letting him in on the plan. She didn't want Fey to know she was there until she had secured Gilbert's affections. Until then, she would lay low. She knew it would be a while before the wedding. That would give her the time she needed to win his heart.

"Oh, silly me," she added, looking, she hoped, sufficiently abashed. "You probably already have a girlfriend, though."

"No, no. It's fine, really," he assured her. He smiled, apparently willing to be complicit in her scheme, and admitted, "I really love surprises." He drew closer to her with a crooked smile and a raised eyebrow.

She held her ground, dizzy with desire, as he stood less than two feet from her. She handed him her phone number, which he reached out slowly to take, their hands both grasping the slip of paper as if it were charged. Their gazes locked for a moment; it felt like time had stopped. She saw the fear in his eyes and let go of the paper.

She knew what he was going through, and it broke her heart. She loved him to distraction and had come in the hope that, knowing him so well from all of the time she had surreptitiously watched as he argued with his father, hid his panic attacks from the world, and continued to fill his body with poison because his heart was empty, she could help to steer him away from his destruction before it was too late. The strain of it was taking its toll on him already. His hair had lost its shine and was falling out from poor nutrition. He was growing too thin, and he now always looked tired. Even his lively sense of humor was dulled under the weight of his self-abuse.

Yasmine looked at him with compassion on her face. He read her name on the paper, pocketed it, and again met her eyes.

"So, would it be all right if I called to, you know, spend a little time together first, so we can get to know each other before the wedding?" he asked in an unusually hesitant tone.

"Tomorrow night," she told him, "after work," knowing full well that Friday night was "date night" in his mind. It worked out well, as she didn't want to wait any more than he probably did to get the ball rolling.

He smiled, taking her hand in his, and then playfully pressed it to his lips. "Tomorrow night, then, Yasmine."

She smiled like a dimpled Mona Lisa, tilting her head in flirtatious response. Not saying another word, she gracefully sauntered out of the shop with the unseen knowledge that he was watching her every step with hungry anticipation.

Once outside, she ducked around the side of the shop and leaned against the wall in the alley, holding her hand over her heart, hoping he hadn't noticed that it was practically throbbing out of her chest. She felt so dizzy that she was afraid she would pass out, then and there. She held the back of her hand to her face, savoring how his lips had grazed her skin.

Her breathing slowly calming itself, Yasmine made her way to the tiny apartment she had rented, feeling hopeful, yet afraid. She had given up everything with no promise of success. Fey had come sure in the knowledge that Paolo loved her to the depths of his soul. With Gilbert, well, she had only her own love to give him, with no promise that he would ever return her feelings. She hurried home, her heels tapping a rhythm on the pavement that matched the rapid thrumming of her heart, accompanied by the dry leaves of autumn, swirling playfully about her kitten-heeled feet.

Gilbert picked Yasmine up directly after work. She looked, to him, absolutely ravishing in one of those clingy red shift dresses that showed off every luscious curve. She noted his appreciative glance, smiling at him seductively, her beautiful dimple making an appearance on her cheek. He had made reservations at Denis à Achères for dinner. He ordered champagne and then asked her with courteous forethought if she, too, was a vegetarian like her friends. *You only get one chance at a first impression,* he thought, and he really liked this beautiful, assertive woman.

He kept the conversation light, regaling her with his best stories, enjoying the sight of her brilliant smile and the sound of her deep, sensual laugh. She was, to him, absolutely fascinating, exciting even. She made him laugh more than any other girl he had dated. She was funny, but not a dumb blonde by any means. A lively intelligence lay below her silly bluster. She was like ecstasy, in human form. He had to have more. He was addicted after the first dose of her.

He tried his hardest to make their date a success. This girl was different from anyone he had ever met. It was odd. They had never even seen each other before, yet, in some strange way, there was a comfort level as if they had known each other all their lives. He had dressed carefully that day in his best suit. Like some bizarre textile karma, his bright-red tie, again, matched her dress to perfection. Weird, he usually never wore a tie on a date, but then, he had never dated a girl like Yasmine.

"So, what do you do, for a living?" he asked her. She already knew what he did, obviously.

"Well ..." She paused for thought, studying her right hand, examining her manicured fingers. "How do I explain this? I'm kind of a relationship expert."

"Really?" he asked, appreciating the irony of it. *Imagine, the king of failed relationships dating a "relationship expert"? Too funny,* he reflected silently. Also, he noted with ingrained discernment, *She's hiding something.*

"I'm sort of looking for work right now," she admitted with a hint of desperation in her voice.

"Good luck with that." He rolled his eyes dismissively. "My friend Latif has been looking for something that pays decent for months, with no luck.

My dad finally gave him some work part-time at the store. He seems really happy with it, though, and at least he isn't whining so much about money anymore."

"Any suggestions?" she asked, hopefully. "You probably know lots of businesspeople in town. There must be somebody hiring. I'm really not in a position to be picky," she went on nervously.

"Hmm … The only place I can think of off the top of my head is the café across the street from the store, The Little Penguin. They're looking for a barista. I think it might be perfect for a 'people person' such as yourself, until you can find something more permanent."

"Do you think you could give me a recommendation?" she asked him, leaning forward in her seat eagerly.

Gilbert leaned back, enjoying the moment. He smiled wickedly at her and raised an eyebrow. *How badly do you want it?* he refrained from asking, rolling his tongue against the inside of his lip, fingers steepled. "Sure," he told her, behaving himself for his friends' sake.

But Yasmine caught his naughty glance, and biting her lower lip, she shot him a seductive look in return. Her correct interpretation of his unspoken innuendo was like throwing gasoline on the fire. He couldn't wait to get her back to his apartment, to touch her. He had never wanted a girl this badly in his life.

They lingered over dinner, truly enjoying each other's company. When Gilbert asked his date to his apartment for a drink, she hesitantly accepted. He wondered if deep down, she was secretly shy. He hoped not. He had never had much luck with shy girls. Too hard to get past first base.

After paying the check, he helped his date into her coat, and they walked the short distance to his flat. Feeling very comfortable with her, he reached for her hand and noted with relief that she beamed at him with genuine pleasure. He liked the way her dimples showed when she was happy. It was really cute. He grinned back at her as they took a leisurely stroll through the darkened streets, his pulse quickening at her closeness and the lovely smell of her perfume.

His second-floor flat above the flower shop was tasteful, neat, and masculine: dark, rich colors; leather furniture; and spare in design. It smelled of lemony furniture wax, as the cleaning person always came on Fridays. Yasmine seemed, for all her hesitancy at accepting his invitation, strangely at home, and after hanging her coat on the rack in the entry, she sank gracefully onto the end of the sofa. It was kind of confusing, just where he stood with her. She had the same mysterious air that Fey and Paolo had. Why would Fey not invite her to the wedding, if they were such good friends? Why did Fey refuse to talk about their past, pushing away his inquiries? These people were a beautiful, fascinating enigma that he resolved to figure out. Perhaps this girl would be the key.

To tilt the odds in his favor, he mixed two double-strength, amber-colored drinks from top-shelf scotch and handed her one with a smile before sitting down next to her on the middle seat. She smiled back coyly, taking a sip.

"Oh, you naughty boy," she scolded, looking over at him with her baby-blue, almond-shaped eyes narrowed accusingly. "Trying to loosen me up, are you?"

He shrugged apologetically, flushing at having been seen through so clearly. She had seemed so tense when he had suggested she come over and acted like she had her guard up. What else was he to do?

She placed the glass on the end table on a green, marble coaster, watching him as he took a generous swallow of the pungent liquid. An awkward silence followed. He placed his own glass on the coffee table and then leaned into her, the perfumey sweetness of the whiskey flavoring their first kiss. He wasn't trying to be aggressive or pushy but, rather, inviting and confident. He drew her in, his hands caressing her face and neck, not touching her anywhere off-limits, yet.

Patience, de Gaul, he reminded himself.

She responded warmly as he kissed her with practiced skill, hungrily, but with courteous restraint. She put her hands on his chest, and he inhaled sharply. His heart began to beat hard and fast. It was as if she had shot him up with adrenaline through her fingertips. Her touch was literally an aphrodisiac. He acted as if it was an invitation and reached down to deftly unzip her dress as he continued to taste her lips like they were dessert. His brain began to shut down, intoxicated by her like no other girl he had ever been with.

Unexpectedly, he felt her push him away. He looked confused, disappointment clouding his flushed features, his breath coming heavy. *No* was a word he rarely heard from anyone, but he was man enough to understand that when a woman said no, you backed off, no matter how badly you wanted her. And he did want her so, so badly.

"But I thought—" he began, his heart sinking with dismay.

"You thought I wanted to hook up with you," Yasmine interrupted angrily, reaching behind herself to pull her zipper back up with the flexibility of a yoga instructor demonstrating gomukhasana.

He hung his head, looking apologetic. He really liked Yasmine and didn't want to come across as a jerk. "We don't have to, if you don't want," he protested meekly, sincerely meaning it. He could wait. He wasn't some kind of perverted sex addict, after all.

"Listen, Gilbert," she explained in an expert tone of voice, "remember, this is what I do, what I'm good at. How have your relationships worked out so far?" As she looked at him with her head tucked down, her eyes searching his, he thought about his long line of failed relationships.

Ouch! he thought, pressing his lips together, surveying her with respect mingled with intimidation. He realized he was playing with a formidable adversary here, and the ball was now in his court. He looked away and gave a self-deprecatory laugh.

"Hmm, thought so," she nodded. "Let's try something different, shall we? Slow things down a little and take our time."

Now it was his turn to hit the ball back over, returning her serve. "If you know so much about me—and I'm assuming Fey has told you what you know—then why do you want to go out with me?" he asked, truly wondering. She would, of course, know of his many, many flaws—his self-indulgence, his bossiness with his friends, and, not least by any means, his addictions. He made no effort to hide any of this from anyone except his father.

"Oh, Gilbert, you are such a sweet guy!" she exclaimed, pulling him close so that his head rested comfortably on her shoulder, twining her arm through his. "You've been such a fine friend to Paolo. Fey is so grateful to you for that, I know. I see a warm, generous person with an incredibly kind heart and an amazing sense of fun."

He stared at the melting ice in the glass on the coffee table as she questioned him. "What do you see?"

He saw the second son, who would never measure up to his older brother, who would forever be a hero in his father's eyes. Gilbert knew in his heart that, if his brother had lived, Tristan would have been groomed to take over the family business instead of him. His father's constant criticism was a hurtful reminder of how inadequate he was. He saw a man who couldn't control his own appetites and didn't even try. He loosened his tie with a few rough movements, a sulk on his face.

Why is she doing this to me? he wondered. She was being sadistic, toying with him like a cat with a poor, helpless mouse. If he wanted a therapist, he would pay for one. He reached over to the coffee table, picked up his drink, and downed it in a few gulps. He looked over at her, his face awash in pain. He hated thinking about all of this crap. It hurt too much, and she had no right digging into his psyche. Why, she barely knew him and here she was, digging out all of his demons.

"You seem to know a lot about me," he admitted. "But if you say you want to go out with me because of my fabulous inner qualities, well, you're going to be very disappointed."

"Oh, now. You don't really believe that, do you?" she countered in a soft voice, giving his hand a squeeze.

He didn't respond but just looked at her with a tight frown. Then the whiskey began to wash the harsher thoughts from his brain. Gilbert eyed Yasmine's glass sitting, untouched, on the end table. He had to resist the urge to reach across her and take it. He still, in spite of his outburst, really liked her and didn't want to do anything overly rude that might spoil his chances. She was a lot more refined than most of the girls he went out with, and of course, he concluded, her expectations of his behavior would be higher as a result.

"Listen," she coaxed him softly, breaking the silence that had ensued, "I think we have something here, you and I, and you're right, I do know a lot about you—from Fey," she interjected quickly. "But if you really want to see me again, which I'd like very much," she added, "I'd like to try a real relationship, if you don't mind."

A real relationship? he thought, still studying his hands. *What does she mean by that?* he wondered. *Psychobabble, or just girl talk for "here's the fine print"?*

"I don't understand," he answered. "What do you want from me?" He met her gaze, his eyes still full of the hurt she had stirred up.

"I know you're using," she told him frankly.

He looked down at his hands and frowned uncomfortably. Somehow, with her, it didn't seem so insignificant as it had with other girls, whom he had invited to do lines with him in his apartment, including that last hookup

246

with Jocelyn. To have Yasmine confirm she knew this about him was kind of embarrassing really.

"If you really think I'm worth your time," she then challenged as he looked sheepishly over at her, "I want you to quit, and …" She turned his face to her own, her voice deadly serious, "I will not share you with anyone."

Oh, so she had heard about Jocelyn too. *There must be some social networking site just for girls, where they post all of a guy's flaws like an ingredient list,* he thought sarcastically. After his disastrous mishap with Marie-David, there was no way he was going to try juggling two relationships at one time anyway. It was too complicated and not worth the backlash.

"Sure, babe," he answered, skepticism evident on his face. "I'm all yours."

As for his habit, it was getting pretty expensive anyway. Even he realized he had better start cutting back or he would be in a pile of debt. His credit card balance was already getting alarmingly high from the advances he had had to put on it between paychecks.

So, she wasn't shy. She was just canny, this one. Well, he would wear her down. He could tell she was attracted to him, and yes, she was right—there was some amazing chemistry going on between the two of them. He wasn't going to give up on the first serve. This was one match he was going to win. It would be interesting, going nose to nose with a relationship counselor. A mischievous expression effaced his look of hurt. She smiled to see it.

"If I promise to behave," he asked with a look of longing, "can I have another kiss?"

He wasn't about to let her leave just yet. It was nice having a girl around again. His world was overloaded with men right now.

"Mmm, you're hard to resist," she cooed playfully, "as yummy as a sweet little bonbon."

She reached over, grabbed his loosened tie, and pulled him toward her. He contented himself with a nice, innocent game of tonsil hockey before walking her back to her apartment for the night, a much more satisfying pastime than her choice of mental tennis.

Fleur returned to Fey's bower, which she had claimed as her own, as the closet was the only one in their domain large enough to contain the combined wardrobes of herself, Yasmine, and Fey. She had watched with delight as the haberdasher of Achères succumbed handily to the siren allure of a daughter of the Fae. She had sprinkled a drop of enchantment on the paper the two lovers had gripped, thus binding their souls' destinies. Did Yasmine notice, or was she, herself, so besotted by the object of her desires that she hadn't even thought of her old pupil? Fleur guessed the latter, giggling with vicarious enjoyment of her former teacher's face as she became lost in the blue sea of her man's eyes.

Flopping down on the bed, she smiled in satisfaction at a job well done, but then, as the darkness swallowed the forest, her own heart was gripped with loneliness. They say the cobbler's children go barefoot. The new matchmaker was about to find out the verity of this old chestnut.

Manon sat in the club where she had met René, makeup partially covering her black eye. She wore her hair over that side, obscuring the damage so people wouldn't stare. A woman sat down next to her, though other seats were available, and ordered a glass of wine. Taking a furtive peek, she noticed that, even though it was dark in the nightclub, the woman wore dark sunglasses. Maybe she was blind.

"Does he hit you often?" the stranger asked. Her voice was unusually clear over the pulsing music, though she spoke softly.

Manon was taken aback. Ex-girlfriend, perhaps? "No," she responded defensively, looking down into her drink.

"What did he tell you he does for a living?" the woman went on, staring straight ahead at the dancing throng on the floor.

"He's a day trader," she lied.

The woman snorted in derision. *Yes, definitely an ex-girlfriend,* she thought. *No use covering up for him.*

Manon took a sip of her martini. "I don't get involved in his business dealings," she informed the woman beside her.

"Nonetheless," the pale, dark-haired woman instructed, "you may end up wishing you hadn't gotten involved with him at all."

Manon couldn't argue with that. There was something weird going on with that guy. She couldn't pin it down, but the longer she was around him, the more uncomfortable he made her.

"You're the only one who knows where he lives, besides his business partner," she went on in a dismissive tone, running her finger, with its long, painted nail, over the rim of her glass, which was filled with chardonnay.

This was said with pointed inference. *What is this woman getting at?* Manon wondered.

"Look up René le Roux on the Internet," the shrouded female suggested. "And Michelle Bertrand, and hope, dear girl," she finished, "that you don't end up like her."

The woman paid for the drink she hadn't touched, as well as Manon's, and then swept out with regal elegance, the crowd parting for her, yet seeming, at the same time, completely unaware of her presence. She turned to give Manon a pointed look, her crimson lips tight and tense. Manon looked away for a second, unnerved. When she glanced back, the figure had disappeared from sight.

A warm breeze ruffled the canvas awning. The morning sun was peeking overtop the buildings. No array of fruit appeared to entice the appetite. The wooden crates remained empty. A woman strolled by, her lush, dark hair swaying as she walked. It was Michelle. She disappeared under the awning.

Paolo felt compelled to follow and swooped down from above. Upon facing the door to the shop, though, he found it shut tightly. A paper fluttered on the door. Turning to go, he found that he couldn't move. His arms were bound tightly by an unseen force. He gasped as he stared straight into the eyes of René, who held a paving brick in his hand. He sneered and heaved it with all his might.

Paolo awoke with a jolt. He lay for some time, thinking. Sleep refused to return, so he switched on the light. Making his way in the semidarkness, he sat in front of the computer and pulled up the Internet search engine. It was time to start figuring out the truth, whether Fey wanted to help him or not. Whatever it was, he would face it. Anything was better than not knowing.

He trusted her completely, feeling strongly that she wouldn't want to be with him if he had been a bad person before. He also believed Gilbert's explanation that dreams didn't mean what they seemed to. If they did, it would be completely ridiculous, because, aside from this recurring dream about Paolo the murdered fruit vendor, he dreamed he could fly and dreamed of a weird, surreal childhood peopled with bats and a profound spiritual peace that could only exist in heaven.

Sophie groaned in her sleep, stretched out on the living room rug. In the darkness, Paolo began the time-consuming search for his past.

40

Office Visits

Fey agreed to meet with the priest. They had decided to have the wedding at St. Fare, though she would have preferred to hold it in the forest. In the Catholic faith, she discovered, weddings had to be held in a church, It seemed strange to her, as nature made her feel closer to the Creator than a man-made building, but, to Paolo, it was important and she didn't want to cause him any additional anxiety.

She surveyed Father Lambert's office with a glance. It was a somber, wood-paneled closet of a room, lined with bookshelves holding sanctioned literature. The priest himself struck Fey as an uninspired thinker, dishing out the fare he had ingested his whole life. Still, there was an intrinsic sensibility to him that prevented her from dismissing him entirely. She gave the graying but fit man the benefit of the doubt, deciding to remain silent for the better part of the visit.

"Please tell me you're kidding, Father."

As the engaged couple sat in his office on a rainy Saturday afternoon in early November, the water beating against the solitary window, Father Lambert had just told him that they would have to wait six months before getting married.

"But, why?" he protested, some of his old petulance flaring up.

The priest proceeded to explain the sad fact that over half of all marriages ended in divorce. The Church attempted to stem this tide of failure by slowing things down and arming the newly married with strategies for success.

"But that won't happen with Fey and me," he continued to argue in an outraged tone.

"Hah, if I had a sou for every time I heard that!" The priest laughed wryly. "Listen, Paolo. Just look at Jacob, who waited seven years for his bride, only to end up with the wrong woman. Six months is nothing."

Paolo snorted in disagreement and slouched in his chair, arms crossed, a look of utter disgust on his face. Fey just looked at him sympathetically. She knew he would wait, if he had to, but that didn't mean he would enjoy it. She was learning to understand his beliefs but had not fully embraced them herself. The restrictions he felt bound by were too harsh for her free-spirited nature, and she could see that the scruples he endured, along with the unnecessary hardships he put himself through as penances, caused him more suffering than they eased.

She liked his Jesus, thinking him without compare in his ideals and practices, but the rest of Guy's well-used book, not so much. It was too overloaded with yang. She had dismissively muttered a quotation from the Bard on their first visit to St. Fare:

> Was ever book containing such vile matter
> So fairly bound? O, that deceit should dwell
> In such a gorgeous palace!

Paolo, lost in his own contemplations, had not heard her.

Also, she viewed the idea of submissiveness by way of gender to be uncivilized and inferior, as her own people viewed each other's decision-making status based on an honest assessment of a person's level of wisdom and expertise in the topic being discussed. A mate was chosen who would balance deficiencies in one's own character, and one humbly and gratefully followed the advice of the better judge of a particular situation. That was why Guiscard had taken such pains to make a good choice, which he, in her estimation, definitely had.

She felt that St. Paul's view of marriage tainted it, turning what should be a loving, mutually respectful relationship into a power struggle, with the physically stronger mate taking control by might. She looked over at her sturdy, large man with a critical glance. She could have never married him if she had had the least suspicion he would see things that way and, truth be told, would have preferred her own beautiful tradition of handfasting, where the betrothed couple had their hands bound together by the matchmaker with a silken cord, representing the joining of their hearts and destinies, under the silvery light of the full moon. Paolo, though, had been taught that such pagan beliefs were inherently sinful.

She knew that his religion's hair-splitting baffled him, as he saw everything with the purity of spirit of a child. He had assured her as much when she had called him on this issue. He had said, with a look of humility on his face, "God help me, if I ever get so full of pride that I feel I deserve the final say in all things that concern the both of us. I just want back that feeling of perfect peace that I know in my heart was once mine, and this is the only way I know to get there," he had explained. He now sat, stewing and frustrated at Father Lambert's harsh dictum. The way back would not be easy.

"You might even learn something along the way," the priest counseled, seeing Paolo's frustration.

He answered with an uncharacteristically sarcastic retort, "Yes, I have just now learned why people move in together without getting married," looking down with barely disguised hostility at this unforeseen roadblock.

Father Lambert folded his arms and frowned, but Fey laughed, enjoying the rare moment of rebellion her fiancé displayed.

Natalie started therapy that week for post-traumatic stress disorder. She liked her therapist and was relieved to be able to talk to a woman about what had happened to her. She could tell when she had talked with Paolo that, although he sympathized with her pain, he didn't really understand it fully. She was pretty sure he was still a virgin himself, and he saw the world through his own filter. She didn't really expect him to understand the depravity she had been forced to take part in. He was like a kid sometimes, as if he had been sheltered from all of life's ugliness until the day he had walked into Achères.

An older woman along the same vein as Marie Durrand, Dr. Fournier wore a pair of black readers perched on the middle of the bridge of her nose. Her dark hair was pulled back in a ponytail and swept elegantly to one side of her face. She wore just enough makeup to look nice, without making the mistake of overdoing it, which, in Natalie's opinion, only made the over-forty set seem ten years older, rather than the opposite. She was tall and slim and wore a pencil skirt and fitted, sky-blue sweater, finished off by a pair of black stilettos. It was a very confident look.

She should take Marie shopping, Natalie thought with condescension toward Mrs. Grizzly and admiration toward the navigator of her psyche.

Dr. Fournier perched on the edge of her desk, an ornate piece with curved, carved legs. The office, overall, was decorated in a feminine, European style, with a crystal chandelier suspended from the high white ceiling, framed in numerous layers of woodwork. Paintings of eighteenth-century women smiled coyly from their vantage points on the walls. A sideboard with a large, porcelain swain wooing a shepherdess was lit by a shaft of sunlight that had filtered through the sheer, airy curtains swathing the long, narrow windows overlooking a large park.

"So, let me understand," Dr. Fournier clarified in her soft, feminine voice, clutching her readers, "you didn't report the attack because you felt ashamed. Can you tell me, exactly, why you feel this way?"

Natalie shifted her weight in the comfortable, crewel-adorned chair.

"I just do," she replied, not very helpfully.

"Tell me what you think you did wrong. If you feel ashamed, you must think you were at fault in some way."

"I fought as hard as I could, but he was just too strong for me," she lamented, looking out the window to avoid her gaze.

"So, you blame yourself for being weaker than your attacker? Considering the fact that you were only twelve years old when it happened, do you think that maybe you are being a little harsh on yourself?"

Natalie looked up at her therapist, her gray eyes wide. All of a sudden, she felt that she was not being fair to herself. Why should she take the blame for what René had done? She certainly hadn't chosen this. Why should she feel guilt for someone else's wrongdoing? She looked at Dr. Fournier with a heavy gaze.

"I just want to feel clean." She sighed and began tearing up, her lower lip trembling. That was the crux of it. "All the saints seem to be pure, and I feel dirty, because of what he did to me. My best friend values this, even though he's a guy, and they usually don't have the same feelings about it. He's very religious," she explained, cutting straight to the heart of what was eating at her. She wiped at her eyes with her sleeve.

"Does he know what happened to you?" the therapist asked, handing her a tissue.

"Yes." Natalie nodded. "I told him so he wouldn't find out from someone else. If you don't think that was hard to do …" She wiped her eyes and nose, regaining her composure.

"Does he judge you, make you feel badly about what happened?"

"Oh, no, not at all," she protested, not wanting her to think ill of him. "The first thing he did was to hug me. I was surprised. He's so, um …" She wasn't sure of the right word. Too many of the words they used to describe the "window saints" were loaded with bad meaning in her mind. *Pious, holy, good*—they were all words she never wanted to hear again. "He's what I wish I was," she explained. "Maybe that's why I got this crush on him, that I had when we first met." She paused. "Now he's like my brother, though. I think it's better that way, because he's so much older than me. But anyway, he didn't think I was too dirty to touch, and that meant the world to me."

To Yasmine's delight, Gilbert kept his promise, not only giving her a recommendation for the job she sought, but also doing his best to make sure she got it. Within a week, Achères's newest resident had gainful employment. She had stopped by to thank him at his workplace, telling him with enthusiasm that she was to start training the next day.

"I'm afraid Fey will see me," the new barista fretted. Gilbert had warned her that she, too, frequented the café on her way to her job as Michelle's replacement as a natural remedies expert in the herb store.

"I've got that all figured out," Gilbert boasted. "Come with me," he directed her.

He led her to the changing rooms and handed her a small box. Upon opening it, she seemed confused and returned his smug look of satisfaction with a puzzled stare.

"They're colored contact lenses," he explained, "to change your eye color. We're going to disguise you." He grinned.

"Oh, Bonbon, you're so clever!" she exclaimed, giving him a quick kiss on the cheek, which he quickly returned before she could back away.

"Go ahead," he urged her. "Put them in. I can't wait to see."

He explained to her how to put them in her eyes, as he himself wore contacts. After a frustrating struggle, she got them in and turned to face him. He nodded approvingly and held up his finger for her to wait. He ran into the storeroom and brought out another, larger box.

"Close your eyes, Yasi," he instructed her excitedly and turned her to face the mirror.

She could feel him putting something on her head, playing with her hair. She giggled, as it tickled.

"No peeking," he warned her in a playful tone.

"Okay, done!" he exclaimed.

Standing before her was a brunette with long, silky hair and heavy bangs that brushed over the tops of her eyebrows. Her eyes were a light brown. She squealed with delight and threw herself into his arms.

"Oh, you are amazing!" she cried.

"Yes, I know," he purred, brushing back her faux hair to nibble on her ear.

She giggled and quoted in English: "All the world's a stage, and all the men and women merely players. That's from *As You Like It*," she informed him.

He nodded, admiration clearly written on his face, though it was obvious the reference escaped him.

Jacques, hearing the commotion, glanced in to make sure everything was all right. Yasmine saw him over her boyfriend's shoulder, a stern look of disapproval on his face. He coughed loudly to get his son's attention, appearing seriously annoyed at their noisy shenanigans.

Gilbert, hearing the gruff warning, turned sheepishly to face his father. "Oh, Dad, uh, this is Yasmine du Bois. She's my new girlfriend. Yasi, this is my dad, Jacques de Gaul."

Jacques nodded curtly, glancing with hostility at the source of the disturbance. Yasmine was embarrassed. She knew it looked really bad, her hanging all over Gilbert in the changing room like this. She didn't want Jacques to think she was trashy. So much for first impressions.

"Son, do you think you could continue your personal life after work? I need to do the banking, and someone needs to be out there, waiting on customers," he scolded.

Gilbert nodded. To Yasmine, he appeared literally to shrink under his father's rebuke. He shot an apologetic look at her and fled to the front of the store, where several customers awaited his assistance. She hung back to watch, enjoying just being in the same room with him.

He was helping an older gentleman pick out a suit. He looked like a wealthy businessman, maybe a lawyer. Gilbert was very reserved and respectful. He handled himself with pleasant seriousness, mirroring the mood of his conservative customer. She admired his ability to adapt himself to so many different situations. He was like a chameleon, ever changing to his surroundings.

He went to measure the man, to check for sleeve and pant lengths, reaching into his coat pocket for his tape measure, only to find it wasn't there.

"Oh, Yasi, be a dear, would you, and run up to my dad's desk? There's an extra measuring tape in the top right drawer."

She climbed the stairs to the office, looking in hesitantly. She had never gone up there before. She spotted the desk and pulled the drawer open, spying several bottles of pills. Curious, she reached in and removed them, reading the labels. A powerful pain medication dated from over a year ago, yet still full, lay next to a bottle of antidepressants, recently purchased. Her intuition went off, and she suspected that Jacques was in as bad of shape, in his own way, as Gilbert. He buried his pain in work, Gilbert, in self-abuse. She placed both cylinders carefully back in their original position and then found the measuring tape in the back of the drawer and hurried to give it to her boyfriend.

41

New Job

Yasmine had just finished her first day at work. She couldn't wait to cross over to the haberdashery to find Gilbert and thank him for his help. Upon entering J. de Gaul and Son, she saw that he was busy with customers, so she waited unobtrusively until he was finished. He saw her, and his face brightened. She smiled her dimpled smile and pushed her fingers forward to gesture, "Go on, then. I'll wait," which he answered with a grateful nod.

She couldn't get enough of the sight of him, so beautiful and polished looking. He took his time, knowing she was there, but focused, nonetheless, on his work. He was, she thought, showing off for her. After selling his customer several items and packaging everything up neatly with a courteous smile gracing his face, he looked eagerly in her direction.

Yasmine revealed herself, sauntering over to where he stood. He leaned over the counter in her direction with a look of pleasant anticipation on his face.

"Yasi!" he exclaimed, drinking in the sight of her with a beaming smile. "How was your first day?"

She peeled off the brunette wig, stuffing it into her satchel and fluffing up her blonde curls. "I absolutely love it," she assured him. "Thank you so much for your help, Bonbon. Claude is a pleasure to work for, and I get to meet so many Achérois, working there. It seems to be a real hub for our little corner of the world."

"You really want to thank me?" he crooned, leaning even farther over the top of the counter toward her with his cocky smirk.

She tilted her head with a flirtatious smile and pulled in closer, meeting him halfway, breathing in deeply of the smell of him. He was like a man-flower, so clean and perfumey. She wasn't sure how he pulled it off, as he smoked at least a half a pack of cigarettes a day, but it drove her wild with desire. He probably did it on purpose, just to attract her, she thought, leaning in to meet him.

Unfortunately, Jacques chose just that moment to descend the stairs from the office. Yasmine saw him from the corner of her eye. He looked scandalized to see his son in a liplock with what appeared to be yet another girl and scowled at Gilbert with a look of utter disgust.

Gilbert, sensing her tense up, caught sight of his father glaring at him from the stairs and backed away from his girlfriend with a look of horror.

"Dad, please," he begged, wanting to explain, as his father stormed back up the stairs.

Yasmine noticed that the bellowed words that flowed down the stairs in Jacques's wake made his son blanch.

"Isn't it enough that you look like her? Do you have to act like her as well?"

He looked at Yasmine apologetically, cringing as the office door slammed.

Gilbert laughed nervously, shrugging his shoulders. Yasmine saw, though, as he glanced up at the stairs, he looked absolutely crushed. His jaw was working in frustrated humiliation.

"Go talk to him," she suggested, as he took a deep breath, leaning back over the counter. She could see the sheen of perspiration that had appeared on his brow and feared he was headed for an anxiety attack. If only Jacques could see what power he held over his son, surely he would temper his stern ways.

"What good would it do?" he lamented. "I can never do anything right, according to him."

She came around the counter and wrapped him in a hug, and he melted against her gratefully. Releasing him, she looked to make sure he was okay.

Gilbert seemed suddenly tired. Sighing, he raked his hand through his silky brown hair.

In spite of his gruffness, Yasmine liked Jacques immensely. She could see to the heart of a person and knew there was an incredibly kind and loving man hiding behind a wall of reserve. Someday, she vowed, she would break through it like the Berlinermauer. No wall was impregnable. She'd bust him out. She would!

The next morning, she eyed him like prey, handing him his morning coffee as he tried, to no avail, to read her like he did the rest of humanity. The Fae, who could read a person's mind like a book with a single touch, had learned over the centuries to guard their thoughts to maintain some semblance of privacy among their own kind. A human, no matter how experienced a judge of human nature, was no match for her.

Fey had also just been handed a cup of cappuccino by Yasmine, who feigned bored indifference under the veil of her dark bangs, her brown eyes expressing condescension and just a smidge of contempt. Fey had tried to ignore her as she took her cup, but Yasmine caught her snatching glances with those big purple eyes of hers. Yes, the bride-to-be recognized a familiar face, if not a friendly one. The new barista hugged her snobby, gothic veneer overtop of her like a cloak on a cold day. Gilbert's disguise had worked.

Speak of the devil, he walked in a few minutes later, greeting Fey with a wink. He looked longingly at Yasmine with his round blue eyes but betrayed no recognition. His cheery composure vanished upon catching Claude's eye, though, and he flushed crimson. The coffee vendor personally fixed his customer's favorite drink, pushing Gilbert's hand away when he tried to pay. The latter flinched as if he had been burned. *What is going on between the two of them?* she wondered, as Gilbert skulked off with his café au lait. Claude, himself, looked on with compassionate benevolence at the retreating figure of his fellow businessman.

She came up behind the short, dark-haired man as he stood, lost in thought. "What was that all about?" she asked.

Claude turned toward her, his head tilted a bit, as if in reflection. "I've never seen him so smitten with a girl before," he admitted with admiration. "What's your secret?"

"Know your adversary," she truthfully responded, shrugging her shoulders as if it were oh-so-simple.

"Oh, I think you still have a bit to learn about de Gaul, yet," Claude challenged with a knowing look, his arms folded across his chest.

Yasmine tossed her head dismissively, turning back to her work. She began grinding coffee beans for the next customer. She felt she knew him better than her new boss could ever imagine.

42

Announcement

The solstice came and went, the Forest of Fontainebleau trading her ascetic brown garb for soft, pure white. Far from the nurturing folds of her confines, snow swirled around a couple hurrying along the sidewalk. Paolo, wearing a long black dress coat, held the door for Fey, who contrasted sharply in a white, knee-length trench that blended with the fresh drifts on the sidewalk. In the doorway of their destination, Paolo stood, transfixed, as he saw his fiancée's hair veiled in soft, downy flakes, a vision of what was to come. She noticed his awestruck silence as he reached out and took a tendril of her hair in his hand, his lips parted in wonder. Her beautiful indigo eyes twinkled up at him. He looked away, as if he had been awakened from a hypnotic state. He said nothing, however, but closed his eyes in reflection, committing the lovely vision to memory, a poem forming in his mind. Fey brushed the snow from Paolo's shoulders as his hair was beginning to drip.

Sister Phillipa walked out to greet them. "Paolo, dear!" she exclaimed with pleasure.

He introduced his fiancée to the old nun, who beamed at Fey with joyous delight, taking her hands warmly in her own. "I've heard so much about you," she gushed. Fey smiled back shyly.

Turning back to Paolo, she told him, "I'll let Natalie know you're here. She is doing so much better. She's even starting to let some of the other girls get to know her."

"That's great, Sister." He looked genuinely pleased, glancing uncertainly at her from under his wet black hair. He always felt profoundly inferior around Sister Phillipa, as she seemed so composed and unruffled all the time. He was overjoyed at her words. It had been harder seeing Natalie in pain than going through the aftereffects of Rene's attack. He hoped she was ready for the news he came to bring.

Paolo smiled encouragingly at Fey. She looked up at him nervously.

"Don't worry, Fey," he assured her with undiluted optimism, his hands on her shoulders. "She'll love you, of course."

Fey didn't look so sure. Paolo was somewhat sorry he had told her of the zingers Natalie could launch when it suited her and of how he had admitted that he often felt intimidated by his young friend.

"Wait here," he whispered, seeing Natalie in the common room. Sister Phillipa led Fey into her office. Paolo walked over to Natalie slowly, hands in his coat pockets, head tilted to the side, his wet hair dripping.

"What's up?" she asked, sensing his hesitancy. "Hey, silly, you're soaking wet." She reached up and shook the water from his hair. It sprayed everywhere, and he laughed at her playfulness.

"S'okay," he said, backing away, holding his hands up. He sat down on the sofa, looked up at her, and sighed, his expression betraying his fear. Then, he turned away and stared out the window at the falling snow, nervously dusting his palms over the tops of his trousers.

"What's wrong? You're definitely not yourself today," she remarked. Sitting down next to him, she folded his hand in her small, warm grasp.

He turned back to face her, and the corners of his mouth turned down in a thoughtful frown.

"I want you to know that when I offered to be your big brother, I meant that to be for always."

"Yes, I know," she assured him quietly, confusion evident in her tone.

He closed his eyes for a minute, summoning the courage to tell her. This was so hard for him to do. He looked back to see her gray eyes, large and alert, studying him.

"Someone I knew, before I met you and Michelle, has come back into my life. Amazingly, she doesn't care that I don't remember anything from my old life, though I always would dream about her."

He paused to see what her thoughts were, but waiting for him to continue, she didn't stir.

"I didn't want to tell you this before, but now that you're stronger, I want you to meet her. We're getting married this spring." There, it was out. He breathed a sigh of relief.

"Paolo, you are so dumb sometimes," she condescended. "Your girlfriend has been living in my house for, what? Five months? Don't you think I've figured it out by now?" She rolled her eyes at his naïveté.

"Did you guys do the nasty?" she asked, a look of judgment on her face.

Paolo was shocked, before he remembered that Natalie, unfortunately, had been through more than anyone her age should.

"I thought not," she said smugly, her eyes narrowed in discernment.

He looked aside, not knowing what to say, exhaling sharply. Sometimes Natalie took him by surprise. She was like a sucker punch that he never blocked, because he loved her so much. He knew he was different, but each time it was pointed out to him, it hurt. He, like anyone else, just wanted to fit in. It was only natural.

"Sorry," she apologized. "Please, Paolo, I'm really sorry," she begged, as she saw the look of pain on his face. She had again, without meaning to, stuck a knife in him and twisted it. "I just hope she's good enough for you. Do you love her?"

"More than my own life."

"Gosh, you're always so overdramatic." She laughed.

He laughed in his characteristic, wry snort, visibly relieved.

"I really can't wait," he admitted.

She arched her eyebrow, wise beyond her years. He reddened. She had caught him again.

"It's really hard, living alone," he explained, trying to shrug off his embarrassment. "I'm not sure how Guy did it for so many years."

He felt like hiding. Natalie could make him feel so uncomfortable sometimes.

"I want you to be happy," she said softly.

She made him look at her. His face was full of mortification that she should guess the desire he felt.

"I am," he replied, hunching his shoulders defensively. "But I want you to know, I will never forget your sister. A part of me will always love Michelle."

A tear trickled down her cheek. She hugged him tightly as the snow fell over the somber campus of her school, cleansing everything like God's forgiveness. Hesitantly, after a pause of surprise at her kaleidoscope of emotions, he put his arms around her as well.

"And now," he spoke into her hair, "I would like my two favorite girls in the whole world to meet."

The snow continued into the afternoon, coating all of Paris, covering her sins with false purity. René roughly shoved a few necessities into a duffle bag and fled his apartment, not bothering to lock the door. They would probably just break it down anyway. He took the stairs two at a time and ran for his car, which he had parked a few blocks away.

His boss had called him a few minutes ago. He had a guy whose sole job it was to monitor police scanner frequencies. It seemed that someone had tipped the cops off to his real identity. Fortunately, he had friends, as well as enemies. He had just enough time to scurry out of sight before hearing sirens, muffled by the falling snow. The car was on the roof of the garage, and he brushed the snow quickly off the windows with his sleeve. After fumbling with his keys, he pressed furiously on the fob, setting the alarm off.

He swore and then dropped the keys in the snow.

After frantically digging around for them, his icy hands wet, he retrieved the keys and opened the car door. The alarm went silent, but now his heart was racing. Gunning the engine, he skidded out of the parking garage but found he was too late. A blast of sirens followed him into the swirling snow.

René wove through the light traffic, the volume diminished by the bad weather. The car skidded and hit a parked van. He didn't stop but kept on going, trying to elude the relentless call that came closer, backed off, and then came closer again, tormenting his ears, making his heart pound. He dodged traffic, causing several accidents on the slick pavement, but he felt no remorse for those he left careening in his wake. Their inconvenience would be minor compared with what awaited him should he fail to elude the blaring menace that coursed after him.

He narrowly missed hitting an old woman, who was ambling across the street in a black coat and kerchief. He blasted his horn at her and watched as she fell, startled, in the road. The stupid police cruiser stopped, and a man emerged to help her up. Perfect. He skidded around a corner, hit the bumper of a parked car and then gained speed.

The sound of the sirens faded. René could scarcely believe his luck. He laughed out loud and then switched on the GPS. Aided by the snowstorm, he wouldn't be pursued by air. He would slip out of Paris on the back streets and then head for the sprawling city of Lille, where his boss had a hideout.

He rounded a corner, making his way to the outskirts of the city but then slammed on his brakes. The street was completely blocked off. Turning around, he noted, with a sick feeling in the pit of his stomach, that two police cars had moved in behind him. He saw, with a feeling of despair, that several pistols were aimed at him. He killed the engine and raised his hands.

He felt the blood drain from his face as the cops approached his car. He sat, still as stone, while they barked orders at him. He was afraid to move, as they appeared to be waiting for an excuse to riddle him with bullets. He heard the car door open and felt the rush of cold air on his face, and the next thing he realized, he was standing, stunned, as handcuffs were roughly braceleted onto his wrists.

A big, burly, middle-aged man was standing triumphantly over him as if he had just bagged his first hunting trophy, and René felt sick. Now he knew how an animal must feel as its pursuers closed in. Hopeless. Longing for a swift, painless death. He wished he had never been born as he was practically shoved into the back of the police cruiser and hauled away like so much garbage.

Glancing in the rearview mirror, he did a double take. Where he had expected to meet the gaze of the cop, taking him to his doom, he thought he saw a pair of crimson eyes narrowed at him with delight. Upon looking back, though, he saw that they were shrewd and steely gray and met his own alarmed stare with confident satisfaction.

Paolo took Fey and Natalie to a local restaurant, one they thought she would enjoy. It served Italian food, including an excellent five-cheese lasagna. There was a slightly meaty smell hanging in the air, and Fey saw Paolo sniff disdainfully, his nostrils flared in disgust. She, too, found the smell of meat off-putting but was learning to deal with that kind of unpleasantness, in the same way as residents of factory towns learned to ignore the sulfurous fumes that enveloped them on a regular basis. Faeries, with their wispy, delicate builds, not being equipped for hunting, were vegetarians, as well. Also, it is quite difficult to eat a creature that you could communicate with, a gift more common than not among her people.

The establishment was cozy, though, with cheery, red-checked tablecloths, pictures of Venice lining the walls, and soft accordion music in the background. Fey expressed appreciation for the attempt at romance it strove for. It made her feel closer to her Italian-ish fiancé.

The pretty girl whom Paolo viewed as a sister was giving Fey a cautious chance, and she vowed to do her best to make a good first impression. Fey was quiet and courteous, and let the others do most of the talking. Natalie was, as he had told her, very bright and discerning. She could see why he felt humbled by her.

The atmosphere at their table was way too serious for a festive outing, and Natalie took it upon herself to remedy the situation.

"Y'know," she said, looking somberly at Fey, "you are probably going to regret this."

The couple exchanged a worried look. Had she changed her mind about accepting their engagement? Fey hadn't said anything amiss.

"He snores like a chainsaw," she quipped, raising her eyebrow and glancing at Paolo smugly.

He sat, looking shocked. Fey, after a surprised silence, burst out laughing.

Paolo, miffed, warned her with a wag of his finger, "Someday, you are going to bring your boyfriend home to meet us, and, be sure, I'll remember this."

She just laughed, enjoying his discomfort and Fey's amusement.

Paolo's cell phone rang, and he excused himself to answer it, leaving the girls to talk. Natalie watched him leave. At that point, she focused her attention on Fey like a hunting spaniel, and she immediately began launching questions at her.

"So, you know where Paolo came from!" she exclaimed. "Did you tell him? Does he remember now? Did you both go to school together?"

Fey opened her mouth to speak, not quite sure what she was going to say, but Paolo came striding back purposefully to the table, a look of import on his face.

"Ah, that was Vin. It seems that René has been captured," he told them, gazing directly at Natalie, a shared look of victory passing between them.

The shop door shut, the bell jingling. Yasmine had just left, heading back to her apartment for the evening. She never asked him up but always met him at the pub for dinner or at his place, with the understanding that he had to behave himself. She was growing more and more important to him with each passing day. He loved how she looked in her disguise, with her brunette hair and rich brown eyes, dressed in simple black and white for her barista job.

Even after they had learned that the wedding wouldn't be held until the summer because of Paolo's insistence on a Catholic ceremony, she still wanted to hold off until the big day to reveal herself to Fey, saying that six months was nothing and she was enjoying the anticipation. She had, at least, let him tell Fey and Paolo they were dating, though when she was around anyone but him, she wore her cool persona like a mask. His friends, as a result, didn't really like her too well. He didn't care, though. They would know the real Yasi soon enough.

She looked so dark and mysterious. Then, when she would spend time with him in the evenings, she would be revealed in her sparkly, blonde, blue-eyed form, ready to make him laugh with stories of Achères and its inhabitants and to share a well-behaved kiss. It was like having two, equally gorgeous girlfriends in one, each with her own personality and look. He was really enjoying this.

It did bother him, though, that although they had an amazingly good chemistry, she continued to hold him at arm's length in more ways than one. He, for one, was equally full of anticipation of a completely different sort but was not enjoying it half so much. Whenever he would let his hands stray over her body, to touch her as he longed to, she would take them in her own, her chin tilted downward, and shake her head with an apologetic look. "Sorry, Bonbon, but we're not ready for that yet. Be patient."

Patient. What is she waiting for? he wondered in frustration. She could tell he was crazy about her. He spent every spare minute he had with her. He could feel that she wanted him, as well. He would give her a look of longing that would've melted almost all of the other girls he had dated, but it didn't even make a dent in her iron resolve. Still, he felt that she wasn't toying with him. From the moment he first kissed her, he had felt a bond with her, like she was a friend he could trust, if he would only let himself do so.

Another problem? Yasmine, like Fey, was very secretive about her origins. His dad had expressed concern about him getting involved with her because of this, but he found there was no way he wanted to break things off. He had begun to create a scenario that he would embellish each time they were together, about how she and their friends had grown up in a secret hippie commune deep in the forest and all were sworn to secrecy as to its whereabouts.

From her body language, he actually felt he was on to something with that. He had learned a lot from his old man on how to read people from the subtle physical cues they gave off. The first time he told this story to amuse her at dinner, her cheeks flushed crimson, which looked so pretty, and she began to twist her hair, looking immediately off to his left as if on cue. Bingo! From that night, he began to tweak his story to get a reaction, changing the setting from one part of the forest to another, guessing what occupations her parents had, et cetera, gauging her reaction to each embellishment. It was a lot of fun messing with her.

Sighing with a determination to wait her out, he opened the electrical box and began to flip off the lights. Donning his coat, he left through the snowy alley, lighting up a cigarette as soon as he had locked the back door.

43

Commitment

Now that Natalie knew of Paolo and Fey's engagement, Gilbert and his new girlfriend had taken it upon themselves to surprise the betrothed couple with a party, allowing her in on their plans. Claude had offered them use of the coffee shop, which had been polluted by a sea of roses; baby's breath; pink, red, and white balloons; paper hearts; lace; tulle; champagne; and chocolate. The establishment had been transformed from a fairly intelligent-looking place by an explosion of Valentine's Day kitsch. Together with the smell of the Arabica beans from the back room, it was absolutely heady. Music floated sensuously through the air above the candlelit tables.

It was probably more Gilbert's idea than Yasmine's, Natalie figured. The haughty, distant barista had never seemed overly friendly toward Fey, hardly spoke to her unless she absolutely had to, and rarely spent time with anyone but Gilbert, who seemed completely besotted with her.

As for her part, Natalie was drawn to a kindred spirit in Yasmine, and as much as she still detested her stuck-up, pretty-boy arm candy, she liked Gilbert's new girlfriend, with her icy detachment and super-cool demeanor. The looks she cast at her boyfriend, though, when she thought no one was looking, were anything but frozen. It seemed the two of them were burning hot for each other as he ran his fingers lightly over her arm with a mooning look and she, catching his eye, bit her crimsoned lower lip like a cheap coquette, popping a strawberry into his mouth.

Disgusting, she thought, turning her attentions elsewhere.

The girls from the natural foods store were there, as well as the staff of the coffee shop. A few people she didn't know had come—probably friends of Gilbert—as well as Latif and Luc. The latter was flirting with Jacqueline from the herb store. Natalie rolled her eyes and made her way over to the fondue pot. The ladies were all attired in red or pink dresses, the men in dark suits—the perfect foil, she noted with her artist's discernment, though she thought ungenerously that Gilbert had probably planned a formal event to sell more clothes at his shop. She wouldn't put it past him. Those de Gauls were all about their precious family business.

"La Vie en Rose" began to play, and the teen, heaving a dripping strawberry into her mouth, watched as Paolo took Fey by the hand and led her to the middle of the open space, a dance floor appearing where, on normal days, the queue of coffee drinkers awaited their fix. She wore a fluffy red dress that swooped over her derriere, fanning out in a little train behind, which, she noted with admiration, Paolo didn't step on once. He, of course, wore that black suit that always stood ready at the back of his closet.

When did he learn to dance like that? she wondered with surprise as they waltzed about like characters in one of the old movies they used to watch together.

He and Fey appeared oblivious to everything around them for a magical few minutes, as Edith Piaf crooned just for them. The flames of the red tapers danced along as the couple glided effortlessly across the floor. Even she had to admit it was a beautiful moment. All the ugliness in the world faded away on a pink and fluffy cloud, and love seemed possible.

Up above the pink and red balloons, amid the swathes of tulle adorning the plate rail that edged the ceiling, Guiscard took his betrothed's hand, beckoning her to join him. He pulled her close, and they began to dance. Arenciel was attired in a sheath of raven feathers that flowed to her ankles and cupped her décolletage enticingly. Guiscard had donned a tunic of midnight gray, with black leggings. A gold belt encircled his waist.

Fleur lounged atop a tuft of diaphanous fabric, dressed in a blush-hued shift made of tiny pinfeathers, dangling a blown-glass vial on a cord, watching the goings-on. She grew dreamy-eyed as Paolo and Fey gazed into each other's eyes with rapt intensity, his look full of pent-up longing, hers of open invitation. Oh, but she was a temptress! Fleur noted with a throaty chuckle as they danced with supernatural elegance.

Looking over at her teacher, she noted that Gilbert's attention had strayed from Yasmine to the dancers on the floor. He looked with dreamy pensiveness at Fey and Paolo as they basked in love's soft glow.

You, too, could enjoy such bliss, haberdasher, she thought.

Rising from her perch, she flew overtop the table where he sat and waited for the right moment. Sure enough, Gilbert tore his tortured gaze from his best friend back to Yasmine, who watched patiently as her man grew sheepish under her scrutiny. She smiled and offered him a sweet red strawberry. Fleur, seizing the opportunity, sprinkled it with courage powder. He bit into it and smiled, sucking a stray fluff of whipped cream from her fingertip. Yasmine bit her lip at his playful suggestiveness.

Not interference at all, she justified. *Just giving the poor, frightened human the bravado to act on what already lies within his heart.*

The party was over. Gilbert walked hand in hand with Yasmine, escorting her back to her apartment, ready to catch her should she slip on the icy patches that lay in wait on the frozen sidewalks. She hummed softly as he listened to the seductive alto of her voice. It was a catchy tune and was stuck in his head now, as well.

"Do you have a middle name?" she asked.

He laughed. "Yes. How did you guess?"

"Oh, just that, with your long family history, I thought your parents might have wanted to name you after your grandparents," she responded.

She was right. They had. It was kind of old-fashioned, he thought. "Guiscard," he told her. "Gilbert Guiscard de Gaul. Quite a name to live up to, isn't it?"

Yasmine's mouth opened in shock. "No way!" she exclaimed.

"Oh no, curse of the ex-boyfriend," he guessed with instinctive accuracy, cringing and laughing at the same time.

"Old crush," she admitted with a guilty smile. He returned her smile with a kiss as they arrived at her apartment.

"I'll make you forget all about him, if you'll let me," he offered in a seductive voice, his face close to hers. She put her hand on his cheek, giving him a playful pinch. He flinched, but chuckled.

An uncomfortable silence followed. He suddenly felt overcome with tension. He had behaved himself well at the party, sticking to the one glass of champagne that was used to toast the new couple. He would do nothing to spoil Fey and Paolo's moment. Not letting go of her hand, he stood with her in front of the apartment, his eyes lowered.

"Did you want to say something?" she guessed. He wasn't usually at a loss for words, after all.

He looked up. Fear was written clearly on his face. He twisted his mouth into a thoughtful grimace and nodded. It had affected him deeply, watching his best friend commit himself completely to a woman he obviously adored, and he found himself wanting that kind of connection in his own life. The casual hookups were really, for Gilbert, fulfilling a desperate need he had for physical contact and affection. Now, seeing what could be, he wanted more. Knowing how his father had been hurt by it, though, made it a very scary thing.

"Yasi," he said, pausing, "I, ah, I think I'm falling in love with you." He felt absolutely terrified at the admission. *Like a moth circling a flame*, he thought. His heart was now lying before her. She could stomp on it, like everyone else seemed to do, or she could receive it. He had said it, now. There was no going back. His heart began to pound in his chest, and he felt dizzy.

"You *think*?" she asked.

She wasn't going to make this easy on him, he noted sickly. It was obvious she wanted a full admission. He hesitated, already in the water. Should he lose that last foothold? He searched her face for a reaction, in much the same way as his father searched his own face, when looking for signs of duplicity. She stood, waiting, inscrutable. He swallowed hard and then took a deep breath.

"I love you," he admitted hoarsely, leaving go the safety of his hesitation, feeling like he might just pass out.

"I love you too, Gilbert," she answered, "with all my heart."

He let out his breath, which he had apparently been holding. Yasmine leaned over and kissed him.

"You're trembling," she noted with concern.

"Oh, ah, I'm just really nervous," he admitted with an embarrassed laugh. "Y'know, Yasi, I've never said that to any girl, before you. I may not be the best person, but I never lied to a girl to get my way with her."

He pulled in close to her, pressing his forehead to hers, willing himself to relax, knowing that she loved him back. *Oh, Yasi, please don't hurt me,* he thought. *I can't take any more of these games. Now I understand, I think, what you meant by a "real relationship."*

"You want to come in?" she asked him, her face still pressed to his.

He pulled back, meeting her eyes with surprise. "Really?" *Finally!* Finally, his amazing, uncharacteristic patience would pay off.

"Well, Bonbon, you just look so yummy tonight, all dressed up in your new suit. I just can't resist you." She smoothed her hands over his shoulders.

"Well, it looks like I won't be wearing it much longer," he commented in a liquid voice, raising an eyebrow and biting the inside of his lower lip to suppress his amusement.

"Must you always be so naughty?" she scolded, slapping his chest.

"My dear, it's just the way I am." He shrugged, a happy glow stealing over his features.

She led him up to her apartment, where he learned the answer to the question he had asked himself so many months ago, as he stood over Marie-David's sleeping form—for him, his first real love; for her, the only man she had ever truly loved. They would both find, over time, that a committed relationship has its ups and downs, but riding out the waves is well worth the effort.

44

Handfast

The day before Midsummer's Eve had dawned hot and sultry. This night, Arcenciel would be made handfast with Guiscard, in the large clearing between Achères-la-Forêt and Arbonne-la-Forêt. All members of the clans of the surrounding forest who could make it would be in attendance. There would be feasting, merrymaking, dancing, and rejoicing. To an unsuspecting human, in the unlikely event he or she should stumble upon their celebration, it would appear as if a thousand fireflies had gathered in the field.

Fleur left the cool shelter of her treetop abode that morning to deliver the wedding invitation she had prepared, remembering her promise to send Yasmine to the ceremony in a dream for Arcenciel. She flew to Yasmine's bare, rundown closet of an apartment and placed a sweetly scented pomander under her pillow. Her human friend would not be able to touch them, as their worlds must remain separate, but she would be able to bear witness to the love of two noble members of the Fae, who had decided to join their fates as one.

Done with her task, she flew to the gathering place in the middle of the forest to help prepare the handfasting feast for the betrothed couple.

Guiscard lay on his bed, having escaped the heat of the afternoon by retreating to his loft for a nap. Awakening refreshed, he lay atop the coverings woven of soft milkweed down, sipping an acorn cupful of tea. That day had dawned bright and fierce, matching the fire in his heart. He had made his choice and was truly happy. How lucky he had been to be looked upon favorably by so many. Undeserved, he felt. Now, though, he had shed his vile hubris and humbly felt gratitude for the love of his beautiful Arcenciel, who had given up so much to be with him. She was a gem, his glorious Emerald. The change she had undergone was subtle. To him, she was still amazingly beautiful, even more so, as her inner qualities became revealed. He had, at one time, thought her to be somewhat harsh and stern, but her selfless actions had been anything but. They would, he was sure, be truly happy and complete in each other, a perfect, balanced match of yin and yang.

Swallowing the dregs of his tea, Guiscard hopped up from the bed to begin his ablutions. He wanted to look pleasing to his mate, as much as possible under the dull veil of his changed exterior. He opened his armoire, which held the clothing he had saved for this day. It, like many of the finer outfits the wedding guests would be wearing, had been designed by Fey before she had left to join the human world. He reached in and pulled out the emerald-green, cobweb silk he had chosen to complement his beloved's gorgeous eyes, which still shone with their full intensity, a reflection of her inner beauty. The tunic was woven with tiny ivy leaves vining their way in a bias pattern from the bottom left to the right shoulder. The hem fell just above his knee. It would be belted with a gold rope, tasseled on the ends. A circlet of ivy leaves, fashioned by the bride's cousin, would grace his brow. On his feet would be sandals soled in dragon scale, a generous gift from the clan of Fontainebleau.

Guiscard laid the items on the bed and then went to wash and prepare for his nuptials with a heart light and free from care.

To his great surprise, Gilbert found himself standing at the inner edge of a circle of people in the middle of the night; he was dressed in pajamas the grayish-white color of a moth's wing—not his clothes, he might add. The last thing he remembered, he was lying snuggled up next to Yasi in her bed. What was he doing here? Everyone looked at him with surprise. He felt uncomfortably conspicuous, as no one else was wearing head-to-toe white, and they all stared at him like he was a circus oddity, with eyes full of bold curiosity. Everything looked really weird, to boot. The trees looked like giant stalks with no branches, and the people all were a bit off, as well, though he couldn't quite pin down what it was. He hadn't remembered taking anything that night. Yasi didn't like it when he did, so he only got high when she wasn't around. He was trying to cut back, but it was harder than he had thought it would be.

A couple approached him. The man had the appearance of a medieval hero, his long, wavy hair flowing over his shoulders complemented by a neatly trimmed beard, his features strong and proud. He was dressed oddly, as everyone else was, but the clothing was still beautiful in its bizarre way, like from a movie set. *Kind of Lord of the Rings looking,* Gilbert thought. The woman looked startlingly like Yasmine, with curly blonde hair and knowing, almond-shaped eyes, narrowed upon him with undisguised antipathy.

"You are Yasmine's man, aren't you?" she asked him coldly.

"Well, I guess I am," he answered, thinking it an odd way of putting it. "Are you her sister?" The woman looked about the same age as his girlfriend, maybe a few years older. She laughed that same deep, sensual laugh as Yasi's, looking at the man who stood beside her with a flattered expression on her face.

"Oh, you are a charmer," she admonished him, thawing significantly at his words. "We're her parents, of course," she explained. "Chevalier and Anaïs."

"Gilbert de Gaul. Pleased to meet you," he introduced himself formally, proffering his hand to Yasmine's father, who looked at it with, not quite revulsion, but as if Gilbert had just committed a faux pas. He coughed, withdrew his hand, and stood, mouth pulled into a tense line. An uncomfortable pause ensued.

"I love your dress," he told Anaïs, returning his attention to his girlfriend's mother, sticking with a safe topic. "It's very … Alexander McQueen."

She accepted the compliment with a smile but looked confused at the reference to the famous designer.

"He is surpassingly fair, for his kind, but does he possess a noble soul?" her father asked, studying Gilbert intently, his head turned a bit to the side.

His kind, Gilbert bristled. *Hmm, small-town boy isn't good enough for their little princess, obviously,* he thought, tilting his head back defensively. *Typical snobby Parisians,* he judged.

"I wish I could touch him to find out," her mother stated, as if he weren't there.

Gilbert spread his hands, palms forward. "Go ahead. I don't bite," he said with a smirk. *She can touch me anywhere she likes,* he thought wickedly.

"Do you know what she gave up to be with you?" Anaïs asked, in a reproachful tone.

Gilbert stood there for a moment, unsure how to answer. "No, not really," he admitted, betraying his deep frustration. "She never tells me anything. She should've been an intelligence agent. You could probably pry her fingernails out, before she'd say something she didn't want you to know."

"Yasmine was the matchmaker of Achères. Only the clan leader possesses a higher status," she informed him with a haughty demeanor.

Gilbert furrowed his brow at the information, which made no sense at all to him.

"Do you love her?" Yasmine's father interjected in a tone laced with challenge.

Before he could answer, a flash of white appeared beside him. It was Yasmine herself. He smiled at her like she was an oasis in the desert of confusion he was feeling at the moment.

"Hey," he greeted her cheerfully, relief flooding over him. He leaned toward her to give her a grateful kiss. He was, indeed, profoundly relieved to see a familiar face.

She smiled back at him, returning his affectionate greeting with delighted surprise. "Bonbon, dear! What are you doing here?"

"I don't know," he answered, perplexed. *Where is 'here,' anyway?*

She took his hand reassuringly in her own.

"I see you've met my parents," she noted, as they tried to greet Yasmine without touching her, which Gilbert thought very odd. Why didn't they hug each other? Yasmine was definitely the huggy sort. Joy and sadness mingled in their gaze as they greeted their daughter. A hush fell over the clearing, and all the guests turned their attention forward.

They stood in the front row of the ring of spectators and watched as a beautiful woman with long black hair glided into the center of the circle, accompanied by a sturdy-looking, bearded man. Both, Gilbert thought, were good-looking enough to be actors, but then, so was everyone else he had seen. The woman looked radiantly happy, and the man she was with seemed to mirror her sentiments. *Is this some kind of wedding?* he wondered.

He looked quizzically at Yasmine for clarification, but she was beaming at something in the center of the circle. When he followed her gaze, he found that another woman had appeared, where before there were only the two people. This woman, a gorgeous girl with long, silky blonde hair, dressed in what could only be an haute-couture silk dress, looked at his girlfriend as if they shared some kind of secret. Girls were like that, he noted. They could communicate volumes without saying a single word. The pretty blonde then looked directly at Gilbert, and her eyes flew wide. He saw her mouth form a soundless, "Oops." She bit her lower lip, shrugging guiltily as she looked at Yasmine.

The moon rose over the treetops, bestowing its bright blue light to the scene below. The couple, standing in the middle of the circle, waiting, became bathed in the glow from above. Gilbert's breath caught, and he tightened his grip on Yasmine's hand as the pair shone brilliant in the magic of Midsummer Night. The man became moonlight itself. The beautiful woman at his side seemed as the night sky. Her raven locks fell gracefully to her waist in a silky veil. Her form, clothed in a shimmering shift, sparkled with a thousand inky lights. The garment glistened around her slim, willowy frame belted in pre-Raphaelite style. A circlet of moonflowers created a stark contrast to her dark hair. Gilbert found her breathtakingly beautiful.

It did, as Gilbert had suspected, seem to be some kind of wedding. Yasmine's friend stepped forward to perform the ceremony. The radiant couple professed their love under the stars, with the moon smiling down upon them. The officiator took a long, silken scarf from around her waist as the man laid his hand over his beloved's. She reverently bound the scarf around their entwined hands, as the guests sang a song of blessing.

Gilbert stood transfixed by the magical sight. Yasmine sang along with the other guests, a song he had never before heard, in voices that blended in perfect harmony. Joined in hand and heart, the couple shared a kiss so full of love that it brought a tear to many an eye.

The reception reminded Gilbert of the time he attended the Sterling Renaissance Festival with his history-buff friends when he was living in New York. They had offered to loan him a costume, but he had chickened out, afraid people would laugh at him. When they got there, though, he noted that many people attended in period dress, and they seemed to have more fun actually. It allowed them to become a part of things, rather than just observe. Now, here he stood, in his white pajamas at this amazing party full of incredibly beautiful people all dressed in outlandishly gorgeous clothing. Again, he wasn't properly dressed. Déjà vu.

The party continued long into the night. There was music, feasting, dancing, and, of course, drinking. They danced with the strangest group of people Gilbert had ever seen, all in fantastical costumes, like in an haute-couture photo shoot he had observed when he was a fashion merchandising major in college. He had never been to such an unrestrained party and had a blast, enjoying the company of his girlfriend's amazing, mysterious people. They, in turn, found him irresistibly magnetic—a novelty to be admired. He met the bride's cousin, Honoré, a member of the Arbonne clan, who had long, silky black hair and features strongly resembling the bride's. He expressed a wish that he stay. Yasmine, though, scolded him.

"Even if he could, his daddy would miss him, Honoré. It would break his heart. You should know the value of family, having lost your parents at such a young age."

"They got eaten by a boar as they foolishly napped over a truffle patch," Fleur whispered close to Gilbert's ear.

He stared at Yasmine's friend like she was crazy. *What did she say? I think I had too much of that punch.*

Honoré nodded apologetically. "You're right, of course, Yasmine. It's just that Arbonne has gotten so dull, lately. We could use one such as him to liven things up a bit."

The matchmaker of Arbonne, Odette, felt quite differently about the whole affair.

"It's *outrageous!*" she declared forcefully. "To allow a human to attend a faerie gathering!" She glared at Fleur, who shrank back behind Honoré for protection. "That clan in Achères just does whatever they feel like doing, with no regard for protocol or tradition. They are a lawless bunch of hooligans, the whole lot of them!" she asserted acridly.

"It was an accident, *mon Coeur*," Honoré soothed.

"Faerie gathering?" Gilbert asked weakly.

Odette glared at Gilbert. He instinctively sensed that this woman could be dangerous and forthwith made every effort to avoid being anywhere near her. The hair stood up on his arms when he met her eyes. No one seemed to pay her any mind, though. Honoré struck up another lively song on his lute, and the bodhran and recorder joined in for another noisy, wild tarantella. The musicians whooped and sang as the dancers whirled.

Finally, the newly joined couple bid the partygoers good night and flew off into the darkness to enjoy the consummation of their love. The celebration continued until, one by one, the revelers flew or staggered off to sleep, depending on how much of that potent punch they had had to drink. Yasmine took hold of Gilbert, who was unsteady on his feet, and led him to the center of the faerie ring.

"Did you have a nice time?" she asked him.

"Oh, the best e'er," he admitted enthusiastically, his head spinning.

"It was very naughty of you, though, flirting with my mommy," she scolded him.

His jaw dropped. *Guilty.* "Well, she … she looked so much li' you, I guess I got carried away," he stammered, swaying as he spoke.

Yasmine gave him a pinch on the arm, and her eyes narrowed. He just flinched, laughing at her, too far gone on the singular, enticing beverage he had consumed to care.

Yasmine took his hands in hers, and the two dreamers returned to their own world.

The alarm clock went off at five. Yasmine had started to get used to waking up on the edge of the bed with Gilbert pressed tightly against her, his face on her shoulder, the rough skin of his chin digging into her back like tiny needles. Reaching over sleepily, she shut the noisy contraption off and clicked the chain pull to the light. She heard him yawn as he released her from her human straitjacket and lay back on the pillow in the middle of the mattress.

"I had the weirdest dream last night," he told her in a voice rough with sleep. With sheepish amusement, he caressed her manicured hand with his own soft fingers.

"Oh?" she replied ingenuously, as if she had no idea what he was going to tell her.

"I dreamed we were at a wedding. I think it was one of your friends. She was this gorgeous girl with black hair all the way down to her waist, and both she and the man she was marrying looked like they were made of moonlight."

He yawned and stretched, smiling at the recollection.

Yasmine looked into his eyes with what she hoped was just enough interest to hear more, without betraying what she already knew. "It sounds beautiful," she told him.

It was beautiful, she recalled. Despite their diminished radiance, Arcenciel and Guiscard shone with all the beauty of the full moon on a clear night, encircled by the fiery light of the faerie ring and the wedding guests, all of whom were arrayed in their finest cobweb silks.

"It was," he admitted, cradling his head in the crook of his arm and staring straight ahead, unfocused. "There was this ring around the bride and groom, like candles or something, and the wedding was strange. Pagan, maybe."

"Did we have fun?" she asked.

Gilbert laughed and shook his head shyly, not wanting to share more. Yasmine could see in the animated expression on his face that he had enjoyed himself and understood that he wouldn't want to say too much about it. Their world was, after all, hard for a human to comprehend. The fact that he had fit in so well with her clan had shown her what a rare individual he was.

Then, he looked at her beseechingly. "I dreamed your parents were there," he told her in a wheedling tone. "You ready to let me meet them, hmm?"

"Well, imaginary weddings aside, I have to get to work!" she exclaimed, jumping up from the bed. Gilbert's expression turned sulky, but he said nothing further. She had the feeling he wasn't going to give up easily on uncovering her past. She hoped the love they now shared would be enough to keep him, in spite of her secretiveness. Throwing on her work clothes, she sighed and made ready to return to her new reality, refreshed from the escape she had been given from the workaday world.

As she prepared to leave, tucking her curls under her dark wig, her boyfriend chuckled to himself.

"What's so funny, Bonbon?"

"Wanna know the best part about tying one on in a dream?" he asked, still lying comfortably on the bed, one arm behind his head, the other draped across his chest.

She folded her arms and tilted her head, waiting for him to continue, her silky, dark hair framing her face.

"No hangover!" he exclaimed with a smug expression.

45

Rachel

The best man adjusted the groom's tuxedo until he was satisfied that every detail was perfect—just the right amount of cuff showing, collar and cravat straight, everything lint free. Taking one final swipe with his fabric brush, Gilbert stood back to survey the results with a critical eye.

Paolo, his face reflecting a mixture of anxiety and seriousness, was distracted.

"You sure you're ready for this?" Gilbert cautioned. "You still have time to back out."

The groom nodded slightly, a hint of a nervous smile appearing for a second.

"Nervous?"

"No ... yes."

Paolo's stomach began to twist into a tight knot. He felt queasy. Gilbert, who knew him very well by then, guessed the cause of his anxiety.

"You've never been with a girl, have you?"

Paolo looked him defensively in the eye but wouldn't answer. He felt that his sophisticated friend would think less of him for failing to hook up with any of the girls at the club. He had had more than a few opportunities, but he had worked so hard to fight the sinfulness that had wormed its way into his soul. There was no way he was going to give in and let it win.

"Hey, don't worry, Lambie," he assured the nervous groom, patting him affectionately on the shoulder. "She's crazy about you, though I'm not sure why," he added with mock sarcasm. "You aren't half as good-looking as me, and you always smell like dirt," Gilbert finished, wrinkling his nose in disdain.

Paolo laughed, the knot in his stomach loosening just a little under his friend's good-natured ribbing. He was a farmer, after all, and not everyone could keep up with the clothier's overgroomed exterior.

Then, the latter got a twinkle in his eye. With a wicked smile, he added at the last minute, "Besides, I heard Natalie bought you a study guide. You should be all ready for your big night."

Paolo rolled his eyes, sighing in frustration. Natalie had taken it upon herself to give him a copy of the Kama Sutra, hoping it would help him. Between Natalie's prying and Gilbert's forwardness, he felt like he had absolutely no mental privacy at all. He wondered who had told his friend about his very unusual wedding gift. He took in Gilbert's smug expression while his own face expressed shocked embarrassment.

"C'mon; it's showtime," the best man said and laughed, nearly dragging Paolo out the door of the vestry. "Time to display my magnificent handiwork."

At the altar, Paolo felt like he might just pass out. He noted gratefully that Gilbert stood close by, a reassuring presence. The music started, and Natalie began the slow walk down the aisle. The cut of the lavender shift made her look several years older. Paolo raised an eyebrow at the sight of her. How had she changed that much without him even noticing? She smiled at him, well aware of the effect she had had. He was so proud of how far she had come and so happy to have her share this day with them. A whisper of Michelle passed through his brain, and then the music changed and he looked up.

His anxiety seemed to melt away in an instant. For there in the doorway stood, not Eve, to be both feared and desired, but Rachel, as splendid as the dawn.

Fleur sat with Guiscard and Arcenciel, perched on the railing of the choir loft, surveying the scene below. She exclaimed with delight as Fey's dark-haired boy appeared, looking absolutely dashing in an elegant black tuxedo. The young man was sporting a deep, summer tan. Beside him stood the beautiful, polished Gilbert, watching solicitously over his friend. He looked thin and tired but still impeccable. She smiled down at him, aware of the surprise he and Yasmine had in store for Fey. She watched, enchanted, as a pretty, young girl in lavender floated gracefully up the aisle. Fleur knew, without a doubt, that Fey had made the dress, she herself having been the recipient of so much of her friend's efforts. She watched with joy as Paolo's expression changed from nervous to smitten, knowing that Fey had arrived in the doorway beneath them.

Their dear friend made her way slowly to the front of the church. Fleur couldn't see her face, but could see that her dress would remain one of her finest creations. She had managed to take her human form, and, by the simple arrangement of fabric and choice of texture, transform back to her faerie self. She was dazzling.

The three friends watched the ceremony from their lofty perch, Arcenciel and Fleur giggling as Paolo seemed to forget where he was for a moment, kissing Fey a little too passionately at the end. Then, he tucked his bride's arm in his own, and the two lovers exchanged a broad smile of mixed joy and relief and made their way out, ready to greet their friends and their new life together.

In the church restroom, Yasmine took one last look at her alternate persona. Taking a deep breath, she then peeled off her brown wig and threw it in the waste can. Looking in the mirror, she plucked the brown contacts from her eyes and wiped the crimson lipstick from her lips, replacing it with pink gloss. She made her way to the vestibule, where the wedding party stood, greeting the handful of well-wishers who trickled out into the sunshine of Summer's farewell.

Gilbert caught sight of her peering from behind a stone pillar, his features brightening with anticipation. He whispered something to Fey with a satisfied smile, inclining his head in her direction. This was the moment. Would Fey be pleased to see her, be happy that she now had someone who truly understood her in this world she had chosen to share with her beloved? Or would she still harbor anger against her, for playing a careless game with one she held so dear? She stepped shyly from her hiding place and minced her way over to the bride, head bowed penitently to show she knew the scorn she deserved.

The church grew eerily silent. Yasmine feared the worst. Lifting her gaze to meet Fey's reaction, she noted that the bride's eyes shone with tears. Fey wrapped her in a tight hug, and Yasmine smiled. Even though she could no longer read her aura, she could sense Fey's forgiveness as strongly as if she had voiced it in words.

"I'll explain everything later," Yasmine promised in a whisper. For now, Fey would just have to suffer some anticipation herself.

"Paolo, this is my dear friend Yasmine," Fey introduced her.

In her dark persona, she had kept her distance from everyone but Gilbert, as if she still feared they could read her thoughts, but now Yasmine leaned up to plant a kiss on the groom's cheek—and not one of those air kisses she usually gave. She had never gotten over the sight of him in the forest and wondered what it would feel like to touch him. She knew this was the closest she would ever get, and she took full advantage, shooting Fey a knowing smile, her eyebrow raised in ill-gotten delight. *My, he smells luscious,* she thought, but not like her Gilbert, more earthy and sensual. No wonder Fey was so enamored of him.

"You, my dear, are a lucky woman. Your husband is a beautiful man, inside and out," Yasmine uttered quietly as she hugged her friend, remembering what she had learned about his character that time she had tried to help him so many months ago.

"I know," she replied, looking at him with deep desire as he stood waiting for her, his own eyes filled with mirrored sentiment.

Yasmine watched as Paolo's look turned from confusion to an almost predatory stare as he ate up Fey with his eyes; his hands tensed at his sides. It reminded her of how a cat would stare you down, unflinching. His time of trial was almost over, and from the look on his face, Yasmine thought he would probably just like to skip the wedding reception. She looked at Gilbert and fanned herself. He laughed, catching her meaning, and scooted her out the door.

Gilbert nursed his glass of champagne, pleased to see that Yasmine's surprise had made Fey so happy, yet puzzled anew by the mysterious origins of his friends. The reception was very small, just a catered dinner set out under a rented tent in front of the farmhouse. Fortunately, the weather cooperated. The day was fair, the air crisp and cool. The shorn fields rolled like a lush, tan carpet toward the forest.

Yasmine regaled the guests with her story of how Gilbert had disguised her to keep her presence a secret before the wedding, describing how he had surprised her with the contact lenses and brunette wig. Gilbert swirled the dregs in his glass, watching Jacques's eyes grow wide as he listened. He confronted Gilbert, pulling him aside.

"Why didn't you tell me it was the same girl, and that she was Fey's friend?" he scolded in a loud whisper. "I see you with that brunette barista one day, then kissing a blonde the next. What was I supposed to think?"

"You never gave me a chance to explain," Gilbert shot back with a scowl. "You just stormed up the stairs to your office, remember? Serves you right, Dad," he lectured his parent smugly, growing hostile as he remembered the hurtful barb he had been hit with. "Maybe next time, you'll think about it before you jump all over me about something, hmm?"

Jacques nodded penitently, looking ashamed. Then Gilbert felt badly for being disrespectful and gave his father a pat on the shoulder. He noted that several of the guests were staring anxiously in their direction. This was no time to start an argument with his old man. Situation defused, Gilbert told a randy joke related to the wedding night to get things back on track. Everyone laughed heartily, sneaking a glance at the bride and groom, one blushing, one with eyes twinkling full of merriment.

It came close to the time for Fey and Paolo to leave and catch their train to Paris. The bride went inside to change into her traveling clothes. Yasmine went with her. The two of them wanted to talk privately before she left and had to make completely certain no one else overheard. In the front bedroom, she peered out the window to make sure Natalie hadn't followed them.

No, she was sitting with Gilbert, the two of them engaged in an animated conversation. It seemed the strong-minded girl had begun to thaw toward her sister's former rejected suitor.

"So, you forgive me, for being so stupid?" Yasmine asked, wringing her hands nervously as she stood on the other side of the room.

"Yes, of course," Fey assured her. What use would holding a grudge do? Yasmine realized her foolishness and had come to join her in the human world—the only person she could be completely honest with. "Now, you have to tell me how you came to be here—and how in the world you ended up with Gilbert," Fey asked breathlessly.

"Well," Yasmine began, settling tentatively on the edge of the bed, "Arenciel could see that I had fallen hopelessly in love with my adorable, naughty boy," she recounted. "So, she decided to send me here to be with him. But it wasn't just for me," she went on emphatically. "She also did it for you, so that you would have a friend from your own people, and especially for Guiscard."

"Guiscard? How did your coming here help him? I don't see it," Fey puzzled. It was, she knew well, an enormous gift, and she was, indeed, very grateful to Arenciel, but it seemed so much more than anyone would think to do, unless compelled by conscience.

"Oh, really, Fey dear," Yasmine rolled her sky-blue eyes at her friend's lack of insight. "She wanted to put herself on his level, to share his suffering, so to speak. He's really quite full of himself, if you haven't noticed."

"Now that you mention it," Fey agreed, "I believe you're right. Strange, that I didn't see it when I had my own sights set on him."

Fey realized the great price Arenciel had paid to assuage her mate's ego. Would she have done the same? She would do anything for Paolo, but it was his humility she loved, among his other virtues. Would she have been willing to sacrifice so much if it had only been to feed his hubris? She thought not and pitied her poor friend.

Fey changed the subject. There was nothing she could do for Arenciel at this point. She had made her choice, and a quiet life with Guiscard wasn't exactly a bad prospect, especially since they would be released to their former state when her and Yasmine's human forms expired. Then they, too, would return to their own realm and their youthful splendor. Bittersweet, as the men they both loved would not be able to accompany them.

"So, how do our friends fare?" she asked cheerfully. "I do miss them so very much," she exclaimed, as Yasmine helped her change into her traveling clothes.

Yasmine chuckled, carefully unfastening the lacing on the bride's gown.

"Fleur invited me to the handfasting," she shared, "in a dream. It seems," she continued in an amused voice, "that my boyfriend crashed the wedding."

Fey's eyes flew wide. It was inconceivable. She turned to face Yasmine with open-mouthed shock, and some consternation that Gilbert had acquired an invitation and she hadn't.

"How did Gilbert end up there? I've never heard of such a thing!" she exclaimed.

Yasmine blushed at that. "Fleur sent me an invitation," she explained, "She knew that I had no intentions of exchanging intimacy with a man who had not committed himself to me," she went on, averting her gaze to the bedspread. "But it seems that love makes fools of us all. After he professed his love for me, I invited him to share my bed, which of course he eagerly accepted," she admitted, tracing a pattern absently on the covering. "He fell asleep before I did that night, snuggled up against me, right overtop the sachet, and arrived in the meadow first."

"He really did have a good time, though he clung to me like a child for the first hour," Yasmine remembered fondly, meeting Fey's eyes with a smile, giggling at the memory of it. "He even told me about it the next day, though he, too, remembers it as a dream."

Yasmine helped Fey slip out of her nuptial raiment, hanging the gown on a satin hanger and lacing it neatly as the bride chose a dress for the brief trip to Paris. Fey noticed the usually bubbly blonde looked wistful, maybe afraid. She tilted her head as Yasmine met her inquiring gaze.

"I'm afraid we might have made an enemy in the Matchmaker of Arbonne," Yasmine revealed, her visage expressing genuine concern. "She was furious to see a human at the gathering and didn't seem mollified in the least that his presence was purely accidental. Poor Bonbon was scared witless by her."

"Don't worry about her," Fey assured, taking off her veil and draping it over the bedpost. "Her sphere of influence doesn't stretch to Achères. She would never overstep the bounds of her authority. Kind of a stick-in-the-mud, that way," Fey joked, pulling the hairpins from her coiffure, releasing the lush, ruddy curls from their bondage.

"So, how did you manage to win Gilbert's affections? He seems to me a rather crafty fish—hard to hook. Eat the bait and run," Fey joked, bringing the conversation back to a more cheerful bend.

"Y'know," Yasmine responded softly, "he hides it so well, but deep down, Gilbert feels so unloved."

Fey was surprised to hear this. He was always in a good mood, usually the life of the party. His father spoiled him with every material thing. Girls never seemed to say no when he asked for a date. His friends all listened to him like he was in charge. How could he feel unloved?

"I truly love him, and I think he can feel it." She sighed. "I just hope it's enough to keep him."

Fey thought just then of Arcenciel's premonition that Yasmine and her beloved would both suffer because of what she had inflicted on Paolo with her flippant treatment of the human heart. She held her tongue, though. Nothing she could say would change her friend's fate, as Yasmine, herself, had written it with her deeds. A question did arise in her mind. Fey couldn't help but wonder if the black-haired faerie harbored a desire to send Yasmine to her punishment, in revenge for what her mate was enduring. She wouldn't put it past her. Arcenciel's aura did possess an air of dark magic. It was part and parcel of her nature.

As for Gilbert, his behavior seemed to be leading directly for a train wreck, without needing help from anyone. Fortunately, the two of them would have friends waiting to help them pick up the pieces when it hit.

46

City of Lights

*P*aolo awoke with his arm draped over his face, palm facing upward. Peeking out from under its shelter, he saw Fey smiling at him sleepily. She took a deep breath and stretched with catlike gracefulness.

It was a feeling like no other, to wake up next to her with the sunlight streaming across the bed. He felt such love for her, but it was profoundly strange, too, to go from lovers back to friends again in the morning. It made him revert to his inborn shyness. It had completely fled the night before, only to return with renewed vengeance in the light of morning.

Fey noticed him looking characteristically introverted and was determined to lighten his mood.

"Natalie was right." She grinned. "You do snore really loud."

Paolo laughed and turned away from her gaze.

"Sorry," he apologized from under the pillow, where he had taken refuge.

She pulled the pillow away from his face and snuggled in close to kiss him. "Well, here we are in the City of Lights," she said quietly. "What do you think? Shall we seize the day?"

He nodded, looking more relaxed but still not ready to talk. Instead, he took her hand, placed it over his heart, and wrapped his own overtop. *You can touch me now. I won't have to push you away anymore,* he thought, looking over at her, his face soft and thoughtful. He didn't want her to think that he didn't like her being affectionate. Actually, the opposite was true.

Fey understood. She always did.

The door to the chicken coop groaned in protest as it swung open. Gilbert wrinkled his nose as he entered, basket in hand. *Ugh, disgusting,* he thought to himself with revulsion. The smell of chicken manure permeated the enclosure and invaded his nostrils. He looked around with distaste as the chickens eyed the potential predator with suspicion. Could they sense the carnivore in him? His favorite meal sat, scattered about the room, as his eyes roved for the feed bucket in the dim light. The floor was dusty and covered with strands of straw, among other things. The wall in front of him was lined with cubbies similar to those that held merchandise in the shop, though trousers and golf shirts couldn't peck you when you reached in to extract them. The dark wood absorbed most of the light, which streamed in from the one square, mullioned window to the right of the door.

Searching in the relatively dim light, he spotted a round barrel to his left, with an antique scoop made of wood, polished with age, hanging by a cord from a nail overtop.

He had performed this chore several times while Paolo lay in the hospital, with equal antipathy. After he had had to send a new suit to the cleaners, as well as to clean chicken droppings off of his dress shoes, Gilbert had wisely changed into Paolo's work pants, rolled up several times at the cuff, and oversized shoes, which clumped on the floor on his much smaller feet. He reached into the bin with the wooden scoop and pulled out a generous helping of corn, which he scattered in the fenced-in chicken yard. Several hungry takers tucked in. He watched with satisfaction for a moment and then returned the wooden implement to its spot on the wall.

Suddenly, he felt a warm, wet drip on his neck and cringed. Looking up, he noted a fat old biddy in the rafters, shaking her feathers with pride at her excellent aim. Gilbert glared at her with malevolence.

"You would taste so good with gravy and mashed potatoes," he growled up at her in an empty threat. The dowager flapped her wings defiantly, a cascade of feathers sprinkling down on Gilbert's head and shoulders. He stepped aside, wiping his neck with the hem of his T-shirt, a sneer of disgust on his face.

Moving on, he began the task of looking for eggs. Hearing a crunch under his feet, he looked down. Rolling his eyes in frustration, he noted a runny yellow substance escaping from under Paolo's boot. He shook his foot, which rattled around in the oversized footwear, and moved on to the rows of cubbies full of straw.

Thankfully, he discovered some were empty, and he could just reach in and extract the small brown ellipses, stashing them in the basket, which hung from his arm. The trouble came when he had to reach underneath one of the hens. The fact that they were sitting there after he had scattered their dinner in the yard meant, to him, that they were probably hiding something. Eyeing a pretty brown-and-white-flecked fowl with trepidation, he bit his lower lip and held his breath, sliding his fingers cautiously underneath of her warm feathers to find her secret stash. She seemed to be able to sense his unease, and he got several pecks on the arm for his efforts—a few of which drew blood—as well as a warm egg. Each time one of the little malcontents tried to take a piece of flesh out of him, he would draw back quickly and swear, as if afraid they might take off a finger. Next time, he vowed, he would wear Paolo's leather gloves and maybe a mackintosh.

"Only for you, my friend. Only for you," Gilbert muttered as he rubbed a fresh peck mark on his hand.

The farm's proprietor, steeped in his twin dream of Light and Love, was blissfully unaware of the suffering his friend was willingly undergoing on his behalf.

He sat in the hotel lobby with Fey, the two of them sipping steaming cups of coffee. He was dressed in a white shirt, black tie, and black trousers, because it was Sunday. They would go to Mass at Notre Dame, they had decided. Fey wore a new crimson silk dress of her own creation. The smooth red fabric flowed over her petite, slim form to the knee, where a fringe of fluttering tatters swayed playfully as she walked. He always marveled at her creativity.

He was so proud to have her for his wife, his beautiful Fey, and still felt humbled by her regard for him.

Paolo ate very little, unable to muster an appetite because of the overwhelming rush of feelings coursing through him.

"What's the matter, Paolo?" she asked him, placing her hand over his arm.

"I'm sorry, Fey, but this is all just a little overwhelming for me," he apologized.

"Oh, that's right," she remembered. "You've never been to a large city before. Yes, it is a lot to take in."

"No," he clarified, "I mean being with you. It's weird …" He paused, not sure what to say. "Ah, different."

He was at a loss for the right words and was afraid she would misunderstand. He was, admittedly, not flexible in his thinking, which was why the strongly structured poetry he wrote was his preferred medium of expression.

"Imagine my rustic poet at a loss for words," she mused with a smile.

He laughed depreciatively under his breath and realized the best way to express what he felt, clued by her jest:

> To fall asleep within thine arms embraced,
> Passions spent, without the stain of sin.
> Awake at dawn to see my Love replaced,
> By She who hath mine own friend always been.

He said this with his eyes fixed on hers. He never recited his poetry aloud and wasn't comfortable doing so. The poems weren't meant as anything but a means of figuring out his thoughts, which he only wished to share with Fey. He kept that part of himself locked away from all others, as it didn't seem to fit in the world in which he found himself.

Fey reached over and took his hand in her own. She gave it a squeeze, a look of reassurance on her lovely face. He looked at her with gratitude, the pensiveness still lurking in his eyes.

"Go on," she encouraged.

"Uh, Fey, can I just tell it to you later?" He was feeling conspicuous. His gaze darted about and rested upon the eyes of the woman at the next table, who sat obviously listening. Paolo sucked in his breath, blushed, and put his hand up to his face to hide, leaning his elbow on the table. *Why can't I just be like everyone else?* he thought with frustration. He knew that normal people didn't think in iambic pentameter and was glad that Fey was the only one who knew about his written thoughts, other than Natalie, who didn't seem to mind that he possessed this mental oddity.

"Is it in your journal?" she asked.

"No, just in my mind," he responded, still mortified that someone had overheard this expression of the most intimate moment of his life. It didn't seem to bother Fey, who glanced over at the other couple with a self-satisfied expression.

She picked up the small paper napkin under her coffee mug, pulled a pen out of her purse, and pushed it toward him. He took them from her and quickly wrote the rest of the sonnet down, his features intense and confident. Paolo would look up every few moments to find her watching with a look of rapt adoration that he found mesmerizing and distracting.

"Um, it's just a draft. I can't concentrate, with people around," he told her. The wording was clumsy, he felt.

When he finished, she took the paper and folded it into a neat square. Sliding it into Paolo's shirt pocket, she said, "Why don't you just tuck your thoughts away for a while and let's go have some fun, hmm? They'll still be there later," she assured him, patting his pocket.

"I think I can do that," he answered, looking at her from under his veil of dark, messy hair, reverting to his everyday self. Fey made everything so simple. He could feel his balance shifting just being around her. Swallowing his awkwardness with the last dregs of coffee, he let his new wife lead him away to explore the City of Lights.

Paolo felt like he had on the day he had first arrived at Guy's farm. Everything was new and amazing. He took great pleasure in knowing that this was Fey's first trip to Paris, as well.

"I want to see everything!" he exclaimed with childlike delight, throwing his arms wide.

"Well, I don't think that's going to happen." She laughed. "We only have three days."

"Wanna bet?"

Holding her tightly against the strong wind on the highest outlook of the Eiffel Tower, he swept one hand over the vista, looking very smug.

"Okay." She admitted. "You got me there."

Feeling her shiver in the chill autumn wind, he held her close in the folds of his coat, the two of them looking out over the city, which seemed to stretch on as far as they could see. He thought of his vision of the view over Lake Como, high above the treetops.

"I dream that I can fly, sometimes," he admitted to her. "Though not like a bird. Um, maybe like a bat, if that makes any sense. You know, the way they flap their wings is different." He could tell Fey anything, and she wouldn't think it strange or laugh at him. It was one of the things he loved about her—that he had nothing to hide. It had made the previous night much easier than it otherwise would've been, that feeling of openness that they shared.

Fey nodded, seeming to understand completely, as he knew she would. "I do, too," she concurred. "But with me, it's more like gliding on the air, with no effort at all, like milkweed down."

They stood for a while, enjoying the moment of peace and companionship. She then removed herself from his warm embrace and turned to look up at him. He leaned down and kissed her softly and comfortably, the edge of desperation gone with this new phase of their relationship. The other tourists cast amused glances at the oblivious newlyweds, who lost track of time for a while.

After enjoying lunch at an excellent table in the better of the two restaurants halfway up the Eiffel Tower—a gift arranged by Jacques—they visited the cathedral of Notre Dame. Paolo had recently finished reading Hugo's book with that title, and he was curious to see the actual place and then to attend Mass. Upon entering the gloomy interior, they both looked up at the same time. He heard a low roar, which gave him goose bumps. It sounded to Paolo like the voice of suffering souls that had accumulated over the centuries, hovering just below the vaulted ceiling. They exchanged a charged look, both feeling unnerved, and Fey linked her arm through his.

They walked slowly around the perimeter of the somber stone edifice, silently, as Mass was underway. The artwork was hard to see in the dim light and seemed to be covered in centuries of grime. The stained glass windows, though, were very beautiful, and were, according to Paolo, the only cheery thing about the place—sinister-looking gargoyles lurked outside and stern saints inside.

His attention was arrested by a series of medieval woodcuts with stylized figures. He tilted his head, studying the story laid out before him. He knit his brows, frowning, the obscurity of the theological world working its confusion inside of him.

"What's wrong?" she asked. "It's just a picture."

"There's something not quite right about it," he judged.

Fey looked more closely. It showed the Nativity but was, actually, very different from the way it was usually depicted, especially in the last panel, where Mary lay reclined after giving birth, looking at baby Jesus with what could be interpreted as intense fatigue or weariness.

"Why does she look so tired?" he whispered. She always looked so peaceful and put-together in all the other paintings of the Nativity he had seen.

"Because she just had a baby." She laughed and added under her breath, "And it's not exactly an easy thing to do."

He pondered that for a moment and then whispered back, "But I read that the pain of giving birth is a punishment for our original sin, and she was supposed to be exempt from that, according to Father Lambert."

"Maybe the artist got it wrong." She shrugged.

"Then the painting wouldn't have been allowed to hang here, in this place of honor," he argued in a hushed voice. He wondered if Mary took the punishment for sin, without actually committing it, like her son. He wasn't sure and would ask Father about the picture when he returned to Achères. He looked at her apologetically for a moment, and then they moved on, his mind still lost in contemplation of what he had seen.

"Let's get out of here," he suggested. The aura of gloom and penance that hung over the cavernous interior of the cathedral was downright depressing.

"Yes," she agreed. "This place is giving me the willies."

It was, according to the clock on the nightstand, around two in the morning. Paolo had awakened and looked over at Fey as she slept, her face awash in blue light. A shaft of moonlight pierced the darkness of their room, giving him the gift of her sleeping visage. He longed to reach over and touch her but was afraid she would awaken.

Slipping out of the warm covers, he threw on the shirt that he'd hung on the bedpost against the night chill and made his way over to the square table in the corner that served both as desk and breakfast nook, where his journal lay. Switching the light on its lowest setting, he sat down, opened the cover, and began to write. First, he copied the sonnet from that morning into his journal, reworking it slightly to improve the wording. Next, he sat for about an hour, varying between staring blankly before him and scribbling, erasing, and rewriting. Finally, satisfied that his thoughts were expressed correctly, he laid the pencil down, shut the book, switched off the light, and went back to bed, wrapping himself carefully around his sleeping wife, who shifted to fit beside him.

He closed his eyes and fell asleep with his face buried in her soft, fragrant curls, dreaming of the moon sparkling over the waters of Lake Como, as seen atop the heights of the Eiffel Tower.

Heart's Desire

At last, I live to see my heart's desire
Far beyond what first imagined was.
This place sublime and thee both do conspire
To please me, yet thou art the foremost cause.
To fall asleep within thine arms embraced,
Passions spent, without the stain of sin.
Awake at dawn to see my Love replaced,
By She who hath mine own friend always been.
Far exceeding Solitude so dark—
Her company hath made my thoughts turn bleak;
Thine own bright presence, a delicious spark
That doth warm fire within my soul to pique.
    Such joy this morn that words cannot describe;
    To thee, Beloved, humbly I ascribe.

47

Black and White

The next day, they visited the Louvre. It was massive, overwhelmingly so, and after two hours, Paolo apologized to Fey that he had experienced enough.

"I think my brain can't hold on to all of this," he complained. "It's making my head hurt."

They left after about two hours, retreating to the Tuileries. Fey gave him some aspirin, and they lay on the grass, under a tree, while she smoothed the pain away by combing her fingers through his wavy black hair. Two college students stood nearby, playing a Brandenburg concerto in duet on their violins. The sound of it was sweet and soothing. It was just as he had told her. The streets were, indeed, filled with music here. Even in the subways, there were talented musicians playing for the sheer joy of it and for the donations of the passersby. He fell asleep for a while, lulled by the soft tones of the girls' violins and the touch of her fingers massaging his scalp through his hair.

Their stay quickly came to an end. It was time to return home. A farm did not wait, and they couldn't ask their friends to take care of things forever. Plus, city life was expensive, and the money they had brought, which had seemed so much when they arrived, was running out. They boarded the train that would take them home.

"So, what next?" she asked, as they pulled away from the platform. She knew he had to have a new goal. It would be something difficult, almost unattainable, she was sure. It was how his mind worked. "Visit the South Pole? Climb Mount Kilimanjaro?"

He laughed. "No, Fey. My next journey won't be that easy."

He said this with wistful sadness in his expression, and she knew that he had been thinking about this. She looked at him quizzically, hoping he would explain. He just pulled his journal out of the side pocket of his carry-on and handed it to her. Then he leaned back and shut his eyes as the train rocked them back and forth. The bookmark led her to the appropriate page.

As is my nature, I realize that I can never be content for long.

There exists another City of Light, whose beauty eclipses the one that enfolds us. My desire to experience this place, for which there are no words to describe, absolutely consumes me. Dogged by doubt about the very existence of my soul, I wonder if I will ever see it. Paradise cannot be earned. It is a gift, freely given. Does wanting this gift cause it to be received? With all my heart, I hope so.

Journey's End
In my lover's arms, my journey's end;
To gaze upon such fairness, unsurpassed.
Twin desires of my heart doth blend,
Fulfillment of my passions seen at last.
Alas, my heart is not content for long,
Doth earthly beauty by divine replace.
Adam wouldst his suffering prolong
With thoughts of lofty Paradise to taste.
Dark Night doth overtake to steal my peace.
Hope hath fled beneath her somber gaze.
She grips my thoughts and wilt not grant release;
Casts her shadow o'er all my days.
    That I couldst know, within my heart assured,
    That Paradise wouldst to me be secured.

Fey looked over at him with pity. She wasn't sure what to tell him. Could he handle the truth? She wanted badly to tell him, to share who she really was, who he was. She didn't have to say anything at the moment, though. The train had rocked him to sleep. She was concerned that he slept so much. He could be awake and alert, and then, after sitting down for five minutes, he would be almost comatose. He hadn't complained about not feeling well, but it nagged at her. It just didn't seem right. He leaned against her, deep in slumber, snuggling into her shoulder. She gladly bore the heaviness of his large frame, happy to feel his closeness as the train pulled them toward home.

The silver BMW pulled into the gravel lane in front of the Paysannes' farmhouse the day after the newlyweds returned from Paris. Gilbert made his way up the drive, hand in hand with Yasmine. Both were still dressed for work—Yasmine in her barista uniform of black slacks and crisp, white shirt, and Gilbert in black suit pants and perennial white dress shirt, sans tie, like a matched pair of Parisian waiters. Fey stepped out onto the porch, still wearing the glow of fresh love like a soft, invisible garment. Gilbert noted that she absolutely radiated happiness. He could truly empathize, after having waited longer to be with Yasmine than any other girl he had dated. It did, he realized with amusement, sort of whet one's appetite for the whole experience.

"Hey, there," he greeted the new bride cheerfully, swirling her around in a tight bear hug before setting her lightly back on the ground.

Yasmine graced her friend with air kisses on each cheek and embraced her delicately.

"So ..." Gilbert leaned into her suggestively. "Did you wear our poor Lambie out?"

Fey laughed, pointing inside toward the sofa, where Paolo lay fast asleep, lips slightly parted, one arm casually lying across his chest. His nap buddy, Sophie, was draped across his legs, her head resting against his side. She looked up and wagged her tail listlessly and then closed her eyes again, seeming glad to have her master back home.

Gilbert shook his head, a grin on his face. "You wicked woman!" He laughed with his hearty chuckle.

She and Yasmine joined in, and Paolo, hearing their laughter, was roused from his nap.

"Hey," he greeted them, stifling a yawn. Pushing his hair back, he sat up, rubbing his eyes with the heels of his hands to chase the sleepiness away.

Sophie groaned in protest, shifting her position on the sofa to take up more room.

"Thanks for joining us." Gilbert came over and mussed his hair.

Paolo batted his hand away but smiled at seeing his friend.

"Let's go outside. I need a smoke. We'll leave the ladies to talk about how lucky they are to have ensnared such fabulous catches," he bragged, patting Yasmine familiarly on the rear. She smacked his arm with a pout, the twinkle in her eye betraying that she didn't really mind. He shrugged his apology on the way out the door, the look on his face completely unrepentant.

Paolo nodded to Fey and Yasmine and shuffled out behind him. Gilbert saw Fey shaking her head indulgently at the both of them as she shut the door.

They casually strolled along the drive toward the barn. "So, how was it?" Gilbert asked, exhaling a long plume of silver smoke as he walked, a lit cigarette between his fingers.

"Paris? Oh, it's everything I had heard, and more. I really would like to go back someday. We've just only scratched its surface, I think."

As much as Paolo gushed about his trip, it sounded forced. The career salesman picked up on that right away, looking sympathetic.

"Paris does have its charms, but it's just a big, dirty city, not the end of the rainbow, Paolo."

Paolo nodded but said nothing. *Is he disappointed?* Gilbert wondered. He waved his hand dismissively and then threw down the cigarette stub, snuffing it out with the toe of his shoe. "Anyway, I don't need a travel log. What I really meant was, how did things go with Fey? I want to hear all the details," he said with a playful wink.

Paolo got that scandalized-old-lady look on his face.

Still the same Lambie, Gilbert thought with amusement. He wrapped his arm around Paolo's neck, grabbing him in a headlock. "I'll squeeze it out of you!" He laughed.

Paolo flinched, laughing. "Stop, please!" he begged.

Gilbert released his discomfited friend and backed off. He grew thoughtful. Leaning on the low stone wall by the barn, he asked Paolo, with seriousness in his voice, mingled with admiration, "How did you do it? I mean, I couldn't wait to get the go-ahead from Yasi. Yet, here you are, head over heels in love, and, from what I could see, it was eating holes in your gut—and she would've been more than willing. How in the world did you survive it for six months?"

"Six months?" Paolo questioned dismissively. "Six months, you say? Try almost a whole year, if you count from the time we got engaged," he corrected, scooping up the barn cat, which rubbed up against his legs. The cat purred his thanks, grateful for the unwonted attention.

"First, we waited to tell Natalie until we felt she could handle it. Then, the priest made us wait six months and take classes. By then, Fey decided we should probably just hold off a little longer and have the wedding on the day we got back together, on the last day of summer."

He put the cat down and shook his head. "I couldn't understand what the big deal was about that. It felt to me like my sentence had been extended, but seeing that it was important to her ..." He shrugged. "I just went along with it."

"I can tell you I wouldn't have made it," Gilbert noted honestly.

He lit two cigarettes and offered one to his friend. Paolo took a thoughtful drag on it and then looked pointedly at him.

"My dad, Guy, told me that we are the sum of the choices we make."

Gilbert nodded, his face twisting into a wry frown. *What does that say about me?*

"The hardest thing was, it was not just one difficult choice, but every day the same difficult choice, a hundred times over. It was not easy," Paolo admitted, smoke wafting in a curling cloud around his face. "You and I aren't as different as you think."

Gilbert looked up at that, overcome with admiration. "I wish I had met you years ago," he lamented. "I might not be such a mess right now if I had."

Breathing out smoke like a beautiful dragon, Gilbert had something to tell his newly married friend. "Yasi moved in with me, right after your wedding," he said, meeting Paolo's surprised, and not approving, look with his own.

"She was living in this tiny, rat-hole of an apartment, and, well, it didn't seem right." His voice pitched up defensively. He shrank back as the cat began to rub loose fur all over the cuffs of his pants.

"Do you love her?" Paolo asked, putting out his half-smoked cigarette on the ground and shooing the feline away.

"Yes, I do," Gilbert told him, his expression genuine and sincere.

"Well, why don't you just marry her then?"

"Paolo, in case you haven't noticed, I'm not exactly the most stable person on the planet. Would it be fair to ask her to tie herself down to me, when I can't even handle my own life?"

"My dad said that nobody's perfect," he replied. "If she loves you, she'll understand."

Gilbert shook his head and folded his arms. "Life's not always written in black and white, my friend."

48

Regret

Luc handed Gilbert a small package. He had just returned from Paris. The latter thanked him, paying him in cash for what he had brought. The two men stood outside the pub in the cold, December air, smoking. Smashing out their cigarettes on the sidewalk, they decided to go in for a drink while they were there. Yasmine had gone shopping with Fey and wouldn't be home for hours, anyway. Now that she had moved in with him, Gilbert didn't like being in his apartment alone. The solitude was fast becoming unfamiliar.

They chose a table in the back of the local watering hole and spent their time downing mixed drinks and talking. Luc had subtly made him feel guilty about hanging out so much with Paolo, who never went clubbing after he married Fey. Gilbert had an inkling that the offer to go to Paris and get him his fix was a kind of bribe, as Luc seemed to be jealous of all the time he was now spending at the Paysanne farm. So, he sat and passed a few hours with his oldest friend, who was loyal to a fault and certainly did not deserve to be neglected.

A few hours later, Gilbert made his way unsteadily home. He hoped that Yasmine would be back from her shopping trip, waiting for him. He left his car parked somewhere near the pub. Not one to take that kind of chance, he preferred walking to driving buzzed. Truth be told, he was way beyond that. He would find the BMW the next morning. One of the nice things about living in a small village was that everything was within walking distance.

Stamping noisily up the stairs to his flat, he hummed tunelessly to himself. At the door, he pulled out his keys and dropped them on the floor. He leaned against the wall to pick them up and, after a few attempts, managed to get the door to his apartment open.

"Yasi?" he called loudly.

Silence answered.

Gilbert threw his keys and the package on the mahogany console by the front door, tossed his leather coat on a chair, and poured himself a glass of scotch. He would wait for her to come home before they ordered dinner. Filled with ennui, he sat down on the sofa with his drink.

Ah, well, I might as well check out what Luc brought me, he thought, draining his glass. He plunked it down on the coffee table and heaved himself off of the sofa. He made his way unsteadily over to the console to retrieve the package. Clumsily, he opened it. A small bag of white powder was wrapped in the plain brown paper. He had to work the next day, he reminded himself, but he was so bored without Yasmine to keep him company. The loneliness was oppressive after becoming used to her comforting presence. He missed her so much and hoped she would come home soon.

Sighing, he opened the bag. It spilled out onto the top of the console in a dusty pile. He pulled out his pocket knife, opened the blade, and scraped the soft powder into a messy line, scratching the shiny mahogany top of the piece of furniture along with it. Pulling a rolled-up euro note from his coat pocket, he placed it on the end of the ragged white streak, leaned over, and slowly inhaled. Feeling immediately better, he set up another line …

Yasmine returned home about ten o'clock. She and Fey had had such a nice time. It was the first time she had ever been Christmas shopping. It had been fun and exciting; the shops were crowded with people choosing gifts for each other. She put her purchases by the door and hung her crimson wool coat on the rack; noticing the euro note and the spilled pile of white powder on the scratched surface of the console, she shook her head with a frown.

"Oh, that man," she growled. Would he never grow up?

She walked into the living room to find Gilbert huddled in a corner, in the middle of a full-blown panic attack.

"Bonbon, what's the matter?" she asked, running to help him up.

"Oh, Yasi," he cried, tears streaming down his face, "I thought you left me."

"You knew I went shopping with Fey, darling, remember?" She led him to the sofa, a shaky mess. Gilbert hugged his arms to his sides, breathing heavily and groaning.

"Oh, I'm going to be sick," he warned her. She ran to get the wastebasket and returned just in time. He emptied his stomach as she held her cold palm to his forehead.

"I's bad this time, Yasi. Please, please, don' leave me," he begged in desperation, grabbing hold of her sweater with both hands. "*Mon Dieu*, I feel like I'm going to die."

He sat, trembling, beside her, soaked in sweat, his face contorted in pain.

She dialed 112, the emergency number while he fretted beside her through gritted teeth. "I'm sorry. I'm sorry. Please don' leave me, Yasi."

"I'm right here. Try to calm down, dear," she directed him, her hand stroking his back to soothe him. She calmly requested an ambulance, holding Gilbert as he sat next to her, his breathing heavy and labored. His eyes rolled back in his head, and he passed out, leaning against her.

"Please hurry," she pleaded with the operator, growing suddenly very worried.

When the ambulance arrived, she quickly phoned his father.

Gilbert came to, but when the emergency workers went to put him into the ambulance, he began to hallucinate, shrieking that it was a giant boar, bigger than an elephant, and they were trying to feed him to its gaping maw. Yasmine sought to calm him. She told him she would ride with him and entered first, so he would see it was all right. He screamed as she climbed in, shouting that the giant pig had just swallowed his girlfriend and wasn't anyone going to help her? The team of medics struggled to strap him down as he fought them, with the strength of a madman, and to get him loaded inside. It was, needless to say, a very unpleasant trip.

In the emergency room, Yasmine stayed by Gilbert, holding his hand. Jacques arrived, looking strained and somber. He nodded silently at Yasmine and sat on a stiff chair to the side, gloomy and tense.

Yasmine reached over, placing her face close to Gilbert's as he trembled.

"You can do this, Bonbon. Just a little while longer," she promised.

Gilbert leaned into her. He hid his face against her neck and shivered. He closed his eyes, took a deep breath, and tried to regain his composure. Slowly, he began to calm down. Yasmine held him until he fell asleep, exhausted. He snuggled up against her. Even in sleep, his face looked ravaged with fatigue. Jacques breathed a sigh of relief. The worst was over.

The nurse kept coming in to check on him, seeming satisfied with his progress.

"He's had a very close call, this one," she informed them both.

Hyperthermia was a dangerous side effect of an overdose, but treatable, she explained. She informed them gravely that the patient probably had suffered some heart damage, as serious as his condition had been.

"That already happened a long time ago," Yasmine quipped wryly.

Jacques walked into the hospital room alone with a somber look darkening his face. He had asked Yasmine to give him some time with his son. She had gladly obliged, telling him she would wait in the cafeteria, where he left her drinking coffee and flipping absently through her new copy of *Vogue*. They were both exhausted. It had been a long haul.

Gilbert, who had been sitting on the edge of the bed dressed in a worn blue hospital gown, stood as his father entered and looked away, saying nothing. Jacques sat down, still overcome with tiredness, studying his disheveled son with disgust, his own exterior similarly rough, as he had not left since the previous night.

"Why are you doing this to yourself?" he asked, at the end of his endurance for Gilbert's recklessness. "You almost died!" he yelled, furious at him. "I have tried," he continued, lowering his voice with an effort of will, "to give you everything I could. I know I'm not your mother, but please believe me; I tried my hardest to be there for you boys. I want so much to teach you everything you'll need to know to take over the business, but you just don't seem to care," he finished, waving his arm dismissively in an uncharacteristic physical demonstration, the despair he felt quite evident in his tone.

A bitter look clouded Gilbert's face. "Too bad you got stuck with me to hand it over to. I know Tristan was your first choice."

"What do you mean by that?" Jacques asked, truly perplexed.

His son glared at him. "Oh, Dad, don't even pretend that it's not true. As soon as Mom left, you were all about Tristan, teaching him everything, leaving me to do whatever the hell I wanted, as long as I stayed out of the way. I guess it's because I look like Mom that you loved him more."

The pain on his face told Jacques that he really believed this to be true. He eyed his son with disbelief. Was that why he had become so unmanageable, all because of some stupid misunderstanding? He shook his head.

"Oh, Gilbert, please," he reached out to him with his words, "you were so young. I just wanted to give you some time to be a kid before getting you involved. You see what hard work it is, running a business. I figured you had been through so much, with your mom leaving. I didn't want to put too much pressure on you."

He sighed, looking at his son with a mixture of pity and frustration. "It seems that all I've done, my whole life, is work. I just wanted you to have something more," he explained, looking tired and worn down. "Can't you understand that?"

Gilbert still glared at him, unconvinced. Then, in a flash of recollection, Jacques remembered the barb he had slung at his boy sometime back.

"I am so sorry, for what I said that day, when I saw you kissing Yasmine at the shop. It was stupid and thoughtless of me, and I didn't mean it, Gilbert. Please, Son, I'm not perfect either."

Gilbert looked down with an expression of hurt, his eyes filling. "I can forgive you, but I'll always remember what you told me that day."

"I wish that I could take back what I said, but I can't. As for preferring your brother, I could see it was you who had the real talent for business." Jacques exhaled, shaking his head derisively. "He needed the head start. Unlike you, getting him to understand selling and bookkeeping was like pulling teeth.

It was always you that I knew would eventually have to carry the burden of leadership. Tristan would never have been able to handle being in charge. You probably would've ended up buying him out, like I did with my own brother."

Gilbert sank down on the edge of the bed, his eyes wide with disbelief.

"All these years, I truly thought you loved Tristan more. Oh, Dad, I was so mean and jealous toward him. Now …" His face crumpled as the realization hit. "Now, there's no way to apologize, no way to make it up to him."

Gilbert broke down in tears. "Oh, Tristan, my brother!" he cried, shaking with sobs.

Jacques went over and pulled him close. He rarely showed affection to the boys, but that didn't mean he cared less. Gilbert wept in his father's embrace, and Jacques imagined all the years of useless bitterness washing away with his tears, leaving only regret. Jacques could feel how thin he was and thought, bitterly, *I hope it was worth it, Lucette, because Gilbert has paid a heavy price for your happiness.* As Jacques held his son, he finally saw clearly, with the eyes of his heart, not a twenty-six-year-old, drug-addicted man, but a broken-hearted, twelve-year-old boy, whose mother had abandoned him, leaving him feeling not only unloved but unlovable.

"I'm so sorry," Gilbert apologized in a choked voice.

Jacques took his son by the shoulders, looking down at him with his own regrets in mind.

"I should've made more time for you then. I wasn't thinking straight. I wish I could make it up to you somehow."

"You can," he told him, looking him in the eye, his own bloodshot and sunken. "You can help me get through this."

Jacques nodded and then sank back down onto the chair. Gilbert wiped his face on the bedsheet and balled it up on top of the mattress.

"Dad?" he asked, giving his father a quick, sidelong glance.

"Hmm?"

Gilbert closed his eyes, a look of deep sadness overcoming him.

"Just once, just once, could you tell me?"

What? Jacques wondered. *Tell him what?* Then, looking over at his boy's face, so full of pain, he knew.

"Son," he said and sighed, "I love you. I always have, and no matter what you do, I always will."

A tear slid down Gilbert's face, unchecked. "I love you, too."

Yasmine had returned but stood out of sight, overhearing the exchange going on in the hospital room. The nurse tried to come in to check on Gilbert, but she grabbed her arm and held her finger to her lips, steering her away.

"Just give them a minute, please," she whispered.

The nurse nodded sympathetically. Yasmine waited until she was sure they were done working things out and then slowly, casually, entered the room.

"Hey, Bonbon, you feeling better?" she asked him sweetly. She scooped him into her arms and placed a kiss on top of his head.

"Yasi, you came back," he marveled, his face alight with love.

"I told you I would, silly," she scolded, roughing up his already messy hair. My, he looked awful. His eyes were red and swollen, he needed a shave, and he smelled like stale sweat. "Remember, I'm playing for keeps," she reminded him, kissing her finger and touching it to the tip of his nose.

He looked at her with humility. "I'm so sorry, babe, for what I put you through. You've given me so much and only asked two things in return. I never cheated on you, Yasi," he promised her, looking her in the eyes to make sure she knew he wasn't lying, "and I swear I'm ready to get better."

It had been one of those nights. Fey had awakened to find that her husband had again slipped from the warm coverings to pace the living room floor. In the mornings, he would act like everything was fine, greeting her with an affectionate kiss and a cup of coffee before escaping to the outdoors to work.

She had learned to head for his journal to see what had been eating at him during the sleepless night before. It lay on the desk, facedown.

> *The troubling dream has again returned. I see this Paolo, who doesn't even look like me, murdered brutally and thrown away like garbage while I watch and do nothing. I still wonder if Gilbert is right and that this dream or nightmare, rather, means something else. Is it a desire on my part to keep my past buried? Does self-loathing over my sinfulness spill into my dreams, causing me to fantasize of murdering one who bears my name? I wish I knew.*
>
> *My greatest fear is that, in trusting Fey and Gilbert, who assure me that I am a decent person, I may yet remember my past and find that I regret allowing my beloved to tie her life to my own. As much as I detest Solitude, I would much prefer to suffer her embrace than to defile my sweet Fey by having her consort with a vile, heartless murderer.*

Fey shook her head, grabbing at her hair in frustration. It seemed, whether she would choose to tell him the truth or not, he would still suffer. *If only I could ask Arcenciel,* she wished silently. *She would know the answer.*

But Arcenciel was as far removed from her as Paolo's dreams were from the reality she withheld from her tortured spouse.

49

Matchmaker

It was a bright January day. The snow, which had fallen during the night, hugged the sidewalks in drifts, the plow having scraped its way noisily through the village in the hours before dawn. The scuffing of shovels filled the cold, sharp air, amplified by the simplicity of the winter landscape. Unseen, a fluff of eiderdown floated above the heads of the hurrying pedestrians. It drifted into the coffee shop above Jacques de Gaul as he entered the aromatic establishment for his morning coffee. The interior was crowded, as the Achèrois vied for the few precious tables inside. Business was as brisk as the weather.

"So, how we doing today?" Fleur heard the barista ask her man's father sweetly. Yasmine handed Jacques his morning coffee with a smile.

"About the same," he answered in a dry tone, taking the steaming cup with a bland expression.

"I miss him too," she reminded him with a look of sympathy on her pretty, round face.

Fleur knew that the young haberdasher had been sent away to be healed of his excesses. She felt badly for Yasmine and could only imagine what it must be like to be stuck in human form with her beloved so far away.

314

Doffing her mantle, she made ready with her bow, carefully nocking the arrow for her big moment.

De Gaul, Senior, gave a nod of gratitude and took a sip of the strong, hot black coffee.

"Hey." Yasmine caught his arm as he turned to go.

Fleur's heart began to beat faster. Her instant of action was approaching.

The businessman looked at the barista with a glimmer of surprise. "See that woman out there? The pretty one at the corner?"

"Hmm?" he growled.

The time was ripe. As the haberdasher turned to look at the woman to whom she had been sending Love Wishes for over a year, Fleur launched her arrow with focused attention, watching with delight as it hit the mark.

Now that's how it's done, Guiscard, she boasted triumphantly to herself.

Yasmine narrowed her bright-blue eyes, intently watching Jacques absently scratch at his shirt front as he studied the woman standing on the snow-covered sidewalk.

She possessed an air of confidence and had an attractive figure and neat blonde hair, which she wore in a feminine page-boy style. She might have been about five to ten years younger than he was.

A pretty catch, Fleur thought approvingly.

"Well," Yasmine continued, in a conspiratorial tone, "I just happen to know that she looks holes in you every time she catches sight of you." She winked.

The eyes of Fleur's target widened in surprise, but he remained otherwise unruffled.

"She's an attorney," Yasmine told him. "Makes pretty good money, divorced, two grown daughters, one of whom attends graduate school at the Sorbonne. Nice lady, very sweet. Lonely, though. She's picky when it comes to men. Only wants the very best," she stated emphatically, looking him in the eye with a hint of a smile, her dimple appearing playfully on her cheek. She pushed her index finger into his chest.

Jacques opened his mouth as if to speak, but he was dumbstruck. He studied Yasmine's features as she spoke. She returned his shrewd gaze with one of wide-eyed innocence. He turned with a hint of longing toward the woman, who caught his glance and then looked away, caught in the act.

Flirtation, Fleur noted with a chuckle. She studied him thoughtfully, her heart full of compassion for this lonely man, who seemed to feel himself not much in the way of romantic potential.

"She gets here a half hour before you, just about every day. Come early tomorrow," Yasmine ordered confidently. "Be waiting for her with two cups of coffee. Next day, buy her flowers. She always stops to look in the window at the florist's. Not sure what she likes, just pick something subtle, like freesias. No pressure that way. Roses can be a bit blunt," she mused.

Jacques stood silent, his expression unchanged. The customer behind him in line coughed impatiently.

"Helloooh?" she waved at him.

He laughed, shaking his head as he snapped out of his stupor. Nodding in thanks, he raised his cup in a mock toast, took a sip, and turned to go, a definite spring appearing in his step.

Fleur danced in delight. The haberdasher of Achères would be her finest accomplishment. Anyone could incite passion in the heart of a reckless youth, but to take the broken heart of a person of more tempered reason and find a way to mend the hardened edges, now *that* showed talent. Of course, she had had help, but by the expression on her former teacher's face, the apprentice knew Yasmine was pleased with her work.

Donning her soft mantle woven of airy eiderdown, the faerie flew out through the door as the next customers came in for their morning coffee.

Jacques followed Yasmine's orders, appearing nervously about forty-five minutes earlier than usual. She noticed that he seemed to have dressed with special care and had just gotten a fresh haircut. He smelled nicely of the same cologne that her boyfriend wore to excess. He looked uncertainly at Yasmine, as if seeking her advice.

"Just stand here and talk to me until she gets here," she ordered. "Then, I'll pour your coffees, and you hand her one. I know just how she likes it, so you won't even have to ask. She likes to sit by the window, inside, so she can watch for you. Just sit there. I reserved the table for you until she gets here, so no one else would take it," she rambled on. Claude turned and glared at her as she said this, obviously not happy about his prime table being empty as customers stood about in wait.

Jacques just nodded dumbly, following Yasmine's orders. He approached the pleasant-looking, well-dressed woman with a proffered cup, his hand shaking. The woman smiled her thanks and gladly sat down as Jacques pulled out a chair for her at "their" table, to the chagrin of those who stood waiting for a spot. Claude never allowed anyone to reserve a table in his busy shop, and they wondered who this VIP was. De Gaul. "Figures," they muttered jealously as the wealthy businessman enjoyed the privilege of his social status. Yasmine folded her arms in challenge to anyone who dared look askance, including her boss, who kept silent, preferring to choose his battles when it came to his outspoken employee.

They talked until both were almost late for work. The woman handed Jacques a slip of paper with a smile and a backward glance. He looked ten years younger in just that short span of time.

The Berlinermauer was going down.

50

Homecoming

A rhythmic percussion filled the air as the high-speed train hurried through the French countryside. Gilbert sat slumped in his seat, looking out the window. He had chosen to travel by rail so that Yasmine and his father would not have to see the place where he had spent the last three months. He had wanted to do it on his own, from start to finish. He knew he would need their help later. They would meet him at the station. He stared at the passing landscape, which had become wet and soft as winter melted away. He had the strangest feeling and wondered if it was how prisoners felt at the end of their sentence. He certainly felt like he had done time, even though it was of his own volition.

As he absently watched the villages, fields, and woods go by, all of which hinted at the unfulfilled promise of spring, he thought back to his conversation with Paolo after he had returned from his honeymoon. He had been joking around, trying to pry out some juicy details about his friend's sex life, but he knew that Paolo would be shut like a clam on that topic. He had just wanted to make him squirm a little, for fun.

He had gleaned something much more helpful, though, from that encounter, as Paolo's words played back through his mind. "It was not just one difficult choice, but every day, the same difficult choice, a hundred times over." He had been referring to his decision not to sleep with Fey until after they got married, even though he had wanted to badly, as he had admitted, in his own way. Gilbert had seen the steamy looks that passed between the two of them and was amazed they had actually succeeded until the end, especially since Fey had no problem with it. Well, those words were going to apply even more so to him, as his new life stretched before him. Paolo was married now. His test was over. Gilbert's temptation would never end. It would lurk at the back of his consciousness his whole life. He knew the recidivism rate for drug addicts was very high. It was a scary thought.

Stepping off at the station, suitcase in hand, his eyes searched the platform. The cool March air caressed his hair reassuringly. His heart beat faster as he caught sight of them, standing side by side at the opposite end of the planks—a dainty red figure between two tall, broad men. He just stood for a second, drinking in the sight.

His father stood in his work clothes and dress coat, looking the same as always—maybe better—Gilbert thought. Yasmine was dressed in her crimson coat and black kitten heels, her blonde curls dancing in the March breeze. Paolo stood on her other side, in a barn coat and jeans but possessed of a dignity that his work only seemed to enhance.

His father looked at him blankly for a moment, not recognizing him at first. Gilbert waved at him and smiled broadly. He hadn't cut his hair for the entire three months, and it hung, long and glossy, dusting his shoulders. He had about a three-day beard, tinged reddish gold, and was dressed very casually in his favorite Bob Marley T-shirt, a light leather jacket, and jeans. He had gained some much-needed weight while he was away. It gave his face an appealing, boyish roundness.

They all met in the middle of the platform.

"Oh, Yasi, you did wait for me," he crooned in disbelief and delight. "I love you so much, you know."

She looked like a rose in her scarlet coat, he thought. Her exotic-shaped, baby-blue eyes looked at him with liquid emotion, and her ruby lips parted. He folded her in his arms and kissed her like no one else was there, greedily inhaling the floral scent of her perfume and groaning with release. It felt more like a precursor than a greeting.

Paolo and Jacques exchanged an uncomfortable look.

"Bonbon, dear!" She laughed, pushing him demurely away. "You are making your daddy blush."

He glanced up at his father with a guilty, apologetic expression and a hint of a crooked smile. Jacques chuckled, patting his son on the shoulder. "What's with the new look?" he asked in a pleasant, nonjudgmental tone.

"Oh, I don't know, Dad. I just get tired of looking so perfect all the time," he jested, sighing, though he really did dislike the dress code his father enforced like a schoolteacher: coat, tie, hair neat. Very conservative. It felt too restrictive for him sometimes. "Do I have to get a haircut?" he asked, his features twisting into a disdainful expression. He wanted to sport his "hippie" look for a while. To him, it was now synonymous with his new feeling of wellness. Plus, Yasmine had expressed a liking for guys with long hair. From the look on her face, he could tell it really turned her on.

Jacques studied him with a thoughtful frown, head tilted in consideration.

"Well, at least trim it up a bit," he conceded. Looking his son sternly in the eye, he asked him gruffly, "Do you remember, some months back, what I told you in the hospital?"

Gilbert thought for a moment and then his face brightened. "Yes, Dad, I do." He would never forget what his father had said.

"Good, because I don't like having to repeat myself." Jacques's eyes betrayed a twinkle.

Gilbert noted with amusement that Paolo looked visibly confused that he seemed to glow under his father's rebuke. Yasmine just smiled knowingly, taking her lover's hand.

Paolo stepped forward and gave his friend a warm embrace, which Gilbert returned with equal enthusiasm.

"Hey, it's good to see you!" the tall, broad farmer gushed.

"Let's go home," Jacques suggested, a satisfied look on his face.

He had planned a surprise at the house. Latif was there, as were Fey and Natalie, though Luc was conspicuously absent. An elegant lunch had been catered and was spread out on the buffet in the dining room—a thoughtful gesture, Gilbert noted gratefully. A woman whom he didn't recognize was also there. He guessed she was in her forties. She had a confident, pretty face and well-coiffed blonde hair and looked at his dad with admiration. Jacques introduced her.

"Gilbert, this is my friend, Simone."

Gilbert got a look on his face of shock and delight. "No way! Oh, Dad, I leave you alone for three months and you go and get a life. Incredible!" he exclaimed, taking her hand between his own. "How did you get him to stop working long enough to get to know each other? That's what I'd like to find out." He made a thoughtful face. "Well, he does have a pretty sweet office with a beautiful leather sofa," Gilbert told her with a wink and kissed her on both cheeks.

Simone laughed, a throaty, sensual sound that reminded him comfortably of Yasi. "We're just friends, Gilbert," she insisted with a raised-eyebrow look at Jacques.

Jacques shot him a black scowl that said, "You'd better behave in front of her."

Latif, noticing his employer's frown, sympathized. "He used to say stuff like that to me all the time, Jacques. I've become immune, after many years of abuse."

Paolo respectfully suppressed his amusement, looking down and pressing his lips together.

"Oh, Bonbon, your hair looks prettier than Natalie's," Latif ribbed. "I just want to run my hands through it," he growled, ruffling his friend's silky brown tresses, as Gilbert deflected him, laughing.

His expression became more serious, and he looked at Latif with confusion.

"Dad, if Latif is here, who's minding the store?"

"Oh, I closed down for a few hours," Jacques said casually, looking pointedly at the ceiling.

Closing the shop was a big deal. Only the two of them would understand its significance, though Latif would, as well, in time. Gilbert started to get misty-eyed and saw his father sneaking a satisfied glance his way. He recovered with a sarcastic barb, delivered with a shrug and a frown.

"Well, I guess if you want everything to go to hell in a handbasket, that's okay."

"No, I don't. Latif, I want you back, store opened, ready for business, by five till two. He offered to come on full-time, by the way," Jacques informed the junior partner, who beamed and punched his college chum in the arm with joy. Latif laughed and flinched at the same time.

"Let's eat, or we'll have to send your friend back to work hungry," Jacques ordered.

"One more thing, first," Gilbert told his father, as everyone made ready to sit down.

He stood in front of Yasmine, and the room grew completely silent as he knelt down in front of her on one knee, in classic fashion, holding a simple, one-carat diamond ring between his fingers.

"Yasmine, you have stood by me in the worst moments of my life. I would like you to also share the best, which, I promise, would still be to come with you at my side. Would you do me the honor of being my wife?" He looked up at her with an expression of humility and trust, knowing in his heart that she was the one woman who would never hurt or abandon him. He felt incredibly lucky to be kneeling before her. He wouldn't put the ring on her finger. He was a risk and wanted the choice to be unforced. Gilbert simply knelt, proffering it before her, looking up at her hopefully. She could reject him—should, really—but it was a risk he was willing to take. He would never find another like her, anywhere.

Yasmine stood, looking completely shocked, as did the whole rest of the room. She took hold of the ring, and he let go with a sigh of relief. She slid it on her finger, a perfect fit.

She pulled him to his feet and gazed into his eyes with a look of complete joy on her face, nodding her assent, as she was absolutely speechless. The roomful of well-wishers cheered noisily as the newly engaged couple shared a kiss to seal the bargain.

"Oh, I can't resist you, my yummy little Bonbon," she cooed, finding her voice as she wrapped her arms around him. Natalie put her index finger in her mouth and made gagging noises just loud enough for Paolo and Latif to hear. The two men shook with silent laughter.

They then sat down to lunch, enjoying a moment of great joy at the return of their beloved son and friend and at the happy surprise he had given the woman who had stood faithfully by him. His friends assured Gilbert and his father that they would do their best to help him rework his life into something new and better. The rest was up to him. It seemed, though, that he had already made a pretty good start of it.

Gilbert was so glad to be back. The past three months had been hellishly difficult, and he had missed Yasmine every moment, fearing she would not be there when he returned home. Asking her to marry him had been a huge leap for him, made even more dramatic by proposing to her in front of everyone he cared about. The commitment was scary, but the thought of losing her was even more so.

They all knew that the overwhelming majority of addicts suffered relapses, unfortunately. No one trusted that Gilbert would be any different. They were all very vigilant. Between his dad and Latif at work, Yasmine at home, and Paolo on weekends, he was rarely alone. Even if he had wanted to, there was little chance for backsliding.

Yasmine had tried to make him give up Luc as a friend. She blamed him for almost killing him with that batch of pure, uncut cocaine he had brought back from Paris, but Gilbert had begged her to at least let them play tennis together. No one else could compete with his aggressive game, and he really needed that outlet. She, in turn, pleaded with him to ease up on his intense play. She worried about his heart, which had been weakened by the overdose he had experienced. He promised to go easy but forgot all about it as soon as he hit the first serve.

The betrothed couple had a heated argument over whether Luc should be allowed to attend their wedding.

"You aren't seriously going to ask the man who bought the poison that almost killed you?" she asked in a furious tone.

Gilbert grew uncharacteristically angry, his jaw set, eyes narrowed.

"I don't abandon the people I care about when they happen to become inconvenient," he shot back. He, watching her shrink under his anger, immediately grew meek, afraid he had offended her. He had no right to be overbearing. She had already put up with so much from him.

"Let's not fight, Yasi," he suggested quietly. Pulling her close, he apologized for his wrath. She nodded, letting him hold her. Gilbert had prevailed, explaining that Luc was his oldest friend and that the blame for his behavior could not be foisted off onto someone else. He was loyal to a fault with those he let into his heart. Love, he explained, forgave all offenses.

51

Battle

Paolo stood over Michelle's grave, Fey on his right, Natalie on his left, oblivious to the drizzle of April rain that continued to fall. His head was bowed, his dark hair falling damply over his eyes. Natalie held herself straight; her chin lifted defiantly, a look of grim determination on her pale face. Bending down, she placed a bouquet of herbs from the kitchen garden her sister had planted on the headstone. Dry-eyed, she stood back up, casting a glance at the man she looked up to as a brother.

Paolo drew a single pink rose from inside his black suit coat. Ripping the petals off with one hand, he cast the thorny stem aside and sprinkled them over the wet ground. Fey gently entwined her fingers with his. The three stood, lost in thought and prayer for a few moments, two black-clad figures and one in snowy white.

"You really did love her," Fey stated more than asked.

Paolo nodded silently. "I don't know how to stop loving someone, once I start," he explained, hoping she understood. He wondered if it were even possible.

Fey squeezed his hand reassuringly. Paolo looked at her gratefully. She would never ask him to lie to her.

"It's time to go," Natalie announced, turning to leave.

The rain vied with the trial to see which could endure the longest. The courtroom was starkly plain, virtually devoid of paintings, carving, or any other distractions to the important business at hand. Paolo, who usually liked simplicity, found the barren chamber oppressive. A row of stiff chairs filled with men and women of various ages and situations was lined up next to the wooden judge's bench. Ten rows of hard pews, like a church, faced the proceedings. Two tables with wooden chairs separated the opposing sides. The judge, a graying man with an unsmiling countenance, managed the proceedings with lugubrious sternness. The prosecutor, a slim, plain woman who wore dark suits and practical shoes, squared off against the defense attorney, a bland, light-haired man with a trim beard. René sat, suited and silent, listening intently, but betraying no expression. His hair had returned to its natural auburn shade during his confinement in prison.

Over the course of the next few weeks, Paolo sat with his wife and his little sister in the oppressive box of a room. Gilbert joined them as often as he could, always with Yasmine by his side. It seemed that finding out the truth of a situation from the various personal recollections of all involved was a complicated thing. Considering what Paolo had come to understand about human motivation, this was not surprising to him. As the long list of charges against his foe was read, Paolo wondered how a man could let his life slide into such a moral abyss. It was interesting to him, hearing first the prosecutor then the defense attorney make their opening statements. If he hadn't known better, he would have sworn that they were each referring to a different man.

Next to the charges of drug possession and intent to distribute, Michelle's murder was the easiest to prosecute. René, in his violent rage, had been extremely sloppy. Her body had not even been that hard to find, as a driver of a passing car, a local man who was aware of the unsolved murder, had spotted the knife glinting in the sun by the side of the road and stopped to inspect it. He immediately called the police with a tip. Tire tracks in the frozen mud nearby and bits of clothing scattered in the woods had left a sloppy trail straight to Michelle's battered corpse.

Paolo hugged Natalie protectively as the ugly story was laid out by the prosecutor. Natalie often leaned into her big brother for strength, hiding her face now and then against the front of his dark coat when things got too hard to hear. His other hand was entwined lightly with Fey's.

He sometimes found it hard to pay attention as the prosecutor laid out, in agonizing detail, the evidence against the accused. Often, his mind began to wander to more pleasant climes and he would suddenly come to, gazing vacantly about as if surprised that, yes, they were all still there in the bland confines of the courtroom, the rain still streaking the windows.

At the end of the long, tedious days, he looked forward to stripping off his dress clothes and heading out in his jeans and a chambray shirt to work in the barn. He vowed never again to complain about the little bit of paperwork he had to suffer through. Compared to the cold, soulless atmosphere of the courtroom, sitting at his desk in his own living room was a pleasure.

Finally, it was Paolo's turn to testify about the vicious attack René had inflicted on him. He glanced over at his assailant, who sat, looking uncharacteristically well groomed compared with his appearance that other night. René stared blankly ahead, refusing to meet Paolo's eye.

The judge had to ask Paolo to speak up several times. He really didn't want Fey and Natalie to have to hear what he had to say. He could not look their way but instead sought out his best friend, who sat one row behind with Yasmine. Gilbert gave a nod of encouragement. He would also have to take the stand but now sat supportively with his fiancée in the gallery.

"Can you please tell the jury what aftereffects you have suffered because of the attack?" the prosecutor asked, probably wanting the jury to understand how much trauma the victim had undergone.

Not for himself, but for Michelle, Paolo honestly laid forth the weeks of agony, both physical and mental, he had endured. Glancing over at his friend once in a while, he told of the excruciating pain he had awakened to, the feelings of complete helplessness, and the long, slow recovery.

"Ah, I still get really bad headaches," he reluctantly admitted. "Sometimes they make me sick, though it's better than before. I used to just pass out when the pain got too bad."

Natalie and Fey exchanged a look of shock that he caught out of the corner of his eye. He had kept this hidden, not wanting to worry them.

The prosecutor kept him on the stand for what seemed like a very long time, considering it had only taken René about two minutes to finish him off in the alley. Next, the defense cross-examined him. Several times, the prosecutor voiced strong objections as René's attorney seemed to lead him into admitting that the whole fiasco in the alley had been instigated by him. She also objected when the defense asked pointedly if he were indeed of Roma descent.

Paolo wondered if the man was some kind of mind reader. Did the attorney sense the guilt he felt over his brashness? It seemed possible. He left the witness stand feeling very confused and shaken.

He tried not to think about all the people watching him and looked down at his hands most of the time. Gilbert had told him that trials were sometimes recorded and played on television, kind of a bizarre form of live entertainment. That thought was absolutely horrifying to think about, and he was glad that the judge hadn't allowed it in his courtroom.

A parade of rather tired-looking people made their way up the gravel drive to the Paysanne farmhouse in spite of the cold rain still coming down with enthusiasm. Fey and Paolo had their first real argument that evening as she scolded him roundly for keeping his headaches from her.

"It's no big deal," he answered defensively, looking past her at the door.

"You need to go back to the hospital, for an MRI," she argued, still angry.

Then Paolo looked truly panicked. "Please, Fey, I'm fine," he lied, his face betraying the falsehood by blanching. He made a hasty exit, fleeing the house. Gilbert followed solicitously behind.

Natalie let Fey have it, seeing his horrified expression as he escaped to the familiar comfort of the outdoors. "You weren't there, when he was in the hospital," she lectured his wife. "He was close to dead, and I think it really scared him, to be so helpless. How can you even think of sending him back there? Though I know he would do it if you made him. He'd be a doormat and let you wipe your feet on him, if he thought it would make you happy." She said this with disgust.

Fey, seeing how upset she had made him, backed off. He had been through enough, without her adding to his stress. Instead, she chose the more acceptable alternative. She made a tea for him and Natalie of strong, sleep-inducing herbs.

Paolo returned, looking damp and green, shooting her a glance filled with enough petulance, she could've sworn he was a teenage boy instead of a grown man. She handed him the tea as he slumped morosely on the sofa. Gilbert stood awkwardly in the doorway. Natalie marched up to the guest bedroom with her tea to escape into the peaceful oblivion of sleep.

Now that Paolo was married, Natalie was again allowed to stay at the farm, to the delight of both. She had returned permanently to Achères a week before the trial, deciding not to go back to boarding school—scholarship or no. She was told the trial could possibly take several weeks to complete anyway and vowed to be present for its entirety, as a show of love for her sister. Though their relationship had been strained at first, Fey accepted the teenage girl's presence. She was, in her opinion as well, the closest thing they had to family.

Gilbert, Yasmine, and Fey sat sipping wine as Paolo fell fast asleep, the empty teacup on the table beside him. Fey sat next to her unconscious man. Gilbert held Yasmine on his lap in Guy's chair. They had also had a long, unpleasant day and probably welcomed the chance to unwind.

"Our Lambie had a rough one today," he noted with an indulgent smile, watching his friend snoring peacefully.

Fey shot him a disapproving glance. Sometimes Gilbert's condescension toward her husband could be annoying. He seemed to think he was better, because Paolo was not worldly.

Gilbert, sensing her bristle, let down his usual guard, giving voice to thoughts he would normally suppress.

"Fey, I can't be like Paolo. I am what I am," he apologized. "It's an honor being his best friend, but it's hard, too."

Now it was Fey's turn to apologize. He had stood by Paolo every day, missing a lot of work and never complaining about it. "You've been a fine friend, Gilbert. I'm sorry. I know I'm hard on you sometimes."

Gilbert nodded silently, appearing to let go of his injured feelings. "My lady, it's time to be off," he ordered. Yasmine hopped up lightly. He followed, reaching for her hand. He tickled her palm playfully with his fingers. They all made their way to the front door.

"How are you going to get Sleeping Beauty upstairs?" he asked Fey, who shrugged. She certainly couldn't carry him.

Gilbert went back to the living room, picked up his friend's legs, hauled them up onto the sofa, and yanked him down so his head lay on the armrest. He pulled off his shoes and pitched them under the coffee table. Paolo shifted a bit and then settled back into his deep sleep.

"Can't tell you how many drunks I've put to bed," he joked.

After kissing Fey affectionately on both cheeks, he cast one last look at Paolo, his face the picture of tranquility.

"They're all so cute when they're sleeping," he cooed.

This time, Fey had to laugh. Gilbert was, by his own admission, just being himself. Who was she to say that was a bad thing?

The trial wore on. Gilbert was called as a witness and recounted watching René exit the pub in an agitated state, accompanied by his two friends, and told of finding Paolo in the alley shortly afterward, unsure if he was even still alive until he cut the tape from over his mouth.

Paolo fingered the faint scar on his cheek. *So that was where that had come from. Oh well, Gilbert didn't mean it, and the alley was so dark.* He couldn't blame his best friend, who had saved his life, for something so inconsequential. It wasn't important.

He spoke of his fear for Paolo's life upon hearing the dire comments of the ambulance crew. Gilbert shot an angry glare at René, who continued to avoid eye contact with anyone. He sat, impassive as stone, eyes fixed on some invisible point in front of him.

Fey squeezed Paolo's hand, and he glanced at her with a look he hoped she could interpret. *It's over now,* he wished he could tell her. *Don't think about the past, my love.* Fey, though, bit her lip, holding back her tears.

Unlike Paolo, Gilbert remained unflappable on the stand, returning the defense attorney's questions, which were meant to refute his testimony, with icy sarcasm. No objections were necessary from the prosecutor, though the judge glowered at his friend's condescension from time to time.

Surprisingly enough, the next two witnesses were René's friends, who had restrained Paolo while René had laid into him. They explained that they had been at the pub with René when Michelle and Paolo had appeared in the doorway. René had become very angry, as he and Michelle had been going out for a long time, and Paolo had pretty much asked her out right under his nose. Michelle had agreed, just to make René jealous, which it definitely did. He had asked them for their help to put a little fear into this guy, who didn't respect other people's boundaries. Things got a little bit out of hand, though, probably because René had had his share of beers that night.

"Yes," the prosecution countered, "but he still had enough presence of mind to rob the victim of a substantial sum of money, drive to the home of his former girlfriend, abduct her, slice her throat with a knife, and bury her body in the woods."

Of course, the defense attorney objected, considering the fact that the verdict on Michelle's murder was still out. That comment was stricken from the record, but everyone knew it was a lot more difficult to forget something you had already heard.

Next came testimony from the police, the ambulance crew, and Paolo's doctor. It seemed to Paolo to go on and on. He wondered how the jurors could take it all in. He, for one, decided that if he ever got called for jury duty, he would find a way to get out of it. There was no way he could pay attention long enough to make a decision on something so important as another person's life.

Eventually, it came time for Natalie's story to unfold. She was not forced to take the stand. Rather, the pre-recorded interview with Marie was submitted, and the jury listened carefully as the young girl poured out her nightmarish ordeal to the counselor.

At that moment, the reality of what Natalie had endured was finally revealed to Paolo in its true form. What she had suffered was, to him, pure evil. To steal the innocence from a child, he could fathom nothing worse. He sat, numb with shock, feeling Natalie leaning against him calmly, as if it were someone else on that recording. It made him sorry for every one of their petty, sibling-like squabbles. He pulled her close, his heart aching with his desire to protect her from something that had happened before they had ever met.

The prosecution finally finished. The defense would take up the case the next day. Paolo stood in the hallway with his family and friends. He was seething with indignation for Natalie, who hung close to him but appeared, to his continued surprise, completely unruffled. They hoped to wait out the reporters, who, hungry for a good story, had made something of a sensation out of the murder of the beautiful young woman and the rape of her sweet, orphaned sister—the romantic involvement of the mysterious Roma foreigner adding just the right touch of drama. Every day, they seemed to multiply, even coming from Italy, as they heard that one of the victims was Italian. Such attention was horrifying to Paolo, who wished he could disappear before he exited the building.

Just then, unexpectedly, René was led past them in handcuffs. The deputy escorted the prisoner through the main corridor, instead of around the back way, where he would not be seen by the victims. The courthouse was small. There weren't many places to go. René caught sight of Natalie, who grabbed onto the fabric of Paolo's coat. He looked at her to see her staring intently in front of her. Following her gaze, he noted that René returned her stare with an appraising look up and down.

Having seen men size girls up in the club in just such a way, Paolo became enraged. He body-slammed René with all his might, a growl of seething anger escaping from him as he smacked him hard into the wall. He wanted to rip him apart. Inches from his face, his voice quaking with loathing, he uttered, through gritted teeth, "I don't know what you are, but you are not a human being." Paolo then raised his fist to strike as René spat in his face. Gilbert grabbed his arm, pleading with him to stop.

"No, no, no, Paolo. Please, don't," he soothed, struggling to hold his work-hardened friend off. Paolo fought to shake him off, until Vincent grabbed him by the shoulders, pulling him roughly back.

"I'm sorry, sir," he apologized to Vin, a bit breathlessly. Paolo thought that the officer looked almost sympathetic.

Vin nodded gruffly and then followed René's progress down the hallway.

"Did you see what he did to me?" René shouted indignantly.

"I didn't see anything," the deputy grumbled in irritation, the echo carrying his voice through the halls of justice.

Coming to, Paolo looked almost grateful to have been stopped. Gilbert looked with revulsion at the spit on Paolo's face. Natalie took one of her omnipresent tissues from her purse and wiped it away. Paolo didn't seem to notice; his mind was off somewhere else. He had never felt rage before. It was a frightening emotion, like being drunk with anger. His thoughts flashed to his dream of the murdered grocer, and he wondered just what, if he were to give in to it, he would be capable of.

The deputy quickly moved René along. Vincent's voice could be heard all the way down the hall, scolding him roundly for his careless mistake. René remained silent.

"Why do you think they have that back stairwell?"

"Sorry, sir, but there's a horde of paparazzi waiting at the back door."

"Don't even try to make excuses! Do you know what that little girl has been through? Did you hear anything in there?"

"It won't happen again."

"That's for damn certain."

"Let's go home," Fey pleaded.

Paolo looked at her in a daze and then let her lead him away. He noted with relief that they were halfway done with the whole unpleasant business. He hung back at the doorway, though, upon seeing the throng of reporters.

Gilbert produced a black umbrella at the door and handed it to his shy friend with a smile. Paolo took it gratefully.

"Hey, I have no problem if they want to take my picture," the businessman joked as he opened the door and held it for the ladies. "They say there's no such thing as bad publicity."

Darkness permeated the alley. Was it the alley behind the fruit vendor's shop or the one behind J. de Gaul and Son? It seemed a confusing blend of both. He began to wander into the blackest portion of the narrow cobbled path, canyoned by high, vertical walls on either side. Hearing a noise, he turned to see René, blocking the way out.

"You and I, we aren't so different, after all, are we, farm boy?" he asked.

Paolo shook his head as René handed him the bloody knife. Looking behind his former assailant, he saw Michelle's lifeless body, lying in a shaft of light from the streetlamp. René pressed the knife into his palm, forcing his hand to close overtop of it. Grinning, René indicated that he should look behind him. The fruit vendor stood by the Dumpster, a look of horror on his innocent face.

"No!" Paolo protested, turning back to face René's sneering visage. "I can't!"

"You already did," René answered.

Paolo wheeled around to see the other Paolo slumped on the ground. Looking down at his hand, which was still tightly gripping the knife, he saw that it was dripping with hot black blood.

Perspectives

The next morning, Paolo sat at the kitchen table, looking very dejected. Dark circles showed under his eyes, as if he hadn't slept well the night before. Fey walked in and poured herself a cup of coffee. He raised his eyes slowly to meet her gaze, his aspect full of sadness, and she immediately knew what he was brooding about.

"Headache gone?" she asked solicitously, rubbing his shoulders.

He just shrugged noncommittally.

"You're not very happy about what you did yesterday, are you?" she guessed.

He shook his head slowly, staring down into his empty coffee mug.

"I'm no better than he is," he lamented, leaning his forehead on his folded hands.

Fey sat down next to him. "You made a mistake," she comforted him, laying her hand on his shoulder. "We all do, sometimes."

Paolo looked up, meeting her sympathetic look, his own eyes full of self-recrimination. "No, Fey," he disagreed, his voice shaky with humiliation. "What I did was to attack a man whose hands were bound. I wanted to kill him," he growled. His face twisted into a scowl, and then he turned away, looking back down at the table.

"Now I know how he felt, when he did the same to me."

The defense had begun to present its argument. Fey again sat on the hard pew with Paolo and Natalie, with Gilbert and Yasmine in the seats behind them.

The attorney began, not by denying René's involvement in Michelle's murder, but by explaining the defendant's mental state at the time. Although he had been determined competent to stand trial, he had, over the weeks preceding the incident, become increasingly violent and erratic in his behavior. This was verified by René's two friends, who described his change in personality as both drastic and sudden.

Fey knew all too well the truth behind the testimony. She wished, ungenerously, that Guiscard were present to see the damage he had inflicted on this already seriously flawed man with his flippant archery. As for Yasmine, she swore she could feel her friend's discomfort without even turning around to look at her. She had forgiven her for her folly but felt an insuppressible satisfaction that the matchmaker had to listen to what had transpired as a result of her reckless game.

Next, the defense portrayed the events of that awful night through René's eyes. Already unstable and somewhat neurotic, he watched as another man stepped in and took the woman he loved, right in front of him, with no decency with regard to his feelings. Then, like rubbing salt in his wounds, he had to endure seeing them together in the very place he sought refuge and oblivion, in the companionship of his closest friends and the numbing comfort of alcohol at the pub.

As he was already half inebriated, the drink swept away any inhibitions he may have had. Filled with rage and jealousy, the logical part of his brain shut down and he began to obey his darkest inclinations, coming to only after it was too late, as he held his girlfriend's body in the car. He was afraid and panicked.

Of the entire gathering in that courtroom, only two knew the real truth of what had actually transpired. The oblivious humans would have no idea the number of times they had crossed paths with the Fae over the centuries, Fey noted. Their minds remained stubbornly shut to the spiritual realm, which they professed to believe in but when confronted with evidence of its existence, roundly dismissed it for fear of being ridiculed.

She too felt a stab of guilt for her part in René's demise. She had watched as Guiscard pulled his bowstring taut and had stood silent as he let the arrow fly, too cloaked in her own self-pity to think of anyone else. As much as she pointed the finger at Yasmine, she too had been negligent. She had seen René's boorishness but had offered her opinion too late, after the Love Arrow had hit its mark.

She remembered the quote attributed to Edmund Burke she had recently learned from Paolo that "All that is necessary for the triumph of evil is that good men do nothing." She, on her own part, vowed never again to remain silent when another person seemed ready to commit a wrong action. Would she too suffer, as Arcenciel predicted Yasmine would? She sat pondering the complicated web of culpability as the defense rambled on.

The defender, unable to refute the evidence submitted by Natalie, which had provided an unmistakable DNA match to his client, claimed that the defendant, who had, to his regret, been given a rather strong dose of heroin by a friend, had no recollection whatsoever of the assault on Natalie Bertrand. He had not partaken of that substance before or since and regretted that he had given in to what, at the time, seemed a harmless amusement.

René sat, head slightly bowed. His face betrayed nothing.

Finally, there seemed to be nothing left to say. The courtroom slowly cleared, and everyone stepped out for a much-needed breath of fresh air, except René, who was taken, by the back way this time, to a holding cell where he would while away the deliberations, dismally awaiting his fate.

René sat down on the cot and leaned his back against the wall of the cell. He closed his eyes, the well-tailored suit he wore an incongruous contrast with the stark surroundings of the holding cell. He felt no hope for the future. Michelle was gone, and he was surely going to prison for a very long time. If only that Roma con artist hadn't wandered into Achères.

As for Natalie, he still found it hard to believe that things had happened the way she said. Her words had brought several jury members to tears, to his dismay. He had had trouble containing his emotions as he listened to the girl's testimony. He didn't recognize the man she described, but, then again, he didn't recognize the man who had slit Michelle's throat and thrown her lifeless body into a ditch.

Leaning forward, he put his head in his hands and shuddered to think what he had become, wishing it was he who was dead, instead of her.

53

Judgment

René stood before the judge, somber and still, betraying neither remorse nor belligerence. The jury had taken but two hours to decide his fate and began to reveal their decisions. He was, to his deep dismay, found guilty on all the charges brought against him—even the supposed rape of Natalie, which he didn't even remember. The jury had been swayed by the oafishness of the simple farmhand and the wide-eyed, innocent look of Michelle's sharp-tongued sister. *It is so unfair,* he thought. How could they hold him accountable for things he had done when he was strung out on heroin and drunk out of his mind? And the drug trafficking? Would he have even considered it if he had had any other options at all? He would appeal. He would fight to the end to have these ridiculous convictions overturned. Then, he would find Paysanne and finish him off.

The judge asked the convicted man if he wished to address the gathering. As quiet and emotionless as he had appeared throughout the trial, he said that, yes, he did have something he wanted to say. He stood and faced the judge, but his thoughts went out to the room in general.

"To Natalie, I would like to offer my sincere apology. I assure her that I have no recollection of what I did and hope she will forgive me someday. I wish I had never tried that stuff my friend gave me. It was not worth the cost to her or to myself. Michelle, I loved with all my heart, and when I saw what I had done, it was as if I had awakened to a nightmare, instead of from one. As for the Roma," he finished, a look of loathing on his face, "he can rot in hell, for ruining my life."

René met Paolo's eyes, glaring at him with loathing. The look he returned did not echo the sentiment, however. René was surprised to see his adversary looking abashed, rather than triumphant, at his demise. For the life of him, he couldn't figure the odd stranger out. Looking over at Natalie, René noted that the girl's face looked as bland as his own had been during the trial. Somehow, it was a strange comfort that they did not rejoice at his downfall. He was led away to begin the hardest stretch of his life.

The sentencing occurred a few days later. The judge asked René to stand and addressed him formally. He found that his legs felt shaky. His attorney helped him to his feet. He heard the judge speaking, but it was as if he were hearing his voice through the crowd of voices that shouted for attention within his own mind. Struggling to pay attention, he noted, with something like relief, that his sentences would run concurrently and that the longest stretch of time would be twenty-five years, for Michelle's murder.

René breathed a sigh of something resembling relief. If he could survive, maybe there would be a light at the end of this very long tunnel. After all, with good behavior and the possibility of a successful appeal …

He would often dream of revenge, the fantasy of its fulfillment keeping him going in his darkest days.

It was just before dawn. Paolo found that sleep eluded him that night. It wasn't a headache this time, just a nagging sense of his own inadequacy that kept him awake. Opening a book that he had found in Guy's meager collection, he located a spot he had bookmarked and then opened his journal beside it and began to copy the text. It was the list and explanation of the seven deadly sins. He had it memorized, along with that of the mortal and venial sins, but referred to the lists frequently lest he grow lax in his vigilance against them.

Greed. Now this, to me, is a confusing sin. It seems, in the opinion of the Church, to refer to material possessions. Can one be greedy for that which has no physical form? If so, then I can count myself stained, as I long incessantly for that which I do not possess and, once achieving it, find myself wanting more.

Acedia. This restlessness of my soul, with its accompanying melancholy, is it the manifestation of this vile sin? "Neglect to take care of something that one should do." I often, especially at twilight, feel that there is some compelling task that I have yet left undone. Can it be a sin, if you don't know what it is that you are supposed to do?

Wrath. Recently, I have felt what it is to be drunk with anger. It is as if the mind shuts down, allowing evil to consume the entire being. I have never felt such shame as upon the moment I awoke from its grasp.

The list of my iniquities grows, and I fear that, before long, I will have experienced the full extent of human sinfulness.

He was shaken from his brown study upon hearing his wife retching in the bathroom. He shut the book and went to get her a glass of water. He met her in the hallway as the first light of day brightened the sky. Her long white gown flowed about her as she walked, and her hair hung over her shoulder in a loose, lush braid. Her skin looked creamy pale in the predawn light. She appeared, to him, an ethereal vision, the air of unreality she possessed perhaps loaned to her in his imagination from his dreams.

She took the glass with a murmur of gratitude, sipped the water halfheartedly, and then placed the glass on the console at the top of the stairs.

"Paolo, dear." She spoke quietly, as the dawn began to brighten the sky. He waited patiently, knowing she was going to chide him for staying up so late writing.

"We're going to have a baby," she shared.

Paolo felt himself blanch, the enormity of the responsibility being the first thing to hit him. Then a wave of dizziness overcame him. He held on to the banister, lest he fall over from shock. A baby? He felt so unsure of himself. How would he help guide another human being through the strangeness of a world that he could barely comprehend? Then, he looked at Fey, so composed, so sure of him. With her, he could accomplish anything. God, in his wisdom, knew that man needed a helpmate. He had Fey.

341

Kneeling down before her, he wrapped his arms lightly around her legs and pressed his face to her belly. Closing his eyes, he wanted to feel the presence of their child. Fey placed her cool palm to his cheek, holding him close, the three of them joined for a moment in time as the sunlight kissed them with the first rays of dawn.

PART THREE

— *Redemption* —

Judge not, and ye shall not be judged: condemn not, and ye shall not be condemned: forgive, and ye shall be forgiven.

—Luke 6:38

Beloved

*L*atif heard his employer bellowing from the restroom, just after the shop had opened for the day.

"Gilbert Guiscard!"

He looked over at his friend, who sucked in his breath and then swore.

"I forgot," the younger de Gaul explained nervously. "I-I ... have a lunch date," he sputtered, fleeing the shop.

Jacques stormed in as the front door shut, his hands purple. "Where is my son?" he growled.

"He just left," Latif told him, suppressing a smirk upon seeing his boss's hands, which were obviously tainted with Gilbert's latest prank. "Why are your hands all purple, Jacques?" he dared to venture. Obviously, the prank had been meant for him, but Gilbert had forgotten about it, as luck would have it.

"I think it's beet juice," Jacques guessed, taking a sniff at his stained fingers. "That ungrateful son of mine filled the soap dispenser with it," he groused.

Latif started laughing, surreptitiously at first, and then, unable to contain himself, he leaned on the counter, his shoulders shaking with mirth to see the staid man looking so miffed. Jacques, at first, frowned, and then a reluctant smile stole over his face. Eventually, he too chuckled at Gilbert's ability to come up with new and ingenious ways to make the workplace more interesting.

"He'd better hope this comes off before tonight," he threatened emptily, rubbing his hands together. "I have a date with Simone."

Gilbert sat with his mother at a quiet restaurant near his stepfather's apartment. He was disappointed that Aimée hadn't come, but Lucette explained that she was busy with her dance lessons and wouldn't be finished for several hours. His half-sister always seemed to be busy with some scheduled activity. He doubted she ever had a whole day off—without a piano lesson, dance lesson, riding lesson, or whatever else his mother had signed her up for.

Lucette looked very much like her son—perfect features; the same striking blue eyes; her body slight of build and trim. She, however, had dyed her hair golden blonde. It was styled fashionably and complemented her features. She looked about ten years younger than she was, even by Parisian standards, and wore styles that fit that illusion. She could have been mistaken for his older sister and had been, on occasion. She spent as much money maintaining her appearance as she did spoiling her daughter, a considerable sum, all of it Pierre's.

"What's with your hair?" she criticized. "It makes you look like a factory worker." She sniffed.

"Oh, Yasi likes it, so I keep it that way," he explained.

"You've gained some weight too, I see," she noted with disdain. "Your face looks chubby. You won't be in your twenties forever, Gilbert. Extra kilos have a way of creeping on you when you hit thirty," she lectured.

"I, ah, gained a little weight at rehab. It'll come off quickly enough now that I'm home," he assured her. *Mon Dieu, but she's harsh,* he noted, his eyes narrowing as he bridled at her scrutiny. Everyone else had told him how good he looked. Maybe they were just being polite, trying to make him feel better. His mother, though, would be brutally honest.

"I came to tell you some news," he shared, a bit reluctantly. His mother always put him on guard.

She waited absently for him to continue, stirring saccharin into her tea, seeming uninterested, as if her own thoughts were more pressing.

"Yasi and I are getting married," Gilbert blurted out, looking nervously at his mother.

"Congratulations, dear," she offered, betraying a sense of surprise. "What brought this decision on?"

"Oh, Mom, she's been so good to me." He sighed. "After what I put her through, she stayed with me and supported me. I really didn't deserve it," he admitted, his eyes growing distant at the thought.

"Do you love her?" she asked in a judgmental tone.

"Definitely," he stated emphatically, his face brightening with honest sentiment. "I never thought I would say that, but I do. So, you'll come to the wedding, right?" He looked at her, hopeful but uncertain.

She twisted her face into a thoughtful frown. "Oh, Gilbert, I'm not sure," she demurred. "Pierre, you know …" she trailed off, looking uncomfortable. "He still thinks you're a bad influence on Aimée, and, you have to admit, your behavior hasn't always been acceptable."

Gilbert's stepfather was, according to him, an overbearing brute. He couldn't see how she had left his father, who, despite his compulsive work habits, was a gentle, generous person, to live with this controlling manipulator. She wasn't the same since he had taken her over. It was like she was afraid of him. Pierre kept Gilbert at arm's length. He was never asked to dinner and was not allowed to visit their apartment when he came to Paris but had to meet his mother at a restaurant. He knew he wasn't perfect, but it seemed that Pierre used his substance abuse as an excuse to exclude him from their lives. This kept their relationship to a bare minimum.

He had expected his mother's rejection, but that made it hurt no less. He completely lost his appetite, and when their lunch came, he merely sipped on his water, swirling the liquid in the glass, brooding, wishing he could have a real drink to ease the stab of pain.

Why did she leave Dad anyway? he wondered, watching her dig into her salad. Gilbert could see that, even though his father drove him nuts with his nagging, he was really a teddy bear, deep down. Why would she leave a man like that for a controlling type like Pierre? He had to know. It was, after all, what had kept him from having a real relationship up until now—the fear that he would end up like his own father, hurt and alone. Before, it didn't matter, but now he had Yasmine, and it was all different. Now he had to face up to this stuff, so it wouldn't come back to bite him later.

"Why did you leave Dad?" he asked her, pushing the food around on his plate.

She gave him a guarded look.

"Honestly?" she pondered aloud. "I wanted more than a paycheck. That's all Jacques was, a paycheck. His choice, not mine." She threw her hands in the air defensively.

Gilbert nodded. He could see how things could have gone wrong between them that way.

"So, are you happier now?" he asked pointedly, eyeing her with shrewd discernment.

She turned her gaze to the window, squirming a bit at his perceptive scrutiny.

"I have Aimée," she reminded herself aloud. "And she's such a wonderful child. I wouldn't trade her for the world."

"Mom?" he asked, leaning back in his chair, wanting to rub salt into his wounds.

"Yes, dear?"

"Who picked my sister's name, you or Pierre?"

"What difference would that make?" she asked with a nervous laugh.

"It was you, wasn't it?" he returned her nonanswer with one of his own, folding his arms across his chest.

Lucette remained uncomfortably silent while the scowl on his face grew blacker with each passing moment.

He sighed, looking down at his untouched plate. *Beloved.*

He paid the check and left, not waiting for her to finish her lunch. He would not see her again and vowed, if he ever had kids, that they would all be Beloved, not just one.

Gilbert pressed his back to the wall of the building in the alley behind the restaurant. His heart was racing, and his chest felt that familiar, terrifying tightness. He had, upon exiting the building, made a beeline for a pack of cigarettes and quickly lit up, inhaling deeply of the comforting smoke. He quickly dialed Yasmine and begged her to stay on the phone with him until he could regain his footing.

"Yasi, I could so easily just cross the street to the bar and tie one on," he admitted to her, slumping down against the building. He took another long drag. "It was my birthday yesterday, and she didn't even remember," he complained in a mournful tone.

"Come home, dear," she pleaded.

"It's too hard, being here," he admitted, smoke pouring out of his nose and mouth. "I could get whatever I want. Luc showed me where to go."

He was in a panic, begging her to pull him back.

"What you really want is waiting for you in Achères," she reminded him.

It was so true. He allowed himself to chain smoke about six of the cigarettes, until the grip of panic eased. He talked himself out of it, not letting it win over him, and then he threw the pack in a trash can. He left to catch the next train, not wanting to spend one more minute in the same city with his mother or her poor choice of a homewrecker, fleeing Temptation, who lurked around every corner, waiting to recapture her lost prey.

Yasmine, who knew that her fiancé was coming home early and that he had not had a good meeting with his mother, had dinner ready. Upon returning, though, he had regained his usual good humor, regaling her with what he had discovered upon reentering the family business, mischievous delight in his voice.

"I was going to stop by and see Dad for a few minutes. He always makes me feel better, even though he pretends to be such a grump." Gilbert laughed. "Boy, was I in for a surprise! I walked in on him and Simone, making out like two teenagers. He didn't see me, thank God. I just left, without interrupting them."

Yasmine didn't look surprised; she gazed to his left at a spot on the ceiling, her mouth in a pretty pout.

"You've been practicing your trade, haven't you, Ms. 'Relationship Counselor'?" he chuckled, tickling her to get her to confess.

She giggled and protested, "Stop, Bonbon, stop!"

"Poetic justice," he declared triumphantly. He sprawled on the sofa, arms folded. "Now my mom's miserable, and Dad finally gets to be happy."

"Gilbert, you smell like cigarettes," she scolded, after snuggling up next to him and smelling his shirt.

"C'mon, Yasi, cut me a break," he pleaded. "You know I could have done a lot worse, and, I promise, I just had a few and ditched the rest." He looked at her pleadingly, his head lowered penitently.

She frowned thoughtfully, the coquettish dimple appearing on her cheek. He was right. She should be proud of him for doing so well on his own. She reassuringly put her hand over the curve of his jawline, and he leaned into it, always so hungry for affection.

"So," he asked her seductively, planting a multitude of sloppy, wet kisses on her neck, "is my dad the only one who's going to get lucky tonight?"

Yasmine hit him with a pillow from the sofa, and he laughed.

"Can we please have dinner first?" she protested.

"Y'know? I'm famished," he suddenly realized.

As she watched her hungry fiancé appreciate a generous helping of pasta, she shared with him a bit of gossip.

"It seems, Bonbon, that I'm not the only one skilled in relationship counseling."

"Hmm?" he asked, chewing a delicious mouthful of Alfredo-doused orecchiette.

"Claude has informed me that he and Matthieu are moving in together, and he is ever so grateful to you for the introduction."

"Oh, it was nothing," he waved dismissively, scooping up another forkful of pasta. "It gets me off the hook, so to speak."

He sighed, looking suddenly sad. Yasmine sent him a quizzical glance. He sheepishly caught her look.

"What is it?" she asked, wondering what ghosts had jumped out of his mental closet.

"Oh, it's just ... well ..."

She raised one eyebrow, waiting for him to continue. He frowned, looking a bit hurt. "I know what it feels like to love someone who won't or can't return the affection." He was, of course, referring to Michelle, she knew. She understood him better than he could ever possibly know.

Her work-in-progress sat looking uncertainly at her, afraid of his own candor. "I can't believe I'm telling you this stuff." He rolled his eyes, putting his fork down, half finished with his dinner. "The Americans I went to college with would call it 'diarrhea of the mouth,'" he derided himself.

"I had such a crush on her. I used to close my eyes and think about her, while I was with other girls," he admitted, burying his face in his hands. "I don't do that anymore," he promised, taking another bite of pasta to shut himself up and looking her squarely in the eye, his own way of swearing to his honesty. She believed him.

"I know," she said, narrowing her eyes a bit. "You talk in your sleep all the time. The only name I hear is my own."

Gilbert cringed, looking into her narrowed eyes, his own wide with fear. He struggled to swallow that last forkful, and then letting loose a nervous laugh under his breath, he looked away.

"Mon Dieu!" he exclaimed. "I should just cut my tongue out now."

Yasmine laughed to see him squirm, and he smiled, looking sheepishly at her, his hair falling over his face in a similar fashion to that of his best friend.

"I must say ..." he mused and then paused to swallow a gulp of water to chase the heavy sauce from his palate and, perhaps, the discomfort from his mind. Taking her hand and looking pointedly at her, he continued, "I'm very happy for Claude and Matthieu. It's the best thing in the world, the love and touch of another person."

Looking at the beautiful, vulnerable man she called her own, Yasmine couldn't have agreed more.

55

Redemption

On a beautiful Saturday in October, the groom stood in the vestry of St. Fare, his dad fussing over his tuxedo as his best man looked on, full of admiration. The long hair had been shorn away for this important occasion, and Gilbert looked healthier than he ever had. Paolo grinned at him, brimming with happiness.

Jacques studied his son, wordlessly nodding his approval. Gilbert caught the favorable appraisal in his look and came to terms with the fact that even though his father had never openly demonstrated affection, he had missed, over the years, all of the other ways he did show his love. He looked at the graying, round-faced man as if for the first time. His dad would always be both his rock, secure and strong, and his soft place to land. After being friends with Paolo for so long, he suddenly realized how shy his old man was and felt sympathy for him. He hoped that things worked out between him and Simone. He wanted Jacques to find happiness, too.

"Well," he asked confidently, "how do I look?"

"Perfect," Jacques replied with conviction. Gilbert knew enough now to see that this was the best expression of love he could give, and he smiled at his dad, who, somehow, received the intended thoughts, tugging one last time at his son's cravat.

Paolo gave his best friend a heartfelt embrace, and the three men went to take their places for the ceremony. The church was packed full with his old school friends, relatives from near and far, and business associates from the community and from Paris.

Just as before, so many months ago, Natalie glided down the aisle first, dressed in a flowing crimson gown, which beautifully accentuated her lush, dark hair and newly attained curves. Gilbert winked at her, his infamous smirk gracing his elegant face. He tried not to think about Aimée, who should have been there as well. He wouldn't let his stepfather ruin this day. Natalie smiled back sweetly. Fey approached next, heavy with her first child. Paolo looked over at his wife as she took her place, his fierce gaze locked on this woman whom he adored.

Fey took her place, and the music changed. Gilbert's breath caught as he saw his bride, dressed by Fey in a gown so beautiful it outshone the one she had made for her own wedding. His blithe veneer vanished in an instant, and he stood, stricken with love, his fickle heart coming to rest on the woman before him, who shone with an unearthly radiance like no other he had ever laid eyes on.

Fleur, Arcenciel, and Guiscard again sat perched atop the choir loft. Arcenciel was thrilled to see that Fey and Paolo were expecting a child and could see that it meant the world to her best friend's mate to be so blessed. Things had truly worked out perfectly for them, so much in love and so devoted to each other. Fey definitely brought truth to the term *pregnancy glow*. Her hair was long and glossy, her skin rosy and fresh. Her form was attractively displayed in an empire-waisted crimson gown of wispy silk that flowed enticingly as she walked. She noted with amusement Paolo's famous, frighteningly intense gaze as he looked upon Fey with deep love. Even if he couldn't remember, what he had once been was still such an integral part of who he was, much the same as his debilitating shyness.

Yasmine's own beloved radiated good health. Last time they had seen him, though certainly quite beautiful, he had looked thin and tired. Now, his light-brown hair shone and he had filled out substantially, giving his face a youthful freshness that had been lacking during his time of suffering. He appeared to be overflowing with happiness. They could tell when Yasmine appeared in the back of the church in much the same way they could when Fey had at her wedding. There was something about when a man saw the woman he was to marry dressed just for him in sartorial splendor; there was just something uniquely human about it.

The bride made her way gracefully up the aisle, as only a daughter of the Fae could. Yasmine's jaunty blonde curls were arranged in a crown above her head, wreathed in white baby's breath. The translucent silk fluttered with her every movement. It was not cobweb, but Fey did the best she could with what she could get in her new circumstances. You could hardly tell the difference really. It certainly had the right effect on her man, who stood in awe. Arcenciel noted Fey smiling with satisfaction at his reaction to her handiwork. It had taken countless hours to complete, she was sure.

Arcenciel snuggled close to her beloved Guiscard. They too had found their happiness. Love and admiration for each other were mingled. They were lovers, friends, and helpmates. It was a successful union in every way. Of their group of friends, only Fleur remained unjoined. It was sad, but Arcenciel felt that she still had some maturing to do before she would be ready to settle down anyway. There were plenty of prospects in the forest surrounding Achères, she thought. Given time, she would find what she was looking for. For now, she was the head matchmaker of their clan and had proven her skill with a tough case, who sat happily next to his lady love in the front of the church and, no doubt, would be next to stand where his son now stood. She had a strong premonition about that.

The ceremony over, Yasmine and Gilbert shared a surprisingly decorous kiss and made their way down the aisle. The three secret guests were sorry it was over. They knew their contact with their old friends would grow less and less over the years, as their paths went in separate directions.

"Bring forth men-children only. For thy undaunted mettle should compose nothing but males," Fleur called down jokingly to the bride, quoting Macbeth.

Yasmine certainly possessed undaunted mettle, Arcenciel conceded. She had bravely gone after her man, stood by him as he faced his demons, and secured his undying love.

"That, Fleur, is a foregone conclusion," Guiscard noted. "Remember the curse that still lies upon her mate's family."

Arcenciel chose a more appropriate blessing for the new couple, Sonnet 88, full of tennis metaphors:

And I by this will be a gainer too,
For bending all my loving thoughts on thee,
The injuries that to myself I do,
Doing thee vantage, double vantage me.

Such is my love, to thee I so belong,
That for thy right myself will bear all wrong.

Yes, they would both have wrongs to bear before they grew in wisdom, she foresaw, but through their injuries, she wished upon them, as expressed in these stanzas, that they should both win in the game of love.

The reception was a huge, noisy, elaborate affair. A large tent had been erected behind Denis à Achères for the occasion. The building was too small to house the party. Yasmine's feet were sore after dancing with countless friends of her husband. They seemed to pop out of the woodwork, wild with curiosity about his gorgeous wife, who had come from nowhere. He kept stealing her back, to her relief. She was tired of being interrogated.

The couple had planned a two-week honeymoon in New York. She had looked forward to it, seeing how much he anticipated going back to the city in which he had spent so much time during his college years. He had been a fashion merchandising major in Paris, but at New York University, he had studied business management. He had regaled her with stories of America—the places, people, and their habits. She knew that if his roots hadn't been sunk so deeply in Achères, he wouldn't hesitate to move there permanently. He tried to speak "American" with her, so she wouldn't feel out of place. According to him, she still seemed stuck in a Shakespeare play, where English was concerned.

He had booked a hotel in Manhattan. Their spacious room was done up in beautiful art deco decor and sported a deep, luxurious bath and an impossibly fluffy white king-size bed. Their room had a view of the street, but Yasmine found the unnecessary noise the taxis made very annoying. Gilbert could sleep through an earthquake, she noted enviously, but the constant blasting of their horns was maddening to her, a child of the peaceful forest. She switched on the television to drown them out and fell asleep to the sound of American newscasters babbling on in their strange accent about things she didn't understand, with her oblivious man wrapped around her like a human garment.

The next day, Gilbert and Yasmine stood looking over what the Americans called Ground Zero. She noticed a deep sadness in her husband's eyes as he gazed at the vast, empty pit, which was being slowly reworked into something new. Yasmine knew he was thinking of his brother, Tristan, and that, in spite of his father's assurances to the contrary, he felt responsible for pushing his brother away with his jealous hostility.

She feared that the pain of losing Tristan, the guilt, would never heal. He refused to talk about such things, even with her, but would stuff them to the back of his mind, as was his habit, and let the culpability manifest itself in subtle ways that only she could see. She was reminded of the many times he had used up all of the hot water in their apartment with his overlong showers. She would lie on the bed, thinking of Lady Macbeth, and say aloud to herself, "Out, damned spot!"

Looking out over the water, Gilbert showed Yasmine the Statue of Liberty, proudly reminding her that it was a gift from France commemorating America's first century of independence. He acted surprised that she didn't already know that piece of trivia. She told him she thought it was stunningly beautiful, with its verdigris patina and classical influence. They stood admiring it for quite a while—or so she thought. Glancing at him, she caught him studying her own profile instead.

"I'd rather look at you, Yasi," he complimented her with honest affection. "I've seen all this before, but watching you look at it for the first time, that's what I'll remember, in years to come."

It was Sunday morning—fairly quiet, even by Yasmine's standards. She slept deeply. The sunlight streamed in through the window of their hotel room, the sun itself still low on the horizon.

"Yasi," she heard her husband croon softly.

"Mmmm," she protested, her face buried in the pillow. He used to sleep so late on Sunday mornings, when he was still drinking. Now, though, he often got up before dawn, even on the "day of rest," to go for a run. Usually, though, he let her sleep.

"I want to show you something today," he coaxed her in a loud whisper.

She could tell he was excited about it by the sound of his voice. Upon opening her eyes, she noted that he was already dressed, not in jeans, but a white dress shirt and dark trousers. He held a steaming cup of coffee out to her. "Thought you might need this first."

Yasmine sat up, taking the cup gratefully. *He looks so eager,* she thought and took a few cautious sips of the hot beverage. She set the cup on the nightstand, rose up, and wrapped her arms around him for a brief moment, breathing in. He always smelled so nice, like soap and aftershave lotion, but even more so now that he had quit smoking. The smell of the cigarettes, though he hid it with mints and cologne, had always lurked in the background. His teeth were much whiter, as well.

"I miss your hair," she complained, running her hand over the short stubble on the back of his neck. She had never seen a man with short hair among the Fae. They all grew their hair at least shoulder length. After all, they spent a lot of time outdoors, and it kept their heads warm. It took some getting used to, his clipped, short style.

"I'll grow it back, then," he assured her. "I just got it cut for the wedding, to make Dad happy."

She hurried to get dressed, so he wouldn't have to wait.

"What do you want me to wear?" she called from the bathroom.

"Whatever you want. It doesn't matter."

He hadn't told her where they were going. He said he wanted to surprise her but did mention he had been there before, with friends from college. Considering how much partying he had done back then, by his own admission, she couldn't imagine him having anything to go back to from that time, now that he was done with all of that. He avoided situations that would put him in the way of temptation like a germaphobe avoided touching doorknobs.

As Gilbert paid the cab fare, Yasmine noticed that they were standing in front of a very large, architecturally interesting modern building. It was a kind of church, to her great surprise. Gilbert had never betrayed any religious inclinations to her, and she looked over at him in astonishment. He looked back sheepishly at her.

"It's not like St. Fare," he promised her. "Just give it a chance."

They chose a seat in the middle, blending in with the large congregation. Unlike the hush at the Catholic church before Mass, people milled about, greeting each other, hugging, and talking. The atmosphere was very warm and casual, compared with the air of cool reverence of the centuries-old structure in Achères, and the church was very crowded.

"Is this a special holiday in America?" she asked. It would just be a normal Sunday in France, but with the church so packed, she figured that it must be some kind of feast day.

"No, Yasi, it's always this crowded," he answered, surprising her again. There were many more young people here than attended St. Fare. Most of the congregation was under fifty. A lot of them, to her surprise, were their age or younger.

Everyone began to settle down—but not completely. The socializing continued until a loud wave of music swept over the church. Yasmine had never seen anything like it. It was more like a concert or a celebration than a church service. People were singing along, but they were also clapping in time with the music. The joy of it was infectious, and she looked over at Gilbert and smiled broadly. He grinned back at her, obviously pleased with her reaction.

Yasmine watched with surprise as her husband raised his hands, palms outstretched, like many others in the congregation—his eyes closed, an expression of peace and surrender on his face. He looked so beautiful to her just then, a picture of serenity.

"I am not my own, for I have been made new," the words rang out loudly.

"You believe that?" she asked hopefully.

"Yes, with all my heart," he answered with a deep sincerity in his voice.

She took his soft, warm hand in her own. He was going to be okay.

56

Curse of Eve

*P*aolo watched as Fey lay in agony, pain ripping through her body in waves of ever-increasing intensity. He stood at her side, unshaven and tired. He asked her to grip his hands with her own, closing his eyes and willing the pain to transfer to him. It would not be so. He knew, from his reading of Genesis, as he lay in the hospital, his own body a sea of pain, that what his dear wife was enduring was, as so much of life's suffering seemed to be, a consequence of their fallen nature.

He thought, honestly, that woman's fate was the more severe punishment. Earning his bread by the sweat of his brow was satisfying and brought peaceful sleep at the end of a long day of toil. Remembering his stay in the hospital, comparing it with what Fey was now enduring, he saw too many similarities and, personally, preferred the peaceful isolation of the fields to physical vulnerability and violation.

She cried out, holding tightly to his strong, large hands with her delicate fingers, which whitened with the effort. Every scream she tried to muffle had him cringing. It had been hours, and she was growing tired. It seemed to him to be beyond endurance. Just as she caught her breath, the next wave would hit, incredibly, with even more force than the one that had come before.

Paolo had read that this was the case, but seeing it himself, how she lay there consumed with the searing stabs, he sensed that it was the kind of thing that must be personally experienced to be truly understood. All he could do was stay close, hold her small hands in his own, and meet her agonized look with his own eyes full of apologetic sympathy. What could he say? He knew he was partly responsible for what she was going through and felt really bad about that, but he could no more forego being with her than he could go without eating or sleeping.

It had been one of the happiest moments of his life when she had made her announcement to him. Now though, he felt selfish for the pleasure they had shared.

"Fey, I'm so sorry." He was anguished, full of remorse for his carnal desires, which had inflicted this trial on the woman he loved more than his own life.

"Don't be sorry," she assured him, with a brave but wan smile. "It will all be well; you'll see."

She was coping by completely focusing on the result, he noted. She referred, in her words, to the saying of the beautiful, saintly Julian of Norwich. Paolo also found the writings of the Christian mystic of interest, as he strove to convince his wife to embrace his beliefs.

Finally, after what seemed like hours and hours, her endurance tested to its breaking point, the pain finally directed itself, and their child made ready to arrive. It took three more gut-wrenching attempts, but relief finally flooded over Fey's pale, exhausted face as their baby girl slipped into the world. She smiled wearily at her man, who, forgetting his own tiredness, was filled with joy. It was a blessing he had never dreamed possible. He bent down and kissed her sweaty forehead, tears of happiness and gratitude welling up in his eyes.

When the baby opened her eyes, Fey handed her carefully to Paolo. What he saw, looking into their dark, calm depths, surprisingly enough, was a feminine miniature of himself. He sat and held her in awe, as nature knit the bond between them, Fey looking on with satisfaction.

57

Turned Tables

It was a beautiful Sunday afternoon in May. Paolo sat under the tree in the front yard, baby Michelle propped on his legs, her head resting on his knees. He was still dressed for Mass in a white dress shirt, black tie, and black wool trousers—his only dress clothes, Gilbert noted with frustrated resignation. He sang to her in his melodious, deep, gravelly bass. She smiled at him, and he stopped, midverse, chuckling with delight.

Gilbert lay in the grass, in his favorite Bob Marley T-shirt and jeans, watching. He envied Paolo and hoped he and Yasmine would have children, as well. Michelle was, to him also, absolutely enchanting. He pulled himself up and went over to watch her smile.

"I can't wait to have kids," Gilbert mused, as he tickled the baby's feet. She kicked and cooed, held firmly in her daddy's strong hands.

"She's not a plaything, you know," Paolo admonished. "It's a lot of work, being a parent. She needs to be watched every minute. Even when she's sleeping, we need to check on her. I hope you do have children, but please, please," he lectured seriously, "make sure that you're emotionally ready for this. You need to be strong to handle it."

Gilbert was taken aback. Since when had Paolo gotten the upper hand on him? He had always been the one to tutor his friend in the ways of the world, yet here Paolo was, instructing him. The tables had turned.

Paolo had gone from a naive, unworldly boy with little common sense and a sometimes skewed version of right and wrong to a responsible man who ran a farm on his own, had a wife and child, and had, most important, a firm grasp of reality. He had learned quickly. It seemed that he lived his life with a sense of urgency, as if he appreciated the fleeting nature of happiness. It wasn't surprising, considering the amount of suffering he had gone through.

Paolo resumed his song as Gilbert sat and watched parent and child share a moment of complete bliss. The tree sang along, overhead, as the breeze played through it—nature and humanity, for an instant, in perfect harmony.

A short while later, Fey and Paolo made their way to the sun-dappled clearing where René and Michelle had enjoyed their last picnic. Yasmine had offered to babysit, and they were looking forward to a rare afternoon of leisure. Paolo spread a blanket on the ground as Fey dropped their basket on a nearby flat rock. She began to unpack their lunch in an unhurried fashion but turned around to see Paolo staring at her with a look of hunger that had absolutely nothing to do with food.

He had been patiently watching her, wishing she would just stop fussing and look at him. He knew his thoughts were selfish, but it was hard on him, how much less time she had for him now, after the baby. He refused to give in to such immaturity and took what attention she could give him with gratitude, drinking it in like sips of cool water on a hot, July day—refreshing, but not nearly enough to satisfy.

She approached him slowly, looked up at him, and waited. He pulled her close, kissing her very gently, as was his way. He smiled, a question playing across his mind.

"What?" she asked, laughing.

"Why do your lips always taste so good?" he asked her with a grin. "It used to drive me crazy, when I was trying my best to keep myself from you."

Fey reached into her pocket, uncapped her strawberry lip gloss, and waved it under his nose.

Paolo laughed heartily, shaking his head at his foolishness. "I thought it was some kind of magic you had brought with you from my dreams, just to make you completely irresistible to me."

She giggled in response, her beautiful violet eyes sparkling with merriment. Paolo folded her in his arms for another taste, tangling his fingers in her gingery curls.

58

Transgression

Paolo finished the story of David, finally. It had been hard to read—confusing and sometimes ungenerous thoughts had occasionally passed through his mind. David could be so selfish, as he took Michal away from Paltiel and lusted after Bathsheba, and he could be kind and respectful, as when he treated Saul and his sons with mercy. David had been forgiven by God in the end for the sins he had committed. Paolo figured that all people, himself included, were really a mix of bad and good, and he knew that the forgiveness of God was available to everyone. All a man could hope for, as Guy had told him so long ago, was just to do the best he could.

Sighing, he turned his attention to the computer. Fey was upstairs, giving the baby a bath. The bills were done. A soft, June breeze ruffled the sheer curtain and, beyond, the grassy carpet that stretched toward the forest. He turned his attention again to his neglected quest to find out what had happened to the poor fruit vendor. He was getting much better at using the computer and switched search engines to an Italian-language version, though he continued to tap clumsily at the keyboard, hunt-and-peck style.

His pulse quickened when he saw the name he was looking for. Finally, he had reached a breakthrough, digging out a small article with frustratingly little detail. The blood drained from his face and his lips went white, as he read that Paolo Lombardelli, the longtime owner of a small produce market in Bellano, had disappeared without a trace, leaving behind a wife and two sons. Foul play was strongly suspected, as the office had been ransacked. Neighbors reported seeing a tall, unkempt-looking vagrant, possibly of Roma descent, hanging around the village in the area of the market. He had not been seen since the grocer's disappearance. A telephone number was listed to call with information on either the business owner's whereabouts or that of the person of interest in the case. The article was dated two weeks prior to Paolo's awakening in the forest.

He printed a copy of the article and then shut off the computer as Fey descended the stairs, flowing like a vision from Paradise in her white nightgown, her ruddy curls floating over her shoulders. His heart squeezed tight at the sight of her, so full of contentment, her face suffused with pleasure to see him sitting there, waiting for her to join him for the evening. How would he tell her? He could barely face what he was himself—a *murderer*.

God forgive him, he made love to her one last time, before it would all transpire. Fey pulled him to her like he deserved such bliss, and he, like a man enjoying his last meal before his execution, savored the pleasure of her presence, pushing the guilt he felt to the back of his mind while he pretended, for a brief time, that nothing else mattered. They fell asleep in each other's arms, she with a satisfied smile, he with silent tears that he couldn't hold back, but which the kind darkness concealed.

Before dawn, he arose to finish his task. After throwing on a dark-blue robe, he padded, barefoot, down the stairs and switched on the small hurricane lamp above the desk.

> *It is as I have feared. Despite the assurances of my best friend, whom I love like a brother and look to for advice in navigating the circumstances in which I find myself, our dreams are sometimes just that which they purport to be. I read, with comfort, that God is ready to forgive a contrite heart, but in order to live out my life with honest dignity, I see that I must also reveal my sin to the world.*
>
> *What will become of Fey and of Michelle? So trusting, Fey assured me that I was a good man. The way she looked at me, so full of admiration and love, convinced me that she could not have been mistaken, but Shakespeare, whose words I have read with my beloved until they have become committed to memory, himself had repeated many a time these wise words in one way or another, "But love is*

blind, and lovers cannot see what petty follies they themselves commit."

Hopefully, the stewardship we have exercised over the generous gift of my mentor will make it enough to sustain them through the years ahead. I will tell her to forget me, as I never really was what she so innocently assumed anyway. Deserving no remembrance, I will set her free. Ironically, then I will indeed be what she sees—a man who lives by his principles.

Early that morning, as they sat drinking coffee, Paolo informed Fey that he needed to visit René. It was, he explained, possibly the only chance he would have to do so. He left his journal on the desk, the news article tucked inside, next to the entries he had written during the night.

René had been called to the visitation room. He couldn't imagine who wanted to see him. His family rarely visited, and his buddies on the outside had had no contact with him since that awful night of Michelle's death, which, he noted, was exactly four years ago to the day. He sat impatiently behind the glass wall, waiting. It was hot and muggy that day, and a large fan blew the warm air noisily around the windowless chamber.

The door opened slowly and a tall, sturdily built man dressed in jeans and a T-shirt looked hesitantly in. His black, wavy hair swooped down over his eyes. He was a bit heavier in maturity, not so lanky as before, but René recognized that worthless Roma, Paolo Paysanne, immediately. What the hell did he want anyway?

Paolo strode slowly, hesitantly, over, still betraying a bit of shyness. Taking the seat at the other side of the window, he smoothed back his unruly hair, meeting René's curious glare without malice, his black gypsy eyes full of compassion, oddly enough.

"Uh, hi," Paolo began, in his characteristic, awkward hesitancy.

"What do you want?" René asked defensively, crossing his arms as he leaned back in his chair.

"I never got to apologize to you, for what I did at the courthouse. I'm really sorry. It wasn't very honorable of me, going after you like that, when you couldn't defend yourself."

René thought he was taunting him for the incident in the alley, when his buddies held him so he could pound on him. "You're referring to what happened to you in the alley. Don't think I'm stupid," René spat, irritated with Paolo's use of reverse psychology on him. He had read books while he was in there and would not be sucked into his manipulations.

"Oh, no," Paolo assured him earnestly. "I'm really sorry. I judged you when you looked at Natalie, thinking I knew what was on your mind when you saw her, but I was completely wrong, and for that, I'm truly sorry," he explained. "Only God can know a man's heart."

René sat in silence, unsure how to respond. Paysanne swallowed uncomfortably and went on, as if compelled to fill the silence. "Um, I, ah, think sometimes that maybe we were meant to have that confrontation. That … maybe God had some purpose for us in it," he explained quietly, trailing off to a barely audible mutter at the end, as if the admission were too private to voice. "I hope you'll forgive me, for laying hands on you," he added softly, lowering his gaze, his face flushed with humiliation. Then, after a momentary pause, he looked up, meeting René's incredulous stare. "Oh, and when you're ready to accept it, I gave you my forgiveness a long time ago."

It was delivered almost as an afterthought. René exhaled, unable to believe what he was hearing.

The Roma's expression grew thoughtful, as if he desired to say something else. René was curious. What else would Paysanne throw out to confuse him? He crossed his arms and sat, silent and hostile.

"Did you ever stop to think," he asked, "that your name means *reborn*? I think that should give you some hope," he added, rising from his seat.

He then turned to go without waiting for a response, leaving René to begin his own journey.

> **Forgiven**
> *Across the chasm's span I gaze upon*
> *The face of dark Transgression's angry stare.*
> *My bitter foe wouldst not have me go on,*
> *Canst not today our enmity forswear.*

On his face is writ Confusion's sign,
Doubting my intentions to be true.
Offer of my heart he doth decline
Thereby his own deep peace he doth eschew.
His name doth God's own love indeed portend
As dawn comes after darkness of the night.
O, that he couldst humbly to transcend
In his own soul, as mine, to be contrite.
    Wouldst that he, at last, forgiven me;
    Then couldst he, as well, forgiven be.

Thunder threatened in the distance as Paolo stepped out of the old pickup. Fey peered through the window as he crunched up the gravel to the house. He met her eye grimly as she looked out. Had she read the last entry he had recorded in his journal?

The front door opened as he climbed the porch steps with fatigued resignation.

"How did it go?" Fey asked.

"I said what I needed to say," Paolo shrugged, exchanging a kiss with her. He stood in the doorway, trying to read her unspoken thoughts.

"Did you know about me, about what I had done, before we met?" he asked, studying her with a somber air.

"Paolo—" she began softly.

He shook his head. "I have to turn myself in," he interrupted. "How can I go on, knowing that René is paying for his crime, while I live this false life of ease," he lamented in an anguished tone, walking over to the mantel. He stared vacantly at the array of pictures on its surface. The living room took on a somber hue as the skies grew darker.

"No! You don't understand," Fey pleaded, following him, desperation sounding in her tone. He hated that she was so upset, but then, so was he. He found that calmness eluded him at the moment. It was like trying to stop the tide coming in.

"What is there to understand?" he asked, turning to face her. "I killed a man, took his identity, stole his money, and shoved him in a Dumpster. I'm filth!" he shouted, his face full of anger at himself, nostrils flared in self-loathing. Nature seemed to agree as another flash of lightning followed with a concurring outburst.

"You didn't do it," Fey pleaded with him. "It was someone else, not you! Don't you see, Paolo? All the dreams you had about that night, it was you watching, not committing this murder."

"How do you know?" he shouted back. "You weren't there!"

Fey blanched. To Paolo, it appeared she was struggling against herself. The baby began to cry, and Fey hurried up the stairs to get her. Paolo immediately regretted his outburst of temper. She returned with their daughter in her arms. He saw that tears were streaming down Fey's cheeks.

"It's time to tell you the truth," she whispered. "It's the only thing that will save you from making the biggest mistake of your life. Paolo," she told him in a quiet voice hoarse with fear, "I know who you were."

They both sat down on the sofa. His face was frozen with a look of intense focus, locked on her beautiful indigo eyes, which were wet with tears.

"Think back to all your dreams, all your poems. Think of how the two of us came to be here, so alone in the world," she related in the voice of a storyteller preparing to tell her tale as a cool wind swept through the screen door.

She settled down with their daughter and began to tell her a story, but Paolo knew that the story was meant for him. He listened, wide-eyed with disbelief, as she told of the beautiful, lavender faerie, who crawled into a hollow tree to escape the last storm of summer, and of the huge, frightening bat, who awakened to see her, pasted with fright against the concave surface of the narrow interior.

"The foolish faerie, thinking only to escape with her life from the giant creature, whom she believed wished to devour her, offered to grant him a wish, telling him to choose whatever he wanted, if he would only spare her life."

Michelle soon fell asleep to the soothing sounds of her voice and the rain drumming against the house, but she continued on, telling of the bat's desire to discover the mystical City of Lights and of how he had wished he were human, in order to enjoy its beauty more fully.

"And that wish," she declared, "was the undoing of them both. For she, upon granting it, reduced the poor bat, who meant her no harm at all," she uttered, looking with great love at his face, so full of horrified recognition, "to a state of humanity, where he must suffer the fate of Adam for the rest of his days. And the faerie," she shared, another tear sliding down her cheek, which she wiped away with her fingertips, "fell in love with the beautiful, lofty soul, following him from the magical realm of the Fae, where all enjoy long lives of peace and pleasure, to share his fate, to become his Eve, his helpmate."

No words worked their way to his consciousness. Paolo just sat and stared at her with an expression that had evolved from disbelief to shocked comprehension. Oddly enough, it all made sense to him. He had remembered being in the tree, remembered seeing her in all her faerie radiance; he had dreamed of flying over the forests of Fontainebleau and Lake Como.

"Oh, *Dio*, I think I'm going mad!" he exclaimed, rising from the sofa and fleeing the room. His head began to pound, and he opened the front door. It was raining in earnest, but he staggered down the stairs, legs shaky with the unreality of it all.

"Paolo, wait!" she called after him, the sleeping child in her arms.

He hurriedly made his way from the house, the cool rain soaking his shirt and his hair. His shoes splashed through the puddles as he jogged toward the barn, the pain fogging his thoughts. He reached for the latch on the door, but as he did, the throbbing ache he felt turned into a blinding, searing stab that seemed to go all the way through his brain. He knelt down, gripping the sides of his head. It took his breath away, worse than anything he had been through thus far.

"Fey!" he shouted in a strangled voice, praying that she heard him.

His mind was swept clean, replaced by a feeling of peace that seemed familiar. His last thought was a realization that no matter whether anyone else was present, you didn't die alone. His last feeling was of being lifted gently from the wet ground, held in a familiar embrace. Such love he felt at that moment, for the one whose arms held him close.

EPILOGUE

Fey had him buried in a plot next to Michelle's, so that Natalie could visit them both at the same time. He, sensing deep down that something was wrong, had made sure she was taken care of. He had felt it his duty to do so. Now, she stood with Natalie, watching as the pretty teenager held to her lips and then ripped the petals off a white rose, scattering them over the open pit, casting the thorns aside. She then did the same with a pink rose, sprinkling the petals over the grass of her sister's grave.

His sonnets would finally be published, Natalie providing beautiful illustrations for each one. He had absolutely refused to do so, but now, it seemed the right thing, somehow—something tangible and permanent to show that he had actually existed. Of course, there was little Michelle. She looked more and more like her father every day. Her face would be a comfort in the years to come.

Fey would, as was her nature, find happiness again, but she knew Paolo was right. You didn't stop loving someone. She would always, always be in love with her beautiful, dark-eyed boy to the end of her days.

Back at the house, most of the other mourners had left. Gilbert sat on the sofa, deep in thought. Paolo's journal lay open in his hand. He now understood the mysterious obsession the poet had had with his dreams, though Fey had enigmatically assured him that Paolo was indeed innocent of his imagined crime. He had the impression that he had never really known this very private, introverted man and wished he hadn't been so abrasive with him. Maybe then, his elusive friend would have trusted him more with his deepest thoughts, which he now held before him.

He had misjudged, thinking that Paolo was just this simple innocent, when he, in actuality, was incredibly profound and complex. Reverently closing the book, he set it on the end table and went into the kitchen to check on Natalie. He was, as they all were, very worried about her. He found her cleaning up after the funeral lunch, banging about the kitchen, as if inflicting abuse on the pots and pans would somehow ease her own pain. She threw the dish towel over the edge of the sink and stood in silence in front of the dish water. He walked over to where she stood and hesitated. Natalie bowed her head. Gilbert wrapped his arms around her and closed his eyes as she began to cry.

The newly widowed mother held little Michelle in her arms in front of the mantel, walking slowly past the array of photos lined up along the ledge—first, Guillaume as a young man with his wife, Marguerite, his face rugged and full of character; next, Michelle, as a newborn; Paolo and she, on their wedding day, standing at the altar of St. Fare, looking enrapt and in love, gazing longingly at each other, their hands entwined; Natalie's school picture, her face serious and beautiful; Gilbert and Yasmine in New York, looking full of joy and promise on their honeymoon; and then the portrait that Natalie had made of Paolo as he sat at Mass with Guy. Looking at it always brought a tight feeling to her chest, as she gazed upon him in the fullness of his innocence—even more so now, with him lying under the earth, perfect as in a deep sleep, the onyx ring on his finger. Lastly, there was a black-and-white photo of Paolo that she had taken with Guy's camera as he stood with the Eiffel Tower in the background. She had captured the image the morning after they had first made love. Paolo stood looking at Fey, hands in his coat pockets, his head dipped down sweetly, a shy, yet satisfied smile on his boyish face.

They would never know him, Fey lamented, neither the child she held in her arms nor the one growing inside of her, about whom she had not had a chance to tell him. She turned to leave the house, needing some air. Sitting down on the porch swing, she hummed the melody that Paolo had always sung to make Michelle smile. The baby girl curled up against her, thumb in mouth, relaxing to the gentle movement and sound.

Ripe wheat, planted by his hand, rippled in soft waves over the field. She could almost feel the whisper-soft caress of his touch in the undulating grass. She thought, with heaviness, that Paolo had never really belonged here. She hoped with all her heart that his restless soul had finally found its journey's end in the eternal City of Light.

Acknowledgments

To Jane Pennington, the first to read my very rough draft, thank you for the early encouragement and for giving me the courage to find Paolo's voice in the sonnet form.

To Daniel Pennington, I can't thank you enough for supporting me every step of the way. Your unwavering belief in me has meant so much.

To Rosie Pennington, thank you for begging me to tell you bedtime stories instead of reading to you, even though I was too tired to appreciate the gift you gave me at the time.

To Jessica Wardlow, thank you for challenging me to stretch my boundaries and for encouraging me to paint colorful pictures with words in the minds of my readers.

Thanks to Roy O'Neal, for patiently explaining the complexities of wheat farming in language I could comprehend, so that I could share this understanding with my readers.

To Georget Novak, thank you for your heartfelt support and for your explanations of reading the physical manifestations that, if we are observant, can clue us in to what others are thinking.

To Doug Hale, Maria Kimsey, and Heather Prescott of Mercersburg Academy, thanks for reviewing the sonnets, Italian and French, respectively.

Thanks go out to John Radvak. We sat for hours in a hotel lobby before dawn, two strangers sharing a bit of life. You gave me a clear image of the powerful beauty of distance running, which I have, as accurately as possible, transcribed in these pages.

The cover photos were taken by John Varljen. The author photo was taken by Arlene Craine and edited by John Varljen. Thank you so much for lending your expertise to help me.

Thanks to Bobby Morris for the tennis lessons and for cheerfully and enthusiastically answering my questions. Like my protagonist, I too was completely clueless about the sport.

To my mom, thank you for backing my endeavor without hesitation and for saving my first novel, which I wrote when I was eight years old. Your belief in me is a priceless treasure.

To the people at iUniverse, I thank you for providing me with a medium to tell my story and for mentoring me along the way.

Finally, thanks to the Divine Creator, who sent me this story to lighten my heart. I hope it will bring joy to others, as well.

CPSIA information can be obtained at www.ICGtesting.com
Printed in the USA
BVOW071409090413

317711BV00001B/4/P